A CHRISTMAS WEDDING AT THE CASTLE

ELIZA J SCOTT

For my Family. Thank you for your support and the endless cups of tea! xx

OTHER BOOKS BY ELIZA J SCOTT

LIFE ON THE MOORS SERIES
    The Letter - Kitty's Story
    The Talisman - Molly's Story
    The Secret - Violet's Story
    A Christmas Kiss

HEARTSHAPED SERIES
    Tell That To My Heart

1

LATE JUNE

THE QUAINT MOORLAND village of Lytell Stangdale was basking in the evening sunshine. The bright blue sky of earlier had faded to a gentle water-colour blue, and the achingly-pretty thatched cottages seemed to sigh with relief, glad that the intense heat of the afternoon had given way to a more bearable temperature. Bumble-bees and butter-flies fluttered and hummed in the neatly-tended gardens that were filled with blowsy, country-cottage blooms, their heady perfume filling the air.

A solitary blackbird, perched on the branches of a rowan tree, was singing his heart out, his song lifting on the barely-there breeze, while a ewe and her two lambs ambled down the middle of the road, bleating plaintively.

'Right, here we are.' Zander Gillespie stopped his four-wheel drive in front of the Manor House, an imposing timber-framed prop-erty, its thatched roof glowing in the last of the evening sunshine. He turned to Livvie and smiled. 'Enjoy your pamper session and text me when you want picking up. Oh, and say hi to the girls from me.'

'Will do.' Livvie leaned in for a kiss, the brush of his lips sending an unexpected bolt of electricity through her. She touched his cheek as her hazel eyes roved over his handsome face. His twinkling light-blue eyes, his close-cropped dark hair and the dimple in his chin were a combination that had made her heart leap when she'd first set eyes on him and, six months on, the feeling still burnt with an inten-sity that took her breath away.

A smile tugged at his lips as he tucked a wayward auburn lock behind her ear, setting her silver, beaded earring jangling. 'And you can get those wicked thoughts out of your mind right now, Livvie Weatherill. You're late enough as it is. You'll have to put *that* on hold until you get home tonight.' His eyes loitered on her rosebud lips.

Livvie couldn't help but laugh. 'You're right, but you're to blame for my wicked thoughts.'

'*I'm* to blame?'

'Yep; for looking at me that way.'

Zander threw his palms up. 'Hey, I was only looking at you the way I normally do.'

'Exactly!' Livvie arched her eyebrows at him as she undid her seatbelt with a click. 'And I should probably warn you, I might be a little bit wobbly on my feet by the time you pick me up; the girls have promised tonight's not only going to be our monthly pamper session but it's also going to include some sort of mini celebration of our news. Prosecco has been mentioned – and lots of it.'

'I'll bet it has,' Zander said, laughing. He checked his watch. 'Anyway, it's quarter-past-seven, you'd better get yourself in there before they send out a search party; it's not right being late for your own celebration, mini or otherwise.'

'Yep, I'm going.' She flashed him a smile and grabbed her patchwork slouch bag, hooking it over her shoulder before reaching behind her for the bottle of white wine – her contribution to the get-together. 'See you later.' She turned to the black Labrador in the back whose nose was poking through the bars of the dog guard. 'Bye, Alf, keep an eye on your dad for me. I'm relying on you to make sure he doesn't get up to any mischief.' Alf snorted and wagged his tail.

'What? You're putting that rapscallion mutt in charge?'

'Yup.'

Zander took a side-ways look at Alf and rolled his eyes good-naturedly. 'Great.'

Grinning, Livvie climbed out of the car and watched them drive away, Alf's black, wet nose pressed against the rear window, making her chuckle. With a happy sigh she glanced around the village; she'd fallen in love with this little corner of the North Yorkshire Moors as soon as she'd set eyes on it just before Christmas last year.

There was a sudden lift in the breeze, ruffling the leaves on the trees and wafting the delicious aroma of a barbecue down the road towards her, accompanied by the sound of laughter and children screeching in delight. *Happy times.*

As she hurried down the neat path to the Manor House, the door was flung open and Robbie appeared. 'I thought that was Zander's car I heard,' he said, smiling. 'Come in, Livvie, it's good to see you. Rosie and the others are just setting up but I should warn you, they've already started on the Prosecco, so you'd best get yourself down there before they demolish it all.'

Molly's unmistakable cackle floated down the hallway as Livvie stepped inside. Robbie raised his eyebrows. 'See what I mean?'

Livvie giggled. 'Ooh, I'd better get a move on.' She was enveloped by the luxurious scent of aromatherapy oils that drifted down from Rosie's therapy rooms, alongside Molly's laughter. It sent a wave of happiness washing over her. Livvie had been thrilled when the friends had invited her to join their monthly pamper session at Manor House Sanctuary – the converted rooms from where Rosie ran her beauty business – and always looked forward to them and the good chinwag that ensued. She regularly went home with her cheeks aching from laughing so much.

Robbie leaned towards her. 'And congratulations by the way; Rosie shared your news,' he said quietly.

'Thank you. It was such a surprise.' Livvie felt her cheeks flush with joy at the memory. 'Anyway, I'll see you later; we'll try not to be too noisy for you.'

'Don't worry about me; I've got a cheeky bottle of red and an action series to binge-watch on the telly. I'll be happy as a pig in muck; you lot just enjoy yourselves like you normally do.'

'We'll do our best,' Livvie said, smiling as she followed the sound of laughter and voices chattering away in the familiar flat-vowels of a North Yorkshire accent. 'Knock, knock,' she said, pushing the door open. Her heart was thudding excitedly in her chest; it was the first time she'd seen her friends since she'd shared her news with them via text message.

'Livvie!' four voices chorused.

She looked around at the sea of smiling faces. Rosie, dressed in her beautician's tunic, was setting out pots of jewel-coloured nail varnish, while Kitty, Molly and Vi were wrapped in fluffy white towelling dressing-gowns and snuggled up on the large plum-coloured squishy sofa, tall glasses of fizzing Prosecco in their hands. 'Hi, everyone, sorry I'm late.' Livvie beamed back at them.

'No worries, you're here now. And huge congratulations, chick!' Kitty set her glass down and ran over to Livvie, pulling her into a hug and kissing her on the cheek. 'It's wonderful news. Ollie and me are so thrilled for you; you and Zander are perfect together.'

'Thank you, Kitts.' Before Livvie could say any more, Molly and Vi had wrapped their arms around her, offering their congratulations. Rosie followed up, armed with a freshly-poured glass of Prosecco.

'Congratulations, flower, we're so happy for you. Here you are, we can't have you empty-handed.' She held the glass out for Livvie to take.

'Thanks, Rosie. Can I give you this?' She swapped the bottle of wine for the glass of Prosecco before her friend squeezed in for a hug.

'Yep, get yourself a good old gobful of that, missus; you've got a glass-worth of catching-up to do,' said Molly. 'We'll sip ours slowly while you fill us in on all of the details of how your hot-to-trot doctor proposed to you – and no missing anything out, mind.'

'Can I just say, speak for yourself, Moll, as far as sipping is concerned,' said Vi. 'I've got a pass out for the evening and, as the mother of a four-month-old baby and whose husband is very much in charge until I get up in the morning, I intend to make the most of every minute of it; there'll be no sipping from me.' She grinned broadly, the glossy purple waves of her fifties-style bob shining in the light.

Molly snorted with laughter. 'Vi, hon, I was only joking. Since when have you ever seen me sip?'

'Hmm. Now you come to mention it, that would be never,' said Vi. 'You definitely come under the "guzzler" category, Moll.'

'Takes one to know one.' Molly arched her eyebrows mischievously. 'I think our Kitty's the only one who's ever been seen sipping a drink round these parts.'

'Yep, if it wasn't for the almost identical big brown eyes and dark curly hair, you'd never guess you two were cousins,' said Vi. 'Kitty must definitely be from the "sipping" branch of your family.'

Kitty sighed and looked across at her friends, shaking her head good-naturedly. 'I "sip", as you call it, because I'm such a light-weight, and end up with a lousy hangover without drinking much at all, as well you both know. And since Ollie and I have promised to take the kids to the beach tomorrow, a thumping head's something I can do without.'

'Ah, well, we still love you, chick.' Molly grinned at her.

'We certainly do.' Vi blew Kitty a kiss. Kitty caught it and pressed it to her cheek.

Livvie and Rosie exchanged amused glances, the pair sharing a giggle at the banter flying around the room. 'Oh, I love these Friday pamper nights,' said Livvie.

'Yep, me too,' said Rosie.

Though Livvie had only moved to the area in February, she felt like she'd known the friends far longer. It helped that she worked with Kitty and Violet at Romantique – the business the pair had set up in a studio in the back garden of Vi's parents' house. They designed and made wedding dresses and vintage-style underwear. Vi had a background in burlesque dancing and they'd originally started out making burlesque costumes, but the demand for wedding dresses had mushroomed so they'd decided to focus on that and had put the burlesque side of the business on the back-burner for now. Business was booming, so much so, they'd been struggling to keep up with demand. After seeing Livvie's book of wedding gown sketches and the quality of the clothes she'd made for herself, they'd offered her a job. Livvie hadn't had to think twice about accepting it; after all, there was nothing to keep her in Rickelthorpe; even her best friend, Bryony, had left Blushing Brides at the same time as her, moving down to London with her fiancé, Josh. Livvie had got to know Molly and Rosie better through her work colleagues too; not to mention the regular trips to the local pub, the fabulously cosy Sunne Inne.

Her last-minute booking of the holiday cottage that was now her home just before Christmas last year had changed her life immeasurably. Livvie had gone from being stuck in a dysfunctional relationship with a bone-idle, cheating layabout and working in a job with a grouchy boss and zero prospects, to being head-over-heels in love with Zander and working at her dream job. Win, win. She regularly had to pinch herself to prove she wasn't dreaming and would one day wake up and find herself slap bang in the middle of her old, miserable life. But, thus far, that hadn't happened. Fate, it seemed, had dealt her a lucky hand. And not a day went by when she didn't feel thankful. Not to mention happier than she'd ever thought possible.

'Anyway, back to the matter in hand, let's have a gander at this ring,' said Molly.

Livvie felt a ripple of excitement. She held out her hand, the diamond solitaire in its white-gold setting glinting in the soft light of the room.

Kitty gasped. 'Oh, it's beautiful. And did you say Zander had chosen it himself?'

Livvie nodded. 'Mmm. He did.'

'Well, he's got fabulous taste,' said Vi, taking Livvie's proffered hand.

Molly gave a low whistle. 'Hasn't he just?'

'Ooh, it's gorgeous, and I know just the nail varnish to set that little beauty off perfectly,' said Rosie. 'I'll get rose balm face masks on these three then I'll set to work on your manicure.'

'And while Rosie's doing that, you can tell us how Zander proposed,' said Vi, sitting back on the sofa and tucking her feet underneath her. 'Ooh, I've just had an exciting thought, we can make your wedding dress for you.'

'We can – that's if you'd like us to?' said Kitty, her eyes wide.

'I'd love you to. We're thinking of a Christmas wedding.' Butterflies took off in Livvie's stomach at the thought.

'Fabulous, I'm thinking a velvet cloak, Victorian-style cream leather ankle boots—'

'Hold your horses, Vi, there's plenty of time for designing wedding dresses.' Molly rolled her eyes, smiling. 'Livvie was just about to tell us how Zander proposed, weren't you, chick?'

Livvie loved the good-natured banter. Though they ribbed one another mercilessly at times, it was clear they all thought the world of one another and woe betide anyone who ever upset one of them, the others would come down on them like a ton of bricks. 'I actually love the idea of a cloak and the boots, Vi, so I'm going to keep them in mind. But as far as Zander's proposal goes, well, in truth, he'd been quizzing me about engagement rings for a bit before he actually popped the question; I think he thought he was being subtle.'

'Honestly, men! What are they like? Didn't he realise asking the woman he's so obviously fallen head-over-heels in love with about engagement rings is about as subtle as a sledge-hammer?' Molly said with a snort.

'And this is coming from the woman who wouldn't know subtle if it bit her on the backside, so that's saying something,' said Vi. Molly stuck her tongue out.

'Let Livvie tell us, you two,' said Kitty gently.

Livvie smiled. 'Molly does have a point. Anyway, though Zander had been quizzing me about engagement rings, I really wasn't expecting him to propose that night, but it happened when we were walking back from a meal at the Sunne Inne, along Fower Yatts Lane, holding hands.'

'Ahh, bless,' said Molly earning, herself a whack on the arm from Vi. 'Ouch! What was that for?'

'Sshh!' said Vi. 'Carry on, Livvie.'

'Well, it was a gorgeous balmy evening, and we stood for a while, watching the sunset over the moors; the colours were amazing; I've never seen one like it before.' Livvie cast her mind back to that night, the sky was ablaze with pinks, oranges, reds, and yellows. 'It made the whole of the moors look warm and golden, and there was the most intoxicating scent of wild honeysuckle in the air.' She glanced up to see four sets of eyes looking at her intently, accompanied by four broad smiles.

'So far, so romantic,' said Vi.

'I thought you said we had to be quiet?' Molly said. Vi shrugged her shoulders.

'I honestly couldn't think of a more romantic setting for a proposal,' said Livvie. 'Anyway, we were just talking, when Zander put his arms around me, kissed me and started saying how, even though we've only known each other a short time, he felt like he'd known me forever. Then he went on to say how much he loved me – I was honestly just so happy to hear he felt the same.'

There was a chorus of "ahhs" and Livvie felt her face burn with the heat of a blush. She gave an embarrassed laugh and continued. 'Before I knew what was happening, he was down on one knee and asking me to marry him.'

'Oh, that's so lovely, chick.' Tears glinted in Kitty's eyes and she pressed her hands to her chest.

'Apparently, he'd planned on doing it later on, over a meal or something, but he said the evening just felt so perfect, he couldn't think of a better time to do it. He had the ring in a box at home. It's a little bit loose so I'm going to get it tightened, but I absolutely love it.'

'It's gorgeous,' said Rosie, with a sigh.

'It'll be your turn next, Moll.' Vi nudged her friend with her foot, her green eyes glinting mischievously.

'Give over; I'm quite happy living in sin with Camm. We haven't got time to get married, what with the farm and the glamping site and a stroppy four-year-old to look after.' For all Molly's talk, Livvie noted the two spots of pink colouring her cheeks. Vi had clearly hit a nerve.

'Ah, how is little Emmie?' asked Kitty.

'Sassy, feisty, chatty,' said Molly wryly.

'Like mother like daughter.' Vi earned herself a dirty look from Molly.

'I remember that phase with my three,' said Kitty. 'And you've got it all to look forward to, Vi.'

'I think I'll leave taking care of the sassiness and feistiness to Jimby,' said Vi.

'You're probably right, I can see little Elspeth having that brother of mine wrapped round her little finger by the time it comes to that,' said Kitty.

'She's already got him there, Kitts. He absolutely dotes on her.' Vi smiled fondly.

'I'd expect nothing less from our Jimby.' Molly shifted in her seat. 'He was always a fabulous uncle; he was born to be a dad.'

'And thank goodness it happened,' said Vi. 'I honestly thought it wouldn't at one point.' She smiled at Kitty who leaned across and rubbed her arm.

'We'll all be looking at you next, Livvie.' Molly winked at her.

'Oh, you can calm your jets on that score! I intend to have a good few years, just me, Zander and Alf before I even think about babies.'

'Famous last words.' Vi arched a sculpted purple eyebrow.

3

AUGUST

LIVVIE GAVE the ground around the newly-planted lavender hedge a satisfied pat. 'There, all done.' She sat back on her haunches, blowing away the lock of auburn hair that had escaped her ponytail. It had been hard work, digging, weeding and planting – as the grumbling muscles in her shoulders could testify – and it had taken her longer than she'd expected, but she'd been determined to use her day off to get the job done. And it had been worth it, being out in the sunshine, listening to the sounds of the countryside, breathing in the sweet scent of freshly silaged grass that mingled with the perfume of the lavender. Bliss! Since her arrival at Dale View Cottage in early February, it regularly crossed Livvie's mind that the person who had built it over four hundred years ago must have put great thought into its location, setting it in a south-facing plot that over-looked the stunning valley of Great Stangdale. With its heavily thatched roof, thick, lime-washed walls and sturdy stone mullions, she couldn't think of anywhere more idyllic to call home.

She picked up her mug of tea and headed towards the wooden bench that was tucked neatly below the window on the left-hand-side of the path, rubbing the small of her back as she went. She flopped down, set her mug on the seat beside her then removed her gardening gloves. Her usually pale, creamy skin was flushed pink and her brow was peppered with tiny beads of perspiration. She wiped them away with the back of her hand and gave a contented sigh before taking a gulp of tea. 'Mmm.' Good; it was still drinkable.

Overhead, the sun shone down from a clear blue sky, the perfect foil to the vivid red berries that hung in clusters from the rowan trees in the lane in front of the cottage. Sparrows were chattering away ten-to-the-dozen from its branches. Livvie stretched her legs out in front of her and circled her feet, first the left foot then the right, ironing out the kinks that had resulted from a day's worth of gardening. Smiling, she admired her handiwork; the lavender hedge that ran either side of the flagstone path would look stunning this time next year, once the plants had filled out. The rich purple of the flowerheads complemented the sage-green paint of the gate where the hedge came to an end. Her gaze was drawn to a robin hopping amongst the recent planting, searching for rich pickings in the shape of a juicy worm. It glanced up at her occasionally, its eyes shining like tiny black beads. He'd been watching her with interest for most of the afternoon, waiting for this very moment.

Since early summer, when she'd first started to dabble with gardening, Livvie's confidence had grown quickly. To begin with, she was just happy to busy herself with a spot of weeding until she was sure of what was actually a plant and what was a weed, and she was surprised to find that she quite enjoyed it. In fact, she'd go as far to say she found the simple activity quite soothing and satisfying; offering her an opportunity to get lost in her thoughts and plans, which regularly featured Zander and their wedding that was due to take place the day before Christmas Eve.

Resting her head against the wall, she closed her eyes and let the sunshine warm her face, indulging herself in thoughts of him and, in particular, their tender love-making first thing that morning. A smile spread slowly across her face and she wiggled her toes as the memory sent a delicious shiver of happiness right through her.

'Penny for them.'

'Ooh!' Livvie started. Shielding her eyes with her hand, she looked up to see Freda Easton's weather-beaten face peering over the dry stone wall; she was wearing her familiar gap-toothed smile. As usual, her grubby deerstalker hat was set slightly skew-whiff and her white-grey hair hung beneath it in lank rats' tails. The old lady was Dale View Cottage's nearest neighbour and lived at Moor Top Cottage, the small-holding half a mile away along the tractor track. 'Freda.' Livvie smiled, happy to see her, though penny or no penny, there was no way she could share her thoughts of what Zander's hot kisses had done to her. 'I was just having a breather; I've finished planting the hedge. Look, I followed all your advice.'

'Aye, so I see; it looks grand, lass.' Freda beamed. 'Mind, it's red-hot today, I'm surprised you aren't in a lather what with all the digging and planting you'd have to do. There's no wonder you're looking a bit flushed.'

If only you knew the reason for that! 'I am; I'm going to have a nice cool shower once I'm done. And I'm surprised you're not sweltering in that hat and coat,' said Livvie. Freda always wore the same thing, come rain or shine. Livvie had never seen her without her hat, her tweed overcoat tied round the middle with a length of blue baler-twine, nor her dirty green wellies.

Freda laughed. 'Aye, I'm a bit warm.' She glanced around the garden. 'No young man and no Alfie Labrador with you today?'

'No, it's Zander's day off from the surgery so he's taken Alf for his annual injections at the vets' over in Middleton-le-Moors, then they're meeting up with Zander's old work colleague, Noah, and going for a walk.'

'Ah, right. Good day for a wander.'

'It is.' Livvie paused. 'Fancy joining me for a cuppa? There's plenty of tea in the pot and I could do with a top-up, and I'd appreciate you checking to see if I've set the plants far enough apart.'

'Well, I was just taking Midge here for a walk to the end of the lane.' Freda nodded to the small wire-haired dog of indeterminate breed, 'but that sounds like a grand idea, if you've got time, that is?'

'Freda, I've always got time for you.' The old lady's rheumy blue eyes sparkled happily at Livvie's words. 'Come on, you park yourself here,' Livvie patted the space beside her on the seat, 'and I'll go and grab the teapot and another mug. There's fresh water in the dog bowl there if Midge needs a drink.'

'Right you are, lovey. Come on then, Midge, you look a bit thirsty, lad, let's get you a drink.' Freda waddled up the path with Midge following behind her. He was panting heavily and went straight to the water, lapping it up enthusiastically.

In a matter of moments Livvie returned armed with a tray. 'There you go, Freda, yours is the one with the flowers on.' She leaned towards the old lady, allowing her to take the mug, before setting the tray down between them on the bench. 'Help yourself to a biscuit.'

'Thank you.' Freda took one and dunked it into her tea.

'And here's one of Alf's dog biscuits for you, Midge, but you've got to promise not to go telling him I've been giving his treats out or I'll be in trouble.' Midge took the biscuit gently and Livvie smoothed the wiry hair on his head. 'Good lad.'

Freda nodded to the lavender hedge. 'Looks to me like you've set the plants exactly the right distance apart; about a foot by the looks of things. But mind you don't forget to give them a good watering. Best save it for this evening though, when things are a bit cooler and the sun won't have the chance to dry it off straight away.'

Livvie swallowed her mouthful. 'Mmm. Good thinking.' Her nose twitched at Freda's somewhat fusty aroma which seemed to have intensified in the heat; she wished the old lady didn't live up to her reputation of not taking a bath or washing her clothes. This, together with her, at times, somewhat eccentric behaviour, meant folk in the surrounding moorland villages tended to avoid her or were scornful of her, which was something Livvie found incomprehensibly sad.

Since Livvie had moved in with Zander, she'd become fond of Freda, who walked past the cottage every day, whether it be to venture out to Lytell Stangdale a mile-and-a-half away, or to simply take Midge for a walk. At first, Freda had been reluctant to offer anything more than a hurried "hello", clearly not wanting to stop and talk. But Livvie felt sorry for the old lady. In her mind, Freda had a tough existence, living in a cottage in the middle of the moors and, if rumours were true, in very basic conditions. She was sure Freda must feel isolated and lonely, especially in the long, dark winter months; it didn't seem right for a woman who must be well into her seventies to have such a pitiful existence. It tapped into Livvie's sensitive nature, and made her reach out and offer friendship to the older woman. Conscious of not wanting to appear pushy, she was keen for Freda to know they were here for her if ever she needed help.

Livvie's gentle persistence paid off and, after a couple of weeks, she was thrilled when the old lady stopped at the gate to admire the garden, apparently keen to strike up a conversation. *A breakthrough!* Livvie had finally won Freda's trust and she was delighted. Since that day, the pair had become firm friends and had chatted regularly ever since, much to the surprise of Livvie's friends in the village.

'And be sure to keep them well-watered until they're established, then cut them back in September; that'll stop them from going all leggy and straggly.' Freda pointed her welly-encased foot towards the lavender plants.

'Will do, but I might need you to remind me about the pruning when the time comes; there's a lot to remember with this gardening lark.'

Freda chuckled. 'I reckon it'll be second nature to you before you know it.'

The pair sat in companionable silence for a moment, watching a bumble-bee investigate the newly-planted lavender. The sound of its humming was joined by another that danced around the blooms of the soft-pink rose that scrambled up the low walls of the cottage. Midge tucked himself under the bench, out of the unforgiving heat of the sun. He rested his head on his paws and closed his eyes. The aroma that matched his owner's wafted up and curled around Livvie's nose. She did her best to ignore it.

The peace was broken when Freda took a noisy slurp of her tea. 'So, how are the wedding plans going with that handsome young doctor of yours?'

Livvie's heart flipped with happiness at Freda's words. 'Well, since it's not that long since Zander proposed, it's still early days as far as plans are concerned, but we're hoping to have the ceremony up at Danskelfe Castle.'

'Danskelfe Castle? I didn't know they did weddings.'

'It's just a recent thing. They do all sorts since Lord Hammondely let Lady Carolyn start running events there. Apparently, she's in her element since her father gave her some responsibility. Well, that's what I've heard anyway, but they do things like Halloween parties for children, music in the wood. There's talk of them opening parts of it to the public but I believe hosting weddings is their latest venture and I honestly can't imagine a more perfect place to get married.'

'Oh, right.'

A moment's silence hung between them and Livvie noticed the old lady's expression had become wistful.

Freda turned to her and smiled, a shadow of sadness hovering in her eyes. 'So, lass, tell me again exactly how he proposed.'

Livvie laughed; she'd told Freda the story several times before. It touched her that the old lady appeared to get enormous pleasure from hearing it each time. 'Ah, it was so romantic, Freda, and totally unexpected.' Her heart fluttered at the memory. 'It was a gorgeous evening and we were walking back from Lytell Stangdale after having one of Bea's delicious meals at the Sunne Inne.'

'Aye, I've heard her cooking's good.'

'Ooh, it's so good, she somehow manages to make even simple dishes taste extra special; I've no idea how she does it but I reckon she must have some magic ingredient or something. Anyway, we were walking along Fower Yatts Lane...' As Livvie recounted the story, she stole a glance at Freda who was looking out across the valley. She was pleased to see her expression was once again relaxed, with no trace of the melancholy of moments ago. Livvie's heart squeezed for her elderly friend.

'Aye, it's a beautiful part of the world.'

'It is, I couldn't have wished for a more perfect location to be proposed to.' Livvie looked down at her engagement ring, the diamond glinting at her. Though it looked a little out of place on her mud ingrained hands with their grubby fingernails, it still gave her a thrill to see it sitting there on her finger, like it belonged.

'Sorry, my dear, I interrupted you; carry on.'

'It's okay. Well, we were standing there, just taking it all in...' Livvie continued her story, her eyes dancing.

Freda chuckled. 'Took you right by surprise, didn't it?'

'It did, but I didn't need to think about my answer for even the tiniest of moments. I knew from the first minute I met him that he was the one, so I said "yes" straight away. And, before I could say anything else, he scooped me up and started spinning me around. As you can imagine, Alf was just as excited as we were and was jumping around all over the place, with his tail wagging like crazy.'

Freda clapped her hands together and gave a throaty laugh. 'Ah, such a lovely story. You were meant to be, you two, no doubt about it.'

'It certainly feels that way. I'm a great believer in fate. I didn't just arrive at the cottage that wild winter's night for no reason; I was sent here.'

'I think you were. And it's given you a lovely story to tell your grandchildren.' Freda smiled, her pale-blue eyes shining, giving Livvie a glimpse of the beautiful woman she'd once been.

'It has that.' Livvie sighed happily. 'And what about you, Freda? Have you ever been in love? Ever been married?' Livvie had heard the rumours rumbling around the village, but she wasn't sure of their authenticity. Freda's background certainly kept the gossip rumour-mill busy which was just the sort of thing Livvie despised.

'Ah, you don't want to know about me, lass, I'm not very interesting.' Freda placed her mug on the tray and got to her feet. 'Right, me and Midge had best be off. I've got some vegetables to lift.'

'Oh, okay, but you don't have to rush off on my account, there's plenty of tea left in the pot; if I drink it all myself I'll be awash.' Livvie wished she could take her question back; it had scared Freda off which was the last thing she wanted to do, especially since they'd made so much progress.

'No, we need to get back home.'

'Okay, bye, Freda. And thanks for all the advice about the lavender, I don't know what I'd do without you.' Livvie watched as Freda waddled down the path and out of the gate. She'd hit a nerve with her questions and she felt bad.

4

THE JET of water from the shower-head pounding at the aching muscles in her back was utter bliss. Livvie had been standing beneath it for a several long minutes, her eyes closed while she savoured the cooling effect of the lukewarm water on her skin. She released her thick auburn waves from the grips that had kept them in place on top of her head, and let them tumble over her shoulders. Cranking the temperature up a notch, she shampooed and conditioned her hair, filling the bathroom with the fragrance of summer flowers as she hummed along to the music playing in the background. With the water rinsing away the soapy residue, Livvie found herself getting lost in thoughts of her wedding dress. One afternoon, just after Zander had proposed, she'd found herself sitting around the little kitchen table in the Romantique studio with Kitty and Vi. The three friends were excitedly bouncing ideas about while Kitty scribbled away, producing a sketch of the most perfect gown for a winter wedding. The memory sent a wave of happiness surging through her; she sang aloud to herself, running her fingers through her hair.

'Fancy some company in there?'

'Whaargh!' The shower curtain was pulled back, making Livvie squeal.

'Oh, my god, Zander! You frightened the life out of me!'

He laughed, his eyes glinting mischievously. 'Sorry, I didn't mean to make you jump.'

She flicked water at him. 'Well, you did.'

'Kind of reminds me of the night we first met, me catching you naked in the bath. I have very happy memories of that evening.'

'I have very embarrassing memories of that evening, you seeing me completely starkers like that with all my wobbly bits before you even knew my name.'

'Well, you have no need to be embarrassed, you looked like a goddess to me. Still do actually.' He reached in, clasping his hand around the back of her neck, pulling her towards him so he could kiss her. He pressed his lips against hers, dark splashes appearing on his blue t-shirt from the shower. 'Mmm. You taste good.'

'Zander! You'll get soaked!' she said, giggling.

'Don't care.' He peeled his t-shirt off, quickly followed by the rest of his clothes, leaving them in a pile on the floor. Before Livvie knew what was happening, he was in the shower beside her, his hands warm on her shoulders. 'Hmm. Have I told you how gorgeous you are?' He bent and kissed her again, sending waves of desire rippling through her.

Livvie wrapped her arms around his neck and pressed herself to him, water cascading down her back. She arched her eyebrows as she felt his eagerness. He ran his hands over her curves while he delivered a trail of burning kisses down her neck towards her generous breasts, making her groan in ecstasy.

The pair were lost in the moment when a loud bark brought them back down to earth with a resounding bump. Zander cursed and rested his forehead against Livvie's. 'The little sod.' He pushed the shower curtain back to see Alf sitting in the middle of the room wagging his tail. He looked rather pleased with himself.

'Has anyone ever told you you're an annoying little bugger, Alfred Gillespie?'

Alf wagged his tail.

'I see his trip to the vets doesn't seem to have dampened his spirits,' said Livvie, stifling a giggle.

'It doesn't.'

Alf wagged his tail some more.

'Ahh, but how could you resist that face?' Livvie asked, which made Alf's tail wag harder still, thudding loudly on the polished elm floorboards.

'Very easily, especially given his shocking sense of timing.' He gave Alf a stern look. 'How would you like it if I pulled that kind of stunt on you, eh, buddy? And I thought you knew the bathroom was out of bounds, especially after you burst in on Livvie last year.'

Alf's tail swished across the floorboards as he gave another bark, the happy expression not leaving his face. He trotted towards the bath and went to jump in. 'Don't even think about it!' Zander leapt out, wrapped a towel around his waist and took Alf by the collar. 'Come on, trouble, downstairs,' he said, leading the errant Labrador out of the bathroom. Reaching the door, he looked over his shoulder at Livvie. 'I'll be back in a minute; don't go anywhere.'

'So, how's Noah doing?' Livvie was in the kitchen, still enjoying the after-glow of their spontaneous romantic encounter in the shower. She'd just finished adding fresh chives to a bowl of potato salad and headed out into the garden where Zander was tending steak on the barbecue. The light breeze was wafting the mouth-watering aroma around in the air, making her stomach growl.

'He's doing great. Said he's getting on well with my replacement at the surgery, which is a relief for both of us. I'd have felt pretty guilty if the new GP had been hard to work with.'

'We'll have to invite him and the family over; I'd like to get to know them a bit better before we get married, especially since Noah's going to be your best man.' Livvie's eyes rested on Zander as she made her way over to the picnic table, her pulse quickening at the sight of his broad shoulders and his cropped dark hair still wet from the shower. She set the potato salad down, then lit a citronella candle to deter the midges which, she'd learnt, could be ferocious on the moors of an evening. She cast her eyes around the eating area which was at the right of the cottage, just off the kitchen, set beneath a gazebo offering protection from sun or rain. Livvie smiled, pleased with her handiwork. She'd thrown a hand-made cloth of blue and white striped ticking over the table, setting it with dark-blue fabric napkins, cutlery with cream handles and plain white crockery. Twinkling fairy lights trimmed the edges of the gazebo, while more were woven through the yew hedge and the branches of the bay trees that sat either side of the kitchen door. Candles in jam jars were hung on strategically placed hooks, their flames flickering in the gentle light of the summer evening. It looked magical. Livvie adjusted the bunch of wild flowers in the jug in the centre of the table and sighed happily. 'How long before the steak's ready?'

'Another minute and we'll be good to go.' Zander gave her a heart-melting smile. 'And it's a great idea to get Noah, Jess and the kids over here; we should organise something soon. We could maybe have a barbecue with them.'

'I'd like that.' Livvie beamed back at him. 'By the way, have you noticed a certain young man?' She directed her eyes towards Alf.

'I have.' Zander feigned a look of disapproval at the Labrador who was glancing from him to Livvie, drool hanging from the corners of his mouth, his body shaking in anticipation of food.

Zander couldn't help but laugh. 'Hmm. After your earlier behaviour, you can think again if you expect me to save a sausage or two for you, Alf. I still haven't fully forgiven you for it.'

'Oh, bless him, it'd be cruel not to give him his usual sausage; he'd be devastated,' Livvie said, laughing. 'And look at that pleading expression; how can you resist it?'

Zander harrumphed. 'Don't worry, I'm not immune to his pitiful looks. There's the usual sausage with his name on it; it's been set aside so it can cool.'

'He'll be thrilled.' She filled two glasses with crisp white wine and handed one to Zander. 'There you go, chef's reward.'

'Mmm. Thanks.' He clinked his glass against hers. 'Cheers.'

'Cheers.' Livvie smiled up at him as she took a sip, her heart swelling with love for him. 'The steak looks seriously good. I'm absolutely starving; I could eat a scabby horse between two mattresses!'

Zander roared with laughter. 'I'm not surprised after all that gardening. And you'll be pleased to know I've brought in some of Lucy's chocolate cake from the village shop for pudding.'

'Mmm-hmm, sounds delicious. I knew there was a good reason I agreed to marry you.'

'So, it's got nothing to do with my hot kisses then?'

'Well, maybe a little bit…' she said, her eyes twinkling at him.

'Or, how about that thing I did when we were in the shower earlier, you know, the thing that drives you crazy?' He grinned mischievously at her.

'Okay, I'll give you that.' She giggled.

'And how could I forget what we did last night? You seemed to particularly enjoy how my t—'

'Behave! Delicate ears and all that.' Livvie nodded at Alf whose eyes were boring into the steak. 'And that's going to be frazzled to a crisp if you're not careful.'

'Bugger!' Zander quickly transferred the steak to a plate. 'Got carried away a bit there.'

'I think you did. Now come on, clear that dirty mind of yours and let's eat,' she said, delivering a slap to his backside.

5

LIVVIE AND ZANDER were sitting on the garden swing seat, his arm around her as they gazed out at the view. The heather was in full-swing, covering the moor top, its huge swathes of springy purple blossom scenting the air with the fragrance of honey. The patchwork of green and golden fields, divided by sturdy dry stone walls, lined the base of the valley, reaching up to meet the heather and bracken, the scene punctuated by clusters of dense woodland where secretive deer sought shelter.

The pair looked on as the sun gradually slipped behind the lofty heights of Great Stangdale rigg on the opposite side of the dale, its warmth of earlier still lingering. Birds were heading home to roost, their exuberant chatter of earlier trailing off, leaving the countryside quiet all but for the occasional low baying of the Danks's cows over at Tinkel Top Farm, the bleating of Tom Storr's sheep from two fields away and the low thrum of a tractor heaving its way up the path to Withrin Hill Farm where their friends Molly and Camm lived. They'd been watching Molly's son Ben silaging in one of the lower fields, making the most of the fine weather, before heading back home for his dinner.

'Freda popped by today, she joined me for a cup of tea in the garden. We had a good chinwag, it was really nice talking to her.'

'You've made real headway with her; it'll do her the world of good to socialise and talk to someone, help her to build up her trust in people.'

'You won't think that when I tell you what I did.'

'Oh?'

'Well, she asked me to tell her about how you proposed.'

Zander rolled his eyes, smiling. 'Again?'

'She loves hearing about it. Anyway, after I'd told her, I went and asked her if she'd ever been married or had someone special which I quickly found out was a *big* mistake.'

'Ah.'

'Honestly, it was as if I'd asked her to share some dreadful secret. Her face dropped and she muttered something about there being nothing interesting about her, then before I knew what was happening, she said she had to go. Which she did, in quite a hurry.'

Zander drew his brows together. 'Poor old thing, she doesn't like talking about herself, makes her clam up.'

'So I gather.'

Livvie rested her head on Zander's shoulder. 'I really wish I hadn't said anything to her, I could've kicked myself as soon as the words were out of my mouth. I don't want it to put her off talking to me or joining me for a cup of tea in the garden.'

'I wouldn't worry, I'm sure she'll be back; from what I've seen, I think she values your friendship. The fact she offered you advice about planting up the lavender hedge shows it – it looks good, by the way. I reckon she'll have just wanted to get out of the conversation but because she's kept herself to herself for so long, she'll probably have lost the social skills or the know-how to change the subject or avoid answering the question. She'll have felt awkward; physically leaving would have been the only solution in her mind.'

'Oh, poor Freda. Is that what you really think?'

Zander nodded. 'Mmm.'

'Ah, bless her; I feel guilty for making her feel that way. I wonder where her family are? She must have someone.' Alf was laid out in front of her and she rubbed his tummy with her bare feet. He groaned happily, stretching out and giving a slow wag of his tail.

'You'd think so, wouldn't you?'

'You would.' Livvie heaved a sigh. 'Surely there must be something on her medical records to say as much.'

Zander gave her a look. 'You know I can't discuss anything to do with my patients.'

'Sorry, I didn't mean you should share any details with me.'

Livvie felt her cheeks burn. 'I don't want you to think I was hinting for information or expecting you to be unprofessional, I just—'

Zander squeezed her shoulder. 'I know you weren't; I appreciate you're looking out for her, but if she wanted anything to do with her family, or if they wanted anything to do with her, then I think it would've happened by now.'

'You're right, and I have no intention of meddling. I just feel so sorry for her living along there on her own, especially with her being as sweet and harmless as she is. And she's been so kind, taking time to offer gardening tips; I'd have made a mess of the lavender hedge if it wasn't for her; I'd have planted it too close together and not watered it enough.' Livvie frowned. 'I can't understand why she has no one to look out for her.'

'I know, it beggars belief. What I can say though is that I've never heard her mention anyone, either friend or relative, but I must admit, like you, I worry about her living all alone in that house at her age, without any creature comforts. And it's not as if she comes to the surgery so I can give her a check over or ask how she's doing.'

'It's like she's so unused to anyone caring about her, she just puts up with everything and deals with whatever gets thrown at her.'

Zander took a sip of his wine. 'Which isn't good at her age and which is why I'm pleased she's started talking to you.'

'Which makes me hope I haven't scared her off.'

'I don't think you will have.'

Livvie wasn't so sure.

Zander gently eased his arm from behind her and stood up. 'The temperature's dropped; I'm just going to go and get a couple of blankets then we can stay out here and watch the Perseids showers, if you like?'

'Ooh, sounds lovely!' Livvie welcomed the distraction; she was at risk of dwelling on her conversation with Freda which she knew had the potential to dampen her mood. It had been a lovely evening thus far, and Livvie didn't want to burst the bubble of happiness she'd been enjoying with Zander.

～

LIVVIE YAWNED, she'd been snuggling into Zander for the last forty-five minutes as they'd watched nightfall creep in, the first stars of the night twinkling shyly above the dale. Before they knew it, the sky had become a deep inky-blue; the perfect backdrop to the shooting stars of the Perseids meteor shower that passed by in August. Having grown up in a town afflicted by the associated light-pollution that watered down the night sky, she'd never seen the phenomenon before; she'd never even *heard* of the Perseids before Zander had mentioned them. She felt a ripple of happiness and snuggled closer into him as she gazed out on the dale which was now peppered with golden-yellow lights from the farmhouses.

Something scurried in the hedgerow at the foot of the garden while a pair of tawny owls hooted to one another in the distance. Not long ago, the sounds would have sent a spike of fear through her, but not now. Now she savoured them; her life in a flat in a less-than-salubrious part of Rickelthorpe, stuck in a dysfunctional relationship with Donny – her flaky, cheating ex-boyfriend – felt far behind her. And she had no intention of going back; she was a country girl now and happy to be so.

She yawned again, pulling the blanket closer up to her chin.

'Tired?' Zander pressed a kiss to her cheek.

'Mmm.' She nodded. 'It's all the gardening in fresh moorland air; it wipes me out.'

'I'm not surprised, you're always outdoors.'

'I love it.'

'And I love the little freckles that have appeared across your nose.'

'Ughh! I absolutely slathered myself in factor fifty sunblock too.'

'Oh, and I almost forgot to tell you, I spoke to Lady Carolyn Hammondely and booked an appointment for us to go and look around the castle this Sunday.'

Livvie sat up straight, excitement surging through her, pushing her sleepiness aside. 'Really?'

Zander nodded. 'Really. And, while I was on, I provisionally booked our wedding in with them for the day before Christmas Eve as we'd discussed.'

Livvie threw her blanket off and leapt at him, straddling his lap and cupping his face in her hands, sending the chair rocking violently. 'That's fantastic, Zander, thank you! I can't wait to see what the castle's like inside.' She kissed him hard on the mouth.

'Woah, steady on, Liv, you nearly tipped us onto the floor,' he said, laughing as he dug his feet into the ground, steadying the seat.

Alf jumped up, wondering what the fuss was about, wagging his tail and nudging Zander's leg.

'Sorry, but that's seriously exciting news.' Her eyes shone in the moonlight. 'But how come you didn't tell me straight away?'

'I was going to keep it a surprise and just drive you there on Sunday, but thanks to me having a glass of wine, it forced its way out of me.'

'Well, you did much better than I'd have done; the words would've been out of my mouth when I was half-way up the path,' she said with a chuckle. 'But thank you, thank you, thank you for organising it.' She planted kisses all over his face.

'You don't have to thank me, I just thought we'd better start making some progress; December will be here before we know it.'

'You're absolutely right, we do need to get things moving.' Her heart was thumping. 'I'm so excited, I can't believe we're getting married in an actual castle. I can't wait to see what it's like and what the grounds will be like for outside photos. It'll be magical.'

'It will, it'll be perfect,' Zander said, smoothing her hair off her face. 'But now, much as I hate to be a party-pooper, it's late and we're both at work in the morning, so I think it's time we got to bed.' He pressed a kiss to her lips.

'Yep, you're right.' She carefully pushed herself off his knee and stood up, rubbing the twinge in her shoulder. 'It's been a lovely day but I think I'm going to know about it tomorrow with all the gardening I've done today.' Tiredness crept back in as she took Zander's hand and followed him into the cottage, Alf trotting along close behind. Though, with Zander's news whirling around her mind, Livvie doubted she'd get much sleep that night.

WRAPPED TIGHTLY in Zander's arms, her head tucked under his chin, Livvie lay listening to his deep, rhythmic breathing and the strong, soothing beat of his heart. Their bedroom was cosy, with its sturdy oak cruck-frame reaching up to the age-darkened beams of the sloping roof, and small dormer windows over-looking the dale in front. It was warm, but not uncomfortably so thanks to the thatched roof which kept the house warm in winter and cool in summer. She inhaled the comforting scent of Zander: soap and citrussy cologne. Sleep had claimed him almost as soon as his head had hit the pillow but, tired as she was, excitement at their pending visit to Danskelfe Castle was pulsing through her, pushing sleep out of reach, just as she'd thought it would. Images of a spectacular staircase, of grand turrets, of twinkling windows and rich, dark wood against thick stone walls sprang up in her mind, filling her with happiness. She couldn't wait to share her news with everyone.

Well, maybe not quite everyone. A memory of her last conversation with her mother loomed in her mind, throwing a bucket of cold water over her joy. She didn't approve of Livvie getting married. 'It's too soon,' she'd said. 'You hardly know the man … he's a doctor, you're a machinist; what on earth will you have in common? I'll tell you this, my girl, since you've moved to that place, you've got ideas above your station … it won't last … our Cheryl agrees with me, you should ask her what she thinks…'

Cheryl. *Ughh!* Livvie squeezed her eyes tightly shut and cuddled closer into Zander, making him stir a little; the last thing she needed was to think about what her snooty sister thought of her engagement. She couldn't remember the last time Cheryl had said anything nice about anyone. Her face seemed to be permanently set in a disapproving expression that was growing more like their mother's with every passing day. The pair had threatened not to come to the wedding, citing Livvie's selfishness at the timing of it as the reason. Livvie wondered if it was wrong of her to secretly hope they wouldn't. They never had anything good to say about her, and seemed to get a thrill out of bad-mouthing her to new ears. If only her dad was still here; he'd have a plentiful supply of kind words and love for her, and he'd be over the moon to see her happily settled with a man who made her feel as loved and cherished as Zander did.

"Our Cheryl agrees with me, you should ask her what she thinks…" Livvie wished those words would disappear from her mind; she had a pretty good idea what "our Cheryl" thought, and one thing was for certain, it wouldn't be anything complimentary. She pushed the image of her sister's disapproving face out of her mind and turned her thoughts to the design of her wedding dress; time was marching on, she'd have to get cracking with it.

6

LIVVIE MADE her way along the flagstone path that ran around Sunshine Cottage and through to the back garden where the Romantique studio was situated. It was another gloriously sunny day and she was wearing a light white shirt over a pair of loose-fitting, batik-print harem pants, a pair of chunky brown leather sandals on her feet. Her hair was tied in a thick plait that swished from side to side as she walked. Though it was just before nine o'clock in the morning, there was already a lot of heat in the sun, but it was ever-so-slightly tempered by the light breeze that rustled through the trees.

Opening the door, Livvie inhaled the studio's familiar aroma of Violet's floral perfume mixed with bales of new fabric. It never failed to send a thrill through her, as did the sight of the shelves loaded with jars of sparkling beads and crystals, reels of luxurious trims and sumptuous bolts of fabric and lace. The walls were lined with sketches and photographs of Romantique-designed gowns, while in the far corner was a mannequin wearing a full-skirted wedding dress in creamy raw silk, the latest creation the friends were working on for local bride-to-be, Hetty Johnson.

Livvie had joined the Romantique team as soon as she'd moved to Dale View Cottage in early February and was in her element sketching designs, sourcing fabric and constructing garments; her dream job. It was a far cry from working as a sales assistant for miserable Mrs Harris at Blushing Brides. Livvie didn't have a moment's regret at leaving her old life at Rickelthorpe behind her.

'Morning, ladies,' she said to Kitty and Violet who were chatting away, making a pot of tea in the small kitchen area.

'Morning, Livvie.' Kitty gave her familiar smile that warmed her large brown eyes and lit up her elfin face. 'Cuppa?'

'Mmm. Please.'

'You're looking very happy this morning, young lady. Living with that dishy doctor of yours is obviously doing the trick.' Vi arched an eyebrow at her.

Livvie chuckled and headed over to them. 'Well, funny you should say that…' Her heart leapt in excitement at the thought of sharing her news about the appointment at Danskelfe Castle. 'Actually, I'll just pop these down, then I'll tell you. I called in at the village shop and grabbed some of Lucy's chocolate-dipped flapjacks; they're still warm so the chocolate's a bit melty.'

'Ooh, delicious!' Vi tore open the packet and lifted out a slice. She licked the gooey chocolate from her fingers. 'Mmm-mmm. Oh, yum.'

Kitty looked on in disbelief. 'Vi, it's not even nine o'clock, how can you face eating chocolate at this time?'

'Very easily since I've been breast-feeding Pippin; it's got me constantly starving.' Vi took a bite of the flapjack, chewing on it appreciatively.

'Hmm. I can remember feeling ravenous when I was feeding my three, but never so that I could eat chocolate or cakes for breakfast,' said Kitty.

'Oh, I love how you still call little Elspeth Pippin,' said Livvie. 'And, actually, I could quite happily eat chocolate or cake any time of day and I've never had the excuse of breast-feeding.'

'There, you see, Kitts, it's not just me. Anyway, I had my first breakfast about…' Vi paused, looking up at the clock on the wall, 'three-and-a-half hours ago. Squeezed in a croissant a couple of hours after that, so I'm more than ready for this, which is more than can be said for apples. There's no wonder Jimby nicknamed the baby "Pippin" before she was even born. I honestly didn't realise just how many apples I was getting through; I can't face them now after my crazy pregnancy craving. This, however, is a completely different matter.' She took another large bite out of her flapjack.

'So we see,' said Molly who'd just walked through the door. 'I think your apple consumption was in danger of causing a global shortage; it's just as well you had Pippin when you did.'

'Moll, come in, you've got perfect timing, we've just made a pot of tea,' Kitty said, beaming at her cousin.

'Moll, I swear you can sniff tea out a mile off,' said Vi as she reached for another mug.

'Yep, it's a gift I'm rather proud of.' Molly grinned. 'And I've no idea how you manage to turn yourself out looking so glamorous every day being mum to a six-month-old baby. I was still walking round in baggy leggings and even baggier sweatshirts when mine were that age – still am if I'm honest,' she said with a chuckle.

'Same here,' said Kitty. 'Though I can't imagine Vi in leggings and a sweatshirt, can you? I bet you don't even own any, do you, Vi?'

'No chance! There's no way I'd leave the house without my make-up on and my hair done.' Vi smoothed the rich purple waves of her bob. 'And I wouldn't be seen dead in a pair of leggings. Though, I have to admit, Jimby is a brilliant hands-on dad and my mum's a godsend, having Elspeth as much as she does. I don't think I'd find it so easy to get myself ready without the pair of them; I know how lucky I am.'

'Well, you wouldn't be you without your Hollywood movie-star style, Vi,' said Kitty. 'I think it's fab that you still make the effort.'

'Thanks, chick.' Vi's eyes smiled as she took a bite of her flapjack.

'And it's good to hear that brother of mine is such a help,' Kitty said, seriously.

'Yep, it's pretty obvious he's a totally besotted dad, just like Pip was with our three.' A barely discernible shadow flitted across Molly's face.

'He was, Moll.' Kitty reached across and rubbed her cousin's arm. Molly replied with a small smile.

Livvie felt slightly awkward at the reference to Molly's husband who she knew had died in an accident the previous year. 'Did you get all of your silaging done yesterday? We saw Ben heading home in the tractor last night,' she said, hoping to move Molly's thoughts on.

'Aye, we did, thank goodness; Tom's been doing the same at Rowan Slack, and Ben and Camm are busy gathering the bales up as we speak. And I'd love a cuppa, thanks, Kitts. I've just dropped Emmie off with my mum and dad for the morning. I need to pop to the shop to pick up some bread and milk, then I'm off back home to do the books which is one of my least favourite jobs so I'm using all the delay tactics I can think of.'

Livvie was relieved to see Molly's smile return.

'Ughh! I can't blame you for that,' said Kitty. 'I hate book-keeping; I'm so grateful Vi's good at it and doesn't mind doing it.'

'I know it sounds sad, but I actually like nothing better than getting my teeth stuck into a bit of bookwork,' said Vi.

'Yep, you're totally right there, it sounds very sad.' Molly flashed her a playful smile.

'Thanks for that, dearest friend.' Vi pulled a face at Molly, making them all laugh.

Kitty, Molly and Vi had grown up together and, from what Livvie could gather, they'd been through some pretty tough times which appeared to have galvanised their closeness. The three women couldn't be more different in looks and temperament but they complemented one another perfectly. Being in their mid-to-late thirties meant they were slightly older than Livvie's twenty-nine years, but that hadn't hindered their blossoming friendship, and she'd slotted in as though she'd known them for years, joining in with their banter and the way they bounced off one another. Initially, she'd been a little wary of Molly's feistiness, but it hadn't taken long for her to realise it was just a front and the woman had a heart of gold.

'Actually, Livvie was just about to tell us why living with Zander has made her look so deliriously happy this morning,' said Vi, handing Molly a mug of tea.

'Thanks, chick.' Molly took the mug and pulled out a chair at the little table. 'I think we all know why Liv looks like the cat that got the cream. We all would if we woke up next to Zander; he's flippin' hot-to-trot.'

'Please excuse my cousin,' said Kitty to Livvie.

'I was only stating the obvious!'

'So says the woman who wakes up with Mr Tall, Dark and Handsome.' Vi gave Molly an impish grin.

'Well, I'd say the same about you, Vi, if the bloke you were married to wasn't my cousin and our Kitty's brother.' Molly chuckled into her mug. 'And come to think of it, our Kitty still hasn't lost that loved-up glow since she got married to Ollie, has she? She's clearly benefitting from regular hot and spicy jiggy-jiggy sessions.'

'Molly!' Kitty's face was crimson and Livvie couldn't help but smile despite feeling slightly sorry for her friend.

Vi nodded, a mischievous glint in her eye. 'Mm-hm. You're not wrong there, Moll. There's definitely more than the "I'm just-married so I'm getting loads of sex" look about her.'

'Vi!' said Kitty.

Livvie looked on, biting down on her smile, as Kitty sought refuge behind her mug, her face burning brighter.

'You know full-well Ollie and me have been married for a year so we're not "just-married" as you put it.'

'Our point exactly,' said Vi.

'Woah, look at those blushes! Kitts, we could fry eggs on your cheeks, hon!' Molly turned to Violet. 'I think we've hit the nail on the head, Vi!'

'Stop it!' Despite shaking her head, Kitty couldn't help but smile.

'We're just saying we're chuffed to bits that you're so obviously happy, Kitts. That's all,' said Molly.

'Funny, it feels more like you're torturing me,' she said, laughing.

'You lot are bonkers,' said Livvie. She couldn't help but giggle as Kitty put her mug down and scurried over to the sink to wash her hands.

'Please don't tell me you've only just noticed,' said Vi.

'Erm, nope, I picked up on that pretty much the first night I met you.'

'Takes one to know one.' Molly nudged Livvie with her elbow. 'Anyway, chick, come on, spill the deets on why you're looking so chuffed with yourself.'

Livvie felt butterflies swoop in her stomach. 'Well, Zander's booked us an appointment with Lady Carolyn Hammondely; we're going to have a look around Danskelfe Castle this Sunday, with a view to having our wedding there.'

'Oh, wow!' said Vi. 'Now that definitely explains the massive smile you walked in with.'

Molly gave a low whistle. 'Danskelfe Castle, eh? That's pretty fancy-schmansy.'

'Ooh! How romantic, it'll be a wonderful venue for your wedding; I'm so happy for you,' said Kitty, her face still pink.

7

THE MORNING HAD FLOWN by faster than ever. Molly had reluctantly pulled herself away and gone home to tackle her book-keeping, leaving the three friends to prepare for a final gown fitting with Hetty Johnson. The young woman was a friend of Kitty's twenty-year-old stepdaughter, Anoushka, and a cousin to Molly on her dad's side, though Livvie had struggled to see any resemblance, physically or personality wise. Where Molly was warm and friendly – and, admittedly, a little feisty – Hetty and her mother, Val, were brittle and bitchy. Livvie's first impression of Hetty hadn't been favourable; she'd found her rather spoilt and rude, giving the impression she considered it beneath her to engage the services of Romantique to make her wedding gown and bridesmaids' dresses. Livvie had lost count of the number of times Hetty or Val had mentioned that they were only using Romantique because of the family connection and that they didn't want to cause offence by going elsewhere. 'More like they expect "mates rates" – and I use the word "mates" very loosely,' Molly had said with a snarl.

'You're spot-on there, chick,' Vi had said, slowly removing the pins she'd had pressed between her lips. 'I wish they'd take their money and go and spend it in another bridal boutique; we're rushed off our feet as it is. I don't know who they think they are, expecting to jump the queue and us to drop everything for them.'

'I'm pleased no one else around here's like them.' The memory of

Val looking her up and down disapprovingly when she realised
Livvie was Zander's fiancée had been fresh in Livvie's mind.

'Well, I'd never have put you two together,' Val had said, making
Livvie's cheeks burn scarlet. 'But, I suppose it just goes to show…'

Livvie hadn't wanted to hear what Val thought it just went to
"show" so had made her excuses and withdrawn herself from the
conversation, making a mental note to avoid the woman outside of
the studio as best she could.

Adding to her dislike, Livvie had heard Kitty air her misgivings
about Noushka's friendship with Hetty, concerned that she was
always pulling Anoushka down and making sly digs at her, as if
getting pleasure from undermining her confidence. Livvie had never
heard Kitty say a bad word about anyone, which, in her mind, added
extra weight to her friend's words. And, from what she could gather
whenever the pair called at the studio with an appointment, the girl's
spiteful gossipy nature matched her mother's, which made Livvie
very wary of what she said around them.

The three friends were working in silence, all but for the hum of
Vi's sewing machine, when they were startled by someone trying the
door handle impatiently. A woman's voice could be heard on the
other side of it, and judging by the tone, the owner wasn't
very happy.

'I'll get it.' Kitty put the fabric she was working on to one side
and got to her feet. She was only halfway across the room when the
doorbell started ringing. First once, then again.

'I'll be there in just a moment,' said Kitty, hurrying.

'Jeez, they're keen.' Vi rolled her eyes at Livvie. 'I thought our
next appointment wasn't for a good hour at least.'

'It's not,' said Livvie.

Kitty unlocked the door and stood back, a look of surprise on her
face. 'Oh! Val!'

'Ughh! Thank goodness! I can hardly breathe!' Val burst through
the door, a look of utter disgust on her face. Hetty followed close
behind looking equally displeased. 'That woman ought to be
ashamed of herself.'

Vi glanced at the clock. 'Val, Hetty, you're early; we weren't
expecting you till two o'clock. And who ought to be ashamed of
herself?'

Just as well there wasn't another bride-to-be here, all dressed-up in her wedding gown. Livvie did her best to hide her feelings at their rude arrival. At Romantique, a generous break between appointments was always scheduled in to avoid any potential overlap but it would seem Val had no consideration for anyone else.

'Well, we were in the village so thought we might as well pop in,' said Val. 'Our plans have been scuppered; we were supposed to be going for a coffee and a slice of cake at the tea shop after calling in at the post office, but that revolting woman was heading there too, and we just had to get away from her. If our early arrival's an inconvenience we can always leave.' There was a challenging glint in her eye.

'No, it's not at all inconvenient,' said Kitty, always keen to smooth things over. 'Can I get you both a cup of tea?'

'A coffee would be much appreciated, and a sit down so we can recover from our encounter with that odious old woman,' said Val. 'I honestly don't think she owns any other clothing; I've only ever seen her in that dirty coat. And don't get me started on that ridiculous hat. Why on earth she feels the need to dress for winter in the middle of summer beggars belief. Honestly, someone should take her to one side and speak to her about her personal hygiene.'

'No one's that brave to get close enough to tell her,' said Hetty, making the pair of them cackle.

Livvie glanced across at Kitty and Vi, feeling her anger begin to rise. From what she'd seen of Val and Hetty, it was nothing new for them to be pulling someone apart, and Freda being today's subject riled Livvie more than ever. However, since she still felt like the new girl at Romantique, she resisted the urge to pull the two women up about their unkind comments, but their attitude only served to justify her initial dislike of the pair. And Val, in particular, had a knack of making Livvie feel like she was always doing something wrong; the woman put her in mind of her own sister, Cheryl. And from what she'd seen so far, Hetty was a younger version in training.

'I assume you're referring to Freda Easton?' Vi looked as rattled as Livvie felt.

'Who else would fit that description?' Val wafted her hand in front of her face. 'The vile creature!'

'We hurried across the road when we saw her heading towards us with that grimy little dog of hers, but we still didn't manage to escape her pong,' said Hetty, flicking her long glossy black hair over her shoulder. 'That's the problem with living in a little backwater like this; the place is full of odd-balls.'

'Or "*characters*" as they get referred to, as if it excuses them from not having to behave like *normal* people,' said Val, looking pleased with her comment. 'Like that other weirdo who walks his cow through the village, Hugh Whatsisname? He's no better; it's ridiculous!'

'My point exactly!' Hetty laughed scornfully.

'You mean Hugh Heifer, er, I mean Hugh Danks,' said Kitty. 'He does it to keep busy since he retired from farming. It must be so difficult to go from having your days full of work to them being pretty much empty. I think his daily walks with Daisy are quite endearing.'

'Yes, well, you would. You're nice about everyone, Kitty, so I'm afraid your opinions don't really have much clout,' Val said sniffily.

'Oh,' said Kitty, taken aback. She looked across at Vi whose eyebrows had shot up to her hairline.

'Well, I think we could do with more folk having opinions like Kitty's; the world would be a better place for it,' said Vi.

'Hmph. I'll take your word for it.' Val gave her a haughty look.

Livvie clenched her teeth together in an effort to keep her anger in check, but it was proving hard and the words she was itching to use to put these obnoxious women in their place were on the tip of her tongue, pushing to get out. She focused her attention on tacking a piece of lace trim onto a pair of cami-knickers in an attempt to hide the feelings she knew would be written right across her face. She had an inkling Val and Hetty wouldn't be able to resist goading her, commenting on her expression, and the last thing Livvie wanted was to have words with a customer; this pair would be just the sort to spread spiteful gossip, and she didn't want to be responsible for that.

'Freda's actually really lovely when you get to know her,' said Kitty, giving an appeasing smile. 'And I feel sorry for her, she's had a rough life and she must be lonely living in that isolated little farmhouse.'

'Best place for her,' said Val. 'Out of the way, where she can't offend anyone with her scruffy appearance. She's as mad as a box of monkeys; I have no time for her.'

'Val!' Vi looked at the woman in disbelief. 'That's a bit harsh.'

'Well, it's true. Anyway, we're not here to discuss her, we're here to discuss a couple of changes Hetty would like you to make to her dress. She was worried it might be a bit late but the wedding's not till a week on Saturday, so there's plenty of time.'

'Changes?' Kitty looked from the dress on the mannequin to Vi then to Livvie, a barely discernible hint of impatience in her voice. This wasn't the first alteration the young woman had requested over recent weeks.

'I'm having doubts about the neckline.'

'But you were really happy with it when you tried it on last week,' said Livvie.

'Yes, but I want to be a hundred percent sure I'm happy with the dress before my big day.' Hetty gave a petulant shrug.

'I appreciate how wedding nerves can get the better of you and trigger a last-minute panic, but this will really have to be the last alteration we do on your dress; we're rushed off our feet with orders and there are other brides who need our attention too,' Vi said, pleasantly but firmly.

Val pressed her lips together and gave Livvie a sideways look. 'Yes, I hear you've set a date for your wedding to that doctor of yours; I suppose you'll be needing a dress.'

Livvie bit down on a retort and made her excuses to go to the bathroom.

As soon as Val and Hetty had left, the atmosphere in the room lifted. It wasn't long before there was a light tap at the door and Vi's mum, Mary, appeared, holding baby Elspeth. 'Thought I'd wait for the coast to clear before we popped across; I didn't fancy getting dragged into conversation with that catty pair of madams,' she said, smoothing her hand over the baby's shock of dark corkscrew curls that were just like her daddy's.

'Jeez, I don't blame you, Mum, they're exhausting. Talk about Bridezilla and her mother.' Vi held out her arms to her baby, her face softening. 'Come here, you gorgeous little pudding. Mummy needs to cover you in kisses.'

Livvie smiled as she watched Vi press noisy kisses to six-month-old Elspeth's chubby pink cheeks, the baby cooing in delight and grasping tightly onto her mother's finger. She felt a sudden rush of broodiness sweep through her, taking her by surprise. She'd always loved babies, but had never felt an urgent need to have one of her own, but little Pippin was tapping right into her maternal side.

'Right, well, I don't know about you ladies, but I think that's a perfect cue for our lunchbreak,' Kitty said, interrupting Livvie's musings.

'I think little Pippin here would agree.' Vi nodded to her daughter and made her way over to the comfy seat Jimby had brought in specially for her to sit in while she breastfed Elspeth.

'Right then, I'll just nip back to the house; I made a Victoria sponge and some lemonade while the little one was having a nap earlier,' said Mary, her cheeks ruddy from a life-time of farming and working outdoors, topped-up by her earlier baking session. 'I'll be two ticks, can you pop the kettle on for those who want tea, Kitty, lovey?'

'No probs, Mary.'

Mary soon returned armed with a tray. She set it down on the table and began slicing the cake. 'So what was the problem with Val and Hetty? You all looked right fed-up when I first came over.'

Vi rolled her eyes. 'Ughh! Well, aside from yet more alterations we have to make to that flipping dress, it was just the usual passive-aggressive sniping the pair of them are so skilled at. I'm getting pretty fed up of listening to it. I'll be glad when the wedding's over and we'll be rid of them.' She shared the details of the appointment with her mum who punctuated her story with tuts of disapproval.

'And I'm getting pretty fed up with them having a dig at Anoushka. Hetty passed some comment about her having put on weight, which she hasn't; she's lost it if anything, thanks to Hetty's nasty remarks,' said Kitty.

'Well, things must be bad if you're saying something, lovey,' said Mary. 'And, Noushka certainly hasn't put weight on. Hetty's just jealous because Noushka's gorgeous, with that long blonde hair and model-like figure.'

'Thank you, Mary.' Kitty sighed. 'Ollie's getting riled up enough to want to say something to her, and you know how easy-going he is.'

'Aye, he is that.' Mary nodded.

'It's understandable he's protective of his daughter,' said Molly. 'But it would be something to see Oll getting angry; I can count on one hand the times I've seen that happen, and it was nearly always because of that turkey you used to be married to, Kitts.'

'Ughh! Don't remind me about Dan,' said Kitty, a visible shiver running through her as she hugged her mug of tea to her chest. 'We haven't heard from him for ages, which is just the way I like it.'

'He was a right piece of work. You're lucky you didn't have the misfortune to make his acquaintance, Livvie,' said Molly.

'From what you've all said about him, I think I am.'

From snatches of conversation since she'd moved to the moors, Livvie had managed to gather that Kitty's first husband had been something of an emotional bully and that Ollie had been her childhood sweetheart. She didn't like to ask too many questions for fear of sounding nosy.

'I honestly don't understand what people gain by being horrible to others,' she said. 'Like Val and Hetty, they were being really nasty about poor old Freda Easton when they first came in. I had to hide in the toilet until I'd calmed down. I was practically stabbing at the fabric I was sewing I was so angry. Freda's such a sweet old soul with a kind heart, and folk like them would realise that if only they'd take the time to find out.'

'Aye, you're right there, lass, but Freda won't give many the time of day, she's that scared of folk turning on her or making fun of her; it's happened before and she got very upset by all accounts. Made her even more of a recluse, it did. You're lucky she talks to you.'

'It's me who's the lucky one; she's sweet and kind-hearted.'

'She is sweet,' said Kitty taking a sip of her tea. 'She's always been pleasant to me when I've spoken to her.'

'But it's true she has a problem with cleanliness; no one can deny that, I'm afraid,' said Vi.

Much as she hated to, Livvie couldn't argue with that. 'Must be difficult to manage that sort of thing if her house is as basic as I've heard it is,' she said. 'And it must be absolutely dreadful in winter; it doesn't bear thinking about.'

Mary bustled over to Vi, setting a glass of lemonade and a plate of sandwiches on the small table beside her, then plumped the cushions behind her daughter's back. 'There you go, lovey.' She turned back to Livvie. 'Well, life wasn't always like that for Freda, you know? The story goes she was actually born with a silver spoon in her mouth.'

Livvie couldn't hide her surprise. 'Freda was?'

'Aye,' Mary said, nodding as she made herself comfortable on one of the kitchen chairs. 'She was that, but her parents sent her away when she was quite young.'

'They sent her away? Why would they do that?'

'Well, I'm not too sure as to how accurate the story is,' said Mary, 'but it's a sad one.'

Livvie felt her heart squeeze for Freda. She steeled herself for what she was about to hear.

8

THE EVENING HAD BEEN BUSY, with barely a moment to sit down and grab five minutes together thanks to numerous phone calls and text messages. One call was from Zander's older sister, Steff, who gave him a gentle telling off for not calling back when he said he would, though the real reason for her getting in touch was to invite them over for a barbecue at their house in Leeds the following weekend. 'Annabel and Joel have been grumbling that they haven't seen you and Livvie for ages. And Annabel's desperate to talk bridesmaids' dresses with Livvie,' she'd said.

There'd been a call from Bryony who had rung for a long-overdue catch-up, which had been lovely but it didn't stop Livvie from feeling relieved when things had calmed down and she and Zander were finally able to tuck into their alfresco dinner: chargrilled chicken cooked by Zander and green salad and herbed potatoes prepared by Livvie. Alf looked on from his vantage point between the kitchen and the table with great interest.

'So, how's your day been?' asked Zander as he poured them each a glass of chilled Pinot Grigio. 'I can't believe it's got to nearly eight o'clock before I've been able to ask you that.' He laughed, his blue eyes edged with thick, dark lashes making Livvie's heart flutter.

'I know, it's been crazy; I thought the phone was never going to stop ringing.'

'Same here. Cheers.' He clinked his glass against hers. 'This chicken smells good, even if I do say so myself.'

Livvie gave an easy smile. 'It does. And cheers to a few hours' peace and quiet. And, since you ask, my day's been quite interesting actually. We were chatting to Vi's mum about Freda – not in a bad, gossipy way. Mary's not like that – she was just telling us what she knew of Freda's past; it's really quite sad actually.'

'Oh?' Zander took a sip of his wine, peering at her over his glass.

'Mmm. Mary seems to think she comes from quite a well-off family from another part of Yorkshire, which might explain how some of her words sound quite well-spoken, even though her accent is mostly Yorkshire. Have you noticed how she pronounces some of her vowels?'

Zander tipped his head to one side as he considered her question. 'Mmm. You've spoken to her more than me, but from the little conversation I've had with her, yes, I'd spotted that. And I'd heard a rumour along the lines of her coming from a well-to-do family, but as far as I was aware, that's all it was, just a rumour that made a good story for the local gossips.' He took another sip of wine. 'So what else did Mary tell you?'

Livvie pushed her fork into a potato, looking thoughtful. 'She said she'd heard Freda had supposedly done something that brought shame on her parents so they sent her away; they essentially disowned her, made her change her name.'

'What? They disowned her? She seems such a gentle soul, I can't imagine her doing anything that would warrant being disowned by her parents.'

'I know, it's hard to believe, isn't it?' Livvie shook her head sadly.

'It's unforgivable; it's a wonder they could live with themselves,' said Zander, a frown creasing his brow.

'I know. Mary said it was as if Freda never existed to her family. I can't imagine how awful that must feel, poor old soul.' Livvie sighed, feeling tears prickle her eyes.

'What a sad story.'

'Which makes me feel even worse about putting my foot in it yesterday; she didn't walk by this evening like she normally does. I know we've been preoccupied by all the phone calls and what-not, but I was looking out for her at the time she usually goes by and there was no sign of her.' A tear spilled over onto Livvie's cheek. Zander reached across and brushed it away with his finger-tips. 'After hearing her story, I hope more than ever I haven't stuffed things up with her.'

'She'll be back, I'm sure of it.'

'I hope you're right; I'd never forgive myself if I've scared her away.' She sniffed. 'Do you think I should go along and see her tomorrow?'

'I don't. I think you should leave her to come to you when she's good and ready. Don't forget she's not used to being close to anyone; it's best not to rush it.'

'Okay.' Livvie nodded, smiling at him. She loved how wise he was, how he could see the bigger picture, whereas she had a tendency to be impulsive, taking an idea and running with it. And, though her intentions were good, Livvie didn't want her actions to backfire. 'Anyhow, you haven't told me about your day yet.'

'It was busy, as ever. I think it's just accepted that appointments are going to over-run; people seem content to wait. In fact, I think a lot of them come in for a natter and a catch-up.'

'What with you, or with other patients in the waiting room?'

'Both!' Zander said, laughing. 'Beth says Greta told her it's been the same as long as she's worked on reception at the surgery and that's a good thirty years.'

'Wow.'

'I'm not complaining; I feel I'm really getting to know my patients and like the fact that I can give them all the time they need – within reason. It's odd, I know I have the same length of time slots per patient as I did at the Runswick Way practice, but there doesn't seem to be the same pressure if you over-run. I guess it's down to the slower pace of life out here.' He shrugged. 'And it's great to be working with Beth. I know we've always got on, but I must admit to having a slight worry about how it would be actually working with my cousin. Turns out it's absolutely fine.'

Livvie knew where he was coming from as far as the slower pace of life was concerned; Rickelthorpe might not be the busiest of towns, but it still had something of the rat-race about it, and it felt good to be well away from it.

Just then, a couple of tractors thundered by on the road in front of the cottage, drowning their conversation. It was Paddy and Ant Ford from the family of farm contractors from the nearby village of Arkleby. They were heading home after a busy day silaging, waving as they went by. Alf jumped up and ran down the garden towards them, barking.

'I see the farmers are making the most of the good weather. Make hay while the sun shines and all that.' Zander nodded in the tractors' direction.

'Ooh, I wonder if that's where the expression comes from,' said Livvie.

'I think it is.'

'I'd never thought about it before now, but I guess it's a job they need to get done before the rain comes.'

Once they'd finished eating and cleared the table, under the close scrutiny of Alf, they made themselves comfortable on the garden swing seat, while Alf was busy giving the ground beneath the table a thorough sniffing for stray juicy crumbs. 'Come on, fella, come and join us here. There might be a little treat for you for being such a good lad while we were eating,' said Zander, clicking his tongue. Alf didn't hesitate and shot down towards them, taking the biscuit gently from Zander's fingers and devouring it in one. 'Might be an idea to taste what you're eating, Alf; just a suggestion, buddy,' said Zander, making Livvie giggle.

Zander sat back and Livvie leaned into him, feeling the warmth of his body, savouring the evening air that was full of the scent of freshly cut hay, courtesy of the fields before the cottage. That morning they'd been a lush sea of green, their tall blades rippling like waves as the breeze skimmed over them, but now they were stripped of their long meadow grass, leaving golden stubble in its place, glowing in the pale light of the moon that was just emerging from behind Great Stangdale rigg.

'I can't imagine ever getting tired of that view,' Livvie said.

'Me neither. When we're old and grey, we'll still be sitting out here, glass of wine in hand, saying those very same words.' Zander pulled her close and pressed a kiss to the top of her head.

'I like the idea of that.' The thought of spending the rest of her life with Zander sent a shiver of happiness through her. And, for a moment, she wondered if the view had the same impact on Freda. Did the old lady look out over the dale of an evening when it was bathed in the warm glow of the sunset? Did she feel happiness at the sheer beauty of it as she and Zander did? Livvie's heart squeezed. She hoped so, it was just a shame Freda had no one to share it with.

∾

THE FOLLOWING EVENING, Livvie was watering the lavender hedge when she suddenly sensed she was being watched. She looked up to see Freda peering over the wall, a hesitant smile on her face.

'Freda! It's lovely to see you.' Happiness rushed through her.

'Now then, lass. You're doing a grand job there.' Freda beamed back at her.

'Would you like a cup of tea? I mean, have you got time? I was going to put the kettle on once I'd finished this. Zander's just taken Alf for a walk.'

Freda shook her head. 'Another time. I just brought you some of these.' She placed a bunch of sweet peas on top of the dry stone wall. 'Thought you'd like them.' With that she turned and headed back in the direction of her home with Midge walking steadily beside her.

Livvie set her watering can down and rushed down to the gate, ready to run after the old lady, but Zander's words advising her to take things slowly started ringing in her ears and she stopped herself. He was right; if Freda had been ready to join her for a cup of tea, she would have done so. Instead, Livvie simply said, 'Thank you, Freda, they're beautiful.'

Freda turned and nodded then continued on her way.

Livvie lifted the blooms to her nose, inhaling their sweet scent, smiling as she watched the old lady walk back along the track. They were still friends and Livvie was enormously relieved.

9

'NOW THEN, YOU TWO,' said Jimby, in a familiar Yorkshire greeting. He was in his Landie, sporting his habitual wide smile. It was infectious and Livvie couldn't remember a time she had seen him without it.

'Now then.' Ollie leaned forward in the passenger seat and raised his hand in a wave, his dark-blond hair sticking up in tufts. The pair looked slightly bedraggled and warm; as if they'd just finished doing some manual labour.

It was just before six o'clock on Sunday evening. Livvie and Zander had encountered them on the twisting country lane between Lytell Stangdale and Danskelfe. Zander had tucked his four-wheel drive into a pull-in place which was getting slowly devoured by cow-parsley and the purple spires of loosestrife, to allow them to pass. Instead, Jimby had stopped his battered old Landie alongside them, his arm resting casually on the open window.

'Hi there, Jimby, Ollie. How's things?' asked Zander.

'They're grand, thanks. We've just been up to our Molly's over at Withrin Hill, helping Camm and Ben move an old horse-box into the yard – it's their latest project to be turned into glamping accommodation, weighs a bloody ton, I can tell you,' said Jimby.

'Aye, should be good when it's all done out though,' said Ollie. 'Moll's got a good eye for that sort of thing.'

'From what I've seen of the other glamping things she definitely does.' Livvie nodded in agreement.

'But now we're heading home to get cleaned up,' said Jimby. 'We're popping out to the Sunne for a pint later on – I think we've earned it; you're very welcome to join us if you fancy?' His eyes danced happily in the way Livvie had come to expect.

He was as exuberant and full of life as his sister Kitty was reserved and shy. But though their temperaments were wildly different, the family resemblance was unmistakable, with them sharing large brown eyes and dark curly hair.

'Much as I'd love to take you up on that offer, lads, I'm afraid I'm going to have to turn you down; we're heading up to Danskelfe Castle for a meeting with Lady Carolyn,' said Zander. 'And I don't know how long it's going to take.'

'We're hoping to have the wedding there, so she's invited us up to have a look around,' said Livvie, excitement pulsing through her as the words left her mouth.

'Wow! The castle would be a fantastic venue for that. I know Vi would've had ours there if they'd been up-and-running last year,' said Jimby.

'Aye, I was fitting a new door for a customer just last week whose daughter had got married there last month and they were very impressed with the place by all accounts,' said Ollie.

'Really? That's so good to hear,' said Livvie.

'I've heard it costs a bob or two, mind,' said Jimby.

Her heart plummeted to the pit of her stomach; this was the part that most concerned her about the wedding, and one she'd tried not to think too much about. Until now.

Though she loved her job at Romantique, and earned more there than she had at Blushing Brides, if she was honest with herself, she doubted her wages would stretch to footing the bill of a wedding at Danskelfe Castle. Even contributing towards half would be tricky. And it wasn't as if she'd got much left in the way of savings; they'd been pretty much depleted by her sponger of an ex-boyfriend, Donny, when she'd lived with him.

Her mind felt suddenly crowded with worries and doubts, muting the conversation between the men, with only the occasional laugh from Jimby coming close to pulling her back. At least she was getting her wedding dress and bridesmaids' dresses done for free with only the fabric to pay for; that would save quite a bit, but nowhere near enough to pay for the actual wedding itself and all it entailed on top of that. Livvie mentally ran through the list: venue, food, flowers, photographer, bridal suite at the castle, and whatever else that hadn't sprung to mind at that moment, for there was bound to be more. *Cars! Of course, how could I forget cars? How the hell am I supposed to get to the castle without a car? Tractor? Quad bike? Landie? But wedding cars won't come cheap.*

She sighed inwardly; she'd let herself get swept away by the excitement of planning a wedding, pushing reality aside in the process. She could see why it had happened. After all, what bride wouldn't love to get married in a real-life fairy-tale castle with the striking moorland scenery, all bold and dramatic, as the backdrop to their wedding photos? Even so, it didn't stop her from feeling a little silly for even thinking they could have their wedding there. And the last thing she wanted was for Zander to think she expected him to foot the bill; she'd hate that. She felt her cheeks burn crimson at the thought.

She gnawed at the side of her mouth as doubt crept in further. *Oh, jeez, what have I started?* How she wished she could retrace her steps to before they'd even talked about the castle. If her lovely dad had still been alive, there would have been no question about who would pay for it; he would've insisted, though she would have wanted to contribute. Thoughts of him triggered a surge of sadness. He'd been gone for over thirteen years and not a day went by when she didn't miss him.

Whereas Cheryl had always been close to their mother, Livvie had always been close to her father, even after he'd left her mother when she was six-years-old and Cheryl was eight. Alan had tolerated his loveless marriage to Delia for ten unhappy years until he was unable to take any more, fearing by staying he was making things worse for the children. He'd remarried a couple of years later to a lovely woman called Rhoda. A primary school teacher, she was five years older than him and completely and utterly adored him. Even at a young age, it hadn't escaped Livvie's attention that Rhoda couldn't have been less like Delia if she'd tried. Where Delia was cold and hard, a permanent pinched angry expression fixed to her face, Rhoda was warm and kind-hearted, her face regularly lit up with a smile. Livvie had never seen her dad look so happy, and she'd loved visiting the pair at weekends; she'd quickly become very fond of her stepmother. And, with Rhoda having no children of her own, she'd grown very fond of Livvie too, showering her in love and affection. Livvie had come to look upon her as a mother-figure and confided in her in a way she wasn't able to with Delia. Since Alan's untimely death from a heart attack at the age of forty-two just seven years later, grief had brought the two women even closer. Rhoda had never remarried, and they'd kept in touch, regularly meeting up for a coffee and a catch-up. It was fair to say Livvie saw more of Rhoda than she did her own mum; a thought that made Livvie feel more than a little guilty from time-to-time. The feeling never lasted for long since whenever Livvie did go to visit her mother, she invariably came away feeling hurt and bad about herself.

The pain of that dreadful day when she'd been in on her own and took the phone call from a tearful Rhoda had never gone away, it had been merely muted by the years that had passed since, the hard edges worn off and smoothed by time like the stone markers on the moor top that had been battered by decades of unforgiving North Yorkshire weather. Rhoda had been reluctant to tell Livvie, asking to speak to Delia, but Livvie had instinctively known it was about her dad, making fear twist in her gut. The agonising memory still had the power to knock the wind right out of her sails. She felt sadness swoop as tears started swimming at the back of her eyes. She blinked quickly, hoping to disperse them before anyone noticed. She needed to rein their plans in before things got totally out of hand. Though she wasn't sure how to put it to Zander.

'Isn't that right, Livvie?' Jimby's voice brought her back to the present.

'Sorry?' Livvie mustered up a smile, hoping she wouldn't be rumbled.

'Jimby thinks we're long-overdue another fund-raising dance in the village,' said Zander, turning to her. 'He's thinking about organising another one.'

With the friendly banter flying around reminding her of the warm and welcoming group she was now a part of, Livvie felt her worries ease their grip.

'Sounds like fun,' she said.

'Fabulous! I'll take that as a yes then. No going back now, Zander.' Jimby winked at him.

'The more the merrier,' said Ollie, chuckling. 'I'm thinking safety in numbers; if the place is packed no one will notice how terrible my attempts at dancing will be.'

'I hate to disappoint you, but I think we all know how bad it is, Oll, mate,' said Jimby.

They were all laughing when John Danks rumbled up in his tractor, and waited behind Jimby's Landie. 'Right then, that's our cue to head off. Hope it goes well up at the castle. And don't forget, we'll be at the Sunne if you get back in time for a pint, Zander.' Jimby waved an apology at John as he pulled away.

'You okay, Liv?' Zander asked as they made their way along the narrow road. 'Just you seemed to go a bit quiet when Jimby and Ollie started talking about the castle.'

Livvie gazed out of the window and heaved a sigh. 'I'm fine, it's just...' She paused for a moment, looking for the right words. 'I just don't want you to feel like I'm pushing you into agreeing to get married at the castle. I mean, it's just one option. There's always St Thomas's church in the village ... and the castle's probably going to be ridiculously expensive. I know it would be lovely to get married there, but, well, I don't want to come across as a Bridezilla; I'm—'

Zander reached across and squeezed her hand. Speaking softly, he said, 'Livvie, sweetheart, you're most definitely not a Bridezilla – I don't know what's given you that idea – and I certainly don't think you're pushing me into anything. Getting married at the castle was my suggestion, if you remember? I mentioned it after hearing the lads talking about it in the pub. And, at this stage, we're only going for a look around, nothing's set in stone; I've only asked Caro to book it provisionally for us. If we think it's the perfect place for our wedding, then we'll confirm the booking, if we're not one hundred per cent struck by it, then we can think about the church, or somewhere else. Okay?'

'Okay.' Livvie nodded, the urge to be completely upfront about it pushing her on. 'But I don't have much in the way of savings, and although Kitty and Vi have been very generous with my wages, I'm a bit worried about being able to contribute my share of the cost of the venue. It's not right that you should shoulder the bulk of it.' She felt her face flush as she fiddled with the fingers in her lap. 'I'm really sorry. I should've said something sooner before it got this far. It's not like my mother would help out with the cost, or even consider lending me the money; she's already put me straight as far as that's concerned.'

Zander pulled the car off the road and brought it to a halt. He stilled the engine and turned to Livvie, cupping her face in his hands, circling his thumbs on the apple of her cheeks. 'Listen, I want you to put all thoughts of cost and money out of your mind. It's our wedding day we're talking about here; a day that I want us both to remember as being perfect for the rest of our lives. I certainly don't want it to be tainted by worries about money, or who's going to pay for what.' His blue eyes looked into hers intently. 'And you need to stop thinking about it in terms of *your* money and *my* money. It's *our* money, okay? I want us to have whatever we want to make our wedding the day we both want, and I don't care how it gets paid for or who pays for it. It's not about that, it's about *us*. Got that?'

Livvie nodded. 'I just don't want you to think I'm sitting back and behaving like a spoilt brat, making demands for everything.'

Zander laughed. 'Livvie, that's the very last thing you could be. And that's part of the reason I love you so much. After Mel and Clara, you're like a breath of fresh air.'

She looked into his eyes, their expression telling her he meant every word. Her heart swelled with love for him. He was as far removed from Donny as it was possible to be. And not a day went by when she didn't marvel at how fate had had a hand in bringing them together. The day just before Christmas the previous year when two complete strangers made the decision to run away from their respective dysfunctional relationships and escape to a cosy little cottage in the middle of the North Yorkshire moors, their mutual attraction sparking instantly in the air around them. That didn't just happen by accident; it wasn't a coincidence or serendipity; it was fate, plain and simple. They often looked back on that day, laughing that it was meant to be. Livvie smiled up at him. 'Well, as long as you know I'll contribute as much as I can.'

'Shush! No more talk like that. Now come on, the Future-Mrs-Gillespie, we've got a castle to look around and a wedding to plan.' He kissed her tenderly, momentarily chasing her worries away.

10

ZANDER'S FOUR-WHEEL drive crunched over the gravel in the parking area of Danskelfe Castle. The ancient building seemed to glow in the early evening sunshine, rendering its great looming sandstone walls less austere than they looked from a distance. It was perched precipitously on a crag half-way along Danskelfe dale, its battlements visible between the dense trees of the wood, a flag at one of its turrets fluttering in the light breeze.

Livvie climbed out of the car, smoothing down the front of her short-sleeved shirt dress. She hovered for a moment, a hint of nerves flickering in her stomach, wondering if she'd need the shrug cardigan that lay on the backseat. Reminding herself it could be cool in the evening and they'd be taking a look at the gardens, she reached in and grabbed it.

'Not sure if I really need to do this up here,' said Zander, aiming the key fob at the car, locking it with a beep.

'Won't hurt I suppose.' He was looking handsome, Livvie thought, in his beige chinos and aquamarine shirt which complemented his short dark hair. She felt a buzz of attraction shoot through her. It hadn't dimmed since the first day they met.

He took her hand in his and they headed towards the archway, the jaws of its foreboding heavy metal gate standing open, its appearance softened by the flowers from the previous day's wedding that were arranged on the lintel above it.

Livvie felt her mouth fall open as they stepped into the courtyard. 'Oh! This place is just amazing.' The castle looked impressive from a distance, but up close like this, there was a real sense of its power and stature.

'It's a bit special, isn't it?' Zander said softly. He looked as stirred by it as she was.

'It is.' Livvie's words came out in a whisper as her eyes devoured the details of the great building before her: the huge stones, covered by centuries of lichen, the arrow-slits that peppered the walls, the leaded mullioned windows of varying size scattered randomly, a large candelabra flickering in one. Gargoyles peered down at them, their gruesome expressions worn smooth thanks to centuries of exposure to the harsh moorland elements. The same could be said of the Hammondely coat of arms that was set about six feet above the door, though recent repair work could be seen in the areas of new stone, and the vivid colours of the paint, in rich shades of gold and blue and red, told that it had been recently refreshed.

'What a place to call home,' said Livvie.

'Hard to imagine, isn't it? Especially compared to our little yeoman's cottage.' Zander laughed, his smile crinkling the corners of his eyes. He gave her hand a squeeze, sending a shiver of excitement through her.

'It is; I still love our home though.'

'Me too.'

As they were nearing the entrance, the vast oak door, grey with age and adorned with black metal studs, was flung open and Lady Carolyn Hammondely's coltish figure appeared, a portly golden Labrador following close behind her. She was dressed in her usual garb of polo shirt with its collar turned up, designer skinny jeans and brown knee-high leather country boots. Her dark hair was tied back in a messy ponytail. 'Zander! Livvie! It's good to see you,' she said in her loud, plummy tone as she ran down the worn stone steps to greet them.

Livvie had only met Lady Carolyn a handful of times, and though she liked the woman, she had to admit, she didn't really know what to make of her. Livvie had heard the various rumours flying around the local villages about her – the most elaborate one that she'd had an affair with a married man and given birth to his child in secret. But no one had ever seen the baby, and as far as Livvie was concerned it was just gossip that fuelled the local rumour-mill. Lady Carolyn seemed to divide opinion and, by all accounts, was a bit of a contradiction. According to some she was a man-eater who you couldn't trust with your husband or boyfriend, while to others she was a reformed character who had worked hard turning the castle into a viable business and the attached estate a success, her marriage to husband Sim having apparently calmed her down. But Livvie didn't like to listen to gossip, she preferred to form her own opinion of folk, especially after what she'd witnessed with Freda.

But it didn't stop her watching closely as Lady Carolyn pulled Zander into a hug and kissed him firmly on each cheek. 'It's wonderful to see you, darling,' she said, before grabbing Livvie by the shoulders and doing the same to her.

Keen not to be left out, the Labrador pushed his nose into the back of Livvie's knee, making her leg buckle. 'Argh!' Livvie grabbed Zander's arm to steady herself. 'And who are you?' She laughed, bending to ruffle the Labrador's ears once she'd got over the surprise.

'Oh, do excuse Mr Tubbs; he can spot a dog-lover a mile-off and wants to make friends, don't you, old boy?' said Lady Carolyn. 'He just forgets his manners from time to time.'

'Well, he's gorgeous, aren't you?' Livvie scratched Mr Tubbs behind the ear taking in his grey muzzle and gentle eyes. He stood beside her, his tail wagging happily.

'Oh, you've made a friend for life there. But, to save you having to tickle his ears for the duration of your visit, I think I'd better give you a quick look around the grounds before it gets too dark to see things properly, if that's okay?' Lady Carolyn stuffed her hands into the back pockets of her jeans. 'And I must apologise for not being able to have you here earlier today, it's just been totally manic – today was the only day all of the team were able to get together for a meeting but since you seemed eager to have a look around as soon as possible, I thought you wouldn't mind being squeezed in a bit later in the day. Of course, you're very welcome to come back for another look around during the daytime, but this evening should give you a flavour of what we have to offer.'

'Please don't apologise,' said Zander. 'We just appreciate you doing this, especially on a Sunday when you could be putting your feet up.'

'Yes, it's really kind of you, Lady Carolyn,' said Livvie.

'Not at all – and please call me Caro. And trust me, there's no way I'll be putting my feet up anytime soon. What with weddings, music events, family-day-out events, vintage car rallies and the like coming out of my ears. I don't have a minute to catch my breath at the moment. Not that I'm complaining; I love it!' She turned to them and smiled, her eyes dancing happily. 'Right, to the gardens.'

'Lead the way,' said Zander smiling and catching Livvie's eye as they followed Lady Carolyn's long strides around the side of the castle.

THE GROUNDS WERE every bit as breath-taking as Livvie had imagined. And, though they were clearly well-tended, there was still an element of moorland wildness to them that she found very appealing. Anything planted up here on this exposed spot would have to be tough to survive, she thought as she looked around her.

The castle grounds offered a plethora of opportunities for stunning wedding photographs, from the walled garden, to the lake complete with fountain in the middle, to the stunning backdrop of the castle or even the moors. Livvie's mind was reeling with it all.

'Looks really quite spectacular when it freezes in the winter.' Caro followed Livvie's gaze to the fountain. 'Remind me to show you the photographs when we get back to the house.'

'Oh, I can imagine.' Much as Livvie would be thrilled with a dusting of snow on her wedding day, she hoped it wouldn't be deep enough to render it impossible to get photographs of them by the lake – it would be quite something to see it frozen. *Maybe a thick velvet cloak wouldn't be such a bad idea if that's what we'll be doing. Hmm. Footwear could be a problem, I'll make a mental note to look into that.*

Stepping over the threshold of the castle, Livvie felt a surge of excitement. The walls had been limewashed, making it lighter than she expected. And, instead of the usual fusty smell she'd come to associate with dark, dusty castles, the scent of lilies hung in the air courtesy of the floral arrangements that were still dotted about from the previous day's wedding. She looked up at Zander and beamed at him; he stole a quick kiss while Caro's back was turned. Livvie sighed happily.

'It's just down here,' said Caro. They followed her down what could only be described as a wide hallway. Mr Tubbs trotted along beside Caro, his tail swishing and his claws clicking on the flagstone floor. Rustic wrought iron wall-lights illuminated the way. They arrived at a sweeping carved oak staircase to the right, its centre carpeted with a plush red runner. 'That's a splendid place for a wedding photograph, lots of our brides have taken advantage of it,' said Caro, pausing with one foot on the stairs.

Livvie could see why; it was stunning, with its backdrop of tapestries and portraits of Caro's ancestors.

The stairs curved round and delivered them to a wide landing area, the walls of which were furnished with more portraits and tapestries, accompanied by weapons and stags' heads. Caro moved with long strides with Livvie having to trot to keep up. They arrived in a large hall, the scent of beeswax polish mingling with the sweet tang of woodsmoke. Here, beneath the ancient vaulted ceiling there was a real sense of the history imbued in the thick castle walls. Livvie couldn't stop the gasp that left her mouth; the room was jaw-droppingly stunning – the photographs on the website simply didn't do it justice. She felt an unexpected surge of emotion at the thought of exchanging her wedding vows here with Zander. She took a moment to steel herself, swallowing the lump that had suddenly lodged in her throat, blinking away the tears that threatened.

'You okay?' asked Zander, giving her shoulder a squeeze.

'Yes, thanks.' She nodded. 'It's just so beautiful in here.'

'You're not the first bride-to-be to be affected in that way.' Caro smiled kindly before moving on to her spiel. 'So, to give you a few details, the castle dates back to the fourteenth century, with later additions at various times through its history. As you've no doubt noticed from the walls outside, it's a little bit battle-scarred and has been under siege at least three times, once during the Civil War. So, you could say its renaissance as a wedding venue is a somewhat more genteel occupation for it.' She stood back, allowing them to take in the full view of the space. 'As you've probably guessed, this is the Grand Hall where the wedding ceremonies take place. The carved panelling was added in the sixteen hundreds.'

Two of the walls were panelled with age-darkened oak, the marks from the ancient adze that had carved the wood still visible in smooth undulations. Thick tapestries hung from the adjacent walls, the colours of their wool still bright despite their age. Great wrought-iron chandeliers were suspended from thick oak beams, their lights glittering warmly. Underfoot were huge flagstones, though a large woven runner in sumptuous shades of red and green ran down the centre of the room, with rows of chairs either side for the guests. A vast mullioned window on the wall to the left overlooked the courtyard, while three smaller ones on the right-hand wall gave views of Danskelfe dale. Livvie peered out. 'Oh!' She gasped, her stomach lurching as she quickly took a step backwards.

'Yes, it's quite a drop down there, isn't it?' Caro chuckled. 'Sorry, I should've warned you about it.'

'That's okay, I just wasn't expecting to be so high up from here,' said Livvie, her stomach swirling with vertigo.

'It takes quite a few people by surprise,' said Caro.

Zander went to peer out of the window. 'Oh, I see what you mean,' he said. 'And what a view; you can see the top end of Lytell Stangdale from here.'

'You can,' Caro said.

Livvie turned her attention back to the room. At the far end was a vast inglenook fireplace where logs the size of small tree trunks were crackling merrily away in an enormous dog grate, sending sparks dancing up the broad chimney. Mr Tubbs hadn't wasted any time and was stretched out in front of it, soaking up the warmth and making Livvie smile. Her eyes roamed the detail of the sandstone fireplace. Sturdy curved stone corbels supported a broad mantel stone upon which the initials "CP" and "EH" had been carved in an old-style hand.

Caro followed her gaze. 'We keep it lit all year round; even though it's the middle of summer, it can get chilly of an evening inside these old walls – they're over six-feet thick in some places.'

'Oh, wow!' said Livvie. Zander whistled through his teeth.

'We do have central heating but I don't think you can beat a real fire.'

'Oh, I agree,' said Livvie, glancing across at Zander who'd been quiet for most of the time. He was looking around, apparently soaking up the atmosphere just as she was. She made her way over to the fireplace to take a closer look. 'We have the stove on in the living room every evening; makes it cosy.'

'It does.' Zander had joined Livvie and was smoothing his fingers over the words that had been carved into the mantel stone.

'Ooh, if walls could speak, imagine the stories they could tell.'

Livvie looked at Zander who was smiling down at her. 'The history that must be steeped into the ones here.'

'I can't tell you how many times I've thought that,' Caro said, smiling. 'Shall I show you the dining room now? Then I can let you see the bedrooms.'

'Sounds good to me,' said Zander, taking Livvie's hand in his.

'Yes, please,' said Livvie.

LIVVIE AND ZANDER waited while Caro fished out the castle's wedding brochure and price-list from the desk in a room just off the entrance. She was chatting about her plans for the next music event in the wood when a nasally cut-glass voice interrupted them. 'Caro, I assume you're almost done with these people? It's nearly eight o'clock.'

Livvie turned to see a tall, thin woman standing imperiously in the doorway. She was wearing a wrap dress in vivid colours that clashed alarmingly with her slash of bright orange lipstick; her rigidly set, over-processed blonde hair put Livvie in mind of a bird's nest. The woman was looking at Caro with eyes that were cold and unfriendly. She had a crystal glass of what Livvie assumed was gin held aloft in her hand, its ice-cubes rattling as she stepped towards Caro. It took Livvie a moment to realise the woman was Lady Davinia, Caro's mother. And she didn't appear to be very happy that they were there.

'Mother!'

Lady Davinia gave a theatrical sigh. 'Surely it's not too much to ask to have one's home to oneself at this hour of a Sunday evening.' She seemed reluctant to make eye contact with Livvie and Zander.

Livvie squirmed, taken aback by the woman's rudeness. She'd heard Lady Davinia could be a frosty old boot, and she appeared to be living up to her reputation. She caught Zander's eye and the subtle twitch of his eyebrows told her he felt the same.

'Yes, yes, we're almost done here, Mother,' Caro said, her cheeks flushing with embarrassment, a flicker of irritation in her eyes.

'Good. Your father wants his dinner. You know very well he's like a bear with a sore head when he's hungry.' Lady Davinia's gaze shifted from Livvie to Zander, her expression suddenly brightening.

'Oh, Dr Gillespie, I had no idea you were here. How are you? Can I offer you a drink?'

'No, thank you, I'm fine. Livvie and I are just leaving. We're sorry to have taken up so much of Lady Carolyn's time.' Zander smiled politely.

'Oh, don't worry about that at all. My daughter doesn't seem to feel the need to tell her family what's happening. Honestly, we never know what's going on, or who's going to be mooching around the place from one day to the next.' She gave an affected laugh.

Caro exhaled noisily and rolled her eyes.

'I don't think there's any need for that, Caro, it's very childish,' said her mother.

Awkwardness hung in the air, stretching out, ready to snap at any moment. Livvie felt embarrassed for Caro. She understood how she felt; Caro wasn't the only one with a difficult mother who treated you like you were the bane of their life, and didn't seem to care who knew it. Not knowing where to look, Livvie trained her gaze on her chunky brown leather sandals, concentrating on a small splash of something on one of the straps.

'Well, maybe if you took an interest in what goes on here, you would have an inkling of the day-to-day happenings, Mother.'

Lady Davinia shot her daughter a dirty look. 'I'm not keen on your tone, dear.' She turned on her heel, her gin sloshing over the side of the glass. 'Right, I'll leave you to it. Lovely to see you, Zander.' She flashed him a smile and flounced off, Caro's eyes boring into the back of her head like laser-beams.

A door slammed shut further down the hall, making Caro flinch. She turned to Livvie and Zander. 'Please excuse my mother, she's struggling to come to terms with the fact that in order to keep the castle in good repair, it's become necessary for us to open it up for weddings and other events. Unfortunately, she prefers to bury her head in the sand and not face reality, whereas my father and I love the fact that it earns its keep – for want of a better way of putting it. She's digging her heels in about us opening some of the rooms to the public which is giving us a bit of a headache.'

'Oh, please don't apologise on our account; it must be difficult for her.' Livvie felt slightly uncomfortable at being caught in the middle of a family drama, albeit a small one.

'Yes, no need to apologise.' Zander smiled. 'Most stately homes and castles appear to be doing exactly that these days. I can imagine the up-keep of places like this is astronomical.'

'You have no idea. Mother would rather sell some of the property attached to the estate, but my father and I aren't keen. There's a risk not all of the tenants could afford to buy them and it would mean having to turf them out of their homes, which is the last thing we want to do. Hosting weddings and events is the better option by far. And organising them has the added bonus of keeping me out of mischief!' She laughed. 'Anyway, you're not here to listen to me waffling on about all of that. Here are the brochures. And I don't know if you've taken a look at the website or our photographs on social media, but they'll give you a better idea of what the place looks like when it's in all its wedding finery. I think you'll like what you see.'

As soon as the car swept out of the castle gates, Zander turned to Livvie. 'Well, that was quite an experience, wasn't it? What do you make of it all?' The windows were wound down and the warm evening air was ruffling Livvie's hair. She took the scrunchie from around her wrist and scooped her auburn waves up into a topknot.

'You could say. I thought the castle and grounds were absolutely amazing...' She surreptitiously inched the price list out of the brochure and blanched. *Bloody hell!* Her heart started pounding; the cost was several thousand pounds more than she had expected.

'Me too.'

She scrambled to recover her composure. 'But the drama between Caro and her mother was a bit awkward, wasn't it?' *That's the way to go; direct his attention towards the dynamics between Caro and her mother, then he won't think your main concern is the cost.*

Zander frowned. 'It was, but I suppose we did call at a bad time and if she wasn't expecting us to be there, then we can excuse her reaction a little; it can't be much fun finding people walking around your home on a Sunday evening.'

'True.' Even so, there was something about the way Lady Davinia had spoken to Caro that gave Livvie the sense it had nothing to do with Zander's explanation; it felt more like it was the norm. She felt an unexpected wave of sympathy for Caro.

'So, how do you feel about us getting married there?' he asked, his smile discernible in his voice.

Oh, I'd love to! She forced a smile. 'Oh, well … the Great Hall … it was just stunning.' Her feelings were in turmoil. 'It's hard to imagine…' Nibbling on a fingernail, Livvie gazed out of the window as an image of her standing beside Zander as they exchanged vows in that spectacular room with their friends and family looking on filled her mind. What her heart was desperate to say was, it was hard to imagine anywhere more perfect to get married. Livvie knew that was all it would take for Zander to book the place right away. But there was no way she'd be able to contribute enough towards the cost, and there was no way she'd countenance letting him foot the lion's share of the bill. Thoughts of what her mother and Cheryl would have to say if they got a sniff that she'd let that happen started ringing in her ears.

Swamped by disappointment, she hurriedly searched for words that wouldn't sound dismissive but wouldn't betray her true feelings either. 'It's such a romantic place…'

'I totally agree, so why am I sensing a "but"?'

'It's just what we've witnessed between Caro and her mother has got me a bit concerned, that's all. It'd be a shame if something like that happened at the wedding, or if the guests overheard them having a squabble. After all, Lady Davinia didn't seem too bothered about sharing her feelings in front of us.' Her eyes slid over to him; he was nodding as he focused on the road, absorbing her words.

'Hmm. It was a bit odd, I have to admit. But are you sure it's enough to put us off having the wedding there? If they did start squabbling, don't you think it would be diluted by our guests? Not to mention all the staff that would be there.'

'Maybe. I just think we should take a couple of days to think it over properly, consider all our options.'

'But what if we lose the booking?' he asked.

'Then it wasn't meant to be.'

Zander nodded slowly. 'Okay, I can see your logic.'

As the lane curved round, Zander slowed the car, his keen eyes spotting a roe deer ready to leap out of the shadows of the wood on their right, and into their path. They watched as it ran gracefully across the road before leaping effortlessly over the dry stone wall. From this vantage point, they could just make out Danskelfe Castle. Livvie craned her neck to get a better view; it loomed out of the sandstone crag as if it had grown out of the very ground it was built on. She felt a tug in her heart; she'd have to accept the wedding wasn't going to take place there, but it wasn't going to be easy.

Zander turned to her. 'At the end of the day, I suppose it doesn't really matter where we get married, does it?'

'It doesn't.' She met his eye and smiled. *Oh, I know you're right, Zander. But why did I have to go and get my hopes built up like some silly little school girl? I got carried away when I should've known better.* She felt relieved that her day off at Romantique had been switched from Thursday to tomorrow; it would give her an extra day to manage her disappointment. She didn't want Kitty and Vi picking up on it and go mentioning it to Ollie and Jimby. The group of friends shared everything and she didn't want to risk it to getting back to Zander, which it invariably would. She knew it wouldn't take much for him to go right ahead and confirm the castle booking if he got the slightest whiff that's what she wanted. Instead Livvie had a visit from Rhoda to look forward to; she'd be a very welcome distraction.

'COME AND GET your gorgeous little body back in this bed so I can have my wicked way with you, Livvie Weatherill,' said Zander, watching as she cranked the windows open a little wider, the moonlight imparting a luminous glow to her creamy skin.

Livvie giggled. 'Give me a chance; I couldn't go to sleep without letting a bit more air in here, it's boiling.'

'And it's about to get a whole lot hotter once I get my hands on you,' he said, his eyes glinting.

When Livvie had lived with Donny, there was no way she'd have had the courage to walk around in front of him naked. His regular taunts about her being overweight and comparing her legs to "massive tree-trunks" had put paid to that. He'd gradually whittled away at her self-confidence reducing it to virtually nothing, which was why she'd found it so excruciating that her first meeting with Zander had been when she was completely naked. But she'd come a long way since then, and in the short time she'd been with Zander and his very obvious appreciation of her curves, she'd grown to embrace them. He made her feel loved and beautiful and her confidence had soared. Now, she didn't think twice about leaping out of bed as naked as the day she was born, feeling his eyes roving her body appreciatively.

'Promises, promises,' she said, slipping back between the sheets. The warmth of his body against her skin sent a pulse of lust shooting through her.

'And it's one I intend to keep.' He turned to her, kissing her deeply.

11

Sunshine flooded in through the open kitchen windows, pooling on the flagstone floor where Alf was currently stretched out, his black glossy head on his paws. Though it was only just after eight in the morning, a sultry promise of the day's warmth hung in the air.

'Right, must dash.' Zander took a final slurp of his tea before picking up his doctor's case. He kissed Livvie full on the mouth, his jaw freshly shaved after the weekend of not troubling a razor. The scent of soap and his citrussy cologne swirled around her nostrils.

'Ooh,' she said, the force of his kiss taking her by surprise, sending a bolt of electricity to her core.

'Mmm.' Zander paused for a moment, his eyes roving her face; he clearly felt it too. He bent and kissed her again, more slowly this time, before reluctantly pulling away. The look in his eyes that never left hers told her exactly what he was thinking.

She smiled back and pressed herself against him, inviting him to take things further.

'Very naughty,' he said huskily. 'Don't suppose you fancy a—' He was cut off by the ping of a text message arriving on his mobile phone, quickly dispersing the sparks of sexual tension that danced around them. 'Bugger!' He rolled his eyes and rested his forehead against hers.

Livvie groaned. 'Talk about bad timing.'

'Too right.' Zander reached into his trouser pocket, pulled out his phone and checked the screen. 'Bloody hell, it's just Noah with a catch-up text. Flaming passion-killing sod. I'll be having words with him next time I see him.' The glint in his eye told Livvie he was joking about his friend.

'Is everything okay? Is Jess any better?' she asked. Zander had mentioned that Noah was concerned about his wife.

Zander quickly scanned the message. 'Seems to be, at least he hasn't mentioned anything to the contrary.'

'That's good.'

'It is.' He sighed and pressed his lips into a half-smile. 'Oh well, much as I don't want to, I suppose I'd better tear myself away from you. Have a great time with Rhoda. And you be a good boy, Alfred Gillespie; keep that mischievous streak of yours under control if you can, buddy.'

Hearing his name, Alf sat up and trotted over to Zander, wagging his tail.

'I'm sure Alf'll be on his best behaviour, won't you, Alf?'

Alf's tail wagged some more.

'Let's hope so, after his last display when Rhoda was here.'

'Oh, yes, good point.' Rhoda had visited only once before and on that occasion Alf had seen fit to hurl himself into the village pond at Lytell Stangdale in pursuit of a wayward cockerel by the name of Reg. Alf had leapt out, covered in pondweed and had proceeded to charge around the village, almost up-skittling Lycra Len who'd been cycling by. Not satisfied with that, Alf had then charged into the Sunne Inne and shook himself all over the soft furnishings. Livvie had been relieved that landlords Bea and Jonty had taken it well, having two dogs of their own. Livvie, however, had been utterly mortified and had apologised profusely, offering to pay for any necessary cleaning bills. Ever since that day, Alf and Reg had been sworn enemies.

'It seems like ages since I last saw Rhoda. I'm so pleased we've got a sunny day for her visit, it'll give her chance to see the moors at their best,' Livvie said, following Zander down the hall.

He nodded, his smile crinkling the corners of his eyes. 'Lots to catch up on; lots of cups of tea in the garden.'

'Too right! And a trip to the tea shop in Lytell Stangdale, and a walk with Alfie boy here. Ah, it's a hard life,' she said jokingly, while Alf's ears pricked at the mention of a walk.

'Well, have fun and I'll see you when I get back tonight, should be around seven-ish.' He kissed her again, sending a ripple of happiness through her. 'Though I'd rather be spending the day with you,' he said, his eyes twinkling. 'I could quite happily take you back to bed for an hour or so.'

'Much as I hate to say it, that moment's passed, and looking at the time, you'll be late for work if you don't get a move on.' She pushed him playfully towards the door. 'What would Greta have to say about you turning up late for work because you've been having a bit of hanky-panky with your girlfriend, eh?'

'Hmm. Good point, lovely as Greta is, she can be a little prudish – not that I'd blame my lateness on *that*! Anyway, I suppose I'd better take myself – and my wayward thoughts – to the surgery.' He arched his eyebrows at her. 'See you later.'

'See you later.' She smiled as she watched him walk down the path, his shoulders broad and muscular beneath his sky-blue shirt, the sleeves rolled up, revealing strong forearms and sun-kissed skin visible through the dark hairs. Leaning against the doorway a sigh slipped through her lips. Much as she was looking forward to seeing Rhoda, she'd be more than happy to spend the morning as Zander had suggested.

AFTER A QUICK TIDY round followed by a refreshing shower, Livvie pulled on a pair of loose ethnic print shorts and a light cotton cami-top with broderie-anglaise straps. She fixed her thick hair into two plaits and fastened them on top of her head in a bid to keep her neck cool.

Armed with a cup of tea she headed out into the front garden to wait for Rhoda's arrival. Alf joined her, finding a spot in the shade beside her. Bees busying themselves on the new lavender hedge were a welcome sight, their hum competing with the birdsong that filled the air. Freda popped into her mind; she doubted the old lady would hang around if she saw Livvie had company when she walked by today. She made a mental note to encourage her friend to meet Rhoda; she thought they'd get on well.

Sitting in contented silence, she watched a wood pigeon industri-ously fly back and forth from the rowan tree in the far corner of the garden. Armed with twigs on its inbound journey, it was clearly intent on building a nest. A grey squirrel scampered along the wall, pausing for a moment, its bushy tail twitching. It looked from her to

Alf as if weighing them up. In a flash, it leapt down and hurried across the lawn before disappearing into the boughs of the holly tree. Livvie chuckled to herself. 'Not sure he liked the look of us, Alf.' Alf's eyes flicked up at her.

The sound of a quad bike and a dog barking drew their attention. Squinting, she saw John Danks and his sheep dog Bess hurtling across the field at the front of the house, rounding up their sheep who were bleating noisily in objection. Before she'd moved to the countryside, Livvie had had no idea that life on the moors could be so busy and vibrant, and positively bursting with life. After growing up in a town, she was surprised at just how quickly she'd settled into rural life here; now she couldn't imagine living anywhere else.

Sunlight glinting off a little red car making its way along the twisting-turning lanes in the distance caught her eye. She watched its journey; every now and then it disappeared from view as the road dipped. She felt her spirits lift as she realised it more than likely belonged to Rhoda.

Before long, the sound of an engine heading along their lane grew louder, the red car appearing and pulling up outside the cottage. Livvie set her mug down on the bench and ran down the path. Alf jumped up and trotted behind her. 'Rhoda!' The woman had barely had time to get out of the car before Livvie had flung her arms around her. 'It's so good to see you.' She inhaled her stepmother's familiar, soothing scent as she sank into the warmth of her embrace. Ooh, it felt so good; Livvie would never stop loving this.

'Ooph! What a welcome!' Rhoda said, the broad smile on her gentle face indicating she was delighted with the greeting. 'It's good to see you too, lovey.' She pressed a kiss to Livvie's cheek before easing herself out of her embrace. 'And don't you just look fantastic? You're positively glowing, your eyes are shining. And I've never seen you in shorts and a little top like that before; they suit you. Your young man is obviously very good for you.'

Livvie was aware of Rhoda holding eye contact a little longer than necessary. She knew she was quietly surveying her step-daughter for any barely-discernible clues that were lurking beneath the surface: a certain flicker in Livvie's eye, a telling way she tilted her head when she spoke.

Mention of Zander made Livvie's smile grow wider. 'I think he is. I honestly don't remember feeling this happy or as comfortable in my own skin.'

'Ah, that's music to my ears, flower. You deserve it, a lovely young girl like you. And I hope he realises how lucky he is to have you.' She smoothed her short salt and pepper hair that had been ruffled by the force of her stepdaughter's greeting.

Livvie's heart surged with affection for this kind-hearted woman. She pulled her in for another hug, planting a noisy kiss on the older woman's cheek. 'Ah, come here, I'm the lucky one, having you in my life, Rhoda.'

'Give over, you'll have me sweating like nobody's business if you keep grabbing hold of me like that.' Her light-blue eyes shone happily.

'And how's retirement suiting you?' asked Livvie. 'Must be strange after being busy for so long.'

'Well, since it's only been a few weeks, and after thirty-five years of teaching let's not forget I'm used to having the six-week summer holidays, it pretty much feels the same as normal. Ask me again at Christmas, I should have a better idea of it then.' After twenty-three years teaching at the same small primary school in Rickelthorpe, Rhoda had been promoted to headteacher for the remaining years of her career. It was a role she'd relished, but now she was ready to enjoy the retirement she'd planned for, though sadly without her beloved Alan.

Livvie laughed. 'Okay, I'll make a mental note to do just that.'

'Now let me have a look at this engagement ring I've been hearing so much about; I've been dying to see it.'

Livvie offered her hand and Rhoda took it, gazing at the diamond that sparkled in the sunshine. 'Oh, my days, that's beautiful, chick. Very classy.'

'I love it; I still can't stop looking at it,' said Livvie, moving her hand from side to side, watching the stone glint.

'I'm not surprised. And I can see how happy you are; you're sparkling almost as much as this diamond, which gladdens my heart.'

'Well, I'm extra happy today because you're here!'

Rhoda gave Livvie's arm a squeeze. 'It's good of you and your young man to invite me.'

The bond between the two women was strong. Stronger and more loving than the one Livvie shared with her natural mother. But she'd learnt early on that Delia seemed to have only enough maternal love to give to one child, and that child was Cheryl. And though it still stung if she thought too hard about it, Livvie had come to terms with this fact some years ago, and it only served to make her appreciate the loving relationship she had with her stepmother. Rhoda loved her fiercely and Livvie knew it.

Rhoda had a handful of nephews and nieces, but she and Livvie's father had never been blessed with children of their own. It meant Livvie filled that gap perfectly, each showering the other with an endless supply of unconditional love.

As their mother-daughter relationship had blossomed, Rhoda had learnt to read Livvie like a book; detecting little nuances that hinted when things weren't right. She'd picked up on the problems between Livvie and Donny before Livvie had even acknowledged them to herself. She'd listened carefully when Livvie had first voiced her misgivings about the relationship, responding to them tactfully, not wanting to alienate Livvie by saying things that she wouldn't be ready to hear. 'Trust your gut, chick,' she'd said. 'It was the best piece of advice my mother ever gave me and it's never let me down. And what I'd add to that is, if someone makes you feel bad about yourself, then it's time to move away from them; they're not good for you and you don't need them in your life.'

Jeez, she'd been right about that. And some, though Livvie hadn't realised it at the time. She always had the feeling Donny knew Rhoda wasn't keen on him, and it was only with the benefit of hindsight that she realised he'd done all he could to keep Livvie away from her, dripping poison into her ear about her stepmother. It had got so bad, it had eventually driven a wedge between the two women, one that Livvie was keen to heal.

She was in the middle of telling Rhoda about how Zander had surprised her with the ring when they were interrupted by a bark from Alf.

'Oops, are we ignoring someone?' asked Rhoda.

'Sounds like it. Don't worry, Alf, we haven't forgotten about you,' said Livvie, shaking her head affectionately.

'Well, hello to you too, young man; it's good to see you again.' Rhoda smiled and bent to give him a rub behind the ears which seemed to appease him.

'He's under strict instructions from Zander to behave himself this time.'

'Oh, really? You mean after his little dip in the pond on my last visit?'

'Mm-hm.'

'Mind, I still get a chuckle out of it.'

'Yes, there's never a dull moment with Alf around, that's for sure.' Livvie couldn't help but smile. 'Right then, let me help you with your bags, then I can make you a cuppa and we can sit in the garden and you can tell me all your news. I thought you might like a bit of a rest after the long drive from Rickelthorpe. But, if you fancy, later on we can go for a walk then grab a bite to eat at the tea shop in Lytell Stangdale? Lucy does some amazing salads – which are a lot naughtier than they sound. But if there's anything else you'd rather do, just let me know and I'd be happy to do it.'

'Your suggestions sound absolutely perfect to me; especially the cup of tea part, I could murder one right now.'

'One pot of tea coming up.'

12

LIVVIE WAS WATERING the geranium in a large pot on the kitchen window sill when Rhoda came downstairs. They'd had their cup of tea and Rhoda was now dressed ready to venture out on a walk. On Livvie's advice, she'd swapped her cotton summer dress and open-toed sandals for a t-shirt and light trousers, and a pair of trainers, which were more suitable for walking on the moorland tracks. She was clutching a straw sunhat trimmed with daisies. 'There's a real problem with ticks out on the moors, and let's not forget there are adders out there, so it's best to keep your feet and ankles covered up,' Livvie had said.

'Right, I'll just finish this, then I'm good to go.' Livvie had swapped her own sandals for a pair of socks and walking boots – she'd invested in a sturdy pair since moving here. Alf was looking on impatiently, dancing from paw-to-paw; he knew her boots equalled a walk and he was ready and waiting for Livvie to grab his lead. Excitement got the better of him and he ran over to Rhoda, attempting to nibble at the daisies on her hat.

'I don't think so, you little rascal.' She lifted the hat out of his way, chuckling. 'I'm not so sure they'll do your insides much good.'

'Alf, what did your dad say about keeping out of mischief?' Livvie spoke in a mock stern tone.

Alf looked on as if to say, 'Well, that's what you get if you keep me waiting.' It made both women smile.

'Running the risk of sounding like a clucking mother-hen, have you got plenty of sun-block on, lovey? You know how that fair skin of yours burns.'

Livvie nodded, setting the little watering can down by the sink. 'I'm absolutely lathered in factor fifty; you're welcome to use it if you need any, it's just over there on the worktop by the door. And you'll be very impressed; I've even got a hat too.' She reached for her phone, tucked it into the back pocket of her shorts and popped a frayed denim bucket hat on her head. Alf leapt about in raptures, whimpering with excitement at the prospect of his walk inching closer.

'Good lass. I think I will have some of that sunblock, actually.' Rhoda made her way to the worktop, doing her best to avoid Alf as he danced around the kitchen.

'Right, Alf looks fit to burst if we don't head out soon.' Livvie grabbed his lead and Alf raced to the open front door and down the path to the gate, making Rhoda chuckle as she rubbed sun-cream into her plump, freckly arms.

'He's a lovely lad; makes me wish I had a Labrador like him to keep me company.'

'He's just the best, I couldn't be without him now. I think a Labrador would be a fab idea for you.'

'Hmm. You've set me thinking now...'

Soon they were making their way along the bumpy track that led to Freda's cottage. Alf was in his element, his nose never leaving the ground as it followed a host of delicious scents. The sun was beating down and Livvie placed a thin scarf over the back of her neck to protect it from the heat. They walked along, chatting away ten-to-the-dozen, only stopping when they reached a wooden seat offering a panoramic view of the majestic dale of Great Stangdale with its lofty rigg looming on the far left. The moors were draped in their summer finery; swathes of thick purple heather reached down to the verdant green fields that were dotted with cows and sheep, its sweet honey fragrance sitting heavy in the warm August air. Swang beck could be seen glittering between the trees as it snaked its way lazily through the base of the valley.

'Oh, my, I don't think I've ever seen anywhere as beautiful as this; it's breathtaking.' Rhoda flopped onto the seat, took her hat off and fanned herself with it.

Livvie was thrilled to hear her stepmother shared her own feelings about this little corner of the North Yorkshire Moors. 'I have to keep pinching myself that I actually live here now.' She wiped the beads of sweat that peppered her brow. Alf was panting heavily and had sought shade under the seat.

'I'm not surprised, chick. Your dad would've loved it here, and he'd be pleased to think you'd made your home somewhere as lovely as this.'

Livvie felt a pang of sadness for Rhoda and for herself too. She reached across and squeezed her stepmother's hand. 'He would, but I tell myself he's looking down and enjoying it from up there, which is an absolutely fantastic vantage point; can you imagine the view he's got of this place?' Livvie looked up at the vast cloudless sky that spread itself out above the endless moorland.

Rhoda sighed. 'I like that,' she said softly.

The two women sat in companionable silence for a while, soaking up the sights and sounds of the countryside. Rhoda was the first to speak. 'So what's that great big building perched rather precariously over there? It looks like a castle to me.'

'It is, it's Danskelfe Castle. Home of the Hammondely family who also own a lot of the land around here, not to mention a whole load of property.' Livvie felt her spirits dip as she recalled her visit there with Zander the previous evening.

'Ooh, is that the place you mentioned you were thinking of as a wedding venue? How romantic would that be?'

'It was one of the options on our list, but I think we're just going to stick with the church in Lytell Stangdale.' There was no way she was going to tell Rhoda the real reason; she didn't want to take the risk she'd think she was tapping her for money. And the more she thought about it, the more she told herself that she was being a diva expecting to get married in a castle. *Just who do you think you are, Livvie Weatherill? What's wrong with that sweet little local church in the village?* And the more she imagined her mother and her sister's scornful reaction, the more she was certain it was the wrong idea to get married there. No, St Thomas's church would be absolutely fine; it was quaint and the grounds would be pretty in the photographs. If it was good enough for Vi and Kitty, it was good enough for her. Livvie had lost count of the times she'd told herself this since last night.

'Weren't you going for a look around there yesterday evening?'

'We did, and don't get me wrong, it was lovely, but we've settled on the church; it seems the most sensible option for lots of reasons.'

Rhoda listened quietly, nodding occasionally. Livvie was relieved she didn't quiz her too closely on the matter.

Feeling refreshed, the pair continued along the track until they came to Freda's cottage. Smoke was curling out of one of the squat chimney pots; Livvie remembered Freda telling her the fire never went out there.

'What a funny little place,' said Rhoda. She gazed around, taking in the ramshackle longhouse with its thatched roof that slumped in places, the stout mullioned windows and low, broad front door with paint peeling from it. It stood in stark contrast to the garden which was well tended, vegetables set out on one side in neat rows, while opposite was what appeared to be an old-style herb garden. Around the walls ran blowsy English country cottage garden flowers. A small orchard, some of the trees laden with plump apples, some a glossy red, some a vivid green, was set at the far side. 'Moor Top Cottage,' she read the roughly painted sign aloud.

'It's Freda's place,' said Livvie, peering over the gate for signs of her friend.

'Ah, is that the old lady you've been telling me about? The one who's very knowledgeable about gardens? Mind, just looking at this one, it's easy to see she knows her stuff. It's like looking at a traditional one from times gone by. Everything looks so healthy.'

Livvie nodded, shielding her eyes from the sun with her hand. 'Yes, that's her, and from what I can gather, she spends a lot of time in it.' If she wasn't mistaken, she could have sworn she'd seen someone peering cautiously around the curtain, a quick flash of grey hair only just visible through the dirty windows, before disappearing again. And, much as she'd love to venture down the path and knock on the door, she held back, Zander's words telling her to let Freda do things at her own pace, clamouring for attention in her mind. Though she was convinced Freda was at home, Livvie knew that if the old lady had wanted to speak to them, she would have opened the door and come down the path. Their friendship was only just recovering from the set-back of the previous week and Livvie didn't want to do anything to jeopardise it. 'I don't think she's in. And maybe it's a good time for us to head back and grab some lunch at the teashop.'

Reading Livvie's unspoken words, Rhoda nodded. 'That sounds like a very good idea to me.'

Walking away, Livvie quietly explained what had happened the other day, and how she didn't want to do anything that would ruin her blossoming friendship with Freda.

'I think you're right,' Rhoda said. 'And it's very kind of you to be so patient, not many would be by all accounts.' She turned to look back at the cottage. 'And did you say there's no bathroom in the place?'

Livvie shook her head. 'Nope, not from what I can gather. Not many people have actually been inside so I don't know how true it is, but I've heard there's an outside toilet.'

'Really? And how on earth does the poor old soul take a bath? It must be a right palaver to fill one. I wonder if she uses a tin one like they did years ago?'

'I think that's the problem, Rhoda, why she gets such a hard time from some unkind folk in the villages round here – not that there are many, but the few that there are certainly make an impact. I don't think she takes a bath very often, nor washes her clothes.' Livvie glanced across at her stepmother, her brow furrowed.

'Oh, right. I suppose the effort must be too much for her.' Rhoda nodded, understanding. She glanced around her, taking in the electric posts and cables that led to the property. 'At least there's electricity to the place, that's something I suppose. Do you know if she owns the house? Please tell me she doesn't rent it and some shoddy landlord is letting her live in a place like that with no creature comforts and an obviously leaking roof?'

'Freda's so private, no one really knows who owns it.'

Rhoda stopped and looked at Livvie, concern troubling her kind face. 'And you say she has no family to look out for her?'

'Well, there are rumours, but no one really knows the truth; she's a bit of an enigma. As far as we're all aware, she's on her own.'

'God love her. Well, I'm just glad she's found a friend in you, petal; she's clearly been drawn to you by your kind nature.'

Livvie smiled. 'Ahh, it's very sweet of you to say that, but I think it's more like she saw my pathetic attempts at gardening and felt obliged to stop and offer advice to save the poor old plants from a terrible fate.'

'Get away with you,' said Rhoda, chuckling along with her. 'Anyway, tell me more about Danskelfe Castle, it sounds like an intriguing place.'

'There's nothing much to say, over and above what I've already told you.' Livvie did her best to keep her voice neutral. She pressed her lips together and gave a small shrug. 'It must be an amazing place to call home. You'd like the gardens, and they're hosting more events to help with the upkeep of the place. That's it really.'

Rhoda gave her a side-long look. 'If you don't mind me saying, you're not doing a very good job of selling it to me.'

'Sorry, it's probably 'cos I'm starving and my rumbling stomach's distracting me. The sooner we get stuck into some of Lucy's fab food the better.'

'Now that's something you have sold well; lead the way!'

13

LIVVIE'S little car pulled up in a parking space on the village green just by the pond and opposite the Sunne Inne in Lytell Stangdale. The sun was beating down and a small flock of hefted sheep that roamed free in the village had sought solace from its unforgiving rays beneath the trailing branches of a weeping willow tree. Ruminating, the creatures watched the pair with bored interest.

'It still makes me laugh to see sheep wandering freely around the village,' said Rhoda. 'And I hadn't realised how funny they look close-up when they've just been sheared.'

'It's a funny sight at first, but it's surprising how quickly you get used to it,' said Livvie.

The pair made their way along the worn flagstone trod. An air of tranquillity hung over the place, quiet all but for the sound of bird-song and the occasional woeful bleating of the sheep. Rhoda glanced around at the thatched cottages that lined the road, their limewashed walls aglow in the sunshine, the cheerful blooms of their neatly tended gardens peering over the fences. 'This is such a pretty village.'

'It is.' Livvie gave a contented sigh.

'And there's a cottage for sale over there. Who on earth would want to leave this place?'

Livvie followed Rhoda's gaze to Fern Cottage on the other side of the road. It was a small, two-bedroomed property with stout mullioned widows. Its walls were painted a rich ochre colour and it's thatched roof hung like heavy eyebrows over the two dormer windows. A short gravel path divided a pretty garden and led to a stable-style door, its top half open, as if welcoming in the sunshine. 'Yes, from what I can gather, houses don't come up for sale very often here. I think that one's been rented out as a holiday cottage for a few years; I don't recall ever meeting the owner and I think I've met most people in the village now.'

'Hmm.' Rhoda nodded. 'It looks very cosy.'

'It does.'

'Morning, Livvie, pet. Morning, Rhoda, nice to see you again.' Gerald's lilting Wearside Geordie accent wafted across the road to them. He and his wife Mary – or Big Mary as she was known, to distinguish her from the two other Marys in the village – had moved to the village a few years earlier. Though the pair were in their early eighties, they had a real zest for life and added a dash of colour to the village. Livvie looked across to see them sitting on deckchairs, large mugs of tea resting on their stomachs, enjoying the sunshine in their little postage-stamp of a garden.

'Morning, Gerald, morning, Mary.' Livvie waved. She leaned into Rhoda and spoke sotto voce. 'And it has more than its fair share of characters, which I love.'

Rhoda stifled a giggle, taking in Gerald's bright-blue dyed hair and matching plaited beard. His equally colourful outfit was smeared in oil paint betraying his occupation as an artist. 'Morning. Enjoying the sunshine?' Rhoda nodded, smiling.

After a nudge from his wife, Gerald reached into the pocket of his trousers and pulled out what appeared to be a pair of false teeth. He pushed them into his mouth, adjusting them with his tongue. 'Aye, that we are, pet, just having a breather before I start on a new canvas; a painting of Withrin Hill Farm for Molly and Camm.'

'You've got a grand day for your visit, Rhoda,' Big Mary said, smiling broadly. Her outfit matched her husband's for brightness.

'I have, that, Mary; couldn't wish for better weather. It's nothing like our usual summers, is it? Usually, the sunshine waits to make an appearance until the schools have gone back after the holiday.'

'Aye, you're right about that one, pet-lamb.' Gerald gave a throaty laugh.

'Anyway, we won't keep you. Enjoy your tea break, you two.' Livvie waved and they continued along the trod to the teashop.

The little bell above the door jangled merrily as Livvie pushed it open, the mouth-watering aroma of freshly-baked scones wafting tantalisingly around the two women as they stepped inside.

'Ooh, what a gorgeous smell,' said Rhoda.

Livvie felt her stomach rumble as she glanced around looking for the table she'd asked Lucy to reserve for them. Already, the teashop was humming with the friendly chatter of customers. It was accompanied by the clink of cutlery against china teacups, while the easy-listening playlist murmured quietly in the background.

'I think that's us over there.' Livvie spotted a table by the window with a reserved sign on it.

They made themselves comfortable and Lucy came over to them armed with a welcoming smile and a couple of menus. 'Hello, ladies, it's good to see you. Have you been having a nice day so far?'

'Hi, Luce.' Livvie beamed back at her. 'We have, thanks, we've just done a three-mile walk with Alf and have worked up a hearty appetite.'

'Hello there, lovey,' said Rhoda, hanging her cardigan on the back of her wicker chair. 'And yes we have, thank you; our walk and the delicious aromas you've got floating around in here have got me feeling ravenous.'

'In that case, I'd better let you have a look at these.' She handed over the menus. 'As usual, the specials are on the board; I can highly recommend the crayfish salad. It comes with crushed herby new-potatoes and the salad dressing is to die for. It's served with a great big wedge of home-made bread too, white or brown, whichever you prefer.'

'Oh, my days, that sounds delicious,' said Livvie. She hoped the food wouldn't take long to arrive; she couldn't remember the last time she felt so hungry.

'But so does everything else on this menu,' said Rhoda, her eyes flicking up and down it. 'How on earth am I going to choose?'

Lucy laughed. 'Shall I get you a pot of tea while you're making your minds up?'

'Sounds like a good plan.' Livvie was torn between the crayfish salad and the quiche which was served warm and was her usual favourite.

'So are you here to talk weddings with Livvie?' Lucy asked as she reached into the pocket of her apron and retrieved her pen and pad, writing down the order for tea. 'Is that milk for you too, Rhoda?'

'Yes please, lovey. And I sure am here to discuss weddings with this gorgeous girl of mine; it's very exciting.'

'We haven't come up for air, have we?' Livvie's eyes twinkled at Rhoda, her heart melting at the woman's words.

'Nope, and we haven't even started on putting the world to rights yet. We thought we needed something to eat before we tackled that.'

'In that case, I'd better leave you to choose in peace. The tea won't be a moment.'

Lucy was right, the tea arrived before they knew it.

Livvie was just pouring tea when the sound of angry voices outside and the noisy squawks of a cockerel pushed their way through the open window catching their attention. 'What on earth's that racket all about?' She looked at Rhoda in puzzlement.

'I've no idea, but someone doesn't sound very happy.'

They looked out of the window, watching in disbelief as a walker stopped in the middle of the road, waving his arms around frantically while an angry-looking cockerel was clinging onto his backpack, its wings flapping alarmingly, its squawking amplifying to ear-splitting levels. 'Get off! Shoo! Shoo! Get off me, you stupid bloody creature!' But the walker's actions only served to increase the bird's annoyance.

Laughter erupted in the tea shop as the diners watched the drama unfold. Livvie set the teapot down and clamped her hand over her mouth, her giggle spluttering from between her fingers. 'Oh, no! It's Jimby's cockerel, Reg. I should've known. He really takes exception to anyone walking past his territory whistling or wearing a backpack.'

Rhoda's attempts at stifling her amusement were as successful as Livvie's. 'I know I shouldn't laugh, it must be quite frightening if you're the subject of Reg's ill humour, but it's such a funny sight I can't help myself.'

Before they knew it, Lycra Len had pulled up on his racing bike. He threw it to the ground and charged over to the walker. 'Oy, you! Off! Now!' He attempted to grab hold of Reg, dodging the bird's sharp beak. 'Ouch! You vicious little shi—' His words were cut off by Jimby who was hurtling down the road towards them, his face creased with concern.

The diners' laughter grew louder and they migrated towards the window to get a better look.

'Reg! Stop! Don't worry, I'll get him off!' Jimby said to the walker who was frantically shrugging his shoulders and spinning around in an attempt to loosen the bird's grip. 'You need to stand still, though, or we'll never be able to get a hold of him.' Jimby had to shout to make himself heard above the commotion.

'Well, can you please bloody-well hurry up then?' said the walker impatiently.

The audience was growing as locals came out of their cottages to watch the drama unfold. Jackie, the postwoman, stopped to film it on her mobile phone, howling with laughter as she did so.

'Ouch, you little bugger!' Jimby pulled his hand away after receiving a stinging peck. 'You're going in a stew, make no mistake, buster.'

Between them, Jimby and Len finally managed to wrestle the bird off his victim, with Reg objecting more and more vociferously. Clutching the cockerel by his scrawny yellow ankles, a look of victory flitted across Jimby's face. Short of breath, he turned to the walker. 'Are you okay?'

'I'm fine, no thanks to that stupid bird.'

'I'm so sorry, it was your whistling and your backpack that upset him, he sees them as a threat,' said Jimby as Reg continued to object, flapping his wings in consternation, taking exception to having his ego bruised.

'That's no excuse. You ought to get the savage bloody thing under control.' The walker began inching quickly away. 'It's a bloody disgrace. You should be reported for having an out-of-control animal.'

'I'm honestly very sorry.' Jimby pulled an apologetic face before turning to Reg, holding the bird aloft. 'Any more of that and you'll be ready for the chop, you obnoxious little bugger.'

Giggles and snorts from the tearoom spilled out into the road. Wearing an expression of surprise, Jimby turned to face it, his familiar broad smile spreading across his face. Ignoring Reg's squawks, he shrugged and took a low bow, then, making a sweeping gesture with his free hand, he motioned for Len to do the same. With a laugh, Len obliged.

Tears of mirth were pouring down Rhoda's cheeks and her shoulders were shaking. 'Oh, honest to goodness, there's never a dull moment here, is there?'

'You're not wrong there,' said Livvie, her cheeks aching from laughing so hard.

'Makes Rickelthorpe seem very dull by comparison.'

'I'm not sure how well a character like Reg would go down there.'

'Ooh, can you imagine? There'd be outrage.'

'There is here!'

'True.' Rhoda wiped her tears away with the back of her hands. 'Ooh, I haven't laughed so much for ages.'

With calm restored and Jimby heading home with a complaining Reg, the teashop bell tinkled and in walked Len. He scanned the room, a look of disappointment on his face when he realised there were no free tables.

Livvie turned to Rhoda. 'You don't mind if Len joins us, do you?'

'Course not, seems a shame to have two empty seats here. And I think he's earned himself a cup of tea after that debacle.'

'Len!' Livvie caught his eye and waved him over. 'You're very welcome to join us, if you'd like?'

Len negotiated his way through the tables. 'Are you sure I won't be intruding?' He glanced between the two women. Livvie noticed that his gaze hovered a little longer on Rhoda.

'Of course not, come and sit yourself down,' said Rhoda, her already rosy face flushing that little bit more.

Len pulled out the chair next to her, beaming at her as he launched into a conversation with her.

Hello, what's all this about then? Could there be a little romance brewing here? Livvie's interest was piqued as she watched the interaction between the pair; there was no doubt about it, her stepmother was suddenly sparkling in his presence. Her eyes were shining and she was touching her hair in a girly, flirtatious way. Livvie felt her heart melt. As for Len, she'd never seen him so animated and chatty. *Oh, how lovely is this!* Excitement swirled in her stomach; she couldn't wait to tell Zander about it.

For a long time, Livvie had thought it a shame Rhoda had never remarried. In fact, as far as she was aware, there'd been no one serious in Rhoda's life since her husband died thirteen years ago. She'd told Livvie of the odd date, but they'd always fizzled out after date number two. In Rhoda's eyes, no one could compare to Alan.

But here, today, there was something different in the air and it gladdened Livvie's heart. *Watch this space, Livvie. Watch this space.*

14

THEIR LUNCH HAD BEEN every bit as delicious as Livvie had expected. Both women had opted for the crayfish salad while Len had chosen the chicken and leek pie. And, while Livvie and Rhoda declared they'd left enough room for a pudding, Len declined, saying he had to get home for a delivery. Livvie noticed a look of disappointment briefly clouding Rhoda's face until Len scribbled something on his paper napkin and passed it to her; then it lit up like the sun had suddenly came out again. 'There's my number if you fancy meeting up for a drink in the Sunne while you're here.'

Livvie's breath caught in her throat. *Oh, wow!* Her eyes were fixed on Rhoda, watching her expression change. *Go on, please say you will.*

'Oh … er … how lovely … thank you, Len, but I'm afraid I'm heading back tomorrow, so maybe another time?' Rhoda looked up at him with what Livvie thought was a hopeful expression in her eye.

'Shame, but yes, next time you're here give me a bell.'

If Livvie wasn't mistaken he looked crestfallen. *Gah! Dratted lousy timing!* And, though Zander had told Livvie she should treat Dale View Cottage as her home, she resisted the temptation to blurt out that Rhoda was welcome to stay longer. Much as she was sure he'd be fine about it, she'd feel better checking with him first. And she wanted to be sure she hadn't read the signs wrong and put Rhoda on the spot – though from the sparks flying between them, she very much doubted it. But, oh my days, this was an exciting development, and she quite liked the idea of playing cupid.

STANDING OUTSIDE THE TEASHOP, Livvie checked her watch, squinting in the bright sunshine. 'Right then, we need to be getting back for Alf soon, but how do you fancy a quick pop over to Romantique to have a peek at the mood-board we've prepared for my wedding dress? It'd be great if you could see it.'

'Ooh, I'd love to, chick.' Rhoda was stuffing her purse back into her handbag, her cheeks still flushed from her flirty session with Len.

'Great; it shouldn't take long.' Livvie stole a look at her step-mother. 'And fancy Len asking you out for a drink, eh? Do you think you'd go if you were staying here longer?'

The older woman's face flushed brighter. 'Oh, I don't know about that. I've been on my own for too long now, I'm set in my ways and then there's...' She was flustered.

Livvie smiled at her fondly. 'I agree that you've been on your own for too long, but not in the sense you mean. And from what I know of him, Len seems like a nice enough bloke – okay, maybe he wears a little too much Lycra, but, hey, you can't have everything,' she said, making them both giggle. 'And I don't want you to think for a second that it would upset me if you did meet up with him. I'd actually be really happy if you did.'

'You would?' Rhoda looked up at her, her eyes shining. 'Are you sure? I mean, I think he's a really nice man; we got chatting last time I was here, got on like a house on fire, but I didn't think any more about it, until now.'

The smile on her face made Livvie's heart swell. 'Go for it. What about tonight? Zander and I won't mind. In fact, I could give you a lift so you can enjoy a cheeky little glass of wine.'

'Much as it's very kind of you to offer, I think, after my long drive and that walk in the fresh air, by the time it gets to six o'clock this evening, I'm going to be absolutely shattered. I'll save it for my next visit; I wouldn't want to go falling asleep on a date. Imagine that.'

'Okay.' Livvie linked Rhoda's arm, kissing her warm cheek as they made their way to Romantique.

They were almost at the gate when a voice calling stopped them. 'Livvie! Rhoda! Wait up a moment.' They turned to see Molly's mother, Annie, heading towards them along the trod. She was wearing a floral cotton summer dress and her wavy bob was pinned back by hair-slides. 'Goodness, it's sweltering. Roll on autumn, that's what I say.' She smiled at the two women, her large brown eyes so like her daughter's.

'Hi, Annie,' said Livvie. 'It is a bit hot.'

'Hello, there, Annie, I couldn't agree more, this heat's a bit much for me too.'

'Ughh! Anyway, I've been meaning to catch you, Livvie. It's just our Molly said you and Zander are planning a winter wedding and I wanted to offer my services to help do the flowers – if you'd like me to, that is. I did them for Kitty's and Violet's weddings so you can take a peek at their photos to see if you like them. I know the theme would be different, but they'd give you an idea of what I can do, so you can see if you like them.'

'Oh, Annie, that's so kind of you, but are you sure?'

'Absolutely, I wouldn't offer if I wasn't. I love doing them; the thought of doing flowers for a winter wedding is very exciting. And honestly, much as I love him to bits, it's a welcome change from listening to my Jack wittering on about his blessed sheep or his sloe gin.' Annie smiled, fanning herself with her hat. 'We've got loads of holly trees up at Withrin Hill and they always get absolutely loaded with berries in winter. I've got pots full of skimmia japonica rubella which should be just perfect for then, there's ivy everywhere, and I've got a friend at my floristry class who can get hold of the most stunning deep-red roses for me, at a good price too, so it should keep costs right down for you.'

'Wow. Thank you, Annie.' Livvie didn't have the foggiest idea what skimmia japonica rubella was, and she hadn't really given much thought to the finer details of the wedding flowers, but holly and ivy sounded perfect, as did keeping the cost down. 'After hearing all that, I'd love you to help with the flowers.' Livvie's mind was reeling. From her initial enquiries, she'd discovered how expensive wedding flowers could be.

Annie looked thrilled that her offer had gone down so well. 'I left a couple of my flower arranging books with our Molly for you to have a look at – I think she's dropped them off at Romantique. They've got some lovely arrangements in them, and some photos I took of winter flower arrangements I've done in the past. And, of course, you can always mix and match things so you can have them exactly how you want them.'

'I can't wait to have a look at them; we're just heading to the studio now. Thank you, Annie, it's very kind of you.'

Annie smiled at her warmly.

The conversation moved on and as they were having a chuckle about the Jimby and Reg debacle, Little Mary walked by with her miniature dachshund, Pete. 'Hello there, ladies,' she said in her soft voice, smiling sweetly. Her scalp was looking extra pink through her neat rows of snow-white curls thanks to the heat of the sun. She had her usual over-sized shopping bag over her free arm, swamping her tiny bird-like frame. And despite the heat, she was wearing a hand-crocheted cardigan and her usual tan tights that had settled in wrinkles around her slender ankles 'It's nice to see you again, Rhoda.'

'Hi, Little M,' said Livvie, smiling at her.

'Hello there, Mary, it's good to see you too; you're looking well.'

'I could say the same about you, my dear. You've got a sparkle about you almost as bright as young Livvie here. Anyone would think you were in love too.' Little Mary chuckled, blissfully oblivious to how she'd made Rhoda blush.

'It'll be the moorland country air,' said Annie. 'Does us all the world of good.'

'Aye, that it does. You wouldn't catch me living anywhere else,' said Little Mary.

Ah, bless her. Livvie bit down on a smile. From what she'd heard, the furthest Little Mary had ever been was the quaint Georgian market town of Middleton-le-Moors on the edge of the moors ten miles away and that was only a couple of times.

'And isn't it exciting news about Livvie and our lovely young doctor getting married? They're made for each other. I said that the very first time I saw them together.' Little Mary beamed up at Livvie, patting her cheek affectionately.

'It's fantastic news,' said Rhoda. She looked relieved at having the attention directed away from herself.

'It is, and there's nothing like a wedding to look forward to if you ask me,' said Annie.

'True, true.' Little Mary nodded. 'Anyway, me and Pete had best head off; we're on our way to see Aggie for a cup of tea and a biscuit, and to swap books.'

Annie's eyes opened wide at the mention of the books. Despite their advancing years, Little Mary and Aggie were well known for their fondness for racy novels, much to everyone's amusement. 'I'll walk along there with you, if you don't mind, Mary. Our Molly asked me to pop in on Aggie and see how she's getting on with that new mobile phone of hers. Apparently the vicar's still getting some worrying text messages from her. I daren't tell you what the last one said but it would make your eyes water.'

'Well, good luck with that, Annie,' Livvie said, chuckling. 'And thanks so much for the offer of doing the flowers; I'll be in touch soon.'

'Yes, I'm going to need luck if what our Molly told me is true. And there's no rush about the flowers, lovey.'

The women said their goodbyes, leaving Livvie and Rhoda to head through the gate to Romantique.

15

LIVVIE AND RHODA were greeted warmly by Kitty and Vi who seemed pleased to have an excuse for a break. And Livvie and Rhoda were glad to get out of the intense heat outside and into the studio which was pleasantly cool, courtesy of a large fan in the corner.

'I'm not here to disturb you, just to get the mood-board to show to Rhoda, then we'll be off,' said Livvie.

'Hey, no worries, chick, it's always good to see you. And you'll be able to fill us in on how you got on up at the castle last night.' Kitty's smile lit up her pretty face. 'We've been dying to hear about it.'

'Ooh, yes, we have,' said Vi. 'I'm thinking about getting married to Jimby all over again, just so I can have the ceremony up there; I bet it was gorgeous.'

Livvie's heart sank, taking her smile with it. *Bugger!* She quickly fixed her smile back in place, hoping the others hadn't noticed. In her excitement to show Rhoda her mood-board, she'd forgotten that she hadn't seen her friends since her visit to Danskelfe Castle and, though she'd texted them about it, it was only natural they'd want to know all the details as soon as they saw her in person.

She glanced across at Rhoda, relieved to see her attention had been diverted. She was gazing around the room, her expression akin to one of a child in a sweetshop, her eyes lingering on the shelves of sumptuous fabrics and jars of glittering beads. Livvie breathed an inward sigh of relief, thankful that her stepmother was too preoccupied to detect any tell-tale signs that would reveal her true feelings.

Rhoda could be like a bloodhound if she got even the tiniest whiff of a problem, and wasn't satisfied until she'd wheedled it out of you. 'I'll tell you all about it when I'm back here tomorrow; I really don't want to keep you, especially as busy as you are and with all the extra work Hetty Johnson dumped on us. And we need to get back for Alf; he'll be crossing his legs, desperate for a wee.' She decided appearing to be in a rush was the best way to go; it would hopefully postpone further questions about the castle until she was back at work the next day. Nevertheless, she could feel the weight of the enquiring looks from her friends and was grateful that they didn't press the matter.

'Oh, my, it's beautiful in here, what with all of the lovely fabrics and beads and drawings,' Rhoda said, her voice full of awe. 'I had no idea it was like this. No wonder you love working here, Livvie, sweetheart; you'll be in your element in these surroundings.'

'I am, I absolutely love it.' Livvie beamed, distracted for a moment. 'Anyway, let me get my mood-board.' She hurried over to a shelf and pulled out a large portfolio folder. Unzipping it, she carefully took out a piece of A1 card and set it out on her work station.

Rhoda gasped when her eyes landed on it. In the centre was a sketch of the gown which was surrounded by small swatches of fabric and lace, together with samples of trims and beads, all in a rich shade of clotted cream. 'Oh, Livvie, it's absolutely beautiful.' Her voice wavered and she pressed a hand to her chest.

'Kitty did the sketch of the dress while we threw our ideas and suggestions at her,' said Livvie, looking across at her friends who were beaming with delight.

'It's you to a "t", lovey. How clever you are, Kitty.'

Kitty blushed. 'Thank you, but it's all our work, so I can't take full credit.'

'And is this the fabric you're going to use?' Rhoda rubbed a sample between her fingers, tears wetting her lashes.

'Yes, it's raw silk. Though I have been wondering about having a cloak to wear over my dress on the way to the…' Livvie paused, aware of everyone watching her. '…on the way to getting married that I can maybe shrug off at the door. Just in case it snows. And it's bound to be absolutely freezing anyway.' Even to her own ears, her laugh was just that little bit too loud.

'Good idea.' Rhoda nodded, blinking her tears away. Livvie felt her stepmother's eyes lingering on her.

'By the way, we've just seen Annie and she mentioned the

wedding flowers; she said she'd left some books here for me to look at.'

'Oh, yes, they're over here.' Vi went over to a unit by the door, her kitten heels clickety-clacking on the floor. As ever, she looked glamorous in her fifties style pedal-pushers and lilac short-sleeved blouse tied at the waist and emphasising her curves. 'There you go, chick.' She handed two large books to Livvie.

'Thank you.' Livvie flicked through to the pages Annie had marked. 'Wow, these look amazing.'

Vi peered over her shoulder. 'Mmm. They do. Annie's very talented with flowers; just never accept her offer to cook anything. Ever. Trust me, your guts will never recover.'

Livvie scrunched up her face. 'Yeah, I'd heard that from Molly. Still, I'm really touched she offered to do the wedding flowers for me.'

'And she said something about Aggie and texting the vicar.' Rhoda looked puzzled. 'Aggie's her grandmother-*in-law*, am I right?'

'Spot on. She's Pip's grandmother; Pip's Molly's husband who's no longer with us,' said Vi. 'Aggie has a habit of sending racy texts to the vicar and blames it on predictive text or her arthritic fingers and Molly's left to clean up the fall-out from them.'

'Poor old Moll texted me last night to say Granny Aggie had been on to her again. Apparently, she'd sent the vicar a text saying something about seeing him mowing the lawn at the vicarage in the nude.' Kitty burst into a fit of the giggles, making it difficult for her to speak. 'And she told him she wanted to take a bite out of his *plump buns.'*

'No way? Seriously, that woman is a liability.' Vi's face dropped. 'And there's a mental image I wish hadn't appeared in my mind. I'm going to have to think hard about something else to make it go away.'

Livvie caught her eye and the pair of them crumpled with laughter.

'Oh, my goodness. I wasn't expecting to hear anything like that. And is there any truth in it?' asked Rhoda, her eyes wide. 'About him gardening in the nude?'

Livvie shook her head, unable to speak for laughing.

'You clearly haven't seen Rev Nev. He's the most gentle, reserved soul you could ever wish to meet. Honestly, I'm surprised the poor fella hasn't upped-sticks and run for the hills. He's been tortured by that old dear ever since she got her mitts on a mobile phone.' Vi sat back down, raised an amused eyebrow and picked up her mug of tea. 'So, did Molly find out what Granny Aggie really meant?'

'Well, she told Molly it was predictive text getting it all wrong again,' said Kitty.

Vi sniggered. 'Yeah, yeah. It's wearing a bit thin now, that excuse.'

'She reckons what she really meant to say was that she'd seen him in the garden as she was walking by and tried to ask him if he wanted some of her freshly-baked bread buns, but said he couldn't hear 'cos he was mowing the lawn and it was too noisy,' said Kitty.

'What a load of rot!' said Vi. 'And how did she explain the naked bit?'

'And don't forget the taking a bite bit,' Rhoda said, wearing an expression of disbelief.

'Apparently she skimmed over those details,' said Kitty.

'I'll bet she did,' said Vi.

'Convenient,' said Livvie.

'And poor old Molly's been left to smooth things over?' asked Rhoda.

'I think Molly secretly finds it amusing; she's convinced Granny Aggie knows what she's doing and is just being mischievous,' said Kitty. 'She's a right old handful, but adorable with it.'

Vi shook her head and turned to Rhoda. 'Kitty thinks everyone's adorable.'

Kitty smiled and rolled her eyes at her friend. 'Not true.'

'Really?' asked Vi.

'Well then, I always thought the countryside was supposed to be a quiet place, but in my two short visits to this tiny, unassuming little corner of North Yorkshire, there's been an awful lot going on,' said Rhoda, looking amused.

'You'd better believe it,' said Vi.

Livvie was distracted by the ping of a text on her mobile phone. She rooted around in her bag and fished it out. Happiness ricocheted around her stomach when she saw it was from Zander. A smile spread across her face as she read the message.

> *Hi Liv, been thinking about your naughty kisses*
> *all day. Hard to concentrate on anything*
> *else. Hope you're having a good day with Rhoda.*
> *Hope Alf's behaving himself! Zx*

She quickly fired a text back.

> *I think you'll find it was your kisses that*
> *were naughty! Mine were quite innocent!*
> *Having a great time. Alf's been a v good boy xxx*

Before she had chance to put her phone away, it pinged with another text.

> *There was nothing innocent about your kisses!*
> *Looking forward to picking up where we left off … Zx*

Feeling a blush rise in her cheeks, she tapped out a quick reply, asking if it would be okay for Rhoda to stay for a few days more, telling him she'd explain why later.

16

Back at Dale View Cottage, Livvie carried a tray with a pot of tea into the garden where she'd left Rhoda relaxing on the wooden seat. Blowing a wayward curl off her face, she carefully stepped over Alf who was stretched out in the doorway, lying flat on his back, legs akimbo and enjoying the shade. 'Here we are. I know we drank the teapot dry at the teashop, but I'm gasping for another cuppa.' She set the tray down on the bench next to where Rhoda was sitting and picked up the teapot, ready to pour. When she got no response she looked closer to see her stepmother's head was tilted backwards, her mouth slightly open and she was snoring softly.

Carefully lifting the tray, Livvie made her way back into the house; she'd use the time to catch up on a bit of housework and – the thing she was least looking forward to – try to catch hold of her mother to tell her the date of the wedding. She'd tried getting in touch numerous times but her calls were never picked up nor returned. She'd even texted her mum, asking her to call her when she had a spare minute, but that hadn't elicited a reply either. It wasn't the first time, so Livvie didn't know why she was so surprised. Anyone would think her mother didn't want to talk to her. Knowing her news would be met with a scornful response, she wished texting her mum was an acceptable option, but decency told her that it wasn't, so she'd kept on trying. She'd been tempted to call Cheryl and ask her to pass a message on that she'd been trying to get in touch, but she knew Cheryl wouldn't be happy until she'd wheedled the reason out of her, her mother even less so for not hearing it first. Livvie couldn't win with those two. God forbid they ever found out that she'd shared the date with Rhoda first. Livvie winced at that thought.

~

LIVVIE WAS in the kitchen zesting lemons for the lemon chicken she was preparing for the evening meal, their citrussy aroma filling the air, when Rhoda wandered in from outside. Her short hair was sticking up at the back where she'd been leaning against the wall and her eyes were still drowsy with sleep. Alf got up from the vantage point he favoured when food was being prepared and trotted over to her, wagging his tail.

'Hello, young man.' Rhoda patted his velvety head. She looked across at Livvie. 'I'm ever so sorry for falling asleep and leaving you to do all this, lovey.'

Livvie wandered over to her, flinging her arm around her and kissing her cheek. 'Hey, no worries, you were flat out; you must've needed it.'

Rhoda sighed. 'I think you're right. One minute I was watching the bees and the butterflies enjoying your new lavender hedge, feeling my eyes getting heavy, and the next thing I know it's nearly five o'clock and I've lost an hour and a half of the afternoon.'

'Happens to the best of us,' said Livvie, smiling affectionately. 'I've lost count of the times I've sat out there and nodded off.'

'Well, I can't remember the last time it happened to me.' Rhoda chuckled and made her way over to the sink to wash her hands. 'But I'm awake now, and ready to make myself useful; I don't expect you to wait on me hand and foot. What can I do?'

'I know you don't, but if you'd like to wash those potatoes then pop them in the Aga for baking then that would be good.'

'Will do.' Rhoda scooped the potatoes up and started washing them under the tap. 'And I don't know about you, but even though we ate a lot at lunchtime, I'm still looking forward to my dinner.'

'Mmm, me too. Since I moved here I'm always like that. It's all the fresh air and walking; it gives you a hearty appetite.' Livvie went to pop some things in the dishwasher. 'Oh, and while I remember, Zander and I wondered if you'd like to stay on a bit longer? You're very welcome to stay on for the rest of the week if you'd like? It'd give you chance to have a date with Len.'

Rhoda blushed. 'Well, that's very kind of you both, and much as I would love to, I'm afraid I'm going to have to head home as planned tomorrow; there are a couple of things I need to sort out. Oh, and it wouldn't be a "date" with Len, it would be an innocent drink and a chat. Nothing more.' She gave Livvie a mock stern look making the young woman giggle mischievously.

'Hmm. I'll believe you, thousands wouldn't.' Despite her laughter, Livvie couldn't help but feel a pang of disappointment at the thought of Rhoda going home tomorrow; it had been lovely spending time with her.

'WOW! THAT'S A MOUTH-WATERING SMELL.'

Livvie turned to see Zander standing in the doorway, a heart-stopping smile on his face that released a flurry of butterflies in her stomach. 'Zander!' She beamed at him.

Alf shot over to his dad, leaping about, his tail wagging so hard you could beat eggs with it. 'Hello there, fella. What's this I hear about you being a good lad, eh? Wonder's will never cease,' he said, laughing as he set his medical bag down by the door before ruffling Alf's ears. When he'd done, he made his way over to Livvie, glancing around. 'Where's Rhoda?'

'Upstairs, having a shower.' Electricity sparked in the air around them.

'Which means I can do this,' he said huskily as he cupped her face in his hands and pressed his lips against hers, parting them with his tongue.

Livvie felt a bolt of desire shoot right through her, making her groan.

Zander pulled away, looking deep into her eyes. 'I've been wanting to do that all day. Couldn't think of anything else.'

'So I gathered from your texts.' She grinned, toying with the idea of dragging him up to the bedroom where they could take things further, but her plan was dashed when she heard Rhoda coming down the stairs.

'Hold that thought.' Zander pressed a kiss to her forehead and gave her a smile filled with promise.

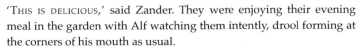

'This is delicious,' said Zander. They were enjoying their evening meal in the garden with Alf watching them intently, drool forming at the corners of his mouth as usual.

'It was a joint effort,' said Livvie, smiling. 'Rhoda and I slaved over it together.'

Rhoda chuckled. 'Well, I'm not so sure there was much slaving involved and there was certainly very little contribution from me; Livvie had most of it done while I was having a doze in the garden.'

'Sounds like the country air's got to you, Rhoda,' said Zander.

'It certainly has. And despite my earlier snooze, I know I'll sleep like a log tonight.'

'There's nothing better than a good night's sleep.' He turned to Livvie. 'Did you tell Rhoda about our trip to the castle yesterday evening?'

Livvie felt her stomach clench but she smiled, hoping to mask her true feelings. 'Erm, yes, I did. I told her it was lovely but that the church was probably the better option for us.' Hard as it was, she resisted meeting Zander's gaze but she could sense him nodding, hear the cogs whirring around his mind.

'Okay. I haven't been in touch with Caro to cancel the booking yet; I wanted to make sure you were absolutely certain before I did that.'

Oh, jeez, here we go.

Rhoda took a sip from her glass of water. 'To be honest, I was quite surprised at how underwhelmed Livvie sounded about it. I was expecting her to be bubbling with excitement after your visit. I mean, getting married in a castle must surely be every girl's dream? But, knowing Livvie as I do, she'll have a good reason for not wanting to have the ceremony there.'

'Hmm.' Zander looked over at Livvie but she still resisted the temptation to meet his eyes.

She gave a small shrug, adopted a casual tone and said, 'It's just … well … when there's a sweet little church like the one in the village, it seems a shame not to use it.' She pushed a piece of chicken onto her fork, keeping her eyes focused on it. She knew if Rhoda looked into them, she'd see straightaway that Livvie wasn't telling the full story.

'All the same, I'm going to leave it a couple of days before I contact Caro, just in case I manage to talk her round. It's a stunning spot; it's just a shame you weren't here last night, you could've gone to see it with us.' Zander winked at Rhoda.

Oh, thank goodness that didn't happen! Livvie knew Rhoda would have been as smitten as she was.

'I haven't told you, but we popped in to Romantique this afternoon. I showed Rhoda the sketch of my dress. And Kitty and Vi told us about Granny Aggie's latest escapades.' *Time to steer the conversation in a different direction, I think.*

Zander paused, his fork half-way to his mouth. 'Don't tell me she's been persecuting Rev Nev again?'

'I'm afraid so.' With Rhoda giggling, Livvie went on to share the conversation.

'And did she tell you about Jimby's cockerel? Honestly, I haven't laughed so much for months; it was the same last time I was here.'

'No, not yet. Who's it been terrorising now?'

'Oh, some poor unsuspecting walker. Luckily Len and Jimby managed to set him free. Actually, Len joined us for lunch; he's such a nice chap.'

'Yes, he's a lot happier since his divorce from what I can gather. And rumours about his ex-wife wanting them to get back together seem to have fizzled out,' said Zander, oblivious to the looks being exchanged between Livvie and Rhoda.

They spent the rest of the meal chatting away, their peals of laughter echoing out down the dale.

THE BEDSIDE LAMPS cast a cosy glow around the room. The air was still but for a light breeze that whispered in through the gap in the open window, the curtains giving a barely discernible flutter as it brushed by, carrying with it the sweet scent of the rose that clambered up the wall outside. The only sounds were a vixen barking in the distance and the gentle snoring that permeated through the wattle and daub wall from Rhoda's room next door. Zander was stretched out on the bed, his hands behind his head. The duvet was thrown back and he was naked but for the sheet that came up to his waist. He was watching Livvie as she slipped off her dressing gown, his eyes roving her naked body appreciatively. Fresh from the shower, she freed her hair from its topknot, letting the auburn waves cascade over her shoulders.

Feeling a frisson of excitement, she climbed into bed beside him, smoothing her hand over the dark hairs of his chest, the warmth of his skin sending a shiver of delight down her spine.

'Well, hello there,' he said, leaning over her and gazing into her eyes, brushing her hair off her face. Livvie clasped her hands around the back of his neck and pulled him towards her, feeling his lips pressing against hers before slowly tracing their way down her neck.

'Zander,' she said in a whisper.

He sat back, looking down at her, his eyes dark pools of desire. 'God, you're beautiful, Livvie.'

'You're not so bad yourself.' She gave a flirtatious smile and pulled him back to her.

17

LIVVIE WAVED RHODA OFF, watching the little red car disappear along the road, swamped by the over-grown hedgerows. She was sorry to see her go, but was offered a little glimmer of hope when Rhoda muttered something cryptic about probably being back sooner than she'd think. But Livvie didn't have much time to dwell on it or she'd be late for work.

Zander had been gone a good hour since; he'd dropped Alf off at his doggy-day-care at Brogan's over at Pond Farm Pooches. A new venture, it had coincided perfectly with Zander's move to the area. By all accounts, Alf had a whale of a time there and was always eager to see his friends, namely a Labradoodle by the name of Dave and a pretty black Lab with a glossy coat called Lulu whom, according to Brogan, both boys were besotted with. Being treated to long walks on the moors, Alf always returned home happy, tired and the edges ever-so-slightly worn off his mischievous streak. Still, on the rare occasions when Livvie was at the cottage and Alf was out, it felt odd without him.

Back inside the cottage, Livvie popped her mug into the dishwasher before quickly fastening her hair up, her mind suddenly occupied by the list of jobs awaiting her at Romantique. 'Right, best crack on.' She grabbed her bag and her keys and headed out to her car, ready to start her week at work.

Kitty and Vi were already at the studio when she burst in through the door. 'I bring gifts,' Livvie said as she made her way over to the kitchen. 'Of the edible variety, that is.'

'They're the best kind.' Vi left her seat and followed her. 'Please tell me you have some of Lucy's delicious flapjacks in that bag.'

Livvie laughed, catching Kitty's eye. 'Okay, I have some of Lucy's delicious flapjacks in this bag.'

'Fabulous! Hand it over! I'm bloody starving again.'

Livvie got a plate out of the cupboard and placed a chunky square of chocolate-dipped flapjack on it. 'There you go, I'll stick the kettle on.'

'You're an angel.'

'Kitty, cuppa?' asked Livvie.

'Ooh, yes, please.'

The three women congregated in the kitchen as they did each morning, talking over their plans for the day, what clients they had coming in and any ideas they'd had. Naturally, it often led to chat about other matters.

'So, if you don't mind me asking, why were we getting vibes you weren't keen on having your wedding up at Danskelfe Castle when you called in yesterday?' asked Vi.

Though Livvie had been anticipating the question, it didn't make it any easier to answer, and she still wasn't keen on sharing the real reason and risk it getting back to Zander. She paused for a moment, marshalling her thoughts. 'Well, it's kind of hard to put my finger on really. But there's a pretty little church sitting there, and I think it would be a shame if we didn't use that. You both got married there, didn't you?'

Both women nodded. 'Yes, I did when I married Ollie,' said Kitty.

'Yep, but trust me, if the castle had been holding weddings when me and Jimby got hitched, I'd have had ours up there, no question,' said Vi.

Livvie shrugged, trying to push images of the castle out of her mind. It had been a struggle to stop her imagination running away with itself, visualising what it would look like dressed for a winter wedding, the fire blazing in the huge inglenook fireplace. 'To be honest, there was a bit of an atmosphere between Lady Carolyn and her mother. They had a bit of a squabble when we were there. I'd be worried if that sort of thing happened at our wedding – but please keep it to yourselves, I don't want to be responsible for starting a rumour that puts folk off booking it for theirs.'

'Oh, don't worry about those two. Lady Davinia's a frosty old bag, everyone knows what she's like,' said Vi.

'And the feedback I've heard from people who've had weddings there has been really good; there's been no mention of squabbling or bad atmospheres, so don't let that put you off. I'm told Lady Davinia stays out of the way.' Kitty looked at her earnestly.

'Hmm. I'm just not sure.' Livvie knew their intentions were well-meant, but they weren't making it easy for her. She was thankful when the phone rang, cutting their conversation short; she'd been getting close to telling her friends the real reason she didn't want to use the castle, and she'd have kicked herself afterwards.

THE DAY PASSED QUICKLY and before she knew it Livvie found herself back at the cottage, watering the lavender hedge. She'd collected Alf from Pond Farm Pooches en route home and they'd had a quick game with the hosepipe – he seemed to get enormous pleasure when Livvie aimed it so he could bite at the jet of water, his eyes wild with mischief as he snapped away, making her laugh. She'd finished watering one side of the plants and was about to start on the other when she caught sight of Freda waddling along the lane towards them. The old lady looked uncomfortably hot in her hat and coat.

'Hello there, Freda, it's a lovely evening for a walk.' Livvie turned off the hose and set it down.

'Aye, it's grand, lass.' She placed a scruffy-looking carrier bag on the garden wall. 'Got some runner beans for you. Just picked them today, nice and fresh they are.'

'Oh, thank you, that's very kind. I can put them with tonight's dinner. Zander will be thrilled when I tell him; he loves homegrown vegetables.'

Freda beamed. 'Was that your stepmother you've been telling me about; the lady that was here yesterday?'

'It was. I was hoping to have the chance to introduce you to her but she couldn't stay long. Maybe next time she's here? She's really lovely.' Livvie realised Freda must have seen them looking into her garden when they were on their walk the previous day. She felt a pang of embarrassment.

'Aye, maybe.' Freda nodded. If Livvie was reading things right, she didn't seem totally averse to the idea.

'Actually, would you mind just waiting there a minute?' Livvie scurried off into the cottage, returning moments later armed with a plastic tub. 'Here, let me give you this; it's some leftover lemon chicken from last night's meal. You can heat it up in the oven; it'll just take twenty minutes or so. Or you could even do it in a pan on the hob.' She handed the carton to Freda. 'In exchange for the gorgeous sweet peas you gave me last week and these delicious looking runner-beans. And you'd be doing us a favour by taking it; I'd hate to think it went to waste.'

Freda looked bewildered, unsure of how to respond. It was almost as if she'd never been given anything before. 'Well, I don't … are you sure? That's very kind of you.'

'You're very welcome, you can have it with rice or potatoes and a bit of a salad.'

'Well, then…' Freda seemed lost for words.

Silence hung in the air between them for a few moments. 'I can't wait to try the runner beans,' said Livvie, for want of something to say.

'Aye, they're best eaten fresh. And thank you very much for this.' With that, Freda set off in the direction of her home with Livvie watching her go.

～

Livvie was flicking through a wedding magazine in the kitchen when she heard the sound of Zander's car pulling up at the side of the cottage. Happiness swept through her as it always did when he returned home. She followed Alf who had jumped up and raced out of the door and into the garden where Zander was walking up the path. He had a smile on his face that made her knees turn to jelly. 'Hi there,' he said.

'Hi.' She beamed at him. 'Good day?'

'Tiring. Busy. Glad to be home.' He bent down to Alf who was dancing around his feet. 'Hi there, fella. Have fun with your buddies today?' He scratched behind the Labrador's ears, laughing as Alf slumped to the floor, offering his tummy up for a tickle, his legs kicking out everywhere. 'What are you like, eh?'

'He's been helping me water the garden.'

'Are you sure "help" is the right word?'

'Hmm. Maybe not quite.' Livvie looked up at him now he was

standing in front of her. His eyes seemed extra blue against the aqua-marine of his shirt, but she noted there was a hint of tiredness in them.

'I'm so happy I have you to come home to.' Placing his hand behind her head, he pulled her in for a kiss, his lips warm and welcoming. Alf whimpered and pressed his paw against his dad's leg. Zander pulled away from Livvie and looked down at him, laughing. 'Yep, and you too, buddy; I'm happy I've got you to come home to as well.'

Livvie stood on her tip-toes and stole another kiss. 'And I'm happy I've got both of you.' She scanned his face, there was some-thing he wasn't telling her, she was sure of it, but she didn't like to pry. Only last week he'd come home, a similar air about him as if something was weighing him down. She'd pressed him about it, worrying that he might be getting fed up of her, regretting it when he'd told her he'd sent a young woman to hospital for tests, only to have his fears confirmed. She couldn't imagine how dreadful that must be. 'And you look like you could do with a relax. Why don't I run you a bath, or set the shower going for you?'

'Only if you join me.' The glint in his eyes had returned. He tilted her chin with his finger and kissed her again, sending a rush of heat through her.

'After such potent kisses, how can I possibly refuse?'

'And that invitation doesn't extend to you, Alfred. Okay? You're staying put downstairs. Don't even think about joining us. Got that?'

On hearing his name, Alf's ears twitched and he cocked his head enquiringly, his tail swishing back and forth on the path.

'He's too adorable for his own good, that boy,' said Livvie, laughing.

'And doesn't he know it?' Zander looked at the Labrador, unmis-takable affection in his eyes.

18

'THAT WAS RHODA,' said Livvie, walking back into the living room, her mobile phone in her hand.

'Oh? Is everything all right?' Zander looked up from his laptop where he'd been catching up on emails.

'She's fine, she just wondered if she could come over for a couple of days. I told her she could; I hope that's okay.'

'Of course it is, you don't have to ask. So any hints at why she's coming back so soon? Is it, by chance, anything to do with a certain Lycra-clad gentleman?'

Livvie grinned. 'Well, I'm secretly hoping that's got something to do with it, though she did say there were a couple of things she wanted to talk to me about.'

'Oh? That sounds ominous.'

'She was in good spirits; I didn't get the impression it was anything bad. She sounded more upbeat than usual actually. She's heading over tomorrow.' Livvie slipped her phone onto the coffee table.

'Ah, so it could be something to do with being keen to see Len again, and the prospect of a little romance bubbling away.' Zander flipped the lid of his laptop down and set it on the table next to Livvie's phone. He watched her as she made her way behind the sofa, leaning into him and draping her arms around his neck, pressing a kiss to his cheek.

The sultry warm notes of his cologne set her hormones dancing.

'Mmm. You could be right.' She nuzzled into him, inhaling deeper. 'And while we're on the subject of romance, how do you fancy getting cosy on the seat outside? It's a beautiful evening; we might as well make the most of it before the weather changes. I gather storms are on their way next week.'

'I like the way you're talking. Lead the way,' he said, his eyes twinkling.

The pair had been ensconced on the swinging seat for the last ten minutes, chatting away and watching the stars slowly appear as light faded from the sky. Livvie was resting her head on Zander's shoulder, he had his arm around her and was twirling a lock of her hair around his finger.

'I meant to tell you, Freda popped by this evening; she brought some runner beans from her garden,' said Livvie.

'That was kind of her.'

'Hmm. I'd intended to serve them with tonight's dinner but got a bit distracted when you got home.'

Zander pulled her closer, giving her a squeeze which made her smile. 'Easy done.'

They sat in silence for a moment, each lost in their own thoughts. Livvie's gaze settled absent-mindedly on a star that was twinkling more brightly over the dale than the others; she was barely aware of Zander's fingers as they brushed the top of her arm. She cast a look Alf's way; he was sitting on the lawn, giving some obscure object his undivided attention, his ears cocked in interest. At least he's not up to mischief, she thought.

Zander was the first to speak. 'I thought I'd check with you one last time that you're certain you don't want to have the wedding up at the castle. Out of courtesy, I don't want to keep Caro dangling any longer than necessary. Are you absolutely sure I can't talk you into it?'

Oh no, not this again. Livvie groaned inwardly.

'For what it's worth I'll just say I think it's the perfect venue, and judging from the look on your face when we were there the other night, I thought you felt the same. Surely that little spat between Caro and her mother hasn't put you off? I was asking around at work today and no one's heard anything negative about their weddings; it's all been very positive.' Zander looked at her hopefully.

I'd love more than anything else to get married to you there, Zander. Livvie sighed, she hated having to disappoint him, but her sense of pride was over-ruling everything else; there was no way she could sit back and let him bear the bulk of the cost. No way at all. 'I agree, it's a gorgeous venue, but I also really like the little church in the village and I can't see any reason why we shouldn't get married there. It's got a lovely lychgate which I can ask Annie to decorate with flowers; it should look stunning, and the grounds will be so pretty for the photos.' She gave him a smile that she hoped would pacify him. And it was true about the church, it was utterly charming; if the castle didn't host weddings, there'd be no way they'd even consider getting married anywhere else.

'Hmm. I'm still not convinced. I'll leave it a few more days before I contact Caro, just in case you change your mind.' He tilted his head to look at her. 'And you promise me it's nothing to do with cost? Because I've already told you, it doesn't matter who pays for it, as long as we get the wedding we want.'

'I promise.' She couldn't quite meet his gaze.

'Good.' He leaned in and kissed her, making her pulse race.

'Warghh!' Livvie pulled away from him, her passion quashed. 'What the…?'

Their romantic moment had been ripped apart by a sudden dousing in icy-cold water. The shower stopped, then started again, not allowing them a moment to catch their breath and marshal their thoughts as a jet of water bounced off Zander's face.

'Alf, you little bugger!' Zander spluttered, holding his hand out in a bid to shield himself.

Livvie squealed as the spray changed direction and was now pointing at her. 'Alf! No!' She couldn't help but laugh as she realised the item that had so occupied him minutes earlier was the hosepipe she'd abandoned on the lawn when Freda turned up at the gate. Her conversation with her friend had distracted her and she'd forgotten to turn the water off at the tap. The temptation to give it a chew while no one was looking must have been too great for Alf to resist, and with the pressure building inside the pipe, it had only taken the slightest nudge of the nozzle for the water to burst forth, spraying everywhere.

'Alf! Stop!' Zander went to stop him but the game was way too much fun for the Labrador and Alf took off around the garden, the hosepipe between his teeth, water flying everywhere. 'Alf! Sit!' Zander raced around after him, ducking the jet of water as Alf bounded about.

'Oh, this is hilarious.' Recovered from her shock, Livvie was in fits of giggles watching Zander pursue Alf, the pair leaping around the garden. 'Arghh! No! Stop!' The water was aimed at her again, making her laugh harder. 'Oh, I wish someone was filming this.' She pushed her drenched hair back off her face; no doubt her mascara would be somewhere round her chin by now.

Zander was laughing hard too. He stopped chasing the wayward Labrador, and rested his hands on his knees, water dripping from him.

'You looked so funny, you two tearing around everywhere,' Livvie said between her giggles. 'It was just like a comedy sketch.'

He grinned at her. 'Yeah, thanks for helping there.'

'I'm sorry, I couldn't move for laughing. It was hilarious, especially when he got you right in the face.'

'Oh, is that right?' he asked playfully.

Livvie hadn't noticed Zander press his foot down hard on the hosepipe, putting an end to Alf's mischief. The Labrador paused for a moment, puzzled as to where the water had gone, before trotting over to Zander, the hose still in his mouth. Zander quickly prised it off him and aimed it at Livvie, removing his foot and dousing her in water before she could work out what was happening.

'Arghh!' Quickly she got to her feet, squealing and giggling. 'Stop! Stop! I'm soaking!'

Alf was leaping about, snapping at the jets of water, his eyes wide with sheer joy.

'Serves you right.' Zander roared with laughter as she ran across to him and tried to wrestle the hose away, water spraying everywhere.

'I'm sorry,' she said, giggling and spluttering as the water poured over her face. 'But please stop!'

'On one condition.'

'Okay,' she said, gasping.

'You kiss me.'

'Done.' Livvie pressed her lips to him, water dripping down both of their faces. Before he could stop her, she'd grabbed the hose off him and gave him one last drenching, before turning it off. 'There, we're quits now.' Happiness danced in her eyes.

Zander wiped his hand down his face as peace was restored. 'I'm absolutely soaked; it's gone right through to my boxer-shorts.' He pulled his drenched shirt away from his skin. 'Alfred Gillespie, I'm holding you responsible, you naughty little hound.'

Alf gazed up at Zander, his tail wagging happily as if to say, 'That was a great game, Dad. How about another round?'

'And there's no need to look so pleased with yourself either, young man.' Zander smiled, glancing over at Livvie. 'After that unexpected bit of fun, I think it's time we headed indoors.'

'Yep, the party's over, Alf, but thanks for giving me a laugh, watching your dad tear about the garden after you. It was hilarious.'

'Cheeky.' Zander looked at her, amusement making his eyes shine. He threw his arm over her shoulder, kissing her cheek. 'I didn't think I'd be doing that when I got up this morning.'

19

WEDNESDAY EVENING FOUND Livvie and Rhoda sitting in the cosy living room sharing a pot of tea while music played softly in the background. Zander had gone to the Sunne Inne in Lytell Stangdale, picking up Camm en route, for a catch-up and a pint or two with Jimby and Ollie. As it was throughout the year, the wood-burner was lit, flames dancing behind the glass.

It had been another busy day at Romantique with more orders flooding in. Livvie had been excited by one for a nineteen-twenties themed wedding, and ideas had been swirling around her mind all evening.

'I won't be a moment, lovey.' Rhoda placed the novel she'd been reading on the coffee table and disappeared upstairs. She returned with an envelope in her hand.

'Is everything okay?' asked Livvie. She was sitting in one of the squishy armchairs that flanked the sofa, her sketchbook in her hand.

'Couldn't be better, or it will be when I get myself comfy.' Rhoda beamed warmly at Livvie as she puffed up the tweed cushion behind her back. 'Right then, that should do.' She paused, setting her hands in her lap. 'So, I've got a couple of things I need to ask you, and I want you to promise me you'll give me your honest answer.'

What on earth could be the matter? Livvie gave her a puzzled look. Though Rhoda sounded serious, the expression on her face said otherwise. 'Of course. Is anything the matter? Are you okay?'

'Yes, I'm absolutely fine, don't go worrying about me. It's just really important you give me your honest answer, and not the answer you think I want to hear.'

'Okay.' *This is getting more and more puzzling.*

'Promise?'

'Cross my heart.' Livvie drew an "X" over her heart with her finger.

Rhoda cleared her throat. 'Good. So, the first thing I want to ask you is about shopping for your wedding bits and bobs, like shoes, jewellery, things like that.' Two dots of colour appeared on her cheeks. 'I hope you don't think I'm being pushy, but if your mum can't go with you, I wondered if you'd consider letting me come along? It's just it's the sort of thing a mother would do with her daughter and I know things haven't always been, well … you know … easy between the two of you, and I certainly don't want to make matters worse, but the thought of you doing that on your own if your mum doesn't want to go with you, well, it just makes me…' She pressed her hand to her chest. 'But, of course, if your friends have offered, and you'd rather go with them, I completely understand. I just don't want you to feel you have to do it on your own.'

Livvie felt a lump form in her throat as tears prickled at the back of her eyes. 'Oh, Rhoda, that's so thoughtful. Thank you. I haven't been able to get hold of my mum or Cheryl to even let them know the date. And, to be honest, I can't imagine my mother would want to go shopping with me for wedding things. As you know, she thinks I'm making a mistake marrying Zander "in such a rush" as she puts it.'

'Well, if she could see the two of you together, she'd know how wrong she was about that.'

Fat chance of that when she's refused to visit here.

Livvie reached out and took Rhoda's hand. 'I'd love to go shopping for my wedding things with you.'

'Oh, lovey, I'm thrilled to bits. Thank you. I know we're not flesh and blood but I love you as if you were my own daughter and I'm so glad we're back on track after your time with that controlling lad, Donny.' Tears shone in her eyes while Livvie's spilled onto her cheeks. She wiped them away with her fingers.

'What are we like?' Livvie said, laughing.

'A right couple of softies, that's what we are. Anyway – and don't forget, I want your honest answer, on this one actually more than the other questions.' Rhoda looked directly into Livvie's eyes. 'How would you feel about me moving closer to you? Say, as close as the village of Lytell Stangdale?'

'What, sell your house in Rickelthorpe and move out here permanently?' Rhoda still lived in the three-bedroomed house she'd shared with Livvie's father. They'd chosen it as it had enough room for the girls to stay over when it was his weekend to have them. Livvie could see the sense in her down-sizing, especially since she'd retired.

Rhoda nodded, a hesitant expression in her eyes. 'Yes, but only if you wouldn't mind.'

'I'd absolutely love it! Having family close would be the best thing – well, maybe not if it was Cheryl and Gavin,' she said making the pair of them laugh. 'But my totally honest answer is, "how soon can you do it?" It would be wonderful to have you living close by.'

Relief washed over Rhoda's face. 'Well, I can't tell you how pleased I am to hear you say that.'

'So what made you decide that?' asked Livvie.

'It was being here the other day, spending time with you and Zander, seeing how happy you are since you've moved here. And then going into the village, actually being made to feel part of the community, made me realise just how lonely I've become at Rickelthorpe. I know I've got all my clubs and things to keep me busy, but it's not the same; it's so vibrant and welcoming here. So,' she sneaked a glance at Livvie, catching her eye, 'one of the reasons I went back home was to get in touch with an estate agent with a view to putting my house on the market – she said she didn't think it would take long to sell and actually had someone in mind she thought would like it.'

'Wow! That sounds promising. So have you got anywhere in mind in the village?' The penny suddenly dropped. 'Ah, the little cottage we saw with the "for sale" sign the other day.'

'The very one, Fern Cottage. I've actually got an appointment to view it tomorrow evening; you can come with me, if you'd like? By the way, I would've cancelled it if you hadn't been keen on me moving here.'

'I'd love to view it with you. I bet it's got loads of character. And there's no way I'd ever not be keen on you moving here.'

'Well, that's settled then, which, very neatly, brings me to the final thing I wanted to talk to you about.'

'Umm. This sounds serious.'

'Well, it is, but in a good way.'

'Okay. Maybe I should make us a fresh pot of tea before we tackle it then.'

'Good plan.'

In the kitchen, Livvie's mind went over what Rhoda had asked her. It had touched her more than she could ever put into words that she would want to go wedding shopping with her. Rhoda was kind and loving and not a day went by when she wasn't grateful to have her in her life.

'Right, here we are.' Livvie poured the tea, adding a splash of milk to both mugs. She passed one to Rhoda. 'There you go, but mind out, it's hot.'

'Thanks, lovey.' She set it down on a coaster on the table, picking up the envelope once more. 'Right then, again I want your absolute honest answer, okay?'

'Yes.'

'Has the reason you're not keen on getting married at the castle got anything to do with cost?'

Oh bugger! Livvie was knocked off kilter by Rhoda's question. Why on earth would she want to know about that? She was struggling to answer when Rhoda spoke again.

'I could tell by your face when you were giving me little details about the place that you were smitten with it; your eyes lit up. So the only reason I could think of that would put you off is if you couldn't afford to pay a chunk towards it – there's no point denying it, I know what you're like.'

'I, er … well, yes.' Livvie paused, knowing when she was defeated. She heaved a sigh and cast her eyes down to the mug of tea she was holding in her lap. 'Cost is the reason. It's much more expensive than I imagined, and I feel really silly for even thinking we could get married there in the first place.' She told Rhoda the amount, wincing as she did so. 'But please don't tell Zander that's why, I think I've got him convinced that there's a different reason and that I'd prefer to get married at the church.'

'I've heard of more expensive places. And, I hope you don't mind, but I took the liberty of having a look at the castle's website; the place is stunning, and I know your dad would've wanted you to get married there. Which leads me very nicely on to the next thing I wanted to discuss with you.'

Oh, hells bells! 'I think I need some whisky in my tea after that.' Livvie took a gulp, forgetting it would still be hot. 'Ouch!'

'Don't worry, it's nothing that's going to upset the apple-cart.' Rhoda smiled kindly at her. 'So, when your dad was still with us, God rest his soul, we had a chat about the future – not in a morbid way, as you know your dad was always upbeat and full of fun. And you'll remember he was a planner, very organised, always liked to think he had everything taken care of, it's almost as if he had a sense he was going to leave this world too young.' She paused for a moment. 'Anyway, we opened a building society account especially for you, so we could put money aside to pay for your wedding when the time came; it's something he would've carried on doing if he was still here. And, just as he would've done, I've been adding a little bit to it over the years, so it's built up into quite a nice little nest-egg.'

Livvie sat listening in disbelief, her mouth hanging open. 'But…'

Rhoda smiled at her, affection glowing in her eyes. 'So, here you are, lovey, this is from your dad and me. It's the real reason I had to pop back to Rickelthorpe. As soon as I cottoned-on to why you weren't keen to get married at the castle, I knew I had to get the cheque out of the building society and give it to you straightaway; there's not a branch in Middleton-le-Moors, and I didn't want you to lose the booking. Hopefully, it should take your worries away and give you the wedding of your dreams, which is exactly what your dad would've wanted.' Her voice sounded thick as she handed the envelope over.

'Rhoda, I don't know what to say, but I can't take it; you're moving house, you've retired. You might need it to live on.'

'Please take it, sweetheart. It's not my money; as I said, it was always intended for you. And please don't worry about me. I should get a good price for my house, and, yes, I'm retired, but I've got a couple of other pensions on top of my one from teaching – another example of your dad's forward planning – and I've got plenty to keep me comfortable for the rest of my life. And, besides, we did the same for Cheryl. Granted there wasn't quite as much in her pot since she got married a good few years ago now.'

'Oh.' Livvie frowned. This was news to her. She distinctly remembered Cheryl telling her in a sanctimonious manner that she and Gavin had paid for their own wedding, insisting that it was only right since their mother was on her own and wouldn't be able to afford it.

'Didn't you know?'

Livvie shook her head. 'No.'

'Well, Cheryl's always been a law unto herself. Anyway, let's not worry about that for now. This is yours, so please open it. I want to be sure it's enough to cover the cost of the wedding up at the castle, because if it's not, I can always add a little bit more.'

Livvie opened the flap and eased the cheque out of the envelope. She gasped, pressing her hand to her mouth as her heart thundered in her chest. It would cover the cost of the castle and some. 'Rhoda! It's too much! I can't take it.'

'Of course you can, I insist, and so would your dad. If you won't take it for my sake, take it for him, and have a day to make him proud – don't forget you were the one who said you think he's looking down on us from his comfy spot up there.' Tears glistened in Rhoda's eyes.

Overcome with emotion, Livvie felt a sob escape her mouth as tears spilled down her cheeks. The generosity of this wonderful woman, and memories of her dad, had her mind reeling; it was almost too much to bear. 'I don't know what to say.'

'No need to say anything, chick. Just come here and give me a hug.'

Neither of them heard Zander walk in. 'Everything okay? Livvie, what's the matter?' He looked between them, concerned.

Livvie wiped the tears away with her fingertips. 'Everything's fine,' she said with a watery smile.

Rhoda patted the back of Livvie's hand. 'Right, lovey, if you don't mind, I think I'll get me an early night. It'll give you and young Zander a chance to have a chat.' She got to her feet, kissed Livvie on the cheek and headed towards the door. 'And I've got a date with Len tomorrow evening, so I need to catch up on my beauty sleep.' She looked up at Zander and squeezed his arm. 'Night, night, sweetheart.'

Zander looked from Rhoda to Livvie, a bemused expression on his face. 'Night, Rhoda.'

'Oh, okay.' The last bit of information Rhoda had imparted had momentarily thrown Livvie's thoughts off course. 'Night, Rhoda, sleep well.' She smiled. 'And thank you.'

Zander waited until Rhoda was upstairs before he closed the door and went to sit beside Livvie, taking her hand, his eyes desperately attempting to read hers. 'You've been crying. Are you okay?'

She nodded, smiling. 'I'm absolutely fine. Just happy.'

'Oh, right.' A frown fleetingly troubled his brow.

'Okay, time to be honest.' Livvie went to sit beside Zander on the sofa. 'So, about the castle…'

20

LIVVIE HAD lain awake for most of the night. Thoughts of getting married to Zander at Danskelfe Castle sent excitement pulsing through her, pushing sleep out of reach. It drowned out the chimes of the grandfather clock in the living room as it counted down the hours until she fell asleep just after three in the morning. The wedding actually felt more real now that she could let loose with her plans and allow herself the indulgence of visualising their day. That grand staircase, that stunning Great Hall with its magnificent fireplace. *Oh, my days!* Strangely, while the castle had been out of the running, she'd suffered from a mental block on the event, her mind seemingly reluctant to give the wedding any headspace, and no matter how hard she'd tried, she'd struggled to summon little more than a sliver of enthusiasm for it. Though she'd been inside St Thomas's several times, she hadn't been able to conjure up an image of how it would be on their wedding day; of standing beside Zander at the altar, how the floral displays would be arranged, the photographs they'd have taken outside. As for the reception, she hadn't known where to start with that, despite the fact she was cutting it fine to book a venue. But now she could let her imagination run free.

~

'IT'S VERY generous of Rhoda to give you that cheque, Livvie. It proves how much she thinks about you,' said Zander. It was just after seven and they were taking Alf for his first walk of the morning. The air was cooler than it had been for the last few weeks, and a fine mist lingered in the valley, a whiff of dampness in the air. It hadn't done anything to hamper the enthusiasm of the birds that were twittering away in the trees.

'Gosh, I know it was. And I think a lot about her too.'

Alf was trotting on ahead, nose down, tail up, the usual jaunty spring in his step. Zander took Livvie's hand, knotting his fingers through hers. 'I'll get straight on to Caro this morning, confirm the booking for the wedding.'

Livvie's chest filled with happiness. 'Sounds like a good plan.' She kept her eyes glued to the ground in front of her, taking a few moments before she spoke again. 'I still can't believe Rhoda and my dad had been saving for my wedding like that.'

'It shows you were always in your dad's thoughts even after he'd split from your mum. And it shows just what a decent person Rhoda is by continuing to pay into it after he passed away. After all, she didn't have to, and a lesser person could've been tempted to keep the money for themselves.'

'I know.' Livvie was still processing the gesture. 'I'm so lucky to have her in my life.'

'She feels the same way about you.'

Livvie smiled, an image of Rhoda's kind face appearing in her mind. 'And I don't just mean because of the money. I'm really looking forward to her moving here; she's been like a mum to me.'

'Seems everything's slotting together nicely.' Zander gave her hand a squeeze, turning his face towards her. 'And dare I ask about your mum?'

Livvie's heart sank. 'Hmm,' she said, pursing her lips. 'She still hasn't returned my calls, but I did get a text from her saying she'd been very busy and would get in touch when she had a spare moment, which is something, I suppose.' She gave a small shrug.

'Oh, right.'

'I'll try getting in touch when I'm on my lunchbreak today.' She was sparing Zander's feelings and didn't want to go into too much detail about what her mum had actually said in the text, but needless to say, it wasn't anything positive. And Livvie wanted to enjoy their bubble of happiness while she could this morning, before her mother got inside her head.

Zander, nodded, holding her gaze.

She looked away and checked her watch, sensing he knew there was something she wasn't telling him. 'Right, I think it's probably best if we head back or you'll be late to the surgery and Beth and Greta will be after you.'

IT HAD BEEN a busy morning at Romantique, dealing with phone calls, emails and last-minute tweaks for the final fitting of a wedding gown. The three women hadn't had chance to catch their breath and Livvie was bursting to share her news. A new client and her mother were leaving the Romantique studio, a huge smile on the bride-to-be's face, when Molly arrived at the door. 'Stick the kettle on, lasses. I've managed to escape the farm for a quick lunch-break,' she said, her chocolate-brown curls bouncing.

'Hiya, Moll, how's things?' asked Vi, slotting the notes she'd just taken into the newly-allocated file.

'Hiya, Molly.' Livvie beamed, thrilled that Molly was there to hear the news.

'Hi, Molly, that's good timing, I was just about to make a pot of tea.' Kitty got up and made her way to the kitchen. 'Is little Emmie with your mum?'

'Yep, they're baking apparently.' Molly pulled a face like she was going to be sick. 'I just hope we don't have to take any of it home. You know what my mother's cooking's like and her baking's even worse.'

'Well, at least she's got little Emmie to keep her right,' said Vi jokingly.

'Trust me, Emmie's the best baker by far out of the two of them. How my poor old dad's survived all these years with the muck my mother serves him, I've no idea. I reckon he's got faulty taste buds or a cast-iron stomach or something.'

'Poor Uncle Jack,' said Kitty, chuckling.

'I might as well grab a quick break before my mum brings Pippin over for her lunch,' said Vi, joining the others at the little table in the kitchen area.

Molly sat back in her chair, cradling her mug of tea. 'So, ladies, what have I missed?' She glanced between them.

'Well, I've got a bit of news.' Livvie felt all eyes turn to her.

'You're pregnant?' asked Vi.

'No!' said Livvie, her cheeks flaming.

'Phew!' Molly feigned wiping her brow. 'We've got a bit of a baby overload amongst us at the minute, I'm struggling to keep up.'

'It'll be your turn next, Moll.' Vi threw her a mischievous look.

'Pfft! No chance. I've done my bit, having my three.'

'I think another baby in our group would be lovely,' said Kitty.

'It's nothing to do with babies, I'm afraid. Zander and me are getting married up at the castle, he's ringing Caro to confirm this morning.' Happiness rushed through Livvie as the words left her mouth.

'Yay! Congratulations, chick,' said Vi, clapping her hands together. 'I bet it'll look gorgeous, decorated for a winter wedding.'

'Good stuff. We can get to have a good old nosy about up there,' said Molly.

'I'm really pleased for you, Livvie,' said Kitty.

'So what changed your mind?' asked Molly.

'Well…'

LIVVIE DRAINED her mug once she'd finished telling her friends of Rhoda's kind gesture. 'Right, if you don't mind, ladies, I'm going to pop outside and see if I can get hold of my mum.' The feeling of joy she'd had as she'd shared her news was leaching away and being quickly replaced by anxiety; her default mode when she had contact with her mother and Cheryl.

'I'm sure she'll be absolutely delighted with your news,' said Mary, who'd popped over with Pippin. 'What mother wouldn't be?'

Er, mine.

21

THOUGH LIVVIE and Cheryl shared the same auburn hair and hazel eyes, Cheryl took after their mother in the personality stakes, both women being prim and proper, aloof and, worst of all, judgmental. Livvie, on the other hand, had inherited their father's warm, easy-going nature, not taking life too seriously, much to Delia's chagrin. Delia and Cheryl's homes were immaculate – clinical almost – in muted shades with nothing out of place, whereas Livvie's home with Zander could be described as characterful and eclectic; with its soft sofas and plump cushions, it was undoubtedly furnished for comfort and relaxation. And though Livvie hadn't lived there long, she'd still had enough time to add her own touch. The warm and friendly personalities of the owners was evident as soon as you walked through the door.

It was true to say the style of their respective homes was reflected in their taste in fashion. Delia and Cheryl were pencil-slim, well-groomed and subscribed to the capsule-wardrobe concept, favouring shades of beige, black, grey and white. They despaired of Livvie's boho, hippy vibe, bright colours and unruly wavy hair, and were scornful of her disregard for watching her weight. Livvie had a hearty appetite and loved her food, with a particular soft-spot for cakes and chocolate, and there was no way she was going to stop eating what she enjoyed just so she could be tiny like them. And, besides, Zander couldn't get enough of her curves; he made her feel beautiful, desirable and loved. *Bring on the chocolate cake!*

Livvie headed out into the garden, sitting on the seat out of earshot of passers-by in the village. She waited a moment, steeling herself before she pressed her mother's number, but it just rang out before going to answerphone. She waited a moment before trying again, startled when her mother answered. 'Livvie! What is it? I'm in Rickelthorpe high street, laden down with shopping.' She sounded short of breath and agitated.

'Hi, Mum, I just wondered if we could have a quick catch-up, you know, about the wedding and everything else? But if you're busy I can alw—'

'It's fine, I'm nearly at my car. Just give me a minute.' There was background noise of traffic, a horn beeping and the sound of her mother's heels clicking along on the pavement accompanied by much huffing and puffing. Before long there was the beep of a key fob unlocking a car, much rustling as shopping was off-loaded before the door slammed and the background noise receded. Then silence.

Livvie waited, the phone pressed to her ear as she listened intently. 'Mum? Are you there, Mum? Is everything okay?'

'Yes, yes, everything's fine. Right, what is it you need to talk to me about?'

Livvie did her best to ignore the impatience in her mum's voice, adding a breezy tone to her own. 'I just wanted to talk to you about the wedding, we haven't really had a chance to discuss it properly. I'd love to come over to see you, to tell you in person, but you seem a bit busy.'

'Yes, I am, I'm rushed off my feet at the moment, hardly a minute to spare. But now you've got me, we might as well have the conversation, save you coming over. Presumably you got my text this morning?'

Livvie felt her shoulders slump. *This is going to be an uphill struggle. Why does everything have to be so difficult with you, Mum?*

Delia listened in silence as Livvie shared the news of the castle, the date and the food they'd planned to have, excitement rearing every now and then only to be quashed by the air of disapproval that was radiating through her phone from her mother. Nerves were making her gabble as she explained how Annie was doing the flowers and Steff and Annabel were making the cake. She hadn't mentioned Rhoda – her name was like a red rag to a bull to her mother and the thought of the woman moving to Lytell Stangdale or going wedding shopping with Livvie would have antagonised her beyond comprehension. Part of Livvie could appreciate why.

'There, that's it; you're all up-to-date with my wedding news.' She was clinging onto the hope that her mum would hear how happy she was and would relent, offering congratulations and being overjoyed that her daughter was so happy.

Silence.

'Mum? Are you still there?'

A sigh came down the phone. 'I'm still here.'

'Oh, good, I thought—'

'All I can say is that you know how I feel, Olivia.' It was always bad news when her mum used her full name. 'I think it's too soon, you hardly know each other. I don't know why you're both in such a rush; he seems as immature as you even though, at thirty-seven, he's a whole eight years older than you. You'll end up in the same mess as your dad and me and it will have cost you a fortune, which is the last thing I want for you. '

Livvie felt her blood boil at the slight to Zander. She bit her tongue, resisting the urge to say her dad hadn't known Rhoda long before he'd married her, and they'd been blissfully happy in the time they'd had together. 'I honestly don't think we will, Mum. And you'd see that if you'd only get to know him.'

'You sound just like your father, looking at things through rose-coloured glasses; you're like him in character just as much as you're like him in looks.'

'Don't say it like it's a bad thing, Mum,' Livvie said, her voice soft. 'I loved Dad. I still do.'

Delia snorted. 'I'm not sure what you expect me to say to that.'

'Just say you'll come to the wedding and you'll be happy for me; for me and Zander. I can book you a room at the castle, they're gorgeous by the way.'

'I'll come to the wedding as long as that dreadful woman isn't there.'

'Oh, Mum, please don't say that.' Livvie felt tears prickle her eyes.

'The harlot has no right to be there.'

'She has every right, Mum. She's been nothing but kind to Cheryl and me.'

From what she could gather, since their father had died, the only contact between Cheryl and Rhoda had been when Rhoda had sent her the cheque for her wedding. Cheryl had replied with a thank you note, but that had been it; she'd always been very firmly in Delia's camp.

Though she knew her mother would be aware of the wedding accounts set up by her ex-husband and Rhoda, Livvie didn't mention them for fear her mother would accuse her of hinting for money from her, or of trying to make her feel guilty. Either reason would only serve to increase Delia's dislike of Rhoda which Livvie was loath to do.

There was a few moments silence on the other end of the phone. 'Have you spoken to our Cheryl about this yet?'

'No, I wanted to talk to you first; being my mum, I thought it was only right. I'm going to ring her after I've finished speaking to you.'

'Right, well, I'd be very interested to hear what she has to say about this. But, as your mother it's my duty to tell you one last time, I think you're making a big mistake. You're rushing into a wedding with a man you've got nothing in common with and who you've only known for five minutes. It's madness. But if, after me telling you this, you still intend to go ahead with your plans I'll reiterate that I'll come to the wedding as long as your father's tart isn't there. Sorry, Olivia, you might think I'm being harsh, but I'm actually only thinking of your happiness.'

Really? I'd never have guessed.

The call ended, leaving Livvie feeling utterly deflated. Why did she always have to feel this way after having a conversation with her mum? It was as if as soon as they started speaking to one another a button was pushed, putting them both on the defensive and they faced each other, hackles raised, prepared for battle. Had it become a habit? What she'd give to have even a tiny share of the close relationship her sister shared with their mother.

'Oh, well, here goes, in for a penny, in for a pound. I might as well get this over with.' With a feeling of dread balling in her stomach, Livvie took a fortifying breath and called Cheryl's number but her sister didn't pick up. After a further two more attempts, Livvie gave up and went back into the studio, half-relieved that she hadn't had to speak to her and half wishing she'd got it over and done with.

22

AT JUST AFTER three-thirty the shrill ring-tone of Livvie's phone spliced through the air of concentration in the studio. She'd been working on a dress for the bridesmaid of a client from Danskelfe, painstakingly stitching handmade rosebuds in a delicate shade of coral-pink onto the bodice, her mind lost in a rabbit-warren of thoughts. Carefully, she set her needle down and reached for her phone at the other side of her workstation, cursing herself for not putting it back in her bag. 'Oh,' she said when she saw the caller ID.

'What's the matter?' asked Vi, looking up from her sewing.

'It's Cheryl's number.'

'You should take it, you've been trying to get hold of her for ages,' said Kitty.

'You sure you don't mind?' Livvie glanced between them both.

'Course not, get it over and done with,' said Vi, giving her an encouraging smile.

Livvie braced herself and pressed the reply button. *Here goes.* Her stomach clenched, there was no way this was going to be an easy conversation.

How right she was.

'Wow,' said Vi when the call had finished. 'That sister of yours doesn't give you much chance to speak, does she? You look bamboozled.'

'Are you okay, chick?' Kitty's eyes were wide with concern.

Livvie put her head in her hands and groaned. 'I'm just so bloody pathetic. Why can't I ever stand up to her? Why does she think it's okay to bulldoze my plans, like my feelings and opinions don't matter? And why the bloody hell do I let her?' Her voice was thick with emotion, her eyes filled with tears.

'I'll stick the kettle on. We can have a break and you can tell us what she said to upset you,' said Kitty.

'Good plan. Come on, flower.' Vi led Livvie to the kitchen, rubbing her arm as they went.

Both women listened in silence as Livvie recounted her one-sided conversation with Cheryl. She was surprised at how much better she felt once she got it off her chest. Her sister had adopted her usual lecture-like, superior tone, reiterating what their mother had said practically word-for-word.

You two have obviously had your heads together.

Cheryl had gone on to give Livvie advice on how she should plan her wedding as if she was in charge and Livvie didn't have a clue, making passive-aggressive comments when Livvie brought up any of her ideas. But what niggled her the most was how she'd spoken as if it was a given that her son, Ryan, would be a groomsman and Gavin would give her away. 'He wasn't wild about the idea, but I've talked him round,' Cheryl had said, her imperious tone grating on Livvie.

I want someone fitting to take the place of my wonderful dad, not someone I don't really like and who can't be bothered!

Cheryl had steamed on, oblivious to Livvie's wishes. She knew the perfect place to get the suits from, she knew the appropriate food to have for a winter wedding. And she'd just assumed she was going to be matron of honour. That had filled Livvie's heart with doom; the thought of her stuck-up sister bossing her around on her wedding day, making snide comments, passing them off with an insincere smile. *Ughh! No thank you!*

Livvie had been sorely tempted to tell her sister where to get off. But, in truth, the conversation had knocked the wind out of her sails and she'd come away from it feeling utterly flat.

'Shit.' Vi pulled a sympathetic face. 'Do you want Gavin to give you away?'

'No! I'd rather walk down the aisle on my own than have him do it. And I'd just assumed that Cheryl wouldn't even consider being matron of honour; but knowing how she is, I'm pretty sure that if I had asked her, she would've refused just to be awkward.' Livvie blew out her cheeks and released a noisy breath. 'She was even telling me what sort of dress she'd like.'

'What a cheek.' Vi shook her head, wearing a look of disapproval.

'Look, chick, it's yours and Zander's special day, nobody else's, you should have it exactly how you two want it, not how other people want it,' said Kitty, giving Livvie's hand a squeeze.

'Yeah, you really mustn't let your sister or your mum browbeat you. And I apologise if it sounds like I'm speaking out of turn, but they never seem to have anything positive to say, you're always upset after you've spoken to them. I can't get my head around that. Your mum and your sister should want the best for you; they should want to help with your wedding, not behave the way they're doing.'

'I agree, they should be absolutely over the moon that you're so happy and in love. We can all see what a perfect match you and Zander are.' Kitty gave her a reassuring smile. 'And they'd see that too if only they'd let themselves.'

Livvie nodded, mulling over their words. 'You know what? You're absolutely right. They should be happy for me, and not make me feel so crappy every time I speak to them. I don't want pompous Gavin to give me away, I'd hate that. I was going to ask Camm, seeing as though he was the very first person I met when I arrived at Lytell Stangdale, and he was so kind to me, helping me get to the cottage. If I can't have my lovely dad, that's who I'd like – if he wants to of course.'

'Oh, I think he'll be chuffed to bits you'd want him to do that. And your reasons for it are so lovely,' said Kitty.

'I think that's a fab idea,' said Vi.

'I'm so pleased you think so, but can you keep it to yourselves until I get chance to ask him?'

'Of course,' said Kitty.

'I'm going to go home tonight and start properly planning the wedding with Zander. We need to talk about who we want for best man, bridesmaids, groomsmen, everyone; the flowers; everything. And there's no way I'm going to let Cheryl interfere with any of it. It's our wedding and we should have it how we want it. But one thing's for certain, I want Rhoda there.'

23

'WHERE ARE THE MENFOLK?' asked Molly as she sat down on the banquette beside Vi. She and Camm had just arrived at the Sunne Inne and had joined Livvie, Kitty and Vi at their usual table in the corner by the large inglenook fireplace. As it did right throughout the year, a fire glowed warmly in the dog-grate. Alf was curled up in front of it with the landlords' rescue dogs, Nomad and Scruff.

'Jimby and Ollie are at the bar but Zander's been waylaid by Anita Matheson.' Livvie giggled mischievously and nodded towards where he was standing with the local vamp. He was nodding politely as Anita fawned and flirted unashamedly, touching his arm at every opportunity.

'Yep, he was innocently making his way to the bar behind Jimby and Ollie when Maneater pounced,' said Vi, a glint in her eye as she turned towards him.

Molly followed her gaze. 'Ughh! She'll have his boxer shorts off as quick as a flash before he can say "keep your mucky paws to yourself". And look at the state of her, why does she think it's okay to stick her knockers in his face?'

'Maybe she's asking for some medical advice,' said Vi, sniggering.

'I could give her all the advice she needs; how about put them away, you mucky old tart. I don't know how Zander's managing to keep a straight face, they're like a couple of wizened old—'

'Molly! Spare us, please,' said Kitty, holding her hands up and pulling a horrified face.

'I think most folk would agree with her, chick,' said Vi.

'Poor bloke,' said Camm with a chuckle. 'I think I need to go and find Jimby and Ollie so we can plan a rescue mission for him pretty sharpish.'

'Good luck with that,' said Molly. 'Once she's got her claws in, she doesn't like to let go. Ask our Jimby, he's been trying to shake her off for years. She's persistent if nothing else.'

'Oh, by the way, Rosie and Robbie can't make it tonight, they're at the theatre in York. Rosie said they're making a night of it, having a nice meal and staying over at a fancy hotel,' said Livvie.

'And we all know what that means, don't we, ladies?' Molly gave a theatrical wink and nudged Vi.

Livvie had been looking forward to tonight; she relished spending time in the welcoming atmosphere of the Sunne, with its cosy tweed soft furnishings in rich, moorland shades, its low-beamed ceilings and thick, wonky walls illuminated by soft light-ing. It's décor was a testament to landlady Bea's previous career as an interior designer. And, though it had been carefully curated, nothing looked contrived, instead it oozed rural charm and comfort. And the fact that the place was permanently infused with the mouth-watering aromas of Bea's delicious home cooking was another plus – even more so when Bea tried out her new creations on the group of friends before she put them on the pub menu. Being a girl who loved her food, this went down very well with Livvie.

Tonight, she'd gathered her friends together for an impromptu drink and a catch-up. Since her chat with Kitty and Vi the previous day, she was determined to put her mother's negativity and Cheryl's domineering nature out of her mind. Kitty's words had struck a chord; it was hers and Zander's day and they should be allowed to celebrate it in the way they saw fit. And now the castle was booked, Livvie was keen to get the wedding plans moving. She and Zander had started making a list of everything they wanted for their wedding – the theme, the food, the guests. Suddenly it felt tangible. Exciting. Finally Livvie allowed herself to believe it was really happening.

The pub was full of locals; there was a huddle of farmers standing at the bar, pints in hand, discussing the price of sheep at the mart held at Middleton-le-Moors earlier in the day. Gerald and Big Mary were having an entertaining conversation with Rhoda and Len at a table in the far corner, Gerald's hearty laugh booming around the room from time to time.

Livvie smiled; it was good to see her stepmother looking so happy, and she'd never seen Len so animated. They went well together; Livvie had her fingers crossed that something would come of it. She'd extended the invitation to Rhoda and Len to join her group of friends, but Rhoda had declined, explaining that not only was she determined not to step on Livvie's toes, but she was keen to forge new friendships in the village she soon hoped to call home.

The friends were sitting around the table, chatting away. Livvie noted the look of relief on Zander's face, having been rescued from Anita's clutches.

'You recovered yet, Zander?' asked Jimby, grinning broadly and slapping his friend on the back.

'I will after a few more mouthfuls of this stuff.' Zander held up his pint and took a long swig.

'You do realise you were seconds away from her grabbing your head and plunging your face right into her cleavage, don't you?' Molly said, sniggering.

Laughter rippled around the group while Zander had a job not to spray his pint over the table and Molly who was sitting opposite.

'Trust you to lower the tone, Moll. You're ever so common.' Vi feigned a look of disdain before turning to Zander. 'Please excuse my friend, she can't help it.'

'Tell me I'm wrong about Maneater.' Molly arched a challenging eyebrow at Vi.

'Hmm. Now you come to mention it, I think you're probably right.'

'See. Say you're sorry for calling me common.'

'Sorry you're common.' Vi flashed her a cheeky grin.

'Very funny. You know what I mean.' Molly nudged Vi with her elbow.

'Okay, sorry for calling you common.'

'Thank you.'

'I know you can't help it.' Vi giggled into her gin and tonic.

'What are you two like?' Kitty shook her head. 'Anyway, I think we should raise a toast to Livvie and Zander for officially booking a date for their wedding.'

'Quite right,' said Ollie, raising his pint of beer. 'To Livvie and Zander.'

'To Livvie and Zander,' the friends chorused, clinking their glasses together and turning heads from nearby tables.

Livvie looked across at Zander whose eyes were glowing with affection, making her heart skip a beat. For a fleeting moment she wished her mother was here to see how he looked at her, but she swept all thoughts of her mother away before they ventured down a different, less palatable path. After their last phone call, she didn't want anything to put the dampeners on tonight. Especially since it was liberating to realise they were now free to plan the wedding they both wanted. She took a deep breath. 'So, now we're all together, Zander and I have got a few wedding-themed things we'd like to ask you.' Livvie felt a thrill ripple down her spine.

'Ey up, sounds ominous,' said Jimby, flashing her a wide grin.

'Don't worry, it's all nice stuff,' said Livvie. 'As you know, we've got the wedding booked at Danskelfe Castle for the twenty-third of December, so don't forget to put that date in your diaries, please – we'll be sorting out invitations soon, but until then, just scribble the date in.'

'Ooh, this is so exciting,' said Vi.

'Liv's on a mission now we've got it booked,' said Zander.

'I so am. Anyway, since my lovely dad isn't with us any more, I need someone to give me away.' Livvie paused for a moment, emotion constricting her throat. She swallowed and took a deep breath before turning to Camm. 'So, the day Zander and I are getting married is almost exactly a year to the day I first arrived in Lytell Stangdale. I'm sure you can all remember it was snowing a blizzard and I was struggling to find my way to the cottage in the pitch black. Anyway, if it hadn't have been for the kindness of a total stranger stopping and showing me the way I think I would've spent the night driving around in circles or getting stuck in a snow-drift. What you did, going out of your way for me that night really meant a lot, Camm, and it would make me so happy if you would give me away.'

Molly was looking at him, smiling, her eyes warm with pride; though she had a tough, jokey exterior, it was obvious to Livvie that she loved Camm deeply.

'It was the least I could do that night; as you know now, the weather can turn nasty pretty quickly out here and I couldn't have seen you stranded. That aside, I'd be honoured to give you away, Livvie.' He beamed at her and, if she wasn't mistaken, his dark eyes were glittering with tears.

'Ah, that's so lovely,' said Kitty.

'It is,' said Livvie, her own tears abating while her heart sang with happiness. She knew her dad would be looking down, pleased with her choice. 'Thank you, Camm, I'm so happy you said yes.'

'And I'm so happy you asked me.' He quickly blinked his tears away, his smile as wide as Livvie's.

Recovered from almost choking on his beer, Zander spoke. 'And, Jimby, Ollie, I'd be honoured if you guys would be my groomsmen; I'm going to ask Robbie too, next time I see him, and I've asked my brother Toby.'

'I'd love to, mate,' said Jimby, raising his pint to Zander.

'Me too,' said Ollie. The three men clinked glasses.

'I think it means we get rewarded with extra beer, Oll.' Jimby gave Zander a cheeky wink.

'Good stuff,' said Ollie.

'And moving on to bridesmaids…' Livvie could barely contain her smiles.

'Wow! You're on a roll tonight, Livvie,' said Molly.

'You'd better believe it.'

'Yep, there's no stopping her now,' Zander said, beaming at her.

'So, as I said, moving on to the subject of bridesmaids. I'm going to ask Zander's niece, Annabel, and I'd love it if Noushka could be chief bridesmaid, and I'd like Emmie, Lily and Abbie if that's okay?'

'Oh, that's lovely, thank you, Noushka and Lily will be over the moon,' said Kitty, glancing happily at Ollie.

'They certainly will. Once Lily and Abbie find out, that's going to be all we hear about till Christmas,' said Ollie good-naturedly. 'Remember what they were like about Vi and Jimby's wedding?'

'How can I forget? My ears were ringing with it,' said Kitty, giggling.

'And Em will be fit to pop when we tell her. But can I just say, I had a horrible feeling you were going to ask Kitts, Vi and me to be maids of honour and I can't tell you how relieved I am you didn't. I mean, who wants to be called a "maid"?' Molly said, laughing. 'And the sight of me in a floaty dress, well, it'd be like putting a carthorse in a fancy frock; I'd ruin your wedding photos, hon.'

'You so wouldn't, Molly,' said Livvie, through her giggles. 'I just thought you'd prefer to sit with your families at the reception and be able to relax and enjoy the day.'

'I can't wait for us to start planning those dresses,' said Vi. 'And I can't wait to get up to that castle and have a good look around.'

'Watch out, Jimby, Vi'll be having you renewing your wedding vows up there before you know it!' said Zander.

Vi hitched up an eyebrow. 'I can't say the thought hadn't crossed my mind for some point in the future.'

'Oh, bloody hell,' said Jimby. 'Rein those thoughts in for now, Mrs Fairfax. I'm a simple bloke and my mind can only cope with thinking about one wedding at a time.'

'Don't worry, I'll be too occupied with planning my outfit for Livvie and Zander's wedding to think about another one of my own. And little Pippin's, of course; we've got to have her dressed in something adorable.'

'Ah, my little angel,' said Jimby.

Their words elicited a chorus of 'ahhs' from the women and the exchange of knowing glances from the men.

'Ladies, I feel a shopping trip coming on,' said Kitty, rubbing her hands together.

'Me and my big mouth. Sorry, fellas.' Jimby clamped his hand to his forehead.

'Can I just squeeze through, please, gents?' Bea appeared between Jimby and Zander. She was dressed in her chef's whites, her blunt, swishy bob held off her face by the tortoiseshell glasses on her head. She had a tray laden with shiny white bowls of steaming food balanced on her hand. 'Thought you might like to give these a try. I'm preparing the autumn menu and they're my latest concoctions for the specials board. I'd appreciate hearing what you all think before I take the plunge and add them to it.'

'Ooh, they look scrumptious.' Vi eyed the bowls appreciatively.

'Wow, the stew looks nice and hearty,' said Zander.

'Don't mind if I do.' Jimby smacked his lips, his eyes lingering on the dumplings.

Bea set the tray down and stepped back, clasping her hands together. 'So, we've got a herby chicken casserole with lemon and thyme dumplings. Then there's a stew with a Mediterranean influence; it's got chorizo, peppers, sweet smoked paprika and a mixed assortment of beans in it. I'm calling it "Warming Chorizo Stew" until I can think of a better name for it.' She looked around the group, smiling, pulling the tea towel from her shoulder.

'I think "Warming Chorizo Stew" sounds nice actually. The name would definitely tempt me to have it,' said Livvie.

'Mmm. Me too,' said Kitty, nodding.

Bea laughed. 'Well, if that's what you think, I'll stick with it; saves me the job of having to think of a new one. But for now, I'd better get back to the kitchen. Enjoy, folks, and let me know what you think.'

Once Bea was out of ear-shot, Molly said, 'Go easy on the beans, Jimby. You know what they do to your insides, and Vi doesn't want to be suffering later.'

Jimby threw his head back and roared with laughter. 'Er, you're a fine one to talk, Moll. So, right back at you, missus.'

'Enough, you two, we're about to eat,' said Kitty, struggling not to giggle.

They dived on the food, devouring it enthusiastically, conversation flowing throughout, excitement bubbling up followed by peals of laughter spilling out into the rest of the pub. Livvie couldn't remember a time when she'd felt so happy.

24

OCTOBER

LIVVIE HAD AWOKEN to find herself alone in bed, a dent in the pillow where Zander's head had been, a lingering hint of warmth suggesting he hadn't been up long. She lay for a while, allowing sleep to clear from her eyes; she was too cosy under the feather duvet to move just yet. Familiar Saturday morning sounds drifted upstairs from the kitchen, the muted hum of music from the radio, Zander whistling along, the occasional clink of crockery, him saying the odd word to Alf and the responding thud of the Labrador's tail wagging. She gave a lazy smile and reached across for Zander's pillow, pulling it close to her and inhaling his delicious familiar scent.

Her thoughts took her back to their tender love-making the previous evening. They were so in tune with one another, she still struggled to believe they'd known each other for less than a year.

The sound of his mobile phone ringing pulled Livvie out of her thoughts. The happy lilt to his voice told her it was someone he knew well. She pulled the duvet up to her chin and snuggled down. She'd give him time to finish his call before she went downstairs; it was no hardship to stay in such a comfy bed for a little while longer.

LIVVIE PULLED her dressing gown on and padded downstairs, her thick hair spread out over her shoulders. She headed into the kitchen to see Zander busy with the coffee machine. The kitchen was warm and he was wearing pyjama bottoms that sat low on his hips; he had his back to her revealing broad shoulders and rippling muscles. A kick of desire pulsed through her. It was quickly dispersed by Alf who trotted over to her, his tail wagging enthusiastically.

'Morning,' she said, bending to ruffle his ears. 'You look happy, young man.'

Zander turned, a smile on his face, his eyes shining, his hair mussed up, making her heart flip. 'Morning. He thinks there'll be food on the go soon, that's why.' He made his way over to her, cupped her face in his hands and kissed her softly on the mouth.

'Mmm. You have no business turning my knees to jelly this early on a morning, you do know that, don't you?' She laughed, pulling him closer.

He gave her a lopsided smile and kissed the end of her nose. 'And you have no business looking so irresistible first thing on a Saturday morning. You've no idea what you do to me, especially when you laugh and scrunch your nose up like that; it drives me crazy.'

'So, what are you going to do about it, Mr Hot-to-Trot?' She looked at him suggestively.

'Hmm. Let me think...' he said, nuzzling his nose against hers. 'Actually, I can think of a couple of things.'

Before he had chance to elaborate, his phone rang again. He rolled his eyes. 'Talk about bad timing.' He picked it up, tutting, frowning at the screen. 'It's a withheld number. There's no way I'm answering one of those after all the scams I've been hearing about recently. If someone wants to speak to me, they can be upfront and show their ID.'

'Don't blame you; I always ignore them.'

Zander put his phone back on the worktop and headed over to the coffee machine. 'How about I make us a coffee each and tell you about the other call I had this morning.'

'Coffee sounds good. I thought I heard you on the phone.'

'Hmm. It was Noah.' Livvie noticed the frown that furrowed his brow.

A few moments later, Zander set a mug of coffee on a coaster in front of her, the rich nutty aroma swirling around her nostrils. 'There you go.'

'Thanks. You look serious, is everything okay with Noah?'

'Noah's fine, he was calling about Jess.'

'Oh?' Livvie lifted her mug and blew across the steaming liquid.

'Seems she's having a few problems with her pregnancy.'

'Oh dear, is she all right?'

'Not really.'

In the summer, Noah had confided in Zander that he was worried about Jess who'd been complaining of feeling unwell for some time. 'She seems really run-down; it's not like her at all, she's always full of beans,' he'd said. It had come as a huge shock to discover the reason for her illness was that she was almost five months pregnant despite having no obvious signs. They'd always thought they couldn't have children themselves so had adopted two babies – Zak, now aged nine and Nina who was now seven. A baby being the cause of Jess's "illness" was the last thing they expected, but it didn't stop Zander from teasing his friend about being a GP who didn't spot his own wife's pregnancy.

'What sort of doctor are you, eh, mate?' he'd said, laughing.

'Ughh! Don't, they're having my life about it at the surgery,' Noah had said, shaking his head. 'I don't think I'm ever going to live it down.'

'Well, at least Jess is okay.'

Noah had puffed out his cheeks and breathed out a huge sigh of relief at that.

But Jess's pregnancy hadn't proceeded smoothly, and she'd been kept under close scrutiny by her consultant.

Livvie glanced up at Zander, awaiting his response. 'What did he say?'

'Jess's due date's been brought forward. She's suffering quite badly with oedema so the hospital's keeping an eye on her; they're worried it could be a symptom of pre-eclampsia which can be dangerous. It means they won't be able to come to the wedding.'

Sensing the disappointment in his voice, she reached across and wrapped her fingers around his. 'I'm really sorry to hear that but I hope Jess and the baby will be okay.' He and Noah had been best friends since they'd met at university and she knew he'd been keen for Noah to be his best man, so the fact he wouldn't even be at the wedding would hit him hard.

'They're in good hands, and Noah's watching her like a hawk, as you can imagine. I'd be exactly the same if it was you and our baby.'

You and our baby. The four words sent a thrill down Livvie's spine;

she'd never felt so cared for by a man before and she was still getting used to it.

They'd discussed having a family, but both agreed they wanted to wait a few years, so they could enjoy spending time just the two of them – and their wayward Labrador – before they considered going down the baby route. But both agreed it was something they were looking forward to in the future; Livvie knew Zander was keen to create the same warm, loving childhood he'd enjoyed growing up and she was looking forward to being part of such a family.

'Do you think we should rearrange the wedding?' she asked.

Zander shook his head. 'No, Noah said not to; he feels bad enough about not being able to come and he'd feel even worse if we did that. I think we should stick with the date we've got, especially since Caro squeezed us in as a special favour; it would seem like we were messing her around if we cancelled.'

'True, it was very good of her.'

'She's an astute business woman. A wedding at the castle is worth a lot of money; she wouldn't want to risk us going elsewhere for ours.'

'Hmm. Despite the fact Lady Davinia gripes about it.'

'I know. I dare say the profit will keep her in designer clothes for quite some time,' said Zander.

Caro had initially told them she wasn't hosting any weddings from mid-December through to the New Year with the next available date being several months after. Seeing the couple's disappointment, she'd relented and agreed to fit them in on the grounds they were having a comparatively small ceremony.

'Anyway, how do you fancy taking this lad for a nice long walk then going to the Sunne for a slap-up lunch? I wouldn't mind popping in on Jimby while we're in the village,' he said, giving her a wide smile.

'I fancy it a lot, but not as much as I fancy hearing about the plans you had before your phone rang.' She gave him a saucy look.

'Then how does a hot and steamy shower sound to you?' he asked, his eyes glittering.

'It sounds pretty darned good.'

25

ZANDER GRABBED Alf's lead from the hook in the utility room, sending the Labrador into raptures. He leapt about, whimpering and spinning in circles before racing down the hall to the front door.

'Someone's keen.' Livvie chuckled as she pushed her hands into a pair of rainbow-striped gloves.

'As always.' Zander looked on fondly as Alf sat by the door quivering with anticipation. 'We'd better not keep him waiting for too much longer; he looks like he could pop with excitement.'

'I'm good to go when you guys are.' She pulled on her emerald green beret, the colour stunning against her rich, auburn hair.

Outside, they were met by a beautiful, crisp autumn day, perfect weather for a leisurely walk. The sun was shining brightly from a clear blue sky, having burnt off the early mists that had hung over the moors first thing. Many of the trees still had their leaves, which were now sumptuous shades of rust, burnished copper, golds and reds. The hedgerows were bedecked with shiny berries and rosehips and spiders' webs with droplets of dew dangling from them like tiny diamonds.

It was Livvie's first autumn living in the countryside, and though she'd loved the freshness and vitality spring brought with it, backend – as locals referred to autumn – was proving to be her favourite season. Every day the scenery was alive with colour. Even the air smelt different; the warm scent of roses and honeysuckle having been replaced with damp earth, woodsmoke and moss; evocative of cosy nights with Zander. She couldn't think of anything better than snuggling up on the sofa with him, flames dancing behind the glass of the wood-burner in the low-beamed ceiling of the living room, the heavy curtains drawn against the night.

The pair made their way along the track, hand in hand, Alf trotting backwards and forwards, his nose bombarded with the myriad trails of scents. Rabbits darted to the safety of the burnished bracken. In the distance smoke curled up from a bonfire at Tinkel Bottom Farm, its tang wafting along the dale on the breeze. The hum of a quad-bike carried across the fields as Camm or Ben rounded up sheep over at Withrin Hill.

They were nearing Freda's cottage where a trail of smoke was spiralling out of the squat chimney pot. 'I wonder if she's in?' said Zander, echoing Livvie's thoughts. Alf raced forwards, his tail wagging enthusiastically.

Just then a bark emanated from the garden followed by the soft tones of Freda's voice. 'Hello there, Alfie Labrador.' She bent over the fence to pat his head.

'Hi, Freda. It's a lovely day.' Livvie gave her a little wave. She noticed the old lady was holding a tub brimming with vibrantly-coloured rosehips.

'Hello there, Freda.' Zander smiled at her.

'Morning. Aye, it's a grand day. We'll be spending as much time out here as we can, me and Midge. Thickening our blood up for winter as they used to say.'

'Your garden looks lovely,' said Livvie, taking in the neatly set out borders, the beetroot and parsnips laid out on the path, earth still clinging to them, and the rosy apples hanging from the trees. She tried not to let her eyes linger on the filthy windows.

'It does. And what are your plans for the rosehips?' asked Zander.

'I'm going to make some rosehip syrup.'

Zander nodded, impressed. 'Full of vitamin C, am I right?'

'Aye, you are; keeps colds away over the winter months.'

'That's what you need now it's getting colder. I bet you have a nice old range to keep your cottage warm,' he said, nodding towards it.

Freda's smiled dropped and she looked suddenly uncomfortable. 'I do.' With that, she turned and headed down the path towards the house, clicking her tongue for Midge to follow.

'What did I say?' Zander looked baffled.

'I think she didn't like you asking about the cottage.' Livvie watched as Freda closed the door firmly behind her. She hoped Zander's comment hadn't set their friendship back.

'I just worry that she's too old to be living like this; I guess she knew what I was thinking. She's so isolated, she could become ill and no one would know for days.'

AFTER THEIR BRIEF conversation with Freda, Livvie promised herself that she'd surreptitiously check on her elderly friend every day. She took note of the times Freda walked by – it turned out she was a creature of habit and walked Midge at the same times each day and headed into the village on a Tuesday and a Friday. Livvie found a variety of excuses to conveniently "bump" into her: some left-over apple pie, a tub of soup that needed using up. In turn, Freda gave her young friend a bag of apples and a variety of homegrown vegetables which tasted unbelievably fresh and had prompted a conversation about Livvie setting up vegetable beds at Dale View Cottage.

A happy consequence was that their friendship bloomed. Freda was a mine of information on gardening and traditional herbal remedies, and Livvie was happy to spend hours listening as the old lady talked away in her soft Yorkshire accent until her voice became hoarse. 'I haven't talked to anyone as much as this for as long as I can remember,' Freda had chuckled, her old eyes dancing with merriment.

'I could listen to you all day long, you're so knowledgeable.' Livvie had meant every word.

As subtly as she was able, Livvie had dropped little hints into their conversations, letting Freda know that if she ever needed help, she and Zander were there for her. It seemed her elderly friend preferred this type of communication to Zander's direct question that had sent her scuttling off.

26

LIVVIE WAS DRIVING along the road to Danskelfe Castle. The weather had taken a turn for the worse. Rain was lashing against the wind-screen of her little car, the wind was rocking the trees that lined the way, fallen leaves were blowing around like copper-coloured confetti. Mist hung in the valley, obscuring the view of the rigg. But it did little to dampen the wedding excitement that had been steadily building inside her over the last month.

She'd had a day in York, shopping for wedding things with Rhoda. There, Livvie had bought the most adorable wedding shoes and silk stockings. And, after much indecision, Rhoda had found her wedding outfit – a beautiful coat-dress in sky-blue silk and a wide-brimmed hat with ostrich feathers. 'I've seen a pair of shoes in a shop in Rickelthorpe that'll go perfectly,' she'd said happily.

Livvie had enjoyed spending the day in Rhoda's company. She'd slotted her arm through her stepmother's as they'd walked along, chattering away. The pair had enjoyed a leisurely lunch, catching up on news of Rhoda's house sale and her fledgling romance with Len. Livvie had thought it sweet how Rhoda's cheeks had flushed when she spoke of him. It had been a lovely day, though Livvie had thought it wise not to mention anything to her mum; she didn't think spending time with Rhoda would go down well. Though her mother had made it clear she was too busy to go wedding shopping with her, loyalty meant Livvie didn't want to hurt her mum's feelings.

Today was her day off work and, after spending the morning

checking her wedding "to-do" list, she was on her way to have a meeting with Caro Hammondely to discuss arrangements for the wedding.

Her heart felt light as she drove along, splashing through the puddles, pausing for the black-faced sheep that roamed the moors. Livvie had come to learn to keep one eye on the road and the other subconsciously scanning for the unpredictable woolly creatures; they either made a sudden bolt for it once they'd seen you heading in their direction, or they stayed put in the middle of the road, staring you out with glassy eyes, ruminating like some sassy teenager chewing on gum as if to say, 'Yeah, and what's your problem?' Livvie regularly found herself chuckling at them.

She pulled up in front of the castle, its great walls looking more austere than they had on her first visit. Rain was slanting against it, turning the stone walls grey. It did little to detract from its imposing appearance and Livvie's mind ran off, envisaging festive flowers around the main door and in large urns in the courtyard.

She stepped out of her car, pulling her coat more tightly around her. With her head bowed against the driving rain she made a dash for it, dodging puddles as she went. Before she reached the castle door it flew open and a voice called, 'Come on in out of this dreadful weather!' She risked a glance up to see Caro standing in the door way with Mr Tubbs peering around her, his tail wagging slowly.

Once inside, and having divested Livvie of her wet coat and hat, Caro leaned in and delivered a noisy air-kiss to each cheek. 'It's lovely to see you, darling. Thanks ever so much for venturing out in such ghastly weather.' Her warm smile crinkled the corners of her eyes.

'It's really not a problem, I'm just happy to be getting things moving with the wedding.'

'I'm not surprised. Come through, let's get out of this draughty hallway and have some tea in the sitting room. We can discuss arrangements in there; there's a roaring fire going.'

Livvie followed Caro and Mr Tubbs along a wide hallway and up a spiral staircase, her eyes wide as she took in the oil paintings and tapestries on the walls. Caro was right, it was chilly here and Livvie resisted the urge to shiver, not wanting to appear rude.

'Right, here we are.' Caro pushed open a heavy oak door revealing a vast room, the warmth rushing out to meet them. Mr Tubbs pushed by and waddled in.

'Oh, this is beautiful.' Livvie gazed around, her mouth open in awe. It was nothing like she'd expected. Here, the floor was covered with a thick, plush carpet, scattered with rugs. The walls were lined with hand-printed wallpaper and the windows dressed in heavy curtains in a sumptuous shade of teal. On the walls, paintings of Hammondely ancestors hung, but their tone was altogether more contemporary and less austere than those that lined the hallway, and suited the mood of the sitting room. One of a young woman wearing an elegant nineteen-thirties style V-neck evening gown stood out above the others. A gasp escaped Livvie's lips as her eyes absorbed the details. The young woman had a long string of pearls dangling from her graceful neck, a creamy-white gardenia held between slim fingers. The artist had painted so skilfully, so delicately, with such a deft hand, the silver fabric of the woman's gown appeared to shine and shimmer like fish-scales; it was as if you could pick out each and every tiny sequin. Tiny brush-strokes captured the soft waves of her honey-blonde bob and the details of the delicate tiara that appeared to sparkle; the gentle curve of her rosebud mouth looked as though it was just about to break out into a wide smile. Indeed, the look in her pale blue eyes suggested the owner had a playful streak.

'That's Great Aunt Veronica on her twenty-first birthday in nine-teen-thirty-four. She's from the very grand Froom-Gillings of Ripskle Hall and married into the Hammondelys. Apparently their combined wealth was out of this world.'

'She's very beautiful … and that gown, it's just stunning.'

'We've still got it,' said Caro. 'I'll show you when we're done here if you'd like?'

'You've still got it?'

'Yes.' Caro nodded. 'It's in immaculate condition.'

'Ooh, I'd love to see it.' Livvie's wedding-gown-designer mind was in over-drive, wondering if she could glean some style ideas from it. Not for her own wedding dress though. With her voluptuous curves, she doubted she could get away with anything as clinging as the debutante's dress.

THE AFTERNOON PASSED QUICKLY and Livvie slid her file into her bag, pleased with what she'd worked through with Caro. The menu had been finalised, as was the allocation of bedrooms. She'd still need to

call back with Annie in tow, so they could discuss flower arrangements, which was something Caro was fine about. 'Pop up whenever
you want, darling. Just give me a call beforehand to make sure
I'm about.'

The two women were finishing off their tea when Livvie's eyes
fell onto a cluster of family photographs set out on a table by the sofa
she was sitting on. She was drawn to a black and white one in a
silver frame. It was of a man and a woman and two children, a girl
and a boy, sitting on a rug in the garden, the castle behind. The
subjects seemed familiar to Livvie, but she couldn't quite place them.

Caro saw her looking. 'That photo was taken in the fifties; it's my
father with his parents and sister, Phaedra. Doesn't my father
look sweet?'

'He does.' Livvie said, looking more closely at the subjects.

'My grandparents made quite a formidable duo from what I can
gather.'

'There you are, Caro!' Both women turned to see Lady Davinia
standing in the door way. 'Have you forgotten what time it is?' She
turned to Livvie and gave her a tight smile. 'Hello, dear.' Her tone
was cool but not as chilly as it had been on Livvie's first visit.

'Hello.' Livvie felt a rush of awkwardness.

Caro looked at her watch. 'Oops. I'd totally lost track of time. I'm
afraid I'm going to have to head off now, Livvie. I do apologise.'

Livvie nodded. 'Of course, I totally understand. It's time I was
heading back too. Thank you for seeing me today.' Her smile masked
her disappointment at not being able to see the dress.

'A pleasure, darling. Here, I'll see you out; and don't forget to call
to arrange a time to bring Annie up to discuss the flowers.'

'I won't.' Livvie was glad to get away from Lady Davinia's
piercing stare; she really hoped the woman would make herself
scarce on the day of their wedding.

∼

IT WAS ALMOST eight o'clock by the time Zander arrived home. He
seemed distracted, and when Livvie asked why, he simply told her it
had been a stressful day at the surgery. She got the impression he
didn't want to talk about it so she thought it best not to pursue
matters.

'Have I got time for a quick shower before we eat? I'm keen to wash away the troubles from work.' Hints of stress shadowed his eyes.

'Of course, dinner can wait a bit longer.' She stood on her tiptoes and kissed him. When she pulled away he gave her a smile that still had the power to send a thrill through her, as tired as he was.

THE GRANDFATHER CLOCK had finished chiming nine o'clock. Livvie and Zander were in the living room, snuggled up on the sofa watching the television. The room was suffused in the warm glow from the table lights and the logs in the wood-burner. Tea lights flickered in mercuried-glass holders, their cosy "Autumn" fragrance filling the air. Alf was lying on his back in front of the stove, snoring gently.

'So how did it go up at the castle?' asked Zander, running his fingers through Livvie's hair.

'It went well. Caro was lovely; I really like her actually.'

'Any sign of old frosty-knickers?'

'From that description I assume you mean her mother? And, yes, she was there but only at the end. She wasn't too bad this time.'

'Good.'

'I'm still not sure of her though.'

'Can't say I blame you.'

'Anyway, we had the meeting in the sitting room which is absolutely gorgeous; it's very homely and has a completely different feel to the parts of the castle we've seen. There was a painting of Caro's great aunt wearing the most amazing pale-silver gown; honestly, it was stunning.' Her face was animated as she spoke. 'They've still got it apparently, the dress, that is, and Caro was going to show me it but her mother arrived and it was time for me to go.'

'Ah, shame.'

'I know. I would love to have seen it.' She pushed her disappointment away and sat forward to look at him. 'So are you feeling any more relaxed after your rough day?'

He smiled, pulling her back to him. 'Yes, being in this room with you and all of your cosy candles is helping.'

'Good.'

He heaved a sigh. 'It's just been one of those days…' He hesitated for a moment. 'Noah rang.'

'Oh? Is everything okay with Jess?'

He nodded. 'Mm. She's doing fine. He just fancied a bit of a chat.'

'Oh.' Livvie waited for him to elaborate but he didn't, and she didn't like to ask any more.

'Have you seen anything of Freda today?'

'Yes, I saw her after you left for work, she was taking Midge for his morning walk when I was taking Alf for his. She was in good spirits.'

'Good.'

They fell silent, Livvie resting her head on Zander's chest, taking comfort from the gentle rise and fall, the sound of his heart beating. Something told her he wasn't concentrating on the programme on the television; she could almost hear the cogs of his mind whirring. She frowned, feeling a little knot of anxiety forming in her gut as her mind started to wander...

SATURDAY HAD ARRIVED WITH A CRISP, frosty morning, the sky a splash of azure blue up above. It was a welcome change from the damp, misty days that had plagued the last week-and-a-half of October, though they had their own beauty.

'You just about ready?' Zander was standing at the foot of the stairs, wrapped up against the cold in his grey tweed coat.

'Yep, I just need to grab my bag.' Livvie checked the mirror in the bedroom one last time, smoothing her hair which fell in luxurious waves over her shoulders.

'Don't be too long, Alf's waiting in the back of the car and is looking very eager to set off; I've got a sneaking suspicion he thinks we're heading to the beach like we did last weekend.'

Livvie ran down the stairs, chuckling. 'Oh, poor Alf. Though I reckon he'll get over it when he realises where he's going; he loves Steff and the gang.' Once in the hallway she reached for her boiled-wool winter coat, lifting it off the peg by the door and shrugging it on. She wiggled her toes, savouring the underfloor heating before she pulled her boots on.

Zander flicked her a grin. 'You mean he loves Steff's cooking and the fact that the kids sneak him a load of food?'

Remembering they'd be spending some of the evening out in the back garden, she grabbed her scarf. 'Yep, plus the fact he'll get the chance to play with a certain dachshund; I love how excited they get when he and Cynthia first see each other.'

Zander rolled his eyes. 'Tell me about it.'

'Right, that's me ready. Come on, let's get cracking.'

Steff had invited them to stay over on the Saturday night with her and her family at their home in Leeds. She'd gently complained that it had been an age since they'd visited and that her children, twelve-year-old Annabel and eight-year-old Joel, had put in a special request that they come and stay with them that weekend.

The sun was out in force by the time they set off, having cleared the frost from the footpaths and lanes as if by magic, pouring its mellow light over the moorland, highlighting its vibrant autumn shades that Livvie so loved. They passed the field at the bottom of Withrin Hill Farm, the scene of the previous evening's Guy Fawkes Night celebration hosted by Molly and Camm. It had been a small affair with their usual group of friends and family and Livvie felt very much a part of it. There had been fireworks and a huge bonfire from which wisps of smoke were still rising, suffusing the air with a sweet tang of burning wood. It had made Livvie's nose tingle. Afterwards, they'd all headed up to the farmhouse for food and drinks, and a noisy game of apple bobbing.

She noted the sheep had been returned to the field next to the one where the bonfire had been, recalling Molly telling her they'd spent much of yesterday moving their livestock to fields further away to ensure they wouldn't be frightened by the noise associated with Bonfire Night. So different to her celebrations in Rickelthorpe, she thought.

'Last night was fun.' Zander interrupted her musings.

'It was, I really enjoyed myself.' They'd had a great time and, as usual, Livvie had come away with her face aching from laughing so hard. Jimby, the joker of the group and the most accident-prone man she'd ever met, had managed to fall backwards into an ancient water-trough carved from a huge lump of sandstone. He'd given himself a thorough soaking and had had to change into some of Camm's clothes.

'Jesus! That water's bloody freezing! My family jewels don't know what's hit 'em,' Jimby had said as Ollie and Zander had helped pull him out, bent double with laughter as they did so.

'Thanks, Moll, but I draw the line at wearing another bloke's underpants,' he'd said when she'd handed him a fresh bundle of clothes in the warmth of the kitchen at Withrin Hill farmhouse, a pair of Camm's boxer-shorts folded neatly on the top.

'And I draw the line at another bloke wearing my underpants,' Camm had said, laughing. 'Can't say I'm exactly comfortable with you going commando in my jeans, but I'll do my best not to think about it.' The friends had roared with laughter at the exchange.

They followed the winding country roads at a steady pace, sunlight glittering on the frost that still lingered on the edges of the lanes, leaving quaint little villages in their wake. Soon, the scenery took on a more suburban air, the roads becoming wider and faster. Zander pressed his foot down on the accelerator, allowing them to be swept up by the traffic and carried off to the city.

Livvie's mind wandered onto the moments she'd caught Zander looking distracted over recent weeks, his face changing as soon as he noticed her watching at him. She'd worked out it was since the phone call from Noah. *He's obviously more upset about his best friend not being at the wedding than he's letting on.* 'Jimby'll be a great best man. He's always so funny; can you imagine his best man's speech? It'll be hilarious,' she'd said, hoping to make him feel more positive about it.

He'd laughed and said, 'Too right, he'll be great. He's already asked for Noah's phone number so he can get some ammunition to use for it. I think I should be scared.'

Livvie felt her stomach squeeze as the car turned into the street where Steff and her husband lived. It was a road lined with large Victorian houses in a well-to-do suburb of Leeds. Much as she loved Zander's family, and they'd been nothing other than warm and welcoming to her, she still felt a frisson of nerves at the thought of meeting up with them.

On the doorstep, flanking the large pillar-box-red front door, they were greeted by the menacing smiles of two carved pumpkins. Alf sniffed at them curiously, not sure what to make of them. On the door was a black, sparkly wreath decorated with small plastic skulls, fake spiders and fir cones hung from the brass door knocker, while a one-foot-tall vampire was hung on the wall beside it, a sign saying, "Press Here" on its stomach. Relics from Halloween a few days earlier.

'Right, here goes,' said Zander pressing the button on the vampire. It emitted a loud, sinister laugh, making Alf jump and the pair of them giggle. Moments later, the door was flung open and Steff stood in the doorway. She was wearing her habitual happy smile, and her glossy hair was swept up into a swinging ponytail, while plastic skeleton earrings dangled from her ears. 'At last, you're here! These two have been driving me mad, asking me how long it would be until you arrived.' She held her arms out, enveloping Livvie into a warm hug. 'It's lovely to see you again, darling.'

Cynthia, their wire-haired dachshund, shot out, dancing around Alf's paws, excitedly weaving in and out of his legs, the pair apparently ecstatic to see each other again.

The mouth-watering aroma of food spilled out onto the doorstep, bombarding Livvie's senses in the nicest of ways; she'd quickly come to learn Steff's house invariably smelt of delicious food. Her nose detected roasting meat, spices and top-notes of something sweet. It tapped into a long-forgotten memory of a weekend visit to her father's and Rhoda's when she was a child, of a Bonfire Night celebration with them. It triggered a nostalgic wave of happiness inside her.

'Yay! Uncle Zandie and Livvie! You're here! We thought you weren't coming.' Joel burst from behind his mother. He was wearing a black cloak and a pair of plastic fangs, a trickle of fake blood pouring from the corner of his mouth.

'Woah! Has anyone seen Joel? I could've sworn I've just heard his voice, but all I can see is a vampire.' Zander looked around as if searching for his nephew, making him giggle.

'Same here,' said Livvie, cottoning on. 'It's a shame he's not here, especially since we've got a treat for him. I wonder if this scary-looking vampire likes gooey sweets?'

'Well, if he doesn't his mother does.' Steff arched a mischievous eyebrow at them. 'Hand 'em over and I'll let you in.' She held the door wide, allowing them to step inside, grabbing a quick hug from Zander as he walked by. 'Hello, you,' she said.

'It's me! Uncle Zandie, Livvie! It's me! Look!' Joel spat the fangs out and pushed them into Zander's hand. 'See!' He gave a wide grin, showing all of his teeth.

'Er, thanks.' Zander glanced down at the saliva-covered false-teeth in his hand, wearing an expression Livvie couldn't quite discern. She caught Steff's eye and the pair giggled.

'The perks of being an uncle, Zandie,' said his sister.

'Hmm. Great.' He handed them to her and winked. 'The perks of being a mum, Steff. And what an awesome disguise, Joel; I'd never have guessed that spooky vampire was you.'

'Joely, what *are* you doing?' His big sister Annabel walked towards them down the hall, an amused smile on her face. At twelve-years-old, she had the poise of someone much older. Livvie could imagine Steff being just like her at that age. As well as sharing the same long dark hair and striking blue eyes, mother and daughter had the same calm, sensible nature.

'Hi, Annabel. I love your hair like that, it looks gorgeous,' said Livvie. She handed Steff a tub so she could take her coat off. 'Toffee apple cake.'

Steff took a peek under the lid. 'Ooh, looks yummy. Thank you.'

Annabel's smile widened, lighting up her eyes. 'I was just trying out some different styles for when I'm your bridesmaid.'

'Well, it's really pretty.' Livvie leaned in to the young girl, lowering her voice to a whisper so Zander couldn't hear. 'And it'll look stunning with the Christmassy flowers you'll be wearing in it.'

'I can't wait to try my dress on next time we're at Romantique.'

'Should be pretty much finished by then; it'll just need the final tweaks.' If Livvie wasn't mistaken, she was sure Annabel had shot up since she'd last seen her.

'And I can't wait for it to get dark so we can show you the sparklers we've got for in the garden,' said Joel. 'We went to an awesome firework display last night; the fireworks were so loud. And then we went to watch the bonfire at the Wentworth's; it was huge! I love Guy Fawkes Night.'

Annabel smiled gently, rolling her eyes at her little brother. Zander ruffled her hair, laughing. 'You're just like your mum, Bells. She used to pull that very same face about me all the time when we were younger; still does, actually.'

Steff grinned at him affectionately. 'I'm sure I don't.'

'I hope you're both ravenous. Steff and Bells have done loads of food, as usual; been cooking away like mad, anyone would think we were feeding the whole street.' Steff's husband, John, came ambling down the hall, an easy smile on his face. 'Hi there, Zandie, good to see you, mate.' He shook Zander's hand, giving him a pat on the shoulder as he went over to Livvie, enveloping her in a hug. 'Lovely to see you too, Livvie. You're looking well, the country air is obviously suiting you.'

'Hi, John, it's good to see you too. And, yes, I'm loving life at Lytell Stangdale. I feel like I've been there forever and I never want to leave.' She looked up at Zander who was smiling down at her.

'Liv's settled in very well; we both have.'

Just then, Alf and Cynthia pushed through them and raced down the hall to the kitchen. 'Don't mind us, you two,' said Steff. 'Anyway, folk, come on through, food's almost ready.'

They followed her down the hallway to the large kitchen at the back of the house. Livvie thought the hallway had been warm, but the heat was cranked up several notches in this room courtesy of the Aga. 'I thought we'd eat in here,' said Steff. 'It's cosier and more relaxed than the dining room.'

'Great,' said Zander.

'Oh, wow! This looks fantastic.' Livvie's eyes were drawn to the long table that had been set with an autumnal theme. In the centre, sat in a pumpkin-shaped pot, was a floral arrangement of vibrant orange gerberas, small red roses and golden-yellow chrysanthemums. Their rich, burnished shades provided the perfect foil to the teasel, fir cones, and poppy heads included in the display. Adding a fun element, bat silhouettes attached to the ends of sticks and made of fluttery black plastic had been strategically placed in it. Fairy lights had been woven through it, emitting a warm glow. Confetti in the shape of pumpkins, black cats and silvery ghosts had been scattered across the crisp white table cloth and goblets in the form of skulls had been placed at each setting. Steff never did anything by halves.

'Not so sure cosy's the word, sis. More like spooky,' Zander said, casting his eyes over the huge fake cobwebs that were draped over the walls and windows and hung from the lights with fat, black spiders and bats dangling from them. They jostled for space with Halloween themed bunting. 'And he looks like he could do with a blooming good meal.' Zander nodded to the large plastic skeleton that was hanging from the wall by the pine dresser, his comment making everyone laugh.

'Oh, but I love the lights on here; they look very cosy.' Livvie nudged Zander and pointed to the pumpkin-shaped LED lights that ran along the huge Victorian pine dresser, suffusing the mugs, jars of spices and party invitations that cluttered it in mellow orange light.

'Ah, we spotted those in that new little shop just along the road. It's full of all sorts of wonderful stuff,' said Steff. 'I could spend a fortune in there.'

'Don't we know it,' said John affectionately.

'Mum and me made these cakes,' Annabel said proudly, pointing towards the worktop. 'They're blood clots and eye-balls.'

'How delicious,' said Zander drily.

Annabel shot him an amused expression. 'The blood clots are really red velvet sponge with strawberry-flavoured icing, Uncle Zandie, and the eyeballs are coconut with vanilla icing.'

'Phew! That's a relief.' Her uncle grinned at her. 'Not sure I fancied biting down on an eyeball.' He made an exaggerated chewing gesture.

Joel laughed hysterically. 'They're for later on, after we've finished with our sparklers out in the garden. And we can have them with some special Bonfire punch Dad and me made. It's got lots of ginger in it and it's *really* spicy.' Joel's voice was shrill with excitement.

'And I helped Mum make some cinder toffee too,' said Annabel.

'You're so clever, Bells.' The loving, family vibe that infused Steff's home gladdened Livvie's heart. It was exactly the sort of atmosphere she hoped one day to recreate with Zander at Dale View Cottage when they had a family of their own, if they were lucky enough to be so blessed. It was a far cry from the cold, clinical show-home that belonged to her sister Cheryl; Livvie had never been able to relax on her few visits there. And the house she'd grown up in had been little better.

28

'THAT WAS DELICIOUS, and now I'm so stuffed I don't think I can move.' Zander patted his stomach. They'd just finished their meal of braised beef cheek in a rich red wine gravy – or "Cheeky Beef" as it was known in the Finlayson household – accompanied by fluffy jacket potatoes and buttery wilted greens. It was topped off by a stickily moreish stem-ginger sponge pudding, served with creamy custard flecked with vanilla and garnished with dark chocolate shavings. The perfect meal for frosty autumn days, thought Livvie.

'It was amazing. Are you sure you don't mind sharing your recipe for Cheeky Beef, Steff?' asked Livvie.

'Not at all, darling. It's so easy, just kind of takes care of itself, bubbling away in the Aga for hours. It's actually a mixture of a few recipes I've encountered over the years, scribbling down ideas as I went along. It's a bit rough, but you get the gist of it. Remind me to take a photocopy before you leave tomorrow.'

'Great, thank you.' Livvie was eager to try making it at home and fill their cottage with its heart-warming aroma.

Soon, with everyone chipping in to help, the table was cleared and the dishwasher filled. The family migrated to the living room, flopping onto two large comfy-looking sofas or the two mismatched chairs with loose-covers. Flames danced behind the glass of the wood-burner while table-lamps cast their cosy glow around the room. Alf and Cynthia wasted no time in curling up on the Persian

Rug in front of the stove, the little dachshund snuggling into the solid curve of the Labrador's belly.

They'd been chatting and laughing for a while when Steff declared she was in urgent need of a mug of coffee in order to stop herself from falling asleep. 'A large meal and a warm and cosy room are a lethal combination for me,' she said, pushing herself up from the sofa with a groan.

'Yes, the last thing Livvie and Zander want is to be serenaded by your snores, darling,' said John, laughing.

'I don't snore,' she said, feigning offence.

John arched an eyebrow at her. 'Really?'

'Need a hand?' asked Livvie, poised to get up.

'No, you stay where you are, my little brother can help me. Come on, Zandie, heave your bones up from that sofa.'

'Yep, I'm happy to help,' he said, removing his arm from around Livvie's shoulders and getting to his feet. 'And I could do with a breath of fresh air; we had a late night last night and I'm getting a bit too comfy here.'

They hadn't been gone long when Annabel brought up the new shop they'd bought their Halloween decorations from. 'They sell jewellery too; you'd love it, Livvie,' she said, her pretty face animated. 'They've got jangly bracelets like the ones you wear, and they have the most gorgeous silver necklace with a daisy on it; I'm hoping to get it for Christmas.'

Annabel's words sent an idea pinging into Livvie's mind. She'd been wondering what to get her bridesmaids as thank you gifts, and she'd been meaning to have a word with Steff about it. Livvie hadn't had much contact with twelve-year-old girls and was keen to get something Annabel would like. The daisy necklace sounded perfect. 'I just need a quick word with your mum,' she said, excusing herself. She was keen to mention it to Steff before it slipped her mind.

'See if you can hurry the pair up with that coffee while you're there,' John said, smiling.

'Will do.'

There was no sign of either Zander or Steff when she reached the kitchen, but she could hear the sound of hushed voices talking outside. She noticed the exterior light was on, illuminating the back garden. Livvie peered out of the large Victorian sash window to see Zander and his sister having what appeared to be a serious conversation, their words suspended in clouds of condensation in the frosty air. Steff had her hand on her brother's arm in a comforting gesture, and he was wearing a concerned expression. Livvie felt her heart start to race. Steff had clearly had an ulterior motive when she'd asked Zander to help her make coffee.

29

Livvie was unable to tear her eyes away from the interaction between Zander and Steff. She watched in morbid fascination as his body-language betrayed the tell-tale signs that he wasn't happy: shaking his head vehemently, running his fingers impatiently through his hair and rubbing his hand over his chin. *What on earth is going on, Zander?* Ignoring the little voice that told her she shouldn't be eavesdropping, she steadied her breathing in an attempt to catch what they were saying. But it was no use; the background hum of the boiler in the kitchen was drowning out their words. Steff said something indiscernible to which her brother replied with a hollow laugh.

Livvie was about to head back to the living room when she noticed the back door at the other end of the room was ajar. She slipped silently down towards it, making sure she could still see the pair from the window. Standing next to the door, she could hear things a little more clearly.

'I'm absolutely positive! She's lying; it's not possible!' Zander threw his arms up in exasperation, his voice ever-so-slightly raised.

Who's "she" and what's "she" lying about? Panic joined the unpalatable mix of emotions that were now swirling around in Livvie's gut.

Steff reached out, touching her brother's arm in a conciliatory gesture. 'I'm only telling you what she said, Zandie, I'm not saying it's true; please don't shoot the messenger.'

'You're right.' He sighed. 'I'm sorry, Steff, it's just Noah said—'

'Any chance of this coffee?' John appeared in the doorway

scratching his head, a hint of drowsiness in his eyes. On hearing his voice, Zander and Steff both turned to the window, shock at being caught writ large across their features. 'What the devil are they doing out there?' asked John.

'I'm not sure. I was going to join them but they looked a bit serious so I thought I'd better leave them to it.'

'Ah, right.' John nodded. 'I suppose I'd better get started on that coffee.'

Livvie couldn't quite put her finger on it, but something told her that John knew what they'd been discussing. It sent a prickle of unease running down her spine. Before she had the chance to quiz him about it, brother and sister came back into the kitchen, the frosty air of the evening lingering on their clothes.

'Everything okay?' she asked, looking between the two of them.

'Everything's fine.' Zander smiled at her.

Steff smiled too and gave Livvie's arm a reassuring squeeze. 'Everything's fine, darling, I just needed to mention something to Zandie about the house he rents out over at Milton Gardens; there've been rumours about some undesirable characters lurking around there. I just thought he might want to nip it in the bud before it becomes a nightmare.' She rolled her eyes, but Livvie detected something in the tone of Steff's voice that was just a little too bright and breezy.

'Oh, right. Well, I hope you can get it sorted out quickly, that's the last thing you need to worry about when we're trying to get organised for our wedding.'

Zander heaved a sigh, a hint of concern dimming his eyes. 'You're absolutely right there, Liv.'

Ignoring the pounding in her chest, she surveyed his expression, hoping to see a little nugget of something that would reassure her. Only a month or so ago, he'd told her he was toying with the idea of selling his Milton Gardens property, so the explanation seemed perfectly plausible. She was aware the doctor who'd replaced him at the surgery in Leeds had rented the house for six months before moving on, and the follow-on tenant had been trouble from the start. But Zander had only mentioned it in passing. He hadn't referred to it since and Livvie had thought no more about it. But today, something was telling her she wasn't being given the full story.

Little nuances in both Zander's and Steff's behaviour only added to her concerns, fuelling the little niggle that was creeping in, vying for her attention, telling Livvie something didn't quite add up. It was a feeling she'd had for the duration of her pathetic excuse of a relationship with Donny, and one she hadn't expected to feel with Zander. *Ughh! Please, not this! Not with Zander.* How she hated it.

For the rest of their stay, Livvie was distracted, her worries sneaking in whenever there was a quiet moment or when her thoughts wandered away from shared conversations. The more she thought about it, the more she just couldn't shake the feeling that it wasn't his old home Steff had been talking to Zander about. It didn't help that she'd caught the pair having more covert chats on a couple of occasions, their conversation coming to an abrupt end whenever she appeared. But Steff and John always put in a huge effort for their visits, so Livvie did her best to push her concerns to the back of her mind and plastered a smile on her face; she didn't want to appear rude or miserable.

Their journey back to Lytell Stangdale had been quiet, with both Livvie and Zander lost in their own thoughts as the miles whizzed by, neither one keen to broach the subject that had placed an invisible wedge between them. The happiness that had filled Livvie's heart less than twenty-four hours ago had been quashed by an indefinable feeling that set ripples of anxiety churning in her stomach. Her insecurity of old was getting its feet firmly under the table once more.

30

'RIGHT THEN, ladies, thanks for the tea but I'd best be heading off now.' Molly headed over to the kitchen and rinsed her mug in the sink. 'Don't forget, I've booked our usual table in the corner by the fire at the Sunne for seven-thirty, so don't be late.' It was Friday morning, a couple of weeks since Livvie and Zander's trip to Leeds. Molly had popped into the Romantique studio on her way to collect Emmie from playgroup.

'No fear of that, I've been looking forward to it all week. I've been counting down the days,' said Vi.

'Ooh, same here. It feels like ages since we had one of Bea's gorgeous meals there,' said Kitty.

'I wasn't sure if Rhoda and Len were joining us, so I asked Jonty if it would be okay to stick a couple of extra chairs either end of the table if they decide to come along; he was absolutely fine about it,' said Molly.

'No, they're having a quiet night in at Len's. Rhoda's offered to drive us so Zander and me can both have a glass of wine,' said Livvie.

'Ah, bless, love's not-quite-so-young dream,' said Molly.

'Moll!' Kitty's eyes widened. 'I think Rhoda looks very young for her age. And I think it's so romantic they've got together. I've never seen Len smile so much.'

'I didn't mean it in a bad way.' Molly looked across at Livvie who giggled and batted the comment away.

'No worries, I know you didn't. But I have to say, it's been great to see the sparkle in Rhoda's eyes and it's been lovely to be seeing so much more of her.'

The sale of Rhoda's house had gone through remarkably quickly. The buyer the estate agent had had in mind had made a fair offer on it which Rhoda accepted straightaway. However, the purchase of Fern Cottage was proceeding a little more slowly thanks to the inexperience of the seller's solicitor who was a trainee. Not wanting to risk the sale of Rhoda's property falling through, Zander and Livvie said she was welcome to stay at Dale View Cottage until the purchase of Fern Cottage was completed, putting the furniture she was bringing with her into storage at one of the barns at Withrin Hill Farm until it was needed.

It was good to have Rhoda share their home, and there was the added bonus of Livvie and Zander returning home from work to the mouth-watering aroma of home-made meals. On top of that, the cottage was spic-and-span and the usual gargantuan pile of ironing non-existent.

'I think I'm going to ring the estate agent for Fern Cottage and tell them you don't want to buy it any more,' Livvie said one evening as they were tucking into Rhoda's delicious shepherd's pie.

'Good idea. I'm afraid there's no way we can let you leave if you carry on spoiling us like this, Rhoda,' Zander said, smiling at her.

'Get away with you. It's the least I can do; you two have made my life so much easier by letting me stay here until I've got the keys to Fern Cottage. All the stress of hanging on and worrying that the sale of my house at Rickelthorpe might fall through if I kept the buyer waiting doesn't bear thinking about. This has taken the bulk of the stress away, and I'm told the purchase of Fern Cottage should go through soon. Touch wood.' Rhoda tapped her hand against the wooden leg of the table.

'There's Jimby at the bar with Ollie and Camm, I'll just go and join them, you go and park yourself with the girls,' said Zander.

'Will do.' Livvie had been looking forward to having a good catch-up and a giggle with them. Work had been full-on and they hadn't had much time to look up never mind have a conversation.

'Prosecco?'

'Sounds good to me.'

The bar of the Sunne was heaving with locals, and Livvie had trouble squeezing her way through to the table where Kitty, Molly and Vi were sitting.

'Here she is.' Molly's strident voice could be heard above the hum of chatter and laughter.

'Hi, everyone,' said Livvie, heading over to the empty space on the banquette next to Kitty. She was greeted by a chorus of hellos and a sea of happy faces. She unwound her scarf and unbuttoned her coat. 'No Rosie and Robbie yet?'

Vi shook her head. 'They're running late. Abbie's not feeling too well, so they've cancelled their usual babysitter and are waiting for Rosie's mum to come over from Middleton-le-Moors so she can look after her instead. Otherwise, Rosie wouldn't come out at all.'

'You and Zander have all this coming to you when you start a family,' said Kitty.

'Too bloody right. Make the most of being sprog-free while you can,' said Molly. 'Don't get me wrong, much as I love my kids to bits – and I know Tom and Ben are grown up now so I don't have to juggle with them – sometimes the logistics and forward-planning that's involved just to have a night out beggars belief.'

'I'm just so glad my parents live close by. My mother loves having little Pippin so much, she practically forces Jimby and me to go out,' said Vi, making them all chuckle.

'Hi, folks, sorry we're late.' Rosie arrived, her nose red from the cold. 'Robbie's with the men-folk at the bar.'

Another chorus of hellos went up as their friend removed her coat and got comfy on the seat next to Vi.

'No worries, chick, we're just glad you could make it,' said Molly.

'How's Abbie?' asked Kitty.

'A bit better, thanks, I'm just relieved my mum could come over and look after her. Robbie and me have been looking forward to this all week, feels like we haven't had a catch-up for ages.' Rosie smiled and turned to Livvie. 'So, how're the wedding plans going?'

'Really well; everything seems to be going okay. I just need to pop up to the castle for a meeting with Caro sometime next week to run through a few things, like the trims we want for the chairs, floral arrangements – I've asked Annie to come with me seeing as she's doing the flowers.'

'Oh, and don't we know it; it's all she's been talking about. She's been dying to have a nosy up there for as long as I can remember,' said Molly.

Livvie glanced across at Zander as he stood at the bar, a preoccupied expression troubling his face. She leaned into her friends. 'While the men aren't here, have any of them mentioned anything to you about Zander? I mean, I can't shake the feeling something's bugging him. He's pretty close to Jimby; do you know if he's said anything, Vi?'

Vi frowned and shook her head. 'No, nothing. Why?'

'It's probably work, now the weather's changed more people are coming down with the usual bugs that float around at this time of year. And some folk make an appointment for the smallest thing,' said Molly.

How Livvie wished she could believe it was that. 'I don't think that's it, and I did originally wonder if it's because Noah can't come to the wedding; they've been best friends for years. But I honestly don't think it's either of those things.'

'He's probably terrified about Jimby's best man speech,' Vi said.

'Well, he's joked about that, but I really don't think so.' Livvie explained about the conversation she'd seen him sharing with Steff and his shocked expression when he realised she'd been watching them.

'If Steff said she was just updating him on the tenant issues with his house in Leeds, I'm sure that's all it was. A problem tenant can be a nightmare,' said Vi.

'True. And, from what Ollie's said, Zander can't wait to get married to you,' said Kitty kindly. 'I'm sure it's nothing and you're worrying unnecessarily.'

'I agree, I think you're reading too much into it,' said Rosie.

'Zander loves you to bits, chick, we can all see that,' said Molly. 'And he probably thinks you've got enough on your plate with organising the wedding and making your wedding dress, not to mention the bridesmaids' dresses.'

Her friends nodded, making sounds of agreement. Livvie wished she shared their conviction.

'Ey up, lasses, here's your drinks.' Jimby arrived holding an ice-bucket containing a bottle of Prosecco, the other men following close behind. 'What's the goss?'

'It's girl-talk, Jimby, I'm afraid I can't tell you.' Vi winked at Livvie.

'Fair enough,' he smiled, setting the ice-bucket down in the centre of the table.

Livvie sighed. In her relationship with Donny, worrying and fretting had become part of her daily life thanks to his womanising ways. And it had been hard to let go of those emotions when she'd first got together with Zander. After all, with her generous curves and wild auburn waves, she bore no resemblance to his glamorous ex, Mel, with her model-like figure and immaculate hair. If Zander's actions hadn't made her feel so loved, it would've been easy to let insecurity and paranoia creep in and take a hold. She'd had no reason to doubt the foundations of their relationship until recently, and her friends' kind words had gone some way to allaying her concerns. So, she loosened her grip on the niggle, feeling it slip away as she allowed herself to join the group as they fell into their usual easy banter.

31

LIVVIE PULLED up outside the barn conversion that was Annie and Jack's home at Withrin Hill Farm to see Annie looking out of the window, waiting for her. Her face lit up when she saw Livvie and she gave her a quick wave. In a matter of minutes she was hurrying down the path.

'Hi, Annie. Thanks for doing this, I really appreciate it.'

'Hello, lovey.' Annie climbed into the car on a subtle waft of rose-scented perfume. 'You don't need to thank me, I'm looking forward to it.'

'Me too. You'll love the castle, it's an amazing place. And I'm keeping my fingers crossed Caro will let us have a look at the dress from the portrait I was telling you about.' Livvie waited for Annie to buckle her seat belt before she pulled away.

'Ooh, yes, I'd love to see that too. From what I've heard Lady Veronica was quite the society girl; her exquisite clothes are legendary, came from some of the top couture houses in France, I believe.'

'Wow. I wonder if the Hammondelys have any more of her dresses?'

'Hmm. I'm not sure; a vague memory tells me they sold them off years ago. They must've had a particular reason to hang on to the one from the portrait,' Annie said.

Before long they were parking up in the courtyard of the castle. Annie was gazing all around her. 'Oh, my goodness, I've never been this close up before. It's really quite a dramatic building, isn't it? I can see why you want to get married here.'

'It's stunning,' said Livvie.

'Hello, darlings.'

They turned to see Caro making her way towards them with long purposeful strides before hugging and air-kissing them like long-lost friends. 'Please excuse me, I absolutely stink of horses; haven't had a chance to get changed since I got back from a quick ride across the moors. I'd only just got through the door when Mother kicked off and I lost all track of time.'

Livvie groaned inwardly. *Oh no.* 'We can come back another time if it's not convenient.' She really wasn't keen on being here if Lady Davinia was skulking about in a foul mood.

'Absolutely not! It's fine. My father was supposed to be taking her shopping to York and he forgot and has taken himself off to heaven-knows-where. Between you and me, I think he was secretly trying to escape; he hates shopping.' Caro gave them a reassuring smile.

'If you're sure?'

'Of course. You need to work out where you want your floral displays; did I tell you we've got lots of vases and bowls you're very welcome to borrow?'

'That would be great, thank you.' Livvie caught Annie's eye, this was welcome news. Only yesterday they were airing their concerns over what to display the arrangements in.

'And I haven't forgotten I promised to show you Great Aunt Veronica's dress. In fact, why don't we do that now before you get lost in thoughts of flowers and bouquets?'

Excitement bubbled up inside Livvie as a wide smile spread across her face. 'Sounds great; I'd love to see it.'

'We have it on display in the Blue Room. Follow me.'

Livvie and Annie exchanged thrilled glances as they trotted after Caro, struggling to keep up with her long strides. She led them along the hallway and up the grand staircase, all the while, Annie looking around her in awe. 'Here we are.' Caro pushed open a dark oak door, revealing a room suspended in a soft light. 'It's dark because we needed to have special blinds made and suitable lighting fitted to protect the fabric in here; your eyes will adjust in a minute,' she said.

They followed Caro into the chamber with a feeling of growing anticipation. 'Oh, wow.' Livvie's eyes danced over the opulent silk fabric in rich shades of blue and grey that lined the walls, picking out the exquisite detail of the chinoiserie pattern. She heard Annie gasp. Underfoot was a soft, deep carpet in a complementary shade of lapis lazuli. But the pièce de résistance was a large glass case in the centre of the room.

It was Livvie's turn to gasp as she turned her gaze on a life-size version of the captivating young woman from the portrait she'd seen on her last visit.

'Oh, my, how beautiful.' Annie's voice was no more than a whisper.

The mannequin's pose echoed that of Lady Veronica's in the portrait, right down to the gardenia and pearls in her hand (though these were fake). Even the blonde wig had been painstakingly styled in the manner of Caro's great aunt, complete with tiara, the fake diamonds sparkling in the soft light.

'Oh, my goodness, it's just stunning.' Livvie felt an unexpected rush of emotion. She moved closer, hardly daring to breathe, her hand clasped to her chest. 'Are the shoes original too?' she asked, admiring the silk T-bar heels. They were shot with silver, had pearl-drop eyelets and were decorated with a diamanté buckle.

Caro nodded. 'They are, but they're not the ones from the portrait, though I do think they go rather well.'

'Mmm. They do.'

The gentle atmosphere of the room was spliced in two as the shrill ring-tone of Livvie's mobile phone spilled from her bag, jolting her out of her musings. 'Drat. I could've sworn I'd put it on silent mode. I'll just leave it to go to answerphone and call back later.' She looked across at Caro, relieved when the phone fell silent. 'Sorry about that.'

'No need to apologise, darling, I'm just amazed you managed to get signal through these thick walls, it's patchy at the best of times.' She clasped her hands together. 'Right, then, shall I show you our stash of vases and bowls?'

'Oh, yes please,' said Annie, her face lighting up. 'It's very good of you to let us borrow them.'

'I don't lend them out to everyone, but as you're locals and I know you, I'm more than happy to let you use them.'

'Thank you, I—' Livvie's words fell on her lips as her phone started ringing again. 'I'm so sorry.' She could feel a blush colour her cheeks. *Who on earth is it?*

'Someone sounds keen to get hold of you,' said Annie.

'They do; you're very welcome to take the call while I show Annie our stuff, if you like?' said Caro.

'Oh, I, erm...' Livvie's mind rushed over who it could possibly be. She doubted it would be Zander, Rhoda or her friends; they all knew she would be here. Would Bryony be calling from Australia at this hour? Livvie didn't think so. Or how about her mum or Cheryl? Livvie wasn't keen to take a call from either of them while she was at the castle; she didn't want to feel embarrassed at the awkwardness if they were calling with more words of disapproval about the wedding. Much to her relief, the ringing stopped. She smiled and was about to speak when it started again, a sense of urgency pulsing through it. *Oh, bugger!*

'I really think you should get that, lovey,' said Annie, looking concerned.

'Me too, someone's being very persistent, which suggests it could be urgent.' Caro's expression matched Annie's.

'You're right.' Livvie went to reach for her phone just as Lady Davinia walked into the room wearing her usual haughty expression. Livvie felt herself bristle.

'Hello, Mother,' said Caro. The rest of her words were lost to Livvie as she answered the call.

'Hi, Mandy, is everything okay?' She listened, her face falling as she took in the woman's words. 'Right, can you tell John I'll be there in ten minutes. Thanks for letting me know.'

She ended the call and looked between Caro and Annie. 'That was Mandy Danks from Tinkel Top Farm. It's Freda, she's had a fall.'

32

LIVVIE'S HEART WAS THUMPING, the thought of Freda being hurt upsetting her more than she expected. 'She's asking for me. I'm really sorry but I'm afraid I'm going to have to go.'

'Oh, God love her, I hope she's okay,' said Annie.

'Of course,' said Caro. 'Is Freda the rather eccentric old lady who lives in the cottage just along from you?'

Livvie nodded, biting back tears. 'Yes, I'm very fond of her and have got to know her quite well since I moved here.'

'Why on earth anyone wants anything to do with that repellent creature is beyond me.' Lady Davinia's face twisted with disapproval. The women looked at her aghast.

'Mother! What a horrible thing to say.'

'Well, I don't think there's any need for that,' said Annie.

Livvie felt her hackles rise as she pushed her phone back into her bag. She bit down on her lip, fighting the urge to give the obnoxious woman a piece of her mind. 'She's actually very sweet and kindhearted, as anyone would find out for themselves if only they gave her a chance.' Her eyes flashed angrily at Lady Davinia. *If anyone's a repellent creature, it's you.*

'Pfft! I doubt that very much.' Lady Davinia flounced out of the room.

Caro rested her hand on Livvie's arm. 'Look, darling, why don't you leave Annie here to discuss floral arrangements with me? I can drop her back home when we're done.' She smiled kindly. 'And I'm terribly sorry about my mother, she can be horrid at times.'

Tell me something I don't know.

'That sounds like a sensible plan to me, Livvie. I know the sort of thing you're after, and I've got my notebook and the camera on my phone so we can discuss any notes and photos I take,' said Annie.

Caro's suggestion raced around Livvie's mind, muddled by the sense of urgency telling her she needed to get to Freda. 'Erm, okay, as long as neither of you mind.' She glanced between them, fishing for her keys in her bag.

'We don't mind at all; you get yourself to Freda.' Annie gave her arm a reassuring squeeze.

'You go, I'll look after Annie. Can you find your way out?'

'I think so.'

Livvie rushed out of the room, down the sweeping staircase and along the hallway, bursting out of the door into the courtyard. She was all fingers and thumbs as she tried to get her key into the ignition. Sending gravel flying she shoved her car into gear and raced off out of the castle grounds on to the road to Lytell Stangdale. She drove faster than she'd ever done before on the narrow, twisting roads, grateful that the hedges had been cut back, improving visibility.

When she reached Freda's cottage, she saw the Danks's tractor parked outside. She ran down the path, pushing open the door, arriving in a cluttered room, its layout reminiscent of the entrance at Dale View Cottage. The smell of damp and decades of grime was overwhelming and momentarily took her breath away. 'Freda? John?'

'In here, Livvie.' John appeared in the door on the left.

'How is she? Is she okay?' Her chest felt tight with panic.

'She hasn't changed much from when I found her. I wanted to call an ambulance but she wouldn't let me. She got upset and said she wanted you.' John spoke in a low voice.

'Oh, poor thing.' A tear spilled onto Livvie's cheek and she swiped it away with her fingers.

'I knew something was wrong as soon as I spotted Midge running around on the lane. Poor little fella seemed right upset with himself. Then I noticed there was no smoke coming out of the chimney like there usually is. I knew straightaway something wasn't right, so I came up here. She doesn't look too good, I'm afraid, bless her, she's had a bit of a shock. I knew Mandy had your number so I rang her as soon as Freda said she wanted you.'

Livvie felt a pang of guilt at not picking up on Freda's change in routine; she'd been distracted, getting ready for her appointment at the castle and had intended to check on Freda later that afternoon.

'Where is she?'

'Through here. I don't know how long she's been there for but she's a bit cold so I put a blanket over her.' John headed back into the room he'd come from and made his way to a door which was ajar at the far end.

'I'm not surprised she's cold, it's freezing in here.' Livvie shivered, noticing ash in the fireplace of the living room, picking up on the clutter and mess of the room in her peripheral vision.

'Aye, it is, poor old soul.'

Freda was laid on the floor in a small, sparsely decorated room by a messily-made bed, her face a deathly white. 'Freda!' Livvie rushed over to her crouching down beside her. 'What happened?'

'I fell.' Her voice was hoarse and dark bruise-like shadows sat beneath her eyes. She held out her hand for Livvie to take.

'Oh, Freda, lovey.' The old lady's hand was icy and Livvie wrapped her fingers around it, rubbing it to warm it up. She struggled to keep tears at bay. 'Do you hurt anywhere?'

'My arm hurts a bit.'

'Right. Do you know how long you've been down here?'

'Not sure. Feels like a long time.'

Gnawing on her bottom lip, Livvie surveyed her elderly friend. 'I'm going to have to call Zander. I think you might have to go to hospital, Freda.'

'No. Not hospital.' There was fear in Freda's voice as she tried to ease herself up. She winced with the pain.

'It's probably best if you just stay where you are, Freda,' said Livvie.

'They'll take my home away.'

'Who will? No one's got the right to take your home away.' She turned to John and mouthed, 'Call an ambulance.' John nodded and slipped out of the room.

'Them up there, they'll take it.' A tear fell from her cheek.

'Listen to me, Freda, there's no way Zander and I will let anyone take your home away from you, okay?'

'You promise?'

'I promise.'

Freda nodded, appeased. 'Okay.'

Livvie rang the surgery but Zander was in with a patient, so she left a brief message with Greta explaining the situation. Before they knew it, the screeching siren of the ambulance from Middleton-le-Moors could be heard as it raced along the dale. Freda became agitated but was too weak to put up much of a fight when the paramedics arrived. They spoke kindly to her as they placed her on a stretcher and lifted her into the back of the ambulance.

'What about Midge?' Freda asked.

'I'll take him home with me; don't you go worrying about him,' said John kindly.

'Can I go in the back with Freda?' Livvie asked the paramedics.

'Of course, love.'

A look of relief passed across Freda's face.

33

AT THE HOSPITAL, Freda was assessed, had blood taken and was sent for an X-ray for a suspected broken wrist. Since she'd had a small bump to her head, the doctor was keen for her to stay in overnight so they could keep an eye on her. She'd looked so frightened at first, sitting there in a hospital gown, and Livvie's heart had gone out to her, but the hospital staff were incredibly kind and patient and, eventually, the terrified expression in her eyes seemed less intense.

'You're very lucky, Freda, it could've been much worse; you could've broken your hip or hit your head badly. You must be made of strong stuff.' The nurse had smiled kindly at her.

'Aye, I never seem to ail anything,' Freda had said, glancing over at Livvie.

Once Freda was settled in a ward and the nurse looking after her had reassured Livvie there was nothing more she could do, she made her way to the on-site café. She ordered a cup of tea to sip while she caught up on all the text messages and phone calls she'd missed. There was one from Annie offering to collect her from the hospital; she'd heard from Mandy Danks that Livvie had accompanied Freda there. She fired off a reply, accepting the offer of a lift and asking if Annie would mind a detour to the shops at Middleton-le-Moors. She'd managed to pick up some basic essentials for Freda in the small hospital shop, but they didn't sell nightdresses and the like and she was keen to bring such things with her on this evening's return visit.

While she waited for Annie, she sent a text to Zander updating him with what had happened. Once that was done, she fished out a pen and scrap of paper from her bag and started making a list of the things she needed to get for Freda. She chewed on the end of her pen, briefly toying with the idea of gathering up some nightwear from Moor Top Cottage. She'd locked up behind them when they'd left for hospital, so she had the key to the house. She quickly dismissed that thought; there was no way she could take anything from there to the hospital. Freda needed new things.

LIVVIE AND ZANDER visited Freda in hospital that evening armed with a couple of nightdresses, a dressing gown, some slippers – Livvie hoped they would fit having had to guess at the size – and a bunch of flowers. Freda had been given a wash and her white hair had been brushed, her pink scalp visible along the parting. Her arm rested across her chest in a sling.

'That was quite a fright you gave us all, Freda,' Zander said, smiling as he placed a basket of fruit on the cupboard by her bed. 'But you're in good hands here. And I hope you're going to let us sign that plaster cast.'

Freda chuckled at that.

Livvie was relieved to see her elderly friend looking brighter, despite still being a little agitated at leaving her home unattended and leaving Midge behind. Several times while they were there, she'd expressed particular concern over an old biscuit tin she had stashed away in a cupboard, albeit a locked one.

'I've had a brainwave, Freda. Why don't Zander and I take the tin and keep it at our place until you get out of hospital? You say the key for the cupboard is the other one on the keyring?' Livvie asked, squeezing the old lady's bony hand.

'We've both got the day off tomorrow, we could go and get it then,' said Zander. Their suggestion appeared to go some way to appeasing Freda.

'HAVE you any idea what she meant by saying she was worried someone would take this place away from her while she's in hospital?' Zander asked Livvie the following day as they headed down the path to Freda's cottage. Both were wrapped up well against the cold. It was late morning and the pair had enjoyed a brisk walk along to the cottage with Alf, the wind blowing Livvie's hair in her face. The weather had turned wintry and the sky bore the threat of snow.

'I have no idea what or who she meant, but she seemed pretty frightened about it. I think if she hadn't been so shocked by her fall she would've put up more of a fight about going into hospital.' Livvie felt a pang of guilt at overriding the old lady's wishes, though she knew it had been the right thing to do. 'Poor old soul, you should've seen the look in her eyes when she heard the ambulance; she looked terrified.'

'I can imagine, but you didn't have a choice, Livvie. Things could've been a lot worse if you hadn't done what you did; she could've ended up with hypothermia or worse. You mustn't go beating yourself up about it.'

'I know … I just wish I knew who she thinks is going to take her house away from her. Making an old lady feel like that is a bloody disgrace. I'd love to give them a piece of my mind.'

Zander flashed her a smile. 'I don't think Freda's ever had a friend like you before. I wonder what she makes of it?'

Arriving at the door, Livvie grinned at him. 'I hope she likes it. I fully intend to make it my mission to make sure she's okay, and to find out who the miserable sod is who thinks they can take her home from her.'

'That sounds like fighting talk to me.'

'You'd better believe it.'

After a brief wrestle with the key in the lock, she was relieved when it clicked open. 'Here goes, brace yourself, I'm afraid it's not a pretty sight.' The door let out a groan as she pushed it wide and stepped inside, the smell of damp and dirt assaulting their nostrils. Alf charged past them, dashing around the place, delighting in the myriad scents that bombarded his nose.

'I'd guessed it was bad,' said Zander, frowning as he scanned the decades' worth of clutter and grime and dusty spiders' webs that hung from the beams. His eyes fell to the floor and the flag-stones that were pitted with dirt. 'But this is a whole different level. Let's hope we can find her biscuit tin.' While they were asking Freda the whereabouts of the cupboard, a nurse had bustled in, announcing visiting hours were coming to an end. Freda had clammed up, reluctant to share the information in front of a stranger.

'Hmm. Let's hope it's not buried under a mound of heaven-knows-what.' Livvie headed through the door on the right-hand-side of the room. 'I think I'll try through here first.' She picked her way across the messy floor.

'Okay,' said Zander, following behind her.

'Jeez.' Livvie stood in the middle of the room, looking around her at the dirty walls, the plaster crumbling in places, the junk piled high. 'I didn't know people still lived like this,' she said sadly.

'Me neither.'

The kitchen, with its sturdy cruck-frame and low-beamed ceiling, was basic. There was a rickety-looking stove, covered in dried-on food with a pan half-full of something unpalatable on the hob. A chipped pot sink with a solitary tap sat beneath a long mullioned window. There was a nineteen-fifties style cupboard that had seen better days pushed alongside it. On the far wall was a dresser, piled high with clutter and dust-covered envelopes and letters. A wooden table and two chairs occupied the centre of the room; on the table was an unfinished plate of food surrounded by jars of jam, earth-covered vegetables and precariously balanced dishes. The flagstone floor was only just visible beneath the old newspapers and clutter that was strewn over it. A couple of buckets were dotted about, half-full of water; they were obviously to catch the rain where the roof leaked. The sight of Midge's food and water bowl by the door made Livvie's heart squeeze.

She took a deep breath, remembering the reason for their visit. 'Right, I'll check the dresser, see if the tin's in there.'

As she suspected, it was full of years' worth of hoarding; bits of paper, an old shoe, knotted-up bits of string, carrier bags, old, yellowing newspapers, but there was no sign of the tin Freda had described. 'Nope, it's not here.'

They made their way through to the living room with Alf trotting beside them, nose down, tail up. Zander flicked the switch of the naked bulb hanging from a beam; it lit up the room with a harsh glow. The room echoed the low beams and cruck-frame of the kitchen; it too was strewn with junk. The only furniture visible was a sagging sofa and chair that sat facing the empty inglenook fireplace.

'Livvie shivered, rubbing her hands together, her breath hanging in a cloud of condensation. 'Brrr. I hope this place feels warmer than this when the fire's lit, it's bloomin' freezing.' She took in the quaint mullioned windows, some of them stuffed with paper and rags where the glass had smashed, her eyes alighting on the L-shaped staircase that was piled high with clutter; it obviously hadn't been used for some time.

'I was wondering how she'd managed to get away without a nasty head injury after that fall, but seeing all this stuff on the floor, I can see why,' said Zander, as they entered the room where Livvie had found Freda the previous day.

'Thank goodness it was there.' Livvie gave an involuntary shudder; Freda with a serious head injury didn't bear thinking about. Scanning the room she saw an ancient-looking oak cupboard on the wall opposite the bed. It was peppered with woodworm holes and had the initials "CH" and the date 1645 carved into it. 'This looks interesting.' She took the key and, after a bit of manoeuvring, the lock surrendered and the door sprang open, spilling an array of fusty-smelling clothing onto the floor. After a quick rummage her hand landed on something cold and metal. 'Umm, this feels promising.' She pushed the other items away and pulled at the metal object. 'Ta-dah! I reckon this is it. It's a bit battered but it's dark blue and has flowers on like she described.'

'Yep, I reckon that's it. And, much as I'd love to know what's inside it that's got her all het up, I don't think we should open it,' said Zander.

'I agree; it's her private stuff, and I respect that.' But Livvie couldn't resist giving it a shake, arching her eyebrows mischievously at him and making them both laugh. 'Right, I'll get this lot tidied away, then we can get out of this freezing cold.'

On their way out, Livvie stopped in the living room, concern for Freda rising, her throat feeling suddenly tight. 'She can't come back to this, Zander; she'll get ill.'

Zander heaved a sigh. 'I know; it's unthinkable that she returns here as it is, though we know the fire and the stove are always lit when she's home, so it wouldn't always be as cold as it is today.'

'Even so, it's grotty and there are no creature comforts an old lady like Freda should be able to enjoy. The place needs a good clean, but that on its own isn't enough. It needs a proper renovation job doing on it like Dale View had.'

He threw his arm around her and pulled her close. 'I agree. It's hard to believe that our place was like this when I first bought it, complete with bracken roots growing through the wall and broken glass in the windows. But I stayed with Beth on the weekends I came over to renovate it.' He pressed his lips together and surveyed the scene. 'There's a lot of potential here with all the original features, which is maybe why Freda's so worried someone wants to take it from her.'

'I hadn't thought of that.' Livvie felt anxiety sweep through her.

Outside, Zander was struggling with the lock while Livvie weighed up the exterior of the cottage, noticing the gaps between the bricks where the pointing had fallen out. 'You know, I think it's actually warmer out here than it is in there.'

'I think you're right. There, that's got it.' He checked the door was locked and stood back. 'Actually, take a look at that sky. I think we should head back sharpish before the snow comes.' Livvie followed his gaze to the foreboding black clouds that were inching their way along the dale. She was relieved Freda was tucked up in a warm, comfy bed in Middleton hospital and not having to spend a chilly night in the cottage.

34

BY THE TIME Livvie and Zander had got back to their cottage, the wind had picked up, and dark, heavy clouds were sprawling across the sky, releasing shards of sleet that stung their skin like hundreds of tiny, spiteful pin-pricks.

'I can't believe how the weather's changed so dramatically since last week.' Livvie hung her coat on its usual peg in the utility room before heeling off her boots, the warmth of the cottage making her skin tingle.

'I'm afraid that's how it is out here; moorland weather's notoriously capricious,' said Zander, doing the same. 'Coffee?'

'I'm going to be naughty and have a hot chocolate.'

After checking his bowl for treats, Alf trotted into the kitchen, sprawling out on the floor and soaking up the under-floor heating. It raised a smile from Zander. 'It's a hard life being a Labrador.'

'He's adorable.' Livvie looked at him fondly.

Alf's tail thudded against the floor.

They had the house to themselves for a change; Rhoda was out, spending the afternoon with Len. Livvie cradled her mug in her hand, a plume of chocolatey steam rising in front of her. It seemed like a long time since Zander and she had enjoyed a quiet moment together, just the two of them; they'd both been so busy recently and Zander had seemed distracted.

She looked across at him, a bolt of attraction firing through her; he was looking ruggedly handsome thanks to the dark stubble that peppered his jaw. 'Freda will be pleased we found her tin and brought it back here,' she said.

'She will.'

'I'm really tempted to give that cottage a good clean, chuck all that rubbish out. Do you think she'd mind?'

'She might, but you could always ask her when we go and see her tonight, I suppose.'

'Yeah, I'd better not do anything before running it by her.'

'It'll be a lot of work, don't underestimate how much will need doing.' He took a sip of his coffee, peering at her over the rim of his cup.

'I'm up for it; I'm off work next week, I could get stuck into it then. I wonder if Rhoda would give me a hand?'

'I dare say she would.'

There was no denying, now they were back home, the conversation between the two was stilted, an air of awkwardness pervading the air. Livvie observed him from behind the safety of her mug. He was distracted, distant even, the hint of worry that had been lurking at the back of his eyes was getting bigger. Livvie felt a knot of anxiety twist in her stomach.

'You okay?' she asked.

'I'm fine.' He flashed her an unconvincing smile. 'There's a lot on at work, I could really have done with going in today. In fact, I think I'll pop by the surgery this afternoon.'

Livvie swept her disappointment away; she'd been looking forward to spending the day with him, of maybe going through their wedding plans. 'Oh, okay.'

∼

FREDA WAS KEPT in Middleton hospital for several days while further tests were carried out. Livvie had been pleased to see the old lady looking a lot brighter and itching to be discharged.

With Freda's reluctant approval, Livvie and Rhoda had made great headway into cleaning her cottage. Annie, Kitty and Molly had helped too. They'd had the chimneys swept, lit the fire and the stove and flung the doors and windows open, giving the house a thorough airing. Zander, Ollie and Jimby had taken several trips to the local recycling centre, offloading the decades' worth of rubbish Freda had accumulated.

'I hardly recognise this place,' said Livvie, with a feeling of satisfaction. She leaned against the mop when she'd finished washing the kitchen floor, the clean bite of disinfectant in the air.

'I hope Freda likes it,' said Rhoda, cloth in hand and standing back from the windows and admiring her handiwork.

'I'm still not keen on her moving back here, it's way too basic for an old lady to live in, what with no hot water, never mind no bathroom and no central heating. And Zander says the walls need re-plastering in places, not to mention the thatch needs fixing where it's leaking.'

'It sounds like a pretty major undertaking,' said Rhoda. 'But at least you got new glass fitted in the windows, that should cut down on quite a few of the draughts.'

'True.' Livvie only half-heard what Rhoda had said, her mind suddenly wandering onto the reason Zander had taken himself off to Leeds that day. She felt a wave of unease wash over her.

35

'THERE YOU GO, ALL DONE.' Livvie slotted Freda's seatbelt into the socket, giving it a quick tug to make sure it was properly secured.

'Thank you, lass.' Freda looked a little uncertain, her face drawn. She'd been discharged from hospital and Livvie had come to collect her and take her back to Lytell Stangdale. Livvie and Zander had given their assurances to the hospital team looking after her that Freda could stay with them until her cast was removed and appropriate help would be provided when she moved back to her cottage.

Livvie had done a double-take when she'd walked into the ward looking for her friend. She'd found Freda sitting on the chair by her bed, her arm across her chest in its sling. She was wrapped up in a spare coat and hat of Rhoda's and beneath that was a pleated skirt and hand-knitted jumper from Vi's mum. Her old tweed overcoat and deerstalker hat were long-forgotten.

Other than her trip in the ambulance, today would be Freda's first car journey in decades. Livvie could see she was feeling anxious.

'Don't worry, we'll take this nice and slowly. The roads are quiet at this time of day and they've been gritted, so there's nothing to worry about.'

Freda gave her a nervous smile, her good hand gripping tightly onto her seat as Livvie took the handbrake off and pulled away. From the corner of her eye, she could see the old lady was glancing around her, wide-eyed as they travelled along.

'How do you fancy taking a look at Middleton-le-Moors? The

Christmas decorations are up and it looks really pretty; we can just have a drive around the square, you don't even need to get out of the car.'

'I think I'd like that,' Freda said.

Arriving in the square of the quaint Georgian market town, Freda was agog, gazing around her with child-like wonder. In the centre was a vast Christmas tree, bedecked with hundreds of tiny white lights, a glowing star balancing precariously on the top. Each of the shops had smaller trees in holders fixed above their doors, and they too were adorned with fairy lights, while yet more white lights were strung from building to building. Each shop had a stunning window display and sumptuous wreaths on the doors. There was a rumour that competition was rife to be the best. No one could accuse the business owners of Middleton-le-Moors of not making an effort.

'Look at that tree! We used to have one as big as that at...' Freda pressed her hand to her lips as if to stop any more words slipping out. But her comment had piqued Livvie's interest, and though she didn't say anything, she was keen to know more.

'And look at the window display!' said Freda, her voice shrill with excitement.

'Has this place changed much since you were last here?'

Freda thought for a moment. 'Well, it's been a lot of years since I came this far, but from what I can remember, it hasn't really. Maybe there's more cars and the shops have different names above the doors, but that's about it.'

'I can believe that.' Livvie gave her an affectionate smile.

For the rest of the journey home, Freda looked around her at the scenery she hadn't seen for so many years, her fingers gripping the seat. Soon they were driving down the lane that led to their cottages. 'So, if it's okay with you, I thought we'd get you settled in at Dale View Cottage first, have a cup of tea, that sort of thing. We've given you the downstairs bedroom; it's nice and cosy.' Livvie sneaked a side-long glance at Freda. 'I can take you along to your cottage later if you like? Or we can save that till the morning? It's entirely up to you.'

'Aye, a cup of tea sounds good. I'll see how I feel about looking at my place after that.'

'That's absolutely fine.'

'What about Midge?'

'He's with Rhoda, waiting at our cottage for you. He'll be over the moon to see you, he's really missed you.'

Freda had agreed without hesitation to stay with Zander and Livvie until she'd made a full recovery. Her decision had surprised both of them; they'd anticipated more resistance after she'd lived on her own for so long. Her fall had clearly frightened her more than they'd expected.

As Livvie and Freda were making their way up the path, the door opened and Midge shot out. The little dog was in raptures at seeing his owner, leaping about and yapping like a puppy. 'Midge! It's good to see you, lad.' Freda's face was alive with happiness as she bent to ruffle his ears. 'Oh, I haven't half missed you, boy.'

'What a welcome,' said Livvie, laughing as she closed the gate.

'Someone looks pleased to see you, Freda.' Rhoda beamed at her.

'And I'm pleased to see him; he's looking very fluffy, aren't you, Midge.'

'He's had a bath and a good pamper session; you should've seen him when it was first done, he was like a little fluffy pom-pom.' Livvie's words made her friend chuckle.

Alf looked on, bemused and quiet for once, his tail swishing from side-to-side. 'Good lad,' Livvie said in a whisper, smoothing her hand over his glossy black head. He nuzzled into her leg.

'Right, how about that cup of tea we were talking about, Freda?' asked Livvie.

'Aye, sounds good.' Freda's cheeks were flushed with happiness.

'I'll put the kettle on.' Rhoda hurried off to the kitchen.

'By, this room's lovely. Are you sure it's okay for me to stay here?' Freda stood in the centre of the snug where two single beds with patchwork quilts were set either side of a small inglenook fireplace. A neat bedside cabinet sat beside each one. The room was toasty thanks to the thick column radiator that sat beneath the small mullioned window. Livvie had placed a jar of autumnal flowers on the deep window sill.

'Of course it is, we got it ready specially for you; we thought you might like the bed by the window so Rhoda put a hot-water bottle in there to air it.' Livvie set Freda's bag down on the small slipper chair by the door. 'You're more than welcome to make use of the wardrobe and drawers, or I could pop everything away while you catch up on your cuddles with Midge?' Livvie was treading carefully, conscious that up to the day of her accident, Freda had coped with everything life had thrown at her without any help or interference. She didn't want to make her friend feel she'd lost her independence or, worse, get the impression people thought she couldn't manage, and rush back to Moor Top Cottage.' She saw Freda glance down at the plaster cast on her arm.

'Well, I suppose it'd be nice to fuss this lad for a bit longer, so if you wouldn't mind…'

Phew! That was easier than Livvie had thought. 'I wouldn't mind at all, you and Midge fill your boots.'

'Fill our boots?' Freda looked at her, non-plussed.

'Ah, it's just a saying. It means go for it, do what you fancy, that sort of thing.'

'Oh, right. Come on then, Midge, lad, let's get our boots filled.'

Livvie bent to unzip the bag, stifling a giggle. 'Oh, and while I remember, the biscuit tin we brought from your cottage is in the drawer of the bedside table.'

Freda looked to where Livvie was pointing and gave a small nod. 'Thank you, sweetheart. I appreciate you getting it for me; it's of great sentimental value.'

Livvie understood, she had a boxful of sentimental stuff relating to her dad.

'How is she?' Rhoda asked when Livvie returned to the kitchen.

'Shattered and a bit overwhelmed; it'll be a lot for her to get used to, bless her. She seems a lot happier now she's seen Midge, she talked about him a lot on the way here. They're both going to have a nap; I said I'd wake her in a couple of hours.' Livvie flopped down on a dining chair with a sigh.

'She'll be emotionally exhausted after what she's been through. There you go.' Rhoda slid a fresh cup of tea towards Livvie.

'Thanks. I'm not surprised, I'm shattered and nothing's happened to me.'

'Did she say when she wanted to see her cottage?'

'She said she'd see how she felt after having a cup of tea but I think tiredness took over and she forgot or wasn't feeling up to it. It might be best if we wait till the morning.'

Rhoda nodded. 'Mmm. I agree, it gets dark pretty sharpish now.'

The two women sat in contemplative silence for a few moments before Rhoda spoke again. 'We need to find some time for you to get the last bits and bobs you need for your wedding. Don't forget you still need something to wear in your hair.'

Livvie puffed out a sigh. 'I know, it's the top of my list. I've been looking online to see if I can find a tiara but I'd rather see what they look like in the flesh, if you know what I mean. I've got an idea in my mind of the sort I'd like; kind of delicate and not too showy. I think we might need another trip to York, though I'm not sure how I'm going to squeeze it in; trust me to leave it so late.'

She was hit by a wave of panic that squeezed in her stomach. Time was marching on and she still had quite a few things to organize. Not least, a trip up to the castle after her last one had been cut short.

Rhoda spotted the change in Livvie's expression. 'Why don't you make a list? I always find that helps. And don't forget, I'm happy to help with anything.'

'Thank you, Rhoda, you're a star.'

36

THE LAST WEEK IN NOVEMBER

THE DAY after she'd been discharged from hospital, Livvie and Rhoda had taken Freda along to Moor Top Cottage in the car. Both women were feeling apprehensive that their efforts there would be construed as interference. They regarded Freda closely as she surveyed her home.

With her hand pressed to her chest, Freda gazed slowly around the kitchen, walking over to the newly-blackened stove, touching it lightly with her finger-tips. 'I can hardly believe this is my house. You've made it look right lovely.'

Livvie and Rhoda exchanged relieved glances, Livvie miming wiping sweat from her brow. 'We're pleased you like it, Freda.'

'We are that,' said Rhoda. 'Oh, and in case you're wondering where the buckets are that you used to catch the rain, you don't need them anymore. Jimby has a contact who's a thatcher and he came and did a temporary fix on the roof to keep the place dry over winter.' For the time being, they'd agreed not to say anything about how he'd said the whole roof needed re-thatching for fear Freda would find it too daunting.

'Oh, that was very good of him; he's a kind lad is Jimby.' She swallowed and bowed her head. 'I'm sorry it was such a mess; it'll have been a right lot of work for you all. I shouldn't have let it get so bad. I'm sorry.'

Livvie's heart lurched and she shot a worried look at Rhoda who gave her a small, reassuring smile.

'You should've seen Livvie's bedroom when she was a teenager; now that's what I'd call a mess. Honestly, it was an absolute tip. Clothes, books, shoes, everything all over the place.' Rhoda caught Livvie's eye and laughed.

'I wish I could say she's joking, Freda, but I'm afraid it's true.'

The old lady's eyes brightened and she chuckled along with them. 'It looks a bit like your cottage now I can see it properly.'

'It could be even more like ours if it had central heating and a bathroom, and some nice soft carpets.' Livvie watched her elderly friend's reaction. It would need a lot more doing to it before it got to the stage where central heating and carpets were fitted, and she had no idea of Freda's financial situation, but Livvie wanted her to see it was possible. Freda continued to look around her, not speaking, her face inscrutable.

∾

FREDA HAD BEEN STAYING at Dale View Cottage for nearly a week. She was in high spirits and had made a good recovery. The colour had returned to her cheeks, her eyes were shiny – the dark circles that had hung beneath them almost gone –and she was starting to fill out thanks to Rhoda's cooking.

On the days Livvie had been at work, Rhoda had been keeping her company and the pair had quickly become friends. They took steady daily walks along the dale with Alf and Midge, swapping notes on gardening, chatting and laughing away.

'What a lovely person she is; it's heart-breaking to think she's lived along there all alone for so long,' Rhoda had said in a whisper when Freda was out of earshot.

'I know; it actually infuriates me that she has family out there somewhere and they've turned their back on her. I wish I knew who they were.' Livvie could feel anger rising inside her, making her cheeks flush.

'Well, don't let that get to you; you've got a wedding to prepare for, and it's inching closer.'

Rhoda's words pushed Livvie's irritation out of the way, sending a frisson of excitement sweeping through her. 'Ooh, I know. I really must get sorted out; I don't want to have a last-minute panic.'

∾

LIVVIE CLIMBED into bed and Zander turned to face her. 'I feel like I never get a minute with you these days; we both seem so busy.' He traced his finger down her cheek before leaning in to kiss her.

Her stomach somersaulted and she pressed herself closer to him, savouring the warmth of his skin, the comforting scent of his cologne. 'I know, things have been crazy-busy recently with everything that's been happening.'

'Tell me about it.' He exhaled noisily.

'Is everything okay at work?'

'Mmhm, but let's not talk about that now. I've got you to myself and I intend to make the most of it.' He pressed his lips to hers, the heat in his kiss sending her heart racing.

LIVVIE LAY back on the pillow, her hair splayed out around her, her heart still pounding. She glanced across at Zander. He had his arm flung up above his head, sweat glistening on his chest, his breathing still heavy. It had been over a week since they'd last made love; the longest time they'd gone since they'd moved in together. It had started to worry her. But right now he was looking as blissed-out as she felt, with no trace of the distracted look that had been haunting him recently.

She snuggled into him and he put his arm around her, smoothing his fingers over the skin on her arm, sending a ripple of happiness through her. She savoured their closeness and the warmth and security his love afforded her. But his recent distance had made the ground beneath her feet feel a little shaky. It had made her glad of Rhoda's company and the distraction Freda's situation had given her.

37

THE THICK CURTAINS of the living room were drawn together, shutting out the frosty evening. Relaxing music played softly in the background. Livvie was sitting in an armchair, her feet curled underneath her; she'd been going through her wedding list, ticking things off, adding question marks next to others, relieved to see there wasn't really much left to do. Tapping her pen against her mouth, she looked up to see Freda dozing on the sofa, her feet propped up on a footstool. She had her head tilted backwards and her mouth slightly open. The image made Livvie smile. A snort from Alf drew her attention to the wood-burner where he and Midge were curled up together in their usual spot in front of it. The pair had become inseparable since Freda's time in hospital.

Thoughts of Bryony flashed through her mind; their communication had been sporadic since her friend's move to Australia, with Livvie's emails and texts regularly going unanswered, followed by huge apologies when Bry eventually got in touch. 'Life's just pretty full-on and I never seem to have a minute, but don't worry, wild horses wouldn't keep me away from your wedding, chick,' she'd said during their last conversation, a slight Aussie twang to her voice. Livvie smiled, she was sure all was well with her friend.

She'd just received a text from Caro confirming a visit up to the castle for tomorrow evening after work; she'd feel better once she knew everything was in place up there. With so many distractions recently, she'd let all things wedding related slide a little, and now she felt a sudden urgency to pick up the reins and get things moving again. After all, it was only a few weeks until the big day. That thought sent nerves rippling in her stomach.

She'd tried on her wedding dress the previous day. Her face had been wreathed in smiles when she'd caught sight of herself in the mirror. It fitted perfectly.

'Come on then, give us a twirl.' Vi had smoothed the skirt down and stood back, giving Livvie some space.

Livvie had felt a blush rising in her cheeks as she swept around, the silk fabric rustling with her movements.

'Oh, Livvie, you look so beautiful. Zander's going to fall in love with you a million times over when he sees you walking towards him,' Kitty had said with a gasp, pressing her fingers to her chest.

Livvie had laughed. 'That would be nice.' *Let's hope so.* 'And thank you for all your help with the design and construction. It's more beautiful than I could ever have imagined.'

'We've loved it, chick. And you look absolutely gorgeous,' Vi had said, stepping towards Livvie and moving a strand of hair that had hooked itself on a crystal bead.

'There's something really special about designing a wedding dress for a friend,' Kitty had said, smiling warmly at her. 'We've done them for the three of us; we just need to do Molly's now.'

'Don't let her hear you say that.' Vi had shot her a warning look.

'There's no fear of that! But I don't think it would hurt to do a little bit of subtle nudging in that direction, do you? She's so happy with Camm.' Kitty had smiled mischievously.

'True, but don't let her know what you're up to; you know how prickly she can get if you mention the "M" word and her in the same sentence.'

Livvie smiled to herself, her thoughts moving on to Zander. He'd popped over to Leeds, telling her there was something he needed to do regarding his Milton Gardens property which he planned to put on the market in the New Year. While he was there, he was going to have a catch-up with Noah and Jess.

Rhoda had taken herself off to Rickelthorpe. She had an appointment with her solicitor there and had been invited to stay over at a friend's to save her making the long journey twice in the same day. The house felt strangely quiet without her happy energy.

Freda stirred and opened her eyes. 'Think I must've had a little snooze.' She yawned and flexed her feet.

'Can I get you anything? Cup of tea?'

'You don't need to jump up for me, lass. I'm fine for the minute.' Her eyes fell to the list in Livvie's lap. 'Have you got far with that?'

'A little. There's just a few things I need to get. I need to find a "something old" and "something borrowed", you know, from the rhyme, "Something old, something new…"'

'Aye, I know the one.'

'And I'm going to have to squeeze in a trip to York.' She unfurled her feet from beneath her and plumped the cushion behind her back.

'Oh, why's that?'

'I'm having trouble finding something to wear on my head. I found a small tiara I really liked but it's out of stock and I'm so disappointed. I know I'm being silly, but I'd kind of got my heart set on it and I can't get it out of my mind so anything else seems like second best.' She shook her head, impatient with herself. 'But I'm being childish; I'm going to have to look past it or I'll end up wearing nothing and my veil will end up looking ridiculous just hanging there.'

Freda rubbed her brow. 'I feel it's my fault you got behind with your wedding plans. I've taken up a lot of your time, what with looking after me and cleaning my home. I'm sorry; I'm always a problem for folk.'

Livvie's heart went out to her. She leaned towards her friend, taking her free hand in hers. 'Please don't think that for a second. You're not a problem at all. You needed some help, like we all do from time to time, and I've been only too happy to do that. After all, look how much help you've given me with the garden; if it wasn't for your advice it would be full of weeds and dead plants.'

Freda looked at Livvie intently as she listened, her last words eliciting a glimmer of a smile.

'I've loved having you here, listening to your stories of how things used to be on the moors, and so have Zander and Rhoda. And the reason I'm not organised is because that's how I always am; remember, I told you I'm the polar opposite of my big sister? Now she's what you'd call organised with a capital "O".' Livvie rolled her eyes and laughed making Freda's smile grow wider. 'Anyway, enough of that, how about that cup of tea?'

'Aye, sounds good.' Flickering light from the fire danced on Freda's face. Livvie felt the overwhelming urge to give her a hug but concern that it might be a step too far for her friend held her back. She gave her arm a reassuring rub instead.

'Righty-ho, one pot of tea coming right up.'

When Livvie returned with the tray, Freda was sitting with her biscuit tin on the sofa beside her. The lid was off and an old-looking leather box was on her lap.

'Here we are, I've brought us a piece of Rhoda's Christmas spiced shortbread. I can't resist it. If I know it's in the house, I'm not happy until I've eaten every last crumb.' She winked at Freda.

'Ooh, sounds lovely. I'd better have some before it's all gone then,' Freda said with a hearty chuckle.

As Livvie poured the tea, she heard her friend take a deep breath. She looked up to see her wrestling with her thoughts, smoothing her hand back and forth over the box. Freda licked her lips nervously before she spoke. 'Well, erm, I think I might have solved a couple of your problems.'

'You do?' Livvie set the teapot down and sat back in her chair.

Freda nodded and handed the box to Livvie. 'There.'

'What is it?'

'Open it.'

Livvie regarded the brown leather box with its slightly battered corners and musty smell. Curious to see what was inside, she pressed the tiny brass button at the front. It released the lid and Livvie lifted it slowly, her mouth making an "o" shape as she gazed in awe at the contents. 'Oh, my goodness, Freda.'

'You can borrow it; it can be your something borrowed. And it's something to wear in your hair … with your veil, so it should solve your other problem.'

'I … I don't know what to say.' She couldn't take her eyes off the exquisite diamond tiara that sat nestled on midnight-blue satin, its brilliant diamonds twinkling up at her.

'Well, I hope you're going to say you like it, and it'll save you having to trek over to York. The stones are still nice and shiny, but you can give them a clean with gin and water if you like.'

'Gin and water?'

'Mmm. It's how everyone used to clean their diamonds. And you can get the dust out with a toothbrush.'

'They're real diamonds?' Livvie's eyebrows flicked up as a curiosity pulsed through her mind. Freda's comment had piqued her interest.

'They are. Go on, try it on.'

'Okay.' Livvie's heart was thudding. The tiara was heavier than she expected, and she did her best to steady the tremble in her hands as she carefully lifted it out of its case. *This is just so incredibly beautiful.* Holding her breath, she brought the tiara closer to her face, allowing her eyes to absorb its beauty. The detailing was incredibly fine, with delicate flowers made of glittering diamonds. 'It's stunning, Freda, I can't pos…' A bolt of recognition shot through her, cutting off her words. She looked at the old lady, then back at the tiara. *Oh, my days! It can't be!*

38

Livvie took a moment to marshal her thoughts. Her brow was knitted together in a frown, her breathing rapid. She swallowed, conscious of her brain being bombarded by a plethora of reasons as to why Freda would be in possession of the tiara. But as they slowly began slotting themselves into place, one pushed its way out in front. *This is unbelievable.*

Livvie composed herself; she knew she would have to handle the situation carefully. The last thing she wanted was to upset Freda and send her scurrying back to her cold cottage. Arranging her face into a smile, she said, 'Freda, this is so beautiful, and it obviously means a great deal to you, but I don't think it's right that I should wear it.'

The old lady's face fell. 'But why? I'd like you to. You've come to mean a lot to me, lass, and it would gladden my heart to know you'll be wearing it on your wedding day.' She looked at Livvie with appealing eyes.

What if someone recognizes it? That would set the cat amongst the pigeons. As she wrestled with her thoughts, one thing she was certain of was that she didn't want to offend or upset her friend. 'Freda, you've come to mean a lot to me too, and I'd be honoured to wear your tiara. Thank you.'

Freda beamed and patted her knee excitedly with her good hand. 'Wonderful! Now come on, lass, let's see what it looks like against that beautiful auburn hair of yours.'

Livvie freed her hair from its ponytail and shook it out before sliding the tiara onto her head, adjusting it until it felt comfortable.

'Oh, my. It's perfect,' Freda said softly, tears shining in her eyes.

Livvie made her way over to the mirror, fighting back a wave of emotion. 'It's beautiful, Freda. Exactly what I was looking for. Thank you.'

A tear trickled down Freda's cheek and she nodded. 'You're welcome. I was going to wear it on my wedding day but...'

Livvie placed the tiara back in its leather case and set it on the coffee table, waiting for Freda to continue. 'But what, Freda?' Her eyes wandered to the biscuit tin beside her friend. She could see it was stuffed with a variety of items, one of which appeared to be a black and white photograph that looked remarkably familiar. She knotted her fingers in her lap, struggling to fight the urge to ask Freda the questions that were filling her mind.

Freda followed her gaze and pulled the photograph out of the box, smoothing it with her fingers. It was a few moments before she spoke. 'It's my mother, father, brother and me. It was taken a long time ago.' She handed the photo to Livvie.

It was almost identical to the one she'd seen up at the castle, of the family sitting in the grounds, the castle looming behind. Livvie looked from the photo to Freda, struggling to find the right words. 'It's a lovely photo, Freda. Where was it taken?'

The old lady met Livvie's eyes and realisation dawned for both of them. Livvie knew Freda's real identity, and Freda was ready to share her story.

39

'I CAN'T BELIEVE you've been through all that.' Livvie snatched the tears away from her eyes, her emotions a melting pot as pity and sadness merged with raw, simmering anger.

'Don't be upset for me, lass, it hasn't all been bad. The people I stayed with were kind and looked after me well. And I've had a happy life living on my beloved moors since I came back.' She patted Livvie's hand.

Livvie shook her head vehemently. 'That doesn't excuse what your parents did. I don't understand how they could do that to you; it was cruel.'

'Well, Harry and me – that was my sweetheart's name – had planned to run away and get married which would've been a terrible scandal; they were such different times we lived in then. I just wish I'd been allowed to keep in touch with my brother, Jeremiah – he's Lord Danskelfe now. He was a lovely lad, and we were very close when we were growing up. I missed him very badly too.'

'Oh, Freda, I can't imagine how it all felt.' Livvie took her hand and squeezed it.

'I can see now why my parents were so concerned, Harry and me were only sixteen, no more than babies, and knew nothing of the world, though we thought we knew it all.' Freda paused, looking pensive. 'And, anyway, I've forgiven them.'

Well, I bloody well haven't.

Freda's story had matched what Vi's mum, Mary, had told them in so far as Freda had been cast out and disowned by her parents. The old lady had elaborated on the scant details; it turned out her only crime was that she'd fallen head-over-heels in love with one of the castle's under-gardeners by the name of Harry Stainthorpe. On hearing of their illicit love affair, her parents had been apoplectic with rage and sacked the boy on the spot. Freda was forbidden from seeing him again.

'I felt like my heart had been ripped out until we found a way to meet in secret. But, unbeknown to us, we were spotted by one of the servants who reported it back to my parents. They were so enraged at me defying them, they said they had no choice but to send me away before I brought shame onto the family. I was absolutely terrified, I'd never seen them so angry before.' Freda sighed, lingering on the memory. 'So that's how come I ended up changing my name from Phaedra Hammondely to Freda Easton and living with a less well-heeled branch of my mother's family in West Yorkshire. My parents carried on as if I'd never existed which still has the power to hurt if I think about it too much.'

Hearing that enraged Livvie and she struggled to keep her feelings under control.

'But how did they explain your disappearance to the locals?'

'Well, that was easy; my father had only recently become Lord Hammondely and we'd only just moved into Danskelfe Castle from our previous home in Skuttleby. I hadn't had the chance to mingle with folk around here and get to know them, so I wasn't missed when I was sent away. Harry was the only person I spent time with.'

'Oh.' Livvie swallowed hard. 'Have you any idea what happened to him?'

Freda shook her head sadly. 'We met one last time – at midnight the night before I was sent away, beneath the huge weeping willow tree by the lake; you know the one?'

Livvie nodded.

'We promised each other as soon as I was old enough to leave my relatives' care, we'd get married; no one would be able to stop us. That's why I took the tiara; all Hammondely brides for the last hundred and fifty years have worn it on their wedding day and I wanted to do the same. Anyway, our promise helped ease the pain of leaving him a little, and at first, I wrote to him as often as I could without arousing suspicion, posting the letters in secret. But they were never replied to, and, after a while, I heard he and his family had moved away almost as soon as I'd left.'

'Do you think your family forced them to leave?'

'Oh, I know so, but they wouldn't have called it "forced". They'd have paid them off, given them enough money to set up somewhere far from here.'

'So Harry would never have received your letters and wouldn't know your address to write to you?'

'Aye, that's about the size of it. Last I heard he and his family had emigrated to Australia.'

'Oh, Freda, I'm so sorry.'

Freda had gone on to say how when she was in her late twenties, the pull of the moors was too strong and she'd decided to move back. Her uncle had contacted her parents and they'd given her Moor Top Cottage to live in and an allowance to live on, with the proviso that she shouldn't attempt to get in touch with them, nor tell anyone who she was. These reasons had resulted in her keeping herself to herself.

'Granted, my return generated a bit of gossip and I was aware of a variety of rumours flying around – the funniest was that I was some sort of white witch and had had to flee my previous home.' Freda laughed at that. 'But, strangely enough, no one ever seemed to link me to the Hammondelys.'

'But that's no excuse for your family to neglect you; even as land-lords to Moor Top Cottage they're obliged to keep it in good repair. Surely they could see the state it was in? I don't mean to be rude, Freda, but it's very basic. Why wouldn't they fix the roof and install a bathroom or central heating for you? Make it comfortable for you to live in?'

Freda hung her head. 'I don't think they knew how bad things were; they had people looking after the estate on their behalf. I kept away, didn't tell them. Didn't want to be a nuisance. And I didn't want to see them, either. I may have forgiven, but I didn't forget.' She paused. 'I can remember one particular day in the early eighties; I was walking back from the village where I'd been shopping and a car stopped beside me on the road. This woman looked at me like I was rubbish. She said she knew who I was and that I was to keep away from her husband and the castle and if she found out I'd been near either of them she'd make sure the cottage was taken away from me.'

'How horrible. Why would she say something like that? Did you know who she was?' Livvie felt her stomach squeeze with anger.

'I didn't know who she was at the time, but I found out later she was married to Jeremiah; our parents had died and he was Lord Hammondely by then.'

'Lady Davinia, your sister-in-law.' *And a toxic witch.*

'Aye, so it would seem. I'd had a wander up there one day, curiosity getting the better of me, hoping I might bump into my brother, but I was chased off by some unfriendly man with a dog, seems she got wind of it. After that, I had no intention of ever going back; I didn't need her to tell me I couldn't.'

'Freda, the way you've been treated is absolutely shocking. That family – your family – are sitting up there in the lap of luxury while you've lived in a cold, damp cottage. Their behaviour is disgusting.' She wondered if Caro knew any of this.

'Please don't be cross. I didn't mean to upset you. I wanted to make you happy, take some worries away by lending you the tiara.'

The pleading expression in Freda's eyes quashed Livvie's anger a little. She knew she needed to rein it in. Her friend had been through enough and the last thing she wanted was to cause her any further anguish. She relaxed her shoulders and sighed. 'I'm sorry, hearing all of that has been a shock, that's all. I'm over the moon that you're lending me the tiara.' She forced a smile. 'And I don't know about you, but I'm ready for another cup of tea.'

'I wouldn't say no.'

40

LIVVIE WAS SITTING in the kitchen mulling over what Freda had told her, the injustice of the situation simmering away in her gut. The old lady had been tucked up in bed for an hour with Midge curled up in a basket on the floor beside her when Livvie was stuck by the urge to contact her mum. Hearing Freda's heart-breaking situation had put her problems with her own mother into perspective. They weren't close by any stretch of the imagination, but Livvie knew her mother had her best interests at heart; she just had a funny way of showing it sometimes.

Feeling a sudden rush of love for her mum, she fired off a quick text.

> *Hi Mum, just to let you know*
> *the wedding plans are going well. Got*
> *an appointment up at the castle tomorrow.*
> *Everything else is organised! So unlike me!! Lol!*
> *Love you lots. L xxx*

She'd just pressed send when she heard Zander's key in the door. Alf jumped up and trotted to the hallway. There soon followed the sound of his tail beating a tattoo on the oak panelling and his dad murmuring a greeting to him. Livvie turned to see Zander, his broad shoulders filling the doorway, a hint of weariness in his eyes.

'Hi,' he said, his lopsided smile sending a buzz of excitement through her.

'Hi. Good day?' She went over and kissed him on the lips. He clasped his hand around the back of her head, pulling her close, her earlier anger momentarily dissipating.

He pulled back, his eyes roving her face appreciatively. 'Mmm. Better now I've seen you.' He shrugged his coat off and hung it on the back of a dining chair. 'Fancy a glass of wine?'

'Please.' Livvie went to the cupboard to get the glasses while Zander reached into the fridge for the half-finished bottle of Pinot Grigio.

'So, how did everything go in Leeds? Did you get your house sorted?' she asked when they were sitting opposite one another at the kitchen table.

Zander's attention was on Alf whose head was in his lap, enjoying having his ears smoothed. 'I did; the estate agent thinks I should wait until the New Year before I put it on the market.'

'Makes sense. And how were Noah and Jess?'

'Both good, Jess looked tired which is understandable.' He sighed, the recent distant look in his eyes returning. 'Anyway, how's your day been?'

Livvie puffed out her cheeks, releasing her breath noisily. 'You won't believe what I found out today.'

Zander's face fell, he swallowed, his glass half-way to his mouth. 'What?'

Livvie's senses responded to his reaction with a tiny flicker of concern but she brushed it away. 'Well, I was talking to Freda about needing to get something to wear in my hair for the wedding and she offered me the loan of this.' She pushed the leather box towards him.

'What is it?'

'Open it and you'll see.'

He pressed the button and lifted the lid revealing the antique tiara. He glanced from it to Livvie, perplexed. 'Something tells me these are real diamonds.'

'They are.'

'Where has she kept it?'

'Wrapped up in some cloth in that biscuit tin.'

Zander grimaced. 'It should really be in a safe; it'll be worth a fortune.'

'Well, make yourself comfy because there's quite a story attached to it.'

'I've got a funny feeling I know where this is heading…'

'SHIT. Poor Freda, or should I say Lady Phaedra?' Zander sat back, pushing his fingers through his hair. His eyes met Livvie's. 'You're thinking you don't want to get married up there, aren't you?'

'I'd be lying if I said I wasn't so keen on it after hearing how that bloody family have treated her, but it's a bit late to do anything about it now. I'll bet it's that snooty cow, Lady Davinia and her toxic influence that's kept Freda and Lord Hammondely apart all these years.'

'We don't know that for sure, and even so, he could've made sure his sister was okay, that the house was in good repair; he sounds quite weak to me.'

'Hmm. Neither of them are coming out of this in a good light. And don't forget, Freda said it was okay for me to tell you, but she didn't want us to mention it to anyone else.'

'Okay, I won't breathe a word.' Zander reached across the table and wove his fingers through Livvie's. 'But after hearing her story, let's promise each other that whatever happens, nothing is going to come between us.'

'I promise.'

'I promise too.' There was a tone to his voice that made Livvie feel ever-so-slightly uneasy.

41

As Livvie made her way along the road to Danskelfe Castle her mind was in turmoil. She drummed her fingers against the steering-wheel; for once, she wasn't looking forward to her visit there. She didn't know what she'd say or how she'd feel if she saw Lord and Lady Hammondely. Livvie liked to think she had an easy-going temperament, preferring to rub along nicely with folk, and she could count on one hand the number of people she didn't like – actually, make that two hands since yesterday's revelations. But if she genuinely didn't like someone, she struggled to pretend that she did; being fake went against her better judgement. And, right now, she genuinely didn't like Lord and Lady Hammondely.

Her mind strayed to Zander; what with everything that had been going on, it felt like they'd had hardly any time together, their moments of intimacy were few and far between which wasn't like them. Granted, their spontaneous love-making had been curtailed by their house guests, but even so, life seemed to be taking over and they were making little time for each other. She decided to make a conscious effort to do something about it.

On arrival at the castle, she was met with the usual effusive greeting from Caro who whisked her off to the sitting room for a cup of tea declaring herself to be "absolutely gasping".

Livvie had grown fond of Caro. She found her warm and friendly with a mischievous sense of humour; she was nothing at all like her mother.

'So, darling, how's your friend? You know, the little old lady you had to rush off for? I do hope she's okay.' Caro poured the tea into the dainty china cups.

Livvie's stomach churned, keeping her eyes firmly away from the photo on the table of Freda – or, rather, Lady Phaedra – and her family. 'She's much better, thank you. She's staying with us while her arm heals.'

'Ah, yes, I heard as much when I popped into the village shop – it's the best place to go if you want to keep up-to-date with what's happening locally.' She laughed, giving no hint that she knew anything of Freda other than what Livvie herself had known two days ago.

Livvie clenched her jaw, resisting the temptation to enlighten her. *Keep schtum, it's not your secret to share, Livvie.* 'You're not wrong; it's certainly the hub of the village, that and the school.'

Caro nodded, taking a sip of her tea. 'So, what do we need to discuss regarding your wedding plans? Are there any little niggles that need ironing out? I assume Annie filled you in on her ideas with the floral arrangements and you're happy with them?'

'She did, and yes, I love her ideas – yours too, thank you for your suggestions.'

'No problem at all.'

'I'd really like to double-check numbers, that we've got enough rooms booked for the guests, the food, etc, just to make sure I haven't forgotten anything.'

'Of course, that's absolutely fine.'

The sound of Lady Davinia's shrill voice approaching made Livvie's hackles rise. She looked at Caro whose shoulders had slumped. 'Uhh. What's the matter with her now?' Caro said, rolling her eyes.

Before they knew it, Davinia had bowled into the room wearing her usual pinched expression. 'Caro, what are you … oh, you're here again?' She scowled at Livvie. 'Surely you must've got everything sorted out by now. Anyone would think we were hosting a royal wedding the amount of times you've been up here.' She laughed, trying to pass it off as a joke, but her eyes revealed her true feelings.

'Mother, please! I invited Livvie to come back here. She had to leave early on her last visit and didn't get the chance for a proper appointment, there were things we still needed to discuss.' Caro looked mortified. 'I'm so sorry, Livvie.'

'Oh, yes, that creature from Moor Top Cottage fell or something, didn't she?' She waved her hand dismissively. 'If you want my opinion, she's too old to be living there on her own, she ought to be in a home. Lord knows that house looks like it could do with gutting and fumigating.'

Livvie listened in silence, her anger boiling. Her hands were balled into fists on her lap and she gnawed on her lip as she struggled to keep control of her feelings.

'That's unkind, Mother.'

'It's the truth.'

It was too much for Livvie to bear, she leapt to her feet. 'How dare you? How dare you speak of Freda in that way? You have no right to judge her, especially when you're partly to blame for her circumstances!' Before she could stop herself, the words had flown out of her mouth in a ball of rage. She stood, glaring at the woman, her body shaking, her breathing shallow.

Davinia clasped her hand to her chest, while Caro looked on, her eyes wide, her mouth hanging open.

'How dare you speak to me like that, you insolent young woman.' Davinia rallied herself and pinned Livvie with a challenging glare.

Livvie's chest was heaving, her face burning. 'I dare because I feel so enraged at the unjust way Freda has been treated by this family. You ought to be ashamed of yourselves, you and your husband.'

Caro glanced between Livvie and her mother, not quite comprehending what was unfurling before her.

'What's all this shouting about? Davinia, you really must calm down, my dear.'

The three women turned to see Lord Hammondely in the doorway, his bushy eyebrows drawn together in confusion. 'Will somebody please tell me what's going on?'

'This rude young woman was just about to leave. Go on, get out of my house. And you can kiss goodbye to having your wedding here. Go on, leave now.' Davinia pointed a red-painted talon at the door.

'Not until I've said my piece.' Livvie flashed daggers at Davinia. 'The reason you heard shouting, Lord Hammondely, is because your wife here passed some spiteful comments about someone I'm very fond of. Someone you know. Someone by the name of Freda, or should I say, Phaedra?'

She heard Caro gasp beside her. 'What?'

'Phaedra?' The colour drained from Lord Hammondely's face as he made his way to the sofa, dropping down onto it. 'Why would you be talking about Phaedra?'

'Don't listen to her. She's come up here with the sole purpose to cause trouble. Just ignore her.' Lady Davinia looked rattled.

Livvie snorted. 'Oh, I think I do know what I'm talking about. Phaedra, or Freda as I know her, is currently staying with me and my fiancé after having a nasty fall at her home and breaking her arm.'

Lord Hammondely looked at Livvie with panic in his eyes. 'Is she okay? Please tell me she's going to be alright,' he said, his voice wavering.

'She's going to be fine, no thanks to you and your wife.'

Lord Hammondely hung his head. 'I see. I suppose I can understand why you think that; our situation must look somewhat unusual to you as an outsider.'

Livvie laughed scornfully. 'Outsider or not, I'm perfectly justified in thinking it unusual that an old lady lives in such a ramshackle, basic house without even a bathroom, and has done so for years. Especially when her brother and his wife are living in the lap of luxury up here. Have you any idea what it's been like for her living there? It's not "unusual", it's downright disgraceful.'

'She chose to live that way, not that it's any of your business. Pay no attention to her, Jeremiah, she's obviously got half a story and made the rest up herself with her vivid imagination. And, for your information, Phaedra lives in that cottage rent-free, as she has done since she returned to the area, and it's up to her to tell us when things need fixing.' Her eyes bulged at Livvie. 'It's not our fault if she hasn't bothered to tell us when things need repairing; we're not mind-readers.'

'So, you stopping Freda when you saw her on the road out of Lytell Stangdale and telling her to keep away from the castle and her brother all those years ago is half a story or a result of my "vivid imagination" is it?' Livvie felt utterly fearless; she was determined to make the Hammondelys see how cruelly they'd treated Freda. And as far as having the wedding here, they could stick it.

Lady Davinia started spluttering. 'I don't know what you mean.'

'Or what about telling her that if she went anywhere near her brother or the castle – which, let's not forget was *her home* before it was yours – that she'd have her cottage taken away from her?'

'What? I didn't know any of this. Is it true?' Lord Hammondely turned to his wife.

'I, er, it wasn't quite like that.'

'Davinia, is it true?' he asked again, anger hovering in his voice.

'It's not how it sounds—'

'I've told you before about taking matters into your own hands without discussing them with me. You had no right to say such things. No right at all.'

'Mother, what have you done? This is terrible.' Caro's face was ashen as she looked at her mother in disbelief.

'She was terrified of leaving her home to go to hospital in case she had no home to go back to when she came out because of what you said. Can you imagine how horrible that would've felt?' Livvie's heart was hurling itself against her ribcage.

'I only said what I did to protect the family and its reputation. To protect Jeremiah from more hurt. I was told he was devastated for years after Phaedra left; he still hadn't got over it when we met. I was frightened she would pursue her idea of marrying the gardener; your parents had been so against it, I thought I was respecting their wishes. I'm so sorry, I didn't mean it to turn out this way.' Lady Davinia put her head in her hands and sobbed.

Livvie was taken aback. She hadn't expected the woman to show an ounce of remorse; part of her wondered if it was genuine or more for herself than anyone else.

'But look at what your words have done; they made my sister too frightened to come anywhere near me.' His voice was barely above a whisper as a tear slipped down his cheek. 'It explains why she always ran away from me whenever I saw her, or hid from me when I called at the cottage. I gave up in the end. All this time I thought she didn't want to see me, when really she was too frightened to. Poor, poor Phaedra.'

'What you did was terrible, Mother. You ought to be ashamed of yourself.' Caro turned to Livvie, her eyes glistening with tears. 'And I'm so sorry you've been dragged into this; you must despise my family.'

Livvie felt her anger leach away at the sadness in Caro's eyes. She placed a reassuring hand on her shoulder. 'No, I don't despise you. I just think you've been trapped in a heart-breaking situation that's dragged on for decades longer than it needed to.'

Caro nodded and cast her gaze over to her father who was sitting on the sofa, sobbing silently into his hands.

Livvie felt suddenly exhausted. She was taken by the overwhelming urge to get out of the castle and back home. She needed to speak to Freda, to tell her what she'd done. *Oh, Lord, I hope she can forgive me.* And she needed the reassuring feel of Zander's arms around her.

She turned to Caro. The sadness on the woman's face touched her heart. 'I'd better go. I'm sorry you're upset. I'll see myself out.'

'I'll be in touch; there's just a lot to take in at the moment.'

'Of course.' Livvie nodded and left the room, running until she reached her car.

42

THE WIPERS WERE SWISHING BACK and forth in a valiant attempt at clearing the windscreen of a soggy blanket of sleet. The wind had picked up and was rocking Livvie's little car as it travelled along the exposed parts of the rigg road from Danskelfe Castle. But she didn't notice; she was on auto-pilot. Her mind was a jumble of thoughts and her stomach was churning as she relived the heated exchange with the Hammondelys. *Shit! I can't believe I did that.* She raked her fingers through her hair. 'Bugger! Bugger! Bugger!' She didn't know what she was going to say to Freda.

The sleet switched to hail, hammering down hard on the roof and intruding on her thoughts. She tried to compile an explanation in readiness, but her brain was too scrambled to think straight. *Uhh! This is hopeless!* Her friend had explicitly asked Livvie not to repeat what she'd told her, and what had she gone and done just twenty-four hours after Freda had trusted her and shared her deepest secret with her? Livvie had blabbed. Big time. And to the worst person possible.

Parking up at the side of the cottage, Livvie took a moment, hoping to compose herself, to find the courage to go and face the music. After all Freda had been through, Livvie wasn't looking forward to adding to her woes.

'Right, here goes.' Huddled into her coat and with her head down, Livvie made a dash for it, wincing as the stinging, icy bullets hit her cheeks. 'Argh! She slipped and grabbed the gate, quickly regaining her balance. She was glad when she reached the front door.

'I thought I heard your car. Come on, get inside, quick.' Zander held the door open, his smile disappearing when he saw her expression. 'Are you okay? Has something happened?'

'Don't ask.' She shrugged her coat off and fell into his embrace, the warmth and solid muscle of his body soothing her. 'Where's Freda?'

'In the living room with Rhoda and the hounds. Why?'

'I've done something I think I'm going to regret and I'm worried about the repercussions for her.'

Zander pulled back, clutching her shoulders. 'What do you mean? I thought you had an appointment with Caro up at the castle?'

Livvie sighed. 'I did, but Lady Davinia barged in when Caro and I were talking and was her usual obnoxious self, which I could put up with, but she passed a nasty comment about Freda and I lost it.'

'I'd say that's not like you, but I know how protective you are of Freda.'

'I know, I can't bear the thought of her being hurt. But … uhh … me and my big mouth.'

'So what happened?'

'Let's go into the kitchen and I'll explain.'

'SHIT! I wonder if Lady Davinia started the rumours that Freda was related to some wealthy family from out of the area, but had shunned them or vice versa.' Zander rubbed his hand across his chin.

'I don't know, but I wouldn't be surprised if she fuelled them. After all, it suited her purposes that no one should connect Freda with Danskelfe Castle.' Livvie nibbled at a hang nail. 'And, much as I'm dreading telling Freda, it's only fair on her I get it over and done with.'

'You're right. And you never know, some good might come of this.'

'You think?'

'Stranger things have happened.'

The pair stood up and Zander pulled her close to him, smoothing her hair. 'You're a wonderful, compassionate person, Livvie, and whatever happens with this don't forget what you did came from a good place.'

She looked up at him, the love in those blue eyes catching her off guard. 'Hmm. I'm not sure Lady Davinia would agree with you.'

'Who cares what that one thinks?' He smiled and kissed the tip of her nose, turning her in the direction of the door. 'Come on, let's go and tell Freda.'

Livvie's stomach was in knots as she sat down on the sofa beside the old lady. Alf trotted over, pleased to see her. He pushed his head onto her lap, sensing her distress. 'Good, lad,' she said, smoothing his ears.

'Hello there, how did it go at the castle?' asked Rhoda, smiling, her face flushed from the warmth of the stove.

Livvie cleared her throat and swallowed down the lump of anxiety that was clogging it. She couldn't bring herself to look at Freda so focused her gaze on Alf. 'I'm afraid it didn't go too well.'

Rhoda sat up straight in her chair, her smile dropping. 'What do you mean? They haven't cancelled on you, have they?'

'More than likely.' Her heart was racing as she felt the weight of their eyes on her. 'I said something, well, several things, which I now regret, and I want to start off by saying how sorry I am, Freda, I never intended to say anything, it's just, well...' She scrunched her eyes together and took a deep breath. 'Lady Davinia passed a comment and I gave her a mouthful. I told her I knew all about what she'd done to you. Your brother was there too, Lord Hammondely. He heard everything.' She turned to Freda who was looking at her, her sweet old face inscrutable.

'Oh, my goodness,' said Rhoda, clasping her hands to her cheeks.

Livvie blinked back the tears that were swimming in her eyes. She took Freda's good hand in hers. 'I'm so sorry. I broke your secret and I had no right to.'

'Tell me everything, lass,' said Freda calmly.

Livvie took a fortifying breath. 'Okay.' A hush fell over the room, with everyone listening intently as Livvie recounted her exchange at the castle, punctuated only by the odd gasp or tut from Rhoda.

'Well, I never,' said her stepmother.

'I'm so sorry, Freda. I wish I could take it all back. I really am sorry.'

Freda squeezed Livvie's hand and mustered a small smile. 'Don't blame yourself, lass. Granted, I'm a bit shocked and I'm still taking it all in, but to be honest, I've never had anyone stick up for me like you do and it makes my heart feel glad.'

'Oh.' Livvie wiped her eyes, glancing from Freda to Zander who smiled and gave a quick flick of his eyebrows.

'And, oddly, the more I think about it, the more it feels like I've had a huge weight lifted off my shoulders. I hadn't realised how heavy my secret was, but I feel light as a feather now.' She chuckled.

Livvie could hardly believe what she was hearing. She looked at Freda, her eyes wide as she absorbed her words. 'I can't tell you how relieved I am to hear you say that. Am I allowed to hug you?'

'I'd like that.' Freda nodded shyly.

Being careful of the sling, Livvie wrapped her arms around Freda and squeezed her gently, happiness and relief radiating through her.

'They wouldn't dare take your home off you now Livvie's on their case,' said Zander, laughing.

'You'd better believe it. She was always an even-tempered girl when she was growing up, but if she felt an injustice had been done, then woe-betide the perpetrator if Livvie Weatherill found out. Remember that lad who used to pick on little Arnie Wilson, Livvie?' Rhoda asked.

'How could I forget Declan Limon? He was a horrible bully.' Livvie curled her lip in disgust.

'So what did Livvie do about Declan Limon then?' asked Zander, his mouth twitching in amusement.

'She found little Arnie sobbing his heart out because Declan had pinched his dinner money. Apparently Livvie marched over to the Limon lad and called him out in the school yard. I gather there was quite an audience. She said how he was a coward because he picked on younger, smaller kids. I'm told she really got stuck into him, got the other kids laughing at him. He left Arnie alone after that.' Pride shone in Rhoda's eyes.

'Well, well, well, who knew there was a fearless warrior lurking behind that sweet exterior, eh?' Zander said, a grin spreading across his face, making Livvie blush.

'I don't make a habit of it.'

'We only see that side of her when it's absolutely necessary,' said Rhoda.

'You've got a good lass there, Dr Gillespie. You hang on to her,' said Freda, affection in her voice.

'Don't worry, I intend to.'

The four of them talked for several hours afterwards, with Freda sharing her story with Zander and Rhoda. Livvie went to bed that night feeling hugely relieved that Freda wasn't upset or angry with her, but apprehensive about what repercussions would rear their head the following day. This certainly wasn't the end of the story.

43

WHEN LIVVIE TURNED her phone on the following morning the last thing she expected to see was a text from Caro Hammondely. Her heart lurched up to her throat when she saw the name and, with one eye closed, she tapped on it and read the message. She was relieved to see it was short and the content kind.

'I've had a text from Caro,' she said to Zander who was busily frying halloumi and spring onions to go with the rest of the Saturday morning brunch he was preparing, filling the kitchen with their delicious aroma. Alf and Midge were watching his every move intently, the pair of them drooling copiously.

'Oh?' He stilled the pan and turned to her. 'Is she okay?'

'She's fine. She just wanted to know if Freda and I were alright after last night, and she apologised for her mother. She said she hoped it hadn't put us off getting married up there.'

'How do you feel about it this morning?'

Livvie pursed her lips. 'We'd got our hearts set on it so it would be a shame not to, but it all depends on Lady Davinia.' Livvie would be devastated not to have her dream wedding at the castle, but she felt torn. It somehow didn't feel right to go ahead with it after what had happened between her and Lady Davinia and, more importantly, their treatment of Freda went against her principles. She couldn't help but feel that going ahead with it would be akin to condoning their behaviour. And that was the last thing she wanted. 'I'll give Caro a call later, see how the land lies.'

'Good plan.'

A sturdy knock at the door had Alf and Midge leaping to their feet and hurtling down the hall, barking loudly.

Livvie started, almost dropping her phone. 'Bloody hell, that frightened the life out of me.'

'Whoever it is, they've got a sturdy knock and terrible timing. This food's just about ready,' said Zander.

'Come on, you two, out of the way, let me get to the door.' Livvie pushed her way through Alf and Midge and pulled the door open. Her mouth fell open when she saw who was standing on the doorstep. 'Oh! Lord Hammondely, Caro.'

'Good morning, Livvie, I hope you don't mind us calling, but I wondered if we'd be able to see Phaedra, please?' said Lord Hammondely.

'Morning, erm, come in.' Livvie was non-plussed; she didn't know if Freda would be keen to see her brother and niece, but she didn't want to be bad mannered and leave them on the doorstep in the cold.

'Thank you.' He wiped his feet on the doormat before removing his tweed flat cap. He bent and scratched Alf and Midge behind their ears which appeared to go down well. Alf soon lost interest and raced back to the kitchen and the food but Midge ran into the living room and sat himself beside Freda.

Caro stepped in behind her father, her usually bubbly, effusive personality subdued for once. 'Morning, Livvie, how are you today?'

'Fine, thank you. How about you?' Livvie felt embarrassment creep up inside her.

Before Caro could answer, Zander popped his head around the door, his eyes widening in surprise at the sight of Lord Hammondely and Caro in the hallway. 'Good morning.'

'Good morning, please excuse us, we don't mean to impose but after what Livvie told me yesterday, well, I just had to come. I haven't slept a wink for thinking ab—'

'Hello, Jemmy.' Freda appeared from the living room. She stood several feet away from him, rooted to the spot, uncertainty flickering in her eyes.

Caro clasped her hand to her mouth, her face twisted with emotion.

'Phaedra. Nobody's called me that since you left,' he said softly, his eyes falling to her arm in the sling. 'Are you okay?'

Freda nodded. 'I am, thank you.' Her eyes searched out Livvie who responded with a smile of encouragement.

Brother and sister stood in awkward silence for a moment, each taking in the other before Lord Hammondely was unable to contain himself any longer. He rushed over to her, his arms outstretched as he towered above her. 'Oh, Phaedra, I'm so terribly sorry for what I've done to you. Please say you can forgive me, please say you can. I want to make amends as best I can. Will you let me do that?'

Livvie looked on, fighting back tears as Freda allowed him to wrap his arms around her.

Rhoda peered around the living room door, her eyes widening as she took in the scene before her. She looked across at Livvie and Zander askance.

'Lord Hammondely.' Livvie mouthed her words and Rhoda nodded in reply.

'Why don't we let you three have a catch-up on your own in the living room?' said Zander. 'We'll just be in here if you need us.'

Lord Hammondely released Freda from their embrace and looked at his sister for guidance.

'If you don't mind,' said Freda.

'Not at all. Can we get you a cup of tea or coffee, Lord Hammondely, Caro?' asked Livvie.

'I'll take your coats,' said Zander.

'A cup of tea would be lovely if it's not too much trouble.' He slipped off his waxed jacket and handed it to Zander. 'Thank you, Dr Gillespie.'

'Tea would be lovely, thanks, Livvie.'

'And this must be Caro, I've heard a lot about you from Livvie,' Freda said, smiling shyly.

'Hello, Aunt Phaedra, it's lovely to meet you at last.' Caro's voice cracked. 'I can see the family resemblance; you have the same eyes as my father.'

Livvie noticed Freda steal a look at her brother. 'I'll go and put that kettle on.' She squeezed Freda's shoulder before disappearing into the kitchen with Zander and Rhoda. She hoped with all her heart that things went well for her friend.

AN HOUR LATER FREDA, her brother and her niece emerged from the living room, their eyes wet with tears, but their faces wreathed in smiles. Livvie breathed an inward sigh of relief. She'd been like a cat on hot bricks while they were having their talk, she so wanted things to turn out well.

'I must apologise for interrupting your brunch, I should've realised by the delicious smells in the air when we first arrived you were about to eat,' said Lord Hammondely.

'No worries, it's still edible. Your conversation with Freda's more important than our food,' said Zander.

'I'm not so sure your Labrador agrees.' Lord Hammondely nodded to where Alf was gazing up at the worktop where the food had been transferred to covered dishes, two lengths of drool swaying from the corners of his mouth.

'Hmm. He's a bit too fond of his stomach, that one.' Zander rolled his eyes affectionately.

'Typical Labrador; Caro's got one, haven't you? Mr Tubbs. I'm sure he'd eat you if you stood still long enough,' he said with a chuckle.

'I have to agree with you there; he's such a glutton, but adorable with it,' said Caro.

'Anyway, before I go, I wonder if I could arrange a time to take a look at Moor Top Cottage?' asked Lord Hammondely.

'Why?' Livvie's voice came out sharper than she intended. She pressed her hand to her mouth and stole a glance at Freda. 'I mean, it's still Freda's cottage, isn't it?'

'Yes, yes, of course, please don't worry about that, but I gather it needs quite a bit of work doing to it and I'd like to have a look around with a view to getting it fixed up.'

About bloody time!

Zander flung the tea towel he was holding over his shoulder. 'I was going to pop along there this afternoon. How about you both join us for brunch...' His eyes flicked to the clock on the wall. '... make that lunch, and we can have a drive along after that?'

'Well, if you wouldn't mind, that sounds like a splendid idea. Thank you. I can take us along there in the Landie.'

∼

LORD HAMMONDELY HAD DRIVEN himself and Zander along to Moor

Top Cottage while Caro stayed and chatted with her aunt, catching up on lost time.

'Jimby Fairfax, the local blacksmith, had a friend come and do a temporary fix on the thatch which was leaking quite badly. Apparently the whole roof needs doing.' Zander brought him up-to-speed with what they'd looked into regarding repairs of the cottage.

Lord Hammondely was mostly silent, his face serious as he took in the basic conditions his sister had been living in for so many years. On several occasions he appeared to be wrestling with tears. 'I can't imagine what Phaedra has endured here while we were living in comfort just a few miles away. I'm ashamed of myself,' he said, rubbing the side of his face. 'The least I can do is get it fixed up so it's comfortable like your cottage. Nobody should be living in conditions like these, least of all an old lady.'

'Least of all your sister,' Zander said gravely.

Livvie and Zander had the living room to themselves that evening, except for Alf who was snoring from his favourite spot in front of the wood-burner. Freda, exhausted by the events of the last twenty-four hours, had turned in early, while Rhoda was on a date with Len.

Livvie gave in to the pull of a yawn, snuggling in closer to Zander.

'Tired?'

'Mmhm. It's been quite a day.'

'It has, and thank goodness it turned out well.'

'So what did Lord Hammondely have to say when you were along at the cottage?'

'You mean after he got over the shock at seeing how run-down it is?'

'I'd love to have seen his face when he first walked in. Freda's adamant that she still wants to live in the cottage and not move up to the castle like Lord Hammondely suggested. Can't say I blame her. Can you imagine having to see the sour face of her sister-in-law on a daily basis?' Livvie pushed her hand under Zander's jumper, smoothing her hand over the warm skin of his taut abdomen.

'Perish the thought. And besides, it would be too much for Freda moving up there after living on her own for so long; her cottage is where she feels comfortable and safe, and she gets so much pleasure being in her garden. And it's kind of Rhoda to say she'll pop in on her and help her with housework and shopping.'

'It is, though I think it'll be just what Rhoda needs; she was feeling a bit lost after retiring. She and Freda share a love of gardening and from what I've seen, the pair can talk away till the cows come home.'

Zander gave a small laugh. 'Who'd have thought reclusive, shy Freda would turn out to be a chatter-box?'

'It's great, isn't it?'

'It is.' He pushed himself up slightly and turned his face to Livvie, cupping his hand at the back of her head and kissing her, turning her insides molten.

'That was nice.'

'We seem to be spending so much time worrying about other people and sorting out problems, we've had hardly any time to concentrate on us.' He kissed her again.

She sat up and straddled him, a playful glint in her eye. 'So, any suggestions for how you'd like to "concentrate" on us?'

'Hmm. How about we take this discussion upstairs?' He grabbed hold of her hips and pulled her closer to him.

'I like the sound of that.'

'Me too.'

44

THE FIRST WEEK IN DECEMBER

'Bloomin' heck, it's nippy out there. I thought you were never going to answer the door.' Molly rushed into the Romantique studio, her nose red despite being wrapped up well against the cold in a thick navy duffle coat and cream bobble hat.

'Ooh, you've brought the cold air in with you,' said Kitty, locking the door behind her cousin.

'I'm not surprised, it's cold enough for snow out there. According to Hugh Heifer, we're in for a hard winter this year.'

'Well, as long as it waits until after the wedding, it can do what it likes,' said Livvie.

'Don't worry, chick, we usually get it worse at the back end of January, so you should be okay,' said Vi who was busily eyeing up the plastic tub Molly was holding. 'What've you got in there, Moll?'

'Mince pies, still warm from the Aga – or I hope they are, I wrapped them up well. I'll stick the kettle on and we can have a chinwag.'

'Fabulous,' said Vi.

In no time the friends were sitting around the kitchen table, sipping tea and tucking into Molly's mince pies.

'These are gorgeous, Molly,' said Livvie.

'Thanks, hon. Anyroad, time's marching on and before we all get bogged down with Christmas stuff, I thought we should finalise the details for Livvie's hen party, which we're all aware is a week on Friday, right?'

'Yep, I think Kitty's got everything pretty much in hand, haven't you, Kitts?' asked Vi.

Kitty finished her mouthful and nodded. 'Mmm. I have indeed. Lucy's closing the teashop early and said we can go and set up from five-ish; it shouldn't take long.'

'And which bloke have you got lined up for "Pin The Penis"?' asked Molly.

'What?' Livvie had all on not to spit her tea over the table, her eyes wide with shock.

Molly burst into a fit of the giggles, nudging Vi. 'I thought you'd all enjoy an X-rated version of "Pin The Tail On The Donkey".'

'Molly! Trust you to come out with something like that. Take no notice of her, Livvie. There aren't going to be any tacky games. What we've organised is very tasteful – "*taste*" being the operative word,' said Kitty.

'Yep, we're going to eat our dinner off the naked body of a hot-looking fella.' Molly flashed Kitty a wicked grin.

Kitty tutted and rolled her eyes. 'Just ignore her.'

'Where do you get these ideas from?' asked Vi.

Molly shrugged. 'Vivid imagination. Anyway, what's happening with the human Bucking Bronco? I thought you said you had Rev Nev signed up for that.' Molly sniggered, taking great pleasure in teasing Kitty and Livvie.

'I think you've been spending too much time with Granny Aggie. Just keep Rev Nev out of this, please.' Kitty shook her head, unable to stop herself from giggling.

'You've got a sick mind. But just wait till you see what we've got in mind for your hen party, Moll.' Vi gave her a victorious look before turning to Kitty and Livvie. 'See, that's shut her up.'

'Thank goodness for that,' said Livvie.

A couple of days had passed since Livvie had shared Freda's situation. Freda and Jeremiah – as he'd asked them to address him – had given their consent to share it, declaring it had been a secret for far too long.

Kitty, Molly and Vi had listened in disbelief as Livvie had told them what she knew.

'Shit a brick,' Molly had said. 'I know it's a shock, but I can't help thinking the worst thing to come out of this is having Lady Davinia as your sister-in-law. She's got a face pinched tighter than a cat's bum. Poor old Freda.' The friends had cackled at that.

'But how sad that she's lived in those awful conditions, almost like she's an outcast, for so long,' Kitty had said.

'At the risk of sounding controversial here, I know what Freda's been through is awful but it didn't mean that she couldn't keep herself and her cottage clean and tidy,' Vi had said, pulling an apologetic face.

Livvie had felt herself bristle a little at her friend's comment but had tried not to show it. 'From what I can gather, Freda felt if no one cared about her, why should she care about herself; basically, she felt she wasn't worth caring about.' Her words had sent Kitty into floods of tears.

∼

LIVVIE RETURNED home that evening in high spirits. She glanced up at the sky above the moors which was already a deep midnight blue, millions of shining stars splashed across it. A pale luminescent moon hung in a perfect circle just above the rigg, illuminating the dale which was sparkling with frost. Smoke curled out of the cottage chimney, while the lights from the Christmas tree in the garden twinkled away quietly. The sight made her heart ache with happiness.

She made her way carefully up the slippery flagstone path, her breath leaving her mouth in a cloud of condensation. The forecasters had predicted a bitterly cold night, and they weren't wrong. She pushed the sneck down and opened the front door, warm air rushing at her infused with the delicious aroma of the Cheeky Beef Rhoda had said she was going to make for dinner that night. Alf charged towards her, his tail wagging so hard it made his rear end wiggle. 'Hey, young man, it's good to see you too.' She smiled, pulling off her woolly hat, and bent to fuss him. 'Where's your dad?'

'I'm here.' Zander poked his head around the door of the living room. Though he smiled, his face looked wan. 'Hi.'

'Hi. Everything okay?'

Before he could reply Rhoda appeared in the hallway, her cheeks ruddy from bending over the Aga. 'Hello, lovey, had a good day?'

'Great thanks. How about you?'

'Busy. Dinner's in half-an-hour. I'd best get back to it.' She smiled and disappeared back into the kitchen.

Livvie followed Zander into the living room, anxiety squirming in the pit of her stomach. 'Freda's having a nap.' He turned to face her, pushing his fingers through his hair.

Livvie felt her heart lurch. 'What's happened? Is it the Hammondelys?'

'No, no, it's nothing to do with them.' He paused, licking his lips nervously. 'It's Mel.'

'Mel? As in your ex-girlfriend Mel?' *What's she got to do with anything?*

'Yes.'

'What about her?' From the look on his face, Livvie didn't think she was going to like his answer.

'She got in touch recently.'

'Oh.' Livvie felt her knees go weak and she dropped down onto the sofa. She swallowed before she spoke. 'It's something bad, isn't it?'

Zander gnawed on his bottom lip. 'It isn't great.'

45

ZANDER SAT down on the chair beside her, his hands on his knees, his breathing shallow. Livvie felt panic rise in her chest, fearful of what he was about to say, a variety of scenarios piling into her mind. *He's going to dump me. He's getting back with Mel. He doesn't want to get married anymore.* Tension crackled in the air between them.

Zander cleared his throat. 'Do you remember when we were at Steff's and you caught us talking in the garden?'

'Yes. Steff said you were talking about your house in Leeds.'

'Well, that was partly true.'

'I had a feeling there was more to it than that.' She twisted the bangle on her wrist, dreading what was coming next.

'What we'd really gone outside to discuss was that she'd bumped into Mel.'

'She'd bumped into her?' Livvie's pulse started whooshing in her ears. 'What, in Leeds?'

'Yes.' He nodded, pressing his lips together. 'She's, erm, she's had a baby. A little boy. He's nearly three months old.' He slid his eyes to meet hers.

'Right,' she said slowly. *Why is this relevant?* Livvie frowned as she tried to make sense of the information Zander had imparted. 'So, that means he was born in September?' she said slowly.

'Yes.'

'Which means she fell pregnant last December?'

He nodded. 'Mmhm.'

'You slept with her when she came here in December.'

'I know.'

Livvie stared distractedly at the fingers she was knotting in her lap. 'You think it's your baby, don't you?'

'She says it is, but I don't know if she's telling the truth.' Zander gnawed his bottom lip some more.

'You mean, you've seen her?'

'Yes; I had to. When someone drops a bombshell like that, what else can you do?'

'When? Why didn't you tell me?' Nausea swirled in her gut as adrenalin coursed around her body. She gave an involuntary shiver.

'I didn't know what to say. I wanted to be sure before I spoke to you about it. I didn't want to upset you, especially when you've been so excited about the wedding; I didn't want to put the dampeners on that.' He tried to reach for Livvie's hand but she snatched it away.

'Well, you failed on that score. How the hell could I feel anything other than upset?' She struggled to keep her voice down. 'Hang on a minute, does Noah know about this?'

'Yes, he's seen her too. That's why he's been in touch so much recently.' He shifted uncomfortably in his seat.

Livvie sat staring at him, her hands pressed to her face, her body shaking. She was too distraught and confused to release the tears that were building up inside her. 'When she was pregnant, did you know about it?'

'No, the first I knew was when Noah told me in October,' he said truthfully.

'*October?* You've know all this time?

He hung his head. 'Yes.'

'So why didn't she tell you before then? Before she even had the baby?'

'I don't know, well, I have my suspicions; it's a long story and a bit of a muddle, to be honest.'

'I think you'd better tell me everything, right from the start. Then we can work out where to go from here.' Livvie tried to ignore the ache in her heart as she steeled herself to hear the worst.

Zander dragged his hand down his face; he looked exhausted. 'I never saw or heard any more from her after she came to collect her stuff from my house in Leeds last January. There'd been complete radio silence which, much as it was a relief, I must admit it surprised me a bit. I'd heard through the grapevine she'd moved to London in the hope of boosting her blogging career, but no more than that until Noah called in October to say he'd seen her.'

A hazy memory of Zander being distracted after taking a call from Noah floated around her mind. 'But why would she get in touch with Noah and not you?'

'Why does Mel do anything? She plays games, tries to manipulate people; she's cunning. She told Noah she'd split up with the man she'd been seeing – apparently she'd met him in London when she was there last Christmas and had bumped into him again in February. She moved in with him and everything was fine until the baby was born; she told him they split up shortly after. By then, she'd decided there was nothing to keep her down in London, so she moved back to Leeds and booked an appointment with Noah. He said she turned up with the baby, saying it was mine but that I'd denied it and refused to speak to her, ignored her calls and messages, the works, so she thought her only hope was to get him to talk to me.'

'And is it?'

'Do you mean is the baby mine?'

'Yes.' *Please, please, please don't say it's yours.*

Zander pushed his fingers through his hair. 'I honestly don't know.'

Her heart fell through the floor. 'Didn't you use protection when you had sex with her?' she asked, trying to steady the shake in her voice.

'She was on the pill; we were in a long-term relationship, I didn't think we needed to use anything else. And she always said she didn't want children, so…' He shrugged wearily.

'And what about her saying you'd ignored her calls and messages, and denied the baby was yours?'

'The messages and calls are all lies; I hadn't communicated with her or seen her till last week. She called the surgery at Danskelfe, I spoke to her and we arranged to meet, which is why I went to Leeds – I did see an estate agent when I was there, before you think I lied about that.'

'There was that number withheld call you got; could that've been her?'

'I don't know, maybe. I've had a few but no messages have been left. I just assumed it was a scam or someone trying to sell me something so I never answered it.'

'I can't believe you've seen her and haven't said anything to me. I'd tell you if I'd met Donny, not that I'd ever be tempted to meet up with that loser.' Livvie was vaguely aware of Rhoda coming out of the kitchen but her footsteps quickly retreated; she must've heard them having words and not wanted to interrupt.

'I'm so sorry, like I said, I just didn't want to upset you; you've had such a lot going on what with Freda, the wedding preparations and work.'

'So what made you tell me now?' she asked, throwing her hands up.

'Mel threatened to come here, to tell you unless I did. I couldn't let you hear it from her. In truth, I don't believe the baby's mine and that's why I've organized a paternity test; I'm just waiting for the results. I didn't want to tell you until they were back. It's taken so long to get one organised because she refused to have one done, but I told her we'd have to get lawyers involved so she reluctantly agreed.'

'When are the results due back? What if the baby's yours? Where does that leave us?' Dread sat in Livvie's stomach like a lead weight. She knew that Zander was big on family and it was only right that if the baby was his, he should be part of his life. But she also knew how pushy Mel could be, and that scared her.

Zander ran his hand over the back of his neck, he was looking more uncomfortable by the minute. 'The test's due back next week; I think we should wait until then before we start making any big decisions.'

'What's that supposed to mean?' she asked, her bottom lip trembling. 'If the baby's yours are you saying we're over? Shit, Zander, we're due to get married in a couple of weeks!' She jumped up. 'I can't believe you kept something as serious as this from me.'

Zander got to his feet, taking hold of her shoulders. 'Please, Livvie, I was only trying to protect you.'

'Protect yourself, more like.' She shrugged herself free and ran out of the room, grabbing her bag as she went.

46

'Livvie! What on earth's the matter? Come on in, it's freezing out there.' Kitty rushed over, pulling her into a hug and rubbing her back in large swirls. 'What is it, chick? Is it Freda?'

Livvie had headed back to the Romantique studio where she knew Kitty was working late. With her face streaked with tears, she rested her head on her friend's shoulder and sobbed. 'It's Zander … the wedding … I think … I think it might be off.'

'What? That can't be right.' Kitty took a step back, surveying Livvie, her brow crumpled in confusion.

'I think it is,' Livvie said through her sobs. 'I don't … know how … we can … get through this.'

'Oh, lovey, come on, let's go and sit down, I'll make us a pot of tea and you can tell me all about it.' She guided Livvie to the sofa, sitting her down and placing a box of tissues on the table in front of her.

Livvie hugged her mug as she brought Kitty up-to-speed with her situation, her friend listening quietly. 'So, as you can see, it all hinges on the results of that dreaded test.'

Kitty squeezed her hand. 'You poor thing, you've had a lot on your plate recently. I bet your brain feels like it's been bombarded.'

'My head's absolutely pounding with it all.' She felt like her head was in a clamp, being squeezed ever tighter.

'There's no wonder. But if you want my opinion, I think things are going to be fine; I can feel it in my bones. And I can totally understand why you're upset with Zander for not telling you, but from where I'm standing, I can see how he was wanting to protect you; you've had such a lot going on, this would be another thing to pile on top of everything else. He'd have been worried about over-loading you until he knew what the score was.'

Livvie listened quietly. She trusted her friend's judgement; she was a decent person with values Livvie respected.

'Zander's a good man, and he won't have kept it secret to protect himself. I think it was to protect you from unnecessary worry. Like I've already said, I'm sure the baby's not his. Don't you think Mel would've rushed back to him as soon as she found out she was preg-nant if she thought for one minute Zander was the father?'

'I hadn't thought of that but, yes, she probably would.' Livvie sniffed and dabbed at her nose with a tissue.

'From what I've heard about her I'm pretty certain she would. And I know it sounds unkind, but the first thing that crossed my mind was that she was being manipulative. She'd turned her back on Zander last Christmas and only wanted him when she suspected there was a spark between the pair of you. That was after she'd had a fling with the man she'd met in London; the very man she went running straight back to when Zander had told her he was in love with you.' Kitty took a deep breath. 'Sorry this is being so long-winded, but you'll see where I'm coming from in a minute.'

Livvie raised a small smile and took a sip of her tea.

'Now, at this point, Mel's either already pregnant by Mr London when she goes back to him, or she falls pregnant pretty soon after – by him or someone else down there. We all know she's not an easy person to live with, but she and Mr London manage to stick together until the baby's born. Everything's hunky-dory for a while till some-thing happens that makes them split up, which is when Mel's thoughts turn to Zander.'

Livvie ran Kitty's theory through her mind; the way she'd put it made it sound plausible. The more she thought about it, the more she could see it happening.

'And I suspect Zander and Noah are thinking the exact same thing.' Kitty squeezed her hand. 'More tea to help you think about it?'

'Please.' Livvie leaned back into the sofa. 'You know, sitting here, hearing that, it makes complete sense. And I can see why Zander would want to protect me, maybe I'd do the same with him if I found out something I didn't think was true. But I can't shake the feeling of … not mistrust but … I don't know how to describe it.'

'Do you think it's because it makes you feel uncomfortable that he's got a kind of … how can I put it?' Kitty tipped her head to one side, tapping her finger against her mouth. 'Do you think it's maybe because they've sort of shared something that you haven't been a part of over the last few weeks?'

'I think you could be right. It's weird, and I don't want to sound pathetic and clingy, but it's like she's got something with him I haven't got, some kind of connection, for want of a better word – and I don't mean a three-month-old baby!' She looked across at Kitty and the pair burst out laughing.

'Well, that makes complete sense, remind me to tell you about Ollie's ex – Noushka's birth mother. Jeez, she was a right piece of work. I know exactly where you're coming from feeling the way you do. But you never know, this whole experience might end up bringing you closer together like Ollie's ex did with us.'

'I hope so.' Livvie glanced at the clock. 'Oh, heck, look at the time. I've stopped you from getting on. Sorry, Kitty.' She drained her tea and rinsed her mug under the tap.

'Hey, no probs, I'd just about finished. Are you feeling any better?'

Livvie sucked in a deep breath. 'Loads, actually. Thank you for being such a good friend. I don't know where things would've gone with Zander if I hadn't spoken to you.'

'You'd have done the same for me, chick. Now get on home to that man who loves you to bits.' Kitty wrapped her arms around Livvie and pressed a kiss to her cheek.

47

THE GRASS VERGES were sparkling with a thick hoar frost making Livvie thankful the gritter had been out spreading salt over the roads. She'd had to wait a few minutes before setting off for home; she had the engine running and air blasting in the hope of clearing the mist from the windscreen of her car. She pulled the visor down and peered in the mirror to see her eyes were puffy and bloodshot from crying, her face streaked with mascara. She thought of Mel, with her immaculate make-up and sleek blonde hair. 'Ughh! Don't go there, Livvie.' She flicked the visor back up, slipped her car into gear and eased it away from the kerb.

Back home, Rhoda flung her arms around her as soon as she got through the door. 'Oh, lovey, we've been so worried about you. Zander told us what had happened.' She'd been anxiously looking out of the window, waiting for Livvie to return.

'Hi, I just went to see Kitty.'

Alf raced to her, nudging her legs with his nose. 'Hello, lad,' she said, bending to stroke his head.

Freda peered around the door of the living room, a look of relief on her face. 'Are you okay? Rhoda was just about to send out a search party.'

'I'm fine, thank you. I'm sorry if I worried you all, I just needed to clear my head.'

'And did it work?' asked Rhoda, scrutinising her stepdaughter's face closely.

'It did, yes.' She gave a small smile. 'Where's Zander?'

'I'm here.'

She turned to see him coming out of the kitchen. He pressed his lips together in a smile, apprehension hovering in his eyes.

'Are you okay?'

'I went to see Kitty.'

'You told her?' he asked.

'Yes.'

As if on cue, Rhoda said, 'Right, well, we'll give you two some privacy to have a chat. Your dinner's in the warming oven when you're ready for it, Livvie. Come on, Freda, why don't we catch up on that programme you like about the Yorkshire moors?' She bustled the old lady into the living room, closing the door behind them.

In the kitchen, Livvie divested herself of her coat and made her way over to the table, her arms wrapped tightly around her middle. She sat down, feeling the weight of Zander's gaze on her.

'Would you like your dinner now?' he asked.

She shook her head. Alf sat himself beside her and she indulged him by smoothing his ears. 'I'd rather we talked first.'

'Okay.' He pulled out the seat opposite and sat down. Slotting his fingers together, he rested his hands on the table, waiting for her to speak.

Livvie glanced at him, the anguish in his eyes triggering a pang of sympathy. 'Talking to Kitty was really helpful; she put everything into perspective for me. I knew she would, which was the main reason I went to see her.'

'Did you tell her everything?'

She knew he was referring to him sleeping with Mel last Christmas. 'Yes, I did.'

'Right.' He winced.

Livvie shared the conversation she'd had with Kitty, Zander never taking his eyes off her. He released a long sigh when she'd finished, rubbing his hand across his brow. 'So where does that leave us?'

'I'm not sure … I have a niggle.'

'Oh?' His eyes met hers.

'The reason I went out was because when I asked does it mean we're over if the baby turns out to be yours, you didn't answer; your reaction kind of gave the impression we would be.' She felt tears sting the back of her eyes and her throat tighten.

'What? No! I love you, Livvie. I want to spend the rest of my life with you. If the baby turns out to be mine, then, of course, I'll have to support him, and I'll want to be in the child's life; it would feel the worst kind of wrong to turn my back on him. But the last thing it means is that I want to get back with Mel. Christ, please tell me you know that?'

She felt suddenly light-headed as relief flooded through her. 'You promise?'

'Of course. I'm sorry I made you feel that way. I'm a bloody idiot. I'm still in shock about it all which is probably why I didn't answer you properly.'

'You're not the only one in shock.' Livvie gave in to her tears and let them flow. Zander rushed around to her, pulling her up into his embrace; she allowed herself to melt into his soothing warmth. He held her close for several moments, before cupping her face in his hands and kissing away her tears. Alf looked up at her and whimpered, touching her leg with his paw.

THAT NIGHT IN BED, Livvie couldn't remember ever being so tightly wrapped in Zander's arms. The pair lay entwined, listening to the nocturnal sounds of the countryside, the ethereal cry of owls calling across the dale, suspended on the frosty air, the scurrying of small mammals over crisp, frozen leaves collected under the hedges in the garden. Though Kitty's words had soothed her, they hadn't completely banished her concerns about Zander keeping something so important to himself. It wasn't helped by the fact that beautiful, confident Mel was suddenly thrust back into their lives, albeit – hopefully – temporarily. The situation had created a background thrum of anxiety running through her body; the day the test results were back wouldn't come too soon.

'Aren't you worried we don't know each other enough?' she asked him.

'What do you mean?' He stilled his hand that had been smoothing circles on her shoulder.

'Maybe, if I'd known you longer, I would've realised that you didn't mean we'd be over if the baby was yours. Or you would've known the need to clarify it to me.'

He took a deep breath, her head lifting with the rise of his chest. 'I honestly think that has nothing to do with it. It's just that we're facing an unusual and difficult situation and there's bound to be some element of misunderstanding. And there's been a lot of other stuff going on.'

'You honestly think that's what it is?'

'I do. But what I know, more than anything, is that I've never felt this way about anyone before. The moment I set eyes on you and felt that "boom" last Christmas, I knew you were the one. What I'd felt with Mel and my previous girlfriends was nothing compared to how I feel about you.'

Happiness bloomed inside her, forcing a smile. 'Do you think we'll get through this?'

'I know we will; we'll come out stronger'

I hope so. 'That's what Kitty said.'

Livvie lay awake, listening as Zander's breathing became slower and deeper. Her mind wandered back to their last serious conversation about starting a family. It had taken place in the summer while they were sitting outside enjoying the last of the day's warmth, sipping wine. They'd agreed to wait a couple of years before thinking about having kids, so they could enjoy some time together, just the two of them, do some travelling and maybe extend the cottage. 'I'd like at least two baby Gillespies,' Zander had said.

Livvie had given her imagination carte blanche to run free. When she got pregnant, she knew exactly how she was going to break the news to him. She was going to get a big box, wrap it up like a present, complete with bows and ribbons. They'd be just about to start their evening meal and she'd say, 'Oh, I almost forgot, I've got a little something for you.' She'd return with the box and place it on the table beside him. 'Go on, open it now,' she'd say, barely able to contain her excitement. He'd ask her what it was, wondering if he'd missed a special occasion. She'd watch him undo the ribbon, glancing up at her, then he'd fish around in the tissue and pull out a smaller wrapped box, scattering sparkly metallic confetti everywhere. Zander would look confused, asking what it was. 'Wait and see,' she'd say, a huge smile splitting her face. Slowly, he'd lift the lid off the box to see a pregnancy test, displaying the word 'pregnant'. She could picture his handsome face so clearly, the happiness in his eyes. He'd look at it in disbelief before glancing back at her. 'Pregnant? Are you telling me you're going to have a baby?' he'd ask in disbelief before the biggest smile would spread over his face. 'Yes,' she'd nod and he would rush around to her, kissing her and spinning her around. Alf would be beside himself at their excitement, leaping around giddily. Zander would tell her how much he loved her and how she'd made him the happiest man on the planet.

But, ughh, things had changed since that happy fantasy had first floated around her mind. If Zander turned out to be the father of Mel's baby, then the shiny edge had been taken off the time when Livvie could share their own baby news with him. It just wouldn't be the same. She wanted him to be a first-time father with *her*. But that luxury could soon be snatched away from them. *Does that make me sound silly? Selfish? Petty?* The thought made her heart twist. She sighed and eased herself out of Zander's arms, turning away from him. He stirred and mumbled something indiscernible. What she'd give to turn the clock back to last year; if she'd given in to temptation with Zander then he wouldn't have slept with Mel, and she wouldn't be part of the equation now. *Oh, sod off, hindsight! You're not a wonderful thing, you're an annoying, "told-you-so" pain in the arse!*

The sexual chemistry that had been sparking between them from the very first moment they met last Christmas had taken Livvie by surprise; it would have been the easiest thing in the world for her to slip between the sheets with Zander. And if it hadn't been for the fact her heart was feeling raw from the very recent break-up of her relationship with Donny, that's exactly what she would have done. But she'd let her head rule her heart and now she regretted it bitterly. With an inward groan, she pulled the duvet over her head and forced herself to think about something else.

48

THE NEW WEEK started with a flurry of wintry weather. Livvie pulled back the kitchen curtains and peered out of the window. Though it was still quite dark, a light dusting of snow illuminated the dale. She gazed out at it, her mind slowly filling with thoughts. Her heart flipped; it was destined to be a big week for the residents of Dale View Cottage.

Rhoda was set to get the keys to her new home on Wednesday, with Freda potentially moving in with her by the end of the week. The two women had become great friends, chatting for hours as they did jigsaw puzzles, crosswords and the like. It had warmed Livvie's heart to see it. Both appeared to be looking forward to the move, though she sensed a little apprehension from Freda. *The poor soul's been through such a lot recently.* She made a mental note to double-check her friend was still happy to move out, she didn't like the thought of her feeling unsettled.

Her thoughts moved on to Friday night; her hen night. She was looking forward to it, despite regularly being teased by Molly that they were planning something raunchy. Livvie was thankful it was Kitty who was in charge of organising it; at least it would be tasteful.

The evening after that was Zander's stag party, organised by Jimby in his capacity as best man. He'd offered the friends the option of a night out in York, a day paintballing or a curry night at the Sunne. The Sunne won the vote hands down, which Zander told Livvie was much to his relief. 'The thought of a night out in a city on the run-up to Christmas just doesn't appeal to me. And how can I resist one of Bea's special curry nights?' He was disappointed Noah couldn't make it, but they'd planned a catch-up when Jess was safely delivered of their baby and the weather less unpredictable.

But one event created a ripple of tension in the cottage, overshadowing everything else: the results of the paternity test.

Livvie's stomach clenched at the thought of it. She'd spent the last few days willing with all her might that the baby wouldn't be Zander's. She'd deliberately not even asked the baby's name, knowing it would have made the situation more "real", the wait even more unbearable.

She hugged her mug of tea to her chest, trying to push the impending test results from her mind, watching as John Danks trundled by in his tractor. He gave her a quick wave which she returned. How perverse, she thought, that she and Zander were awaiting a potentially life-changing event within the walls of this cosy little cottage, but life went on as normal out in the dale.

'Right, I'm heading off to work now.' Zander bowled in from outside, breaking into her musings. He was wrapped up in his padded waxed jacket, his face red from the cold. He rubbed his hands together, breathing warm air onto them. 'I've de-iced your car windows, they should still be clear for when you're ready to leave.'

'Ahh. What would I do without you?' She grinned at him.

'Didn't know there was a chance you were going to be without me?' He grinned back and leaned in to kiss her. 'Have a good day. Hope it goes well up at the castle.'

'You'll let me know if you hear anything, won't you?' She knew she didn't need to clarify she meant the test.

'Of course, though I'm not expecting anything today.' He picked up his doctor's bag and kissed her again, making her rock back on her heels. 'Try not to worry about it; just focus on something fun or happy, like your hen party.'

'I'll try. You have a good day too.' She smiled as she watched him go, aware of the invisible barrier that had wedged itself between them in the days since he'd told her about Mel and the baby. Neither of them acknowledged it, and though Livvie snuggled into Zander in bed at night just as she'd always done, there'd been no intimacy between them; just an unspoken understanding that it didn't seem right.

49

'HAVE YOU NOTICED THE TIME, LIVVIE?' Kitty asked, looking over at her.

But Livvie was too engrossed in her thoughts to hear. She'd been struggling to concentrate all morning, and her mind kept drifting to the possible outcome of the paternity test. It sent her heart galloping like the clappers whenever it popped into her mind.

'Livvie,' Kitty said again, catching Vi's eye.

'What was that you were saying about the strippers Moll's organised for the hen party, Kitty? Are you sure they're all over eighty?' Vi asked in a theatrical whisper.

That got her attention. She looked up, her eyes wide with shock. 'What? Please tell me you're joking.'

Kitty and Vi burst into laughter. 'Kitty's been talking to you but you were away with the fairies.'

Livvie clapped her hand to her brow. 'Sorry, my mind's all over the place. I'll just be glad when we know – about the baby, I mean.'

'Don't worry about it, chick. I was just reminding you of the time, didn't you say you had an appointment up at the castle at two? It's half one now.' Kitty flicked her eyes towards the clock.

'Oh, right, yes, thanks for the reminder; I'd lost track of time.'

Livvie had been hand-stitching a vintage panel of lace onto the bodice of a wedding dress. She slotted her needle into the pincushion and tidied it away. She had mixed feelings about her visit to the castle; she hadn't been there since her confrontation with Lady

Davinia and she wasn't sure what type of reception she'd get if they bumped into one another.

'Wish me luck, and keep your fingers crossed Lady Davinia doesn't bite me,' she said, slinging her bag over her shoulder and pulling an awkward face at Kitty and Vi.

'Good luck, chick, though I don't think you'll need it.' Kitty smiled kindly at her.

'Kitty's right, the old dragon'll be quaking in her boots after you tore a strip off her last time you were there,' said Vi, grinning.

'Ughh! Don't remind me. I still feel bad about that.' Livvie cringed at the memory.

'Don't; she asked for it,' said Vi.

'Maybe, but not in her own home; that was rude of me.'

'She was rude first, Livvie,' said Kitty. 'But get that out of your mind and just focus on your gorgeous wedding that's less than two weeks away.'

'Okay.' Livvie laughed, a frisson of nerves and excitement sweeping through her chest.

MORE SNOW HAD FALLEN since Livvie arrived at work that morning, though it was the slushy, slippery variety which didn't usually hang around for long. After the warmth of the Romantique studio, it was bitterly cold, no thanks to the biting north-easterly wind that was whipping around the village. She pulled her collar up and glanced at the brooding sky overhead. It was a foreboding shade of grey with dense clouds that looked like trouble. Livvie shivered.

As she made her way along the road to Danskelfe, she was glad she'd taken Zander's advice and had winter tyres fitted to her car. She'd experienced first-hand how dangerous these country roads could be. Conditions could change in a heartbeat and, after coming a cropper last winter, it was something she wasn't keen to experience again in a hurry.

She was relieved to find Caro as warm and welcoming as ever, leading her to the sitting room where a tray of tea and cake awaited them. 'Come in, darling, it's so lovely to see you.' She hugged Livvie tightly. Mr Tubbs seemed pleased to see her too, wagging his tail enthusiastically as he waddled along beside her. Coming face-to-face with Lady Davinia wasn't half as bad as she expected. Though the older woman still wore her superior expression her eyes held a less haughty look, and she was civil. Guilt had been gnawing away at Livvie since she'd let her temper fly and she felt compelled to apologise.

'Lady Davinia, I feel I must apologise for my outburst last time we met. I was upset at what you said about Freda, or rather, Lady Phaedra, but I had no right to speak to you in such a way in your own home. I stand by my views, but I'm sorry I aired them in such a forceful way in your home.'

Lady Davinia's cheeks flushed and she flicked an imaginary fleck of dust from the sleeve of her cardigan. 'Yes, well, I may have said a little too much myself. But I appreciate your apology, thank you.' She sniffed. 'I'll leave you to get on with your planning.'

Caro watched her mother leave the room then leaned into Livvie. 'Well, I for one, was bloody well glad you put her in her place. It was time somebody did. I'm just pleased I got to meet Aunt Phaedra. If it wasn't for you, that would never have happened.'

'I just hope it doesn't backfire on Freda.'

'Oh, there's no need to worry about that, darling, you have my word it won't. Mother's absolutely riddled with remorse. My father tore a strip off her; he was bloody brutal and I've never seen her apologise as much. When she met Aunt Phaedra on the road all those years ago I don't think she fully appreciated the effect her spiteful words would have – I actually think she buried her head in the sand rather than face them, which is cowardly, I know – but my father left her in no doubt about their impact.' She pulled a face at the thought.

'Really?' Livvie would have loved to have been a fly on the wall to witness that.

'Really. Don't be fooled by her composed exterior; I can assure you she feels utterly shaken to the core. I've never seen my father lose his temper the way he did, but I watched as every word he threw at her hit their target.'

'That can't have been pleasant for you to witness,' said Livvie.

'To be honest, I was too stunned to think about it; I just found myself watching with a kind of morbid fascination. And I know she's my mother, but I have to say she deserved it; she's been allowed to get away with her appalling behaviour for years. But, credit to her, she stood there and took it. I can hardly believe I'm saying this, but it seems to have knocked the wind out of her sails and smoothed her sharp edges. Long may it continue,' said Caro, with a lift of her eyebrows.

Livvie was uncertain how to respond to this without sounding rude.

'She's hoping to have a word with Aunt Phaedra; she says she wants to apologise and make it up to her.'

Not sure how she's going to do that. 'Gosh.' *She has had a change of heart.*

'Do you think Aunt Phaedra will be prepared to see her?'

'I'm sure she will; she's kind-hearted and doesn't seem to bear a grudge.'

Caro released a sigh. 'Well, that's good to hear; I don't want her to feel scared she's going to lose her home anymore.'

Not only did Livvie welcome this news, but she felt relieved at getting her own apology out of the way; she didn't like to be on bad terms with anyone and her behaviour that afternoon had made her squirm with discomfort whenever she recalled it. She took some solace from Caro's words; it was true, if she hadn't said anything, Freda's house would still be no more than a dilapidated hovel. And that had made her bad manners seem worth all the drama.

By the time she left the castle, Livvie felt more settled. Worrying about whether they'd still be welcome to have their wedding there had been taking up a lot of head-space. But everything was nicely in place; Caro, it seemed, was an efficient organiser and Livvie felt confident at leaving matters in her more than capable hands. As she drove home she breathed a sigh of relief. 'Phew!' It felt good to get that ticked off her wedding list.

50

LIVVIE HAD TAKEN Wednesday off work to help Rhoda move into her new home. Jimby, Ollie and Camm had brought her belongings from their temporary storage place in the barn at Withrin Hill. They'd deposited them in the relevant rooms which was making it easier to wade through the boxes. 'By, it's a quaint little cottage, is this,' said Jimby, looking around him. 'I can see why Rhoda wanted to snap it up.'

'It is, it's got a lovely homely atmosphere,' said Livvie.

'And it's handy for Len.' He shot her a mischievous look. 'Anyway, I'll be off but shout up if there's anything you need a hand with; if something heavy's in the wrong room, we can pop back and shift it for you.'

'Okay, thanks, Jimby, see you later.'

She was emptying boxes in the kitchen when she was startled by a noise behind her. 'Oh! Zander, I didn't hear you come in,' she said, pressing her hand against her chest. The very next thought to leap into her mind was the paternity test. Her heart upped its pace and her knees felt weak. She rested her hand on the worktop, bracing herself for the news. 'Have you heard?'

'Yes.' He strode over to her, wrapping his arms around her, squeezing her like there was no tomorrow.

Livvie's face prickled with fear and her breathing became ragged. 'Oh, God. Are you the … is the baby yours?' Her voice came out in a whisper. Her pulse was whooshing so loudly in her ears, she was fearful it would drown out his words.

He stood back and held her shoulders; it seemed like an eternity before he answered. 'No. I'm not the baby's father,' he said, throwing his head back and puffing out a noisy sigh of relief. 'Thank fuck for that.'

Livvie let his words sink in before a feeling of euphoria swept her up. 'Oh, thank goodness! Thank bloody goodness. Oh, what a reli—' Her words were stifled as he pressed his mouth against hers and kissed her hard. He picked her up and spun her round, making her squeal with joy.

'I knew in my heart of hearts I wasn't the father. If Mel had had a tiny inkling I was, she'd have been back straight away.'

'That's what Kitty said. Does Mel know yet?'

'I've asked Noah to contact her. I don't want anything else to do with her; I never want to speak to her again. I wish her no ill will and I feel sorry for her child, but I want her to leave us alone now.'

'Am I right in thinking you two have had some good news?' Rhoda was standing in the doorway, weighed down by two bulging carrier bags, a beaming smile on her face.

'We have indeed,' said Zander, giving Livvie a squeeze.

'Zander's not the father of Mel's baby.' Speaking those words felt so good.

'Well, thank goodness for that. Now you two are free to enjoy the build-up to your wedding just as you should be able to.' Rhoda made her way into the kitchen and dumped the bags on the worktop. 'Come here, lovey, let me give you a hug.' She wrapped her arms around her stepdaughter and kissed her cheek before patting Zander's arm. 'I'm so happy for the pair of you.'

'Thank you,' they said at the same time. They watched as she headed back out to her car.

'Listen, I have to fly, but how do you fancy celebrating with a meal at the Sunne tonight?' Zander asked.

'Lovely as that sounds, I think I'd rather have a cosy night in at home. Rhoda's going to be getting settled in here and Freda always goes to bed early.' She cocked a flirty eyebrow at him.

'Hmm. I like way you're talking.' He grinned and bent to kiss her, the touch of his lips sending sparks flying in her stomach. 'How about I get some of Lucy's ready-made meals from the teashop?'

'Sounds good to me.' Livvie couldn't stop herself from smiling.

'Chicken casserole?'

'Perfect.' She'd eat carpet burgers and wouldn't care one jot, she was that happy.

'See you, tonight, beautiful.' He kissed her again.

'Don't be late.'

'Don't worry, I won't,' he said with a lopsided smile, his eyes glinting.

It was good to have the old Zander back again, she thought.

∿

'CHEERS TO OUR GOOD NEWS.' Zander clinked his wine glass against Livvie's, his eyes shining, his relief palpable.

'Cheers.' Livvie returned his smile. 'What a couple of weeks we've had, what with Freda, the Hammondely family and the castle drama, and then Mel and her accusations. Jeez, I feel exhausted with it all. We need a break from it now.'

'Yeah, it's been pretty draining.' He sat back in his seat and brushed his hand back and forth over his close-cropped hair. 'We need to put it all behind us and just focus on the good things. We're free to look forward to your hen night, my stag night and our wedding.'

'I'm all for that. I can't believe we can put all that hassle behind us at last; we were getting so bogged down by it all.'

'But not anymore. How about we get this lot into the dishwasher and have an early night? Freda's tucked up and fast asleep – I heard her snoring – so we shouldn't disturb her.'

Livvie giggled, her heart lighter than it had been for weeks. 'Why? Are you planning on making a lot of noise?'

'You'd better believe it.' He grinned at her. 'Actually, sod the dishes. Come on, we can see to them after.'

'After what?'

He got to his feet and pulled her up to him, making her heart swoop. Brushing her hair off her face, he dipped his head to hers and kissed her slowly and tenderly. She felt her insides melt as he parted her mouth with his tongue, emitting a groan from deep inside. 'Let's go upstairs,' he said, huskily. He took her hand and led her up to the bedroom.

∿

'THAT WAS AMAZING,' Livvie said breathlessly. She lay with her head on her pillow, her heart still racing. The barrier between them had been torn down and they'd felt closer and more in tune than ever. She felt inexorably happy as she glanced over at Zander. He looked towards her, and gave her a heart-melting smile.

'It was.'

'Kitty said the trouble with Mel might even bring us closer together; I think she could be right.'

'I think she could too.' He tilted her chin towards him with his finger and kissed her. 'Don't ever forget I don't want to be anywhere else than with you. You're everything to me, and the thought that I might lose you because of not telling you about Mel frightened me more than I ever anticipated.' He pulled her closer to him.

'No more secrets; however well intended they are,' she said.

'No more secrets.'

51

Livvie was gathering her stuff together when there was a knock at the door, making Alf bark excitedly as he charged towards it. 'Come in, Molly, don't mind the tough guy,' she called.

It was the evening of her hen party and Camm had offered to scoop her up with Molly and drop them off at the teashop in Lytell Stangdale, leaving them free to enjoy some Prosecco.

She peered round the kitchen door to see Molly sporting a bright pink deely-bopper hairband complete with two sparkly pink pompoms that bobbed about whenever she moved. 'Now then, missus,' Molly said, flashing a wide smile and opening her coat. 'Ta-dah!' She was sporting the same black t-shirt as Livvie with the words "Livvie's Hen Party" emblazoned across it in bright pink letters. She was wearing black jeans like Livvie too. 'I hope you're all set for this and ready to have some fun.'

'I so am, I've been looking forward to it all day. It's been manic recently what with getting Rhoda and Freda moved into Fern Cottage and everything else. I'm definitely ready to let my hair down.'

'That's what I like to hear,' said Molly, rubbing her hands together.

'Hi there, Molly. Nice head gear.' Zander wandered into the hall wearing an amused expression, glass of wine in hand.

'Thanks, I've got a pair for your betrothed in my bag somewhere.' She had a quick rummage and produced a matching headband, the pom-poms bouncing back and forth. 'There you go, get that on then I won't feel so daft being the only one wearing one.' Molly thrust it into Livvie's hands.

Livvie slid it on and turned to Zander, waggling her head about. 'What do you think?'

'Very fetching.' He grinned at her while Alf looked on, bemused.

'Hehe. Wait till you see what the lads have got in store for you tomorrow night.' Molly shot him a mischievous look.

'Knowing Jimby, it'll be interesting,' he said, laughing.

'You'd better believe it. Anyway, come on, let's get this party started, young lady. See you, Zander, enjoy your peaceful night.' She headed towards the door.

'Thanks, Moll.'

Livvie directed her gaze to Alf. 'Right, Alf, I'm leaving you in charge of your dad, okay?' The Labrador's ears pricked up at the mention of his name, cocking his head to one side as she spoke. 'Make sure he behaves himself; I'll be asking for a report when I get back.' She ruffled his ears.

She turned to Zander who was smiling down at her. 'Enjoy your boys' night in.' She stood on her tiptoes and kissed him.

'Will do, and you have a great time.' He cupped her cheek with his hand and kissed her again, triggering a surge of love for him. She was so relieved they'd been able to put the stress of the last few weeks behind them.

'Will you two give-over with all that mushy stuff.' Molly rolled her eyes. 'Come on, Liv, pull your lips away from your fella for a few hours; there'll be plenty of time for that when you get back.'

Livvie giggled. 'Sorry, Molly.'

The icy air nipped at Livvie's cheeks as she made her way down the path and climbed into the back of the Landie, her deely-boppers clattering against the inside of its roof.

'Hi there, Livvie,' said Camm, his dark curls hidden by a thick woolly hat.

'Hiya, Camm, thanks for doing this, I really appreciate it.'

'Hey, no problem, especially when you're returning the favour tomorrow for the stag night.'

Soon they were deposited in the village, Livvie's excitement building as they headed over to the teashop, the golden glow of its lights spilling out onto the road in front despite the windows being steamed up.

Molly paused at the door. 'Now, before we go in, you've got to promise me you'll approach this with an open mind. Gerald and Rev Nev might be as old as the hills, but they were the only blokes up for it.' Her face was deadly serious

'What?' Livvie couldn't tell if her friend was winding her up.

'You'll see.' Before Livvie could argue, Molly opened the door and pushed her through it, the bell above jangling noisily. 'Hiya, lasses, here's the bride-to-be.'

A cheer went up and Kitty rushed over to Livvie, wrapping her arms around her. 'Happy hen night, petal. I hope you love what we've got in store for you.' Her elfin face was lit up by her smile.

'Thank you, I'm sure I will.' Livvie was met with a sea of happy faces, all wearing "Livvie's Hen Party" t-shirts, and matching deely-boppers that bobbed about in a synchronised Mexican wave. 'And this all looks wonderful, thank you so much.' She gazed happily around the room, touched by the amount of effort that had gone into the decoration. Huge frothy pompoms in shades of pink and white were suspended from the ceiling alongside streamers trimmed with pink sparkly stars. Fairy lights had been trained around the windows and doors, while banners emblazoned with the words "Hen Party" were stuck on the walls. Several tables had been pushed together to create one long one which was covered in pink vinyl table cloths, the phrase "Team Bride" splashed all over them.

'And, since eighties music is your fave, we've put together an eighties playlist for you,' said Rosie, beaming happily. 'Robbie had great fun compiling it.'

'That's so kind.' Livvie had got her love of eighties music from her dad who used to listen to it all the time. A memory of the pair of them singing along in the car sneaked into her mind, sending a wave of emotion sweeping through her. *Pull yourself together, Livvie, you can't bawl your eyes out on your hen night!*

'Any idea what sort of celebration we've organised for you?' Molly grinned.

The frisson of nerves Molly's question generated was enough to send her tears scurrying for the hills. 'No, but I'm sure with your mum and Little Mary here, it's not going to be too raunchy.' She cast a surreptitious eye around the room looking for evidence of Gerald and Rev Nev.

'Here's a clue.' Vi handed her a cocktail glass containing a creamy-coloured drink with chocolate shavings on the top.

Livvie took it. 'Ooh, this looks delicious, what is it?'

'Chocolate martini,' said Vi.

Livvie took a sip, her eyes widening. 'Ooh, that's heavenly.' She licked the creamy liquid off her top lip. 'But I'm still none the wiser.' She took another sip.

'You're having a chocolate party, chick. We're making truffles, lollipops, chocolate-dipped strawberries, anything you fancy. Becca from the Chocolate Cherub in Middleton-le-Moors should be here any minute.'

'Oh, wow! That sounds amazing; I couldn't think of a more perfect hen party. Thank you.' Livvie was genuinely thrilled at the choice.

'Well, as we're all chocoholics, I thought it would suit everyone.' Kitty beamed at her.

'You're right there, pet. I can't go a day without a treating myself to a bar of the stuff,' said Big Mary.

Noushka skipped over to her, her golden waves flying out behind her. She held out a shocking-pink sash with the words "Bride-to-Be" printed on it. 'Livvie, you've got to wear this,' she said.

'Oh, thanks, Noushka.' Holding her drink carefully, she let the young woman slip it over her head, straightening out the kink.

'Perfect.' A huge smile lit up Noushka's pretty face.

'No Rhoda?' asked Little Mary, the bright pink of her deely-boppers a contrast to her white curls. Livvie thought she looked very sweet in her "Livvie's Hen Party" black t-shirt and black slacks.

'No, she's staying in with Freda. They're just getting settled in at the new cottage. I told Freda she was very welcome to join us, but she's still a bit shy.'

'Ah, bless her,' said Lucy.

'From what I've seen of her, I always got the impression she was a kindly soul. It'll nice to get to know her better, when she's ready,' Little Mary said wistfully.

'I'm sure she'd love that, Mary,' said Livvie. 'And you're right, she is kind.'

News of Freda's real identity had spread around the village like wildfire since Caro had called into the village shop and shared the news she'd found her long-lost aunt. The Hammondelys hadn't come out of it looking good but everyone without exception was happy for Freda, knowing that she actually belonged and could be given the love and care she deserved.

'Is Caro coming?' Livvie wasn't certain if the young woman would show up in case she was given a frosty welcome by the other ladies in light of the revelations.

'I'm not sure; I sent her an invitation, but I haven't heard back,' said Kitty.

Before anything further could be said, Becca arrived, a huge box of delights in her hands. She pushed the door open with her elbow admitting an icy blast of air. 'Sorry I'm late, my Sat Nav sent me all over the place.'

Molly strode over to her. 'No worries, loads of folk say that. Here let me help. Is there anything else to bring in?'

Becca nodded. 'There's a couple of boxes on the backseat of my car, if someone wouldn't mind giving me a hand.'

Soon, everything was set out and the ladies crowded around the table wearing the "Livvie's Hen Party" aprons Vi's mum, Mary, had made. There were groans of ecstasy as the delicious aroma of melted chocolate wafted around in the air. 'Oh, man, whoever said chocolate's better than sex is absolutely spot on; even the smell of it's orgasmic,' said Molly, sniffing the air and making them all giggle.

'Molly!' said her mum but she chuckled all the same.

Becca gave a quick demonstration of what they'd be creating that evening. 'Any questions, just shout up. And I'll try not to get all the ladies called Mary mixed up.'

'It's easy, I'm just plain Mary,' said Vi's mum, 'then the little lady there is Little Mary and the tall lady's Big Mary.'

'Oh, okay,' Becca said, laughing. 'Actually, I've just remembered I brought some moulds for you to use. They must still be in the box, I'll just go and fish them out.'

'I hope we're not making anything phallic-shaped; we have ladies of a delicate disposition here,' Molly said, nodding towards Kitty playfully.

'Well, that doesn't include you, Moll. Delicate and you would never be used in the same sentence,' Vi said, making them all laugh.

'Haha.' Molly pulled a face at her.

It wasn't long before they all got stuck in, sampling what Becca had made, and trying the techniques out for themselves. The room was brimming with the happy sound of laughter and banter mingling with the eighties playlist. Livvie's eyes shone as she set to work on the ganache, her cheeks flushed thanks to the couple of chocolate martinis she'd downed in quick succession.

Several times she threw her head back, laughing at the quips and jokes Molly had on tap. She hadn't felt this carefree in months.

Just then, the bell jangled, making them all turn to see Caro holding the door open for Rhoda and Freda. 'Oh, my goodness, it smells absolutely divine in here,' she said, smiling. 'I hope we're not too late to join the fun.'

'Rhoda! Freda!' Livvie ran across to them, hugging them both. 'It's perfect timing. I'm so pleased you came.'

'We'd finished decorating the Christmas tree when Caro called, so we thought, "why not?", didn't we, Freda?' Rhoda gave her friend an encouraging smile.

Freda was standing beside her, looking self-conscious. She nodded shyly. 'We did that. Rhoda said she'd help me seeing as I've still got this pot on my arm.'

Livvie's heart went out to her; she appreciated how much courage it would have taken for her to come here knowing that her secret was now public knowledge.

'Well, I couldn't be happier. Go and hang your coats up and come and join us, we've just started making truffles.' She watched Rhoda and Freda head to the coat stand and leaned in to Caro. 'Thank you for getting your aunt to come,' she said quietly.

'You're very welcome, darling. It was surprisingly easy.' She smiled kindly in Freda's direction. 'And thank you for being so instrumental in us getting to know her; I only wish it had happened years ago. But I don't want to dwell on that tonight.' She waved her hand in the air. 'Especially when there's fun to be had and chocolate to be eaten.'

The ladies had moved on from making chocolate and ganache and were moulding truffles. 'I'm not so sure my efforts look particularly appetising,' said Molly, frowning at the two mis-shaped hazelnut-covered lumps in front of her. Livvie tried not to laugh at the smear of chocolate around her friend's mouth. 'And I hate to say it, but there's something about them that reminds me of Camm, if you know what I mean?' She gave a dirty laugh and held the plate up, showing everyone the two misshapen truffles. 'As you can see, they're not his best feature.'

'Oh, poor Camm,' said Kitty, looking embarrassed on his behalf.

Freda looked on non-plussed while the rest of the group fell about in a fit of the giggles.

'Honestly, our Molly, T.F.I.F.; we don't need to know that sort of stuff,' said Annie, shaking her head and chuckling despite herself.

'T.F.I.F.? Are you sure you mean that, Mother?'

'Isn't it what you say to someone who's shared too much information with you?'

Molly stifled a laugh and glanced over to where Livvie, Kitty and Vi were sitting. 'I'm not so sure about that.'

Livvie pressed her lips together and looked away, fighting the urge to let rip with a guffaw.

'No, Annie, you mean MILF,' said Vi's mum, Mary. 'Isn't that right, Vi?'

'MILF?' Noushka flashed a look of amused disbelief at Vi, who snorted with laughter.

'Oh, my days,' said Bea with a quiet chortle.

'Erm … not quite, Mum.'

'MILF?' Annie looked puzzled. 'So, what does it stand for?'

Big Mary howled with laughter, almost falling back-over in her chair. 'Oh, wait till I tell Gerry about this.'

Molly clapped her hand to her forehead, tears of laughter pouring down her cheeks. 'Oh, sweet Jesus, someone help me, please. Have you two been spending time with Grannie Aggie, or something?'

'No. What do you mean by that?' Annie looked utterly confused as she glanced around at so many amused faces.

'Mum, listen carefully, you mean T.M.I., which stands for "too much information".'

'Oh, that's the one.' She turned to Vi's mother. 'It's not MILF or the other one, Mary, it's T.I.M.'

'No, Mum, it's T.M. … actually, never mind.'

'Oh, right.' Vi's mum looked from Annie to Molly, baffled.

'Oh, this is hilarious.' Molly wiped her tears of mirth from her eyes. 'Now we've got that sorted – kind of – I'd love to know what you think T.F.I.F. stands for, Mum.'

Annie sat thinking for a moment, all eyes on her. 'Let's see, well now, the "T" will be for "too" and the "I" will be for "information" and the … hmm … I'm not sure about the "F"s to be honest. You're going to have to tell me.'

Molly ran over to her mum and whispered the definition in her ear in between splutters of laughter. Annie's eyes widened and both hands flew to her mouth. 'Oh, my goodness, I didn't mean *that*! I'd never use the "eff" word.' Her face burned crimson as everyone fell about laughing at her endearing reaction. 'So what does MILF mean then, or shouldn't I ask?'

Molly held her hand up. 'You definitely shouldn't ask, there's no way I'm going to translate that one for you, but promise me you'll never, ever, under any circumstances, use it.'

'Oh, dear, I think I'll steer clear of the lot. What a minefield, it's like a whole new language.'

'It is with you,' Molly said sotto voce.

'What are they talking about?' asked Little Mary, bemused.

'You don't want to know, pet,' said Big Mary, patting her hand.

Freda looked on, her eyes shining, enjoying listening to the banter bouncing around the room. She caught Livvie's eye and her smile widened, making Livvie's heart swell with happiness. Her friend had been made welcome by the other ladies who didn't quiz her about her past, but made sure to include her in their conversation as if she'd never been away.

'Oh, my goodness, I can't remember the last time I laughed so much, my face is aching,' said Lucy. She and Bea were about to set the table near the kitchen in readiness for their evening meal.

'Same here. And if I eat any more truffles or chocolate I'm not going to fit into my wedding dress.' Livvie patted her stomach wondering how she was going to manage the food they'd planned for later.

'Yeah, I'm feeling a bit stuffed actually. How about we have a bit of a boogie before we eat? Make some space for the food,' said Vi.

'Sounds great, as long as you don't have us doing any burlesque,' said Molly.

'Yikes, I'm too stuffed to do any of those moves. One bend in the wrong direction and the button's in danger of pinging off my jeans,' said Rosie.

'Same here. Crank up the music, Luce, we're going to have a bop before we eat. Come and join us, you two,' Vi said, waving her and Bea over.

The friends, including Becca, spent the next half hour dancing and singing along to the playlist. Even Freda joined in, swaying on the periphery, staying close to Rhoda. They finished off with a riotous version of the conga, hands on the hips of the person in front, laughing and giggling, until they were exhausted and ready to sit down.

'Oh, that was just brilliant.' Livvie fell into her seat. She was out of breath and her face was glowing. The popping of corks got her attention and before she knew it Vi was thrusting a glass of Prosecco into her hand. 'Here, chick, you need one of these.' She tapped the side of her own glass with a knife, getting the room's attention. 'Everyone, I want to make a toast to Livvie here who, as you all know, is getting married in a couple of weeks. So, I'd like you all to raise your glasses to Livvie and wish her all the very best for the future. Here's to Livvie.'

'To Livvie,' the room chorused, followed by a resounding cheer.

'Thank you all for coming and making this the best hen night I could ever imagine. And thank you all for welcoming me into the village and making me feel like I've lived here forever. To friendship.'

'To friendship.' The women raised their glasses.

52

'AFTERNOON.' Zander grinned as Livvie shuffled into the kitchen, her pink dotty pyjamas crumpled and her hair ruffled. 'How're you feeling?' It was twelve-fifteen.

'Rough.' Her voice came out in a croak. She trudged over to the table, pulled out the seat opposite him, wincing as it scraped against the floor, and flopped down.

Alf ran over to her, putting his head in her lap. It took every ounce of her strength to stroke his head.

'Are you up to a coffee?'

'I'll give it a try.'

'So you're not quite ready for a chocolate martini yet then?'

Livvie's stomach heaved. 'Don't. I'm never drinking ever again.'

'Ah, famous last words.' He went to the coffee machine and set it away, pulsing the rich aroma of coffee beans around the kitchen.

Livvie couldn't remember getting home last night. She didn't even remember leaving the tea shop, but she had an overwhelming feeling she'd had a great time. A vague memory of doing the conga crept into her mind, as did Molly laughing at things her mum was saying. She knew they'd had a good dance a couple of times, and she recalled singing along at the top of her voice, which probably explained why she felt like she'd been gargling with gravel this morning.

'Freda came last night. It was lovely so see her. She looked like she was really enjoying herself, bless her.'

Zander set a mug of coffee down in front of her. 'I know, you told me all about it. You were very chatty when you got back.'

'I was?'

'You were.' His mouth twitched with amusement.

Livvie blew across her mug and took a sip. She caught his eye and paused. 'I did something last night, didn't I?'

He was struggling not to smile. 'Let's just say you were very entertaining.'

Livvie covered her eyes with her hand and groaned. 'Oh, no. What did I do?'

'Are you saying you don't remember the lap-dance followed by the striptease you treated me to? Shame, they were pretty unforgettable.'

She eyed him warily. 'No. You're winding me up.' She couldn't remember a thing about it.

'I'm not. Ask Alf, he was mortified when your knickers landed on his head.'

Livvie's giggle quickly morphed into a wince. 'Ouch! Don't make me laugh, it hurts my head.'

'Sorry, I'll do my best not to.' He took a sip of his coffee, amusement dancing in his eyes.

Livvie scrunched her face up. 'Go on then, put me out of my misery, tell me all.'

'You were adorable actually.'

'Why do I doubt that?'

∽

AT JUST BEFORE one in the morning, Livvie landed home, staggering up the garden path slightly worse for wear, Molly under one arm, Camm under the other. Zander was stretched out on the sofa watching an action film when she stumbled through the door, a happy smile on her face, her deely-boppers skew-whiff.

'We've had a brilliant time, but she's jiggered,' Molly said, slurring her words slightly. 'Oh, and it might be wise to have a glass of water and a sick bucket by the bed, just in case.'

'Oh, right, okay. Well, thanks for the heads up and for bringing her home. I'll see you tomorrow, Camm, we'll pick you up around six-thirty.'

'Looking forward to it.' Camm winked, grinning as he left.

When their friends had gone, Livvie insisted she wasn't ready for bed and the pair headed to the living room where she proceeded to give Zander an animated run down of the evening. 'It was the best night ever. We had chocolate martinis, chocolate truffles – I must tell you what Molly said, she was so funny. But best of all Freda was there.'

'I'm pleased you had a good time, sounds like the girls put a lot of thought into it.'

Before he knew what was happening Livvie had straddled his lap and was peeling her chocolate-spattered t-shirt over her head. 'How do you fancy a lap-dance, big boy?' She ran a finger down the side of his face and hiccupped.

Zander pressed his lips together, doing his best not to laugh at the chocolate smears on her face. She hiccupped again.

'I'm gonna give you a treat you'll never forget.' Grinding down on him, she pouted exaggeratedly before pushing her boobs together in her lacy bra. 'What do you think of these bad boys, eh? You don't get many of these to the pound, you know.'

Before Zander could answer, she'd fallen off his knee and onto the floor with a thud. 'Are you okay down there?' he asked.

'S'okay, I'm fine.' She pulled herself up and, fumblingly, undid the top button of her skinny jeans, wiggling her bottom in his face as she unzipped them, pushing them down to her knees, humming some "raunchy" music as she did so. Zander covered his mouth with his hand in an attempt to hide his smile.

Livvie turned and looked at him, licking her lips suggestively as she struggled to get her jeans over her ankles. Zander spluttered with laughter but disguised it as a cough as she hopped around the room trying to yank her jeans off her feet. Eventually she succeeded and stood, swaying in front of him in her knickers and bra and a pair of striped socks. She bent and pulled her socks off, running one across Zander's face before hurling it across the room, hiccupping noisily as she did so. Next was her bra which she removed after a brief wrestle. 'Don't move, I'm nearly ready,' she said, before flinging it behind her, where it landed on a table lamp. 'Ta-dah!' She jiggled her boobs in his face, sending her off balance and falling into him. 'Oops.' Undeterred, she pushed herself up and started humming the "raunchy" tune again, punctuated with yet more hiccups.

All the while, Zander had been struggling to hold back his laughter; his shoulders were shaking and tears of mirth were pooling in his eyes.

Precariously, Livvie stepped out of her lacy knickers and flung them flamboyantly behind her where they landed on Alf's head. The Labrador yelped in shock and ran off to watch proceedings from a safe distance. Unable to contain his amusement a moment longer, Zander roared with laughter until Livvie hiccupped and shot him a dirty look, making him clamp his hand over his mouth.

She flopped down on the sofa, declared herself tired and rested her head on his shoulder. She was asleep within seconds.

LIVVIE GROANED, pressing her hand to her forehead. 'I can't believe I did that. You must've been thinking what a sophisticated, stylish woman you're about to marry.'

'The funniest part was when Alf jumped out of his skin when your knickers landed on his head. It was hilarious.'

Livvie couldn't help but giggle at that. 'Sorry, Alf, I'll make it up to you.' She risked glancing across at Zander. 'And you can get your own back tonight, but please, not with a lap-dance.'

He chuckled. 'I'm afraid I can't make any promises.'

'Well, I don't think Alf could take any more; he'll be packing his bags and moving in with Rhoda.'

'Right.' Zander clapped his hands together and got to his feet. 'How do you fancy my hangover cure in the shape of a mouth-watering fry-up.'

Livvie's stomach growled. 'That sounds surprisingly good.'

53

TWO DAYS BEFORE THE WEDDING

THE WEEK and a half since the hen night had passed in a blur. Zander had enjoyed his stag night celebrations and had returned home merry. He'd jokingly asked Livvie if she'd like him to return the favour of performing a strip-tease or a lap-dance.

'I think one of us making a turkey of themselves this weekend is enough, don't you?' she'd said, laughing.

'Well, I thought your performance was magnificent.'

'Yeah, not sure that's the right word for it.'

Though everything to do with the wedding was organised, Livvie was still relieved that Romantique had closed its doors at the weekend and wouldn't reopen until the New Year. Much as she adored working there, she welcomed the break and time to catch her breath.

After much groundwork on her part, and since sending the impromptu text, Livvie found that relations with her mum had improved. Though her mother's words and attitude stung, Livvie was keen for the wedding to run smoothly and had bitten her tongue whenever Delia made her usual negative remarks, either about Zander, the wedding or Rhoda. She was pleased to see her tactics appeared to have worked. And, though she was eager to keep her mother happy, one thing Livvie had stood firm on was the matter of Rhoda being at the wedding. There was no way was she going to let her mother dictate about that. Livvie wanted Rhoda there whether her mother liked it or not. Realising when she was beat, Delia had surprised her and agreed to come, though there was more than a hint of reluctance in her voice. Nevertheless, her decision had been a massive weight off Livvie's shoulders.

'Thank you, Mum, I understand why it's difficult for you, and it means a lot that you're going to be there.'

'Hmph. Just don't expect me to have much to do with the woman or become friends with her,' Delia had said.

'Don't worry, I won't.' Livvie couldn't ever imagine that happening, but getting along with her mother like this was a whole lot easier than the usual unpleasant dynamics she had to navigate.

Cheryl had surprised her too, apparently relinquishing her role as chief bossy-boots, and backing down over Gavin giving her away and her being matron of honour; it was probably made so much easier because, ultimately, neither of them wanted to do it. And, after much persuasion from Livvie, she'd finally taken on board that her little sister was more than capable of organising her own wedding and didn't need her "guidance" as Cheryl had referred to it – Livvie thought that too mild a word but kept it to herself.

LIVVIE WAS SITTING at the kitchen table, doodling absent-mindedly on her wedding list. Christmas carols were playing merrily in the background, a festive-scented candle was burning in the window and she had mug of freshly-made tea beside her. Alf was asleep, his paws and ears twitching as he dreamed, making her smile. From the look of her list, everything seemed to be in order. But there were two things that gave Livvie cause for concern.

The first one was the lack of communication she'd had with Bryony. Last she'd heard, Bryony's grandmother had taken poorly and her friend had been in two minds as to whether or not to fly back from Australia early. Livvie had sent her several text messages but there'd been no reply to date. She'd thought about emailing, but Bry was terrible at replying to those. Feeling a sudden pang of concern for her friend, Livvie picked up her phone and fired off a breezy text, saying she hoped all was okay and how she couldn't believe the wedding was only days away. That would put the ball in Bryony's court without putting pressure on her and also let her know she was thinking of her. If her grandmother was really poorly, Livvie didn't want to add to her friend's stress.

The second thing to worry her was something with far bigger implications: the weather, or as she'd come to refer to it, the "flipping" weather. The temperature had plummeted over the last few days and the forecasters had been issuing weather warnings with threats of a wave of arctic conditions moving over the UK within the next few days. Livvie hoped with all her might that it would hang on until after the wedding. The only place they were going the day after that was home, having decided to postpone their honeymoon until later in the New Year, so the weather could do what it pleased then.

The room suddenly got darker and she glanced out of the window to see the sky covered in thick foreboding clouds, snowflakes spilling silently from the sky. 'Uh-oh. Please don't do this.'

54

THE DAY OF THE WEDDING

THE FIRST THING Livvie did when she opened her eyes was to clamber out of bed and make a dash for the window. She pushed her head through the curtains and breathed a sigh of relief to see the level of snow on the window sill had hardly changed; there'd been very little fresh snow overnight. Excitement quickly replaced relief; the day she and Zander were getting married had finally arrived. She pressed her hands to her face and gave a little squeal of happiness.

She checked the alarm clock to see it was only just gone six; a while before she needed to be up. But there was no chance she'd get back to sleep. Her mind was already filling with the preparations for the day, excitement thrumming through her. And, besides, there was no Zander to snuggle into since he'd spent the night at Kitty and Jimby's. It had been odd sleeping without him but she'd pulled his pillow close to her and had eventually drifted off in the early hours. She must've only managed about four hours' sleep but adrenalin had kicked in as soon as she sat up and now she felt wide awake.

As she sat on the edge of the bed the water-pipes creaked, signalling the central heating starting up. Livvie slipped her dressing gown on, pushed her feet into her slippers and headed downstairs.

'Hi, Alfie boy, did you sleep okay?' she asked when she reached the kitchen.

Alf yawned and stretched, wagging his tail sleepily.

'I know it's early but we've got a busy day ahead of us so we need to get cracking. But first, a cup of tea.'

She filled the kettle and went to check her list on the table; it sent a ripple of excitement up her spine. She'd made a separate one especially for today, listing every stage up to leaving the house for the castle. She wanted everything to run without a hitch.

Rosie was booked to arrive at nine to do Livvie's hair and makeup before heading back down to the village to do Noushka's and the other bridesmaids; they'd had to alter plans slightly to accommodate the unpredictable weather and, as far as Livvie was concerned, that was fine. Initially, all of the bridesmaids were meant to gather at Dale View Cottage to get their hair done and get ready, with Noushka being around to give Livvie a hand with her dress if needs be. But seeing the change in the weather, they all agreed it would be best if the bridesmaids stayed in the village, having less roads to tackle if conditions changed for the worse. Again, Livvie was fine with this, there was no way she was going to let such small tweaks to her list spoil the day. She wasn't a diva, she didn't mind getting herself dressed and, after all, any adjustments to her veil could be made once she arrived at the castle. Calm and collected was the order of the day; she knew Camm would get her there.

The previous evening, she'd popped up to Danskelfe Castle with Annie and Molly. She'd gasped when she'd seen the floral arrangements; they were beyond her wildest dreams. 'Oh, Annie, they're absolutely stunning, thank you.' She'd wiped a tear from her eye before kissing Annie on the cheek.

'I'm just thrilled you like them, lovey. I've had a ball doing them,' Annie said, her face animated.

Steff, John and the kids had arrived while she was up there and Livvie had her first glimpse of the cake, or rather, the components of it; it wouldn't be fully constructed until it was in situ the following day. But, all the same, the various parts looked fantastic. 'It's mostly Annabel's work,' Steff had said.

'Wowzers, Annabel, you're super-talented. You could make a career out of this,' Livvie had said, making the young girl blush with pride.

Livvie had declined all offers of having anyone stay over-night at the cottage to keep her company, instead she found the idea of having a quiet night, just her and Alf, appealing. It had turned out to be a chilled and peaceful evening; just how she wanted it.

Pre-wedding jitters had taken the edge off her appetite so she'd had a light supper of scrambled eggs on toast, washed down with a mug of tea and followed by a languorous soak in the bath. 'Here's where it all began,' she'd said, laughing to herself as she blew a cluster of bubbles off her hand, reliving the moment when she and Zander had first set eyes on one another.

The last thing she'd seen before turning out the bedside light was a text from him telling her he loved her, making her heart swell with happiness.

Everything seemed to be fitting together nicely, even taking into account their newly-amended schedule.

The wedding wasn't until twelve-thirty and though she didn't feel the least bit hungry, Livvie fixed herself some toast and marmalade. The last thing she wanted was to keel over in the middle of their wedding vows through lack of food.

Just after seven her mobile phone pinged with a text from Zander, her heart leaping when she saw his name.

> *Can't wait to make you Mrs Gillespie.*
> *Love you with all my heart.*
> *Z x*
> *P.S. Hope Alf's behaved himself!*

Livvie read the text, her eyes brimming with tears as she read the first part, laughing at the post script. She fired one straight back.

> *Can't wait to become Mrs Gillespie!*
> *Love you more than I could ever say.*
> *Alf's been a very good lad!*
> *L xxx*

She'd added a flourish of heart-shaped and wedding-themed emojis at the end which she knew would make him smile.

There was one thought that kept skirting around her happiness, one that she was afraid to let in because she knew it would affect her deeply once she started to dwell on it. Her dad. Her wonderful dad. He was going to be so conspicuous by his absence she simply couldn't bear to think about it. She'd shed a few tears for him a couple of days ago and her heart had ached so badly. She didn't want to go there again today. Today was all about being happy, which is exactly what her dad would have wanted.

'Love you, Dad.' She blew a kiss heavenwards, blinking quickly to chase away the threat of tears.

55

LIVVIE HAD JUST FINISHED in the shower when she heard Rosie pull-up in her four-wheel drive. She ran downstairs and opened the front door, an icy-cold wall of air hitting her. 'Brrr! Hiya, Rosie. Noushka, I wasn't expecting to see you but I'm so happy you're here. Come on in out of the cold, it's bloomin' freezing. Beep-beep, out of the way, Alf.' Excitement had got her feeling giddy. Alf stepped back, picking up on the vibes, prancing back and forth as the two women entered the house.

'Happy wedding day, chick.' Rosie bustled into the hallway with her box of tricks, a beaming smile on her face. 'I know last time we spoke we'd planned on Noushka having her hair and make-up done with the younger ones back in the village, but I thought it would be nice for you to get your hair and make-up done with a bit of company.'

'I'm so happy you did that.' She felt a swell of joy in her chest.

'Yay! Happy wedding day, Livvie,' said Noushka; she was wearing a smile to match Rosie's. She had her hands full too.

'Hiya, gorgeous girl, thank you so much for coming.' Livvie stood on her tiptoes and kissed Noushka's cheek. 'I swear you get taller every time I see you.'

Noushka giggled. 'Hey, I wouldn't miss getting ready with you for the world. And I thought you might like a cheeky sip of this.' She pulled a bottle of Prosecco out of the bag she was holding. 'According to Vi, it's absolutely imperative a bride has a glass of bubbles while she's getting ready for her wedding. And Vi's always right about these things.'

'I totally agree with you on both those counts but it's nine o'clock in the morning. I'm not sure my stomach's ready for that just yet,' Livvie said, giggling. 'How about we wait till we're all done, then we can crack it open?'

'Sounds like a good plan. It does seem a bit early to me, I've only just had my porridge,' said Rosie, as she headed into the kitchen.

'Hadn't actually thought of the time,' Noushka said, wrinkling her nose.

The three women spent the next hour and a half chatting and laughing, happiness bubbling up in the air around them. By the time they were done, Livvie was feeling light-headed with excitement.

'You look gorgeous, Livvie,' Noushka said, her eyes shining. 'Your hair's amazing, and the way Rosie's done your eye make-up is subtle but stunning; it really emphasizes the colour of your eyes.'

'Thank you, chick, you look absolutely gorgeous as you always do. Rosie, you've done a great job, thank you so much.'

'It's been a pleasure, hon,' Rosie said warmly, squeezing Livvie's arm.

'Right, time for that Prosecco.' Noushka leapt to her feet and dashed to the fridge. 'Anyone any good at opening these things?' she asked, frowning at the cork.

'Yep, give it here,' said Rosie. Squinting, she eased the cork and it shot off into the hallway with a resounding pop, making Alf bark and the women squeal with laughter.

'I can only have a couple of sips because I'm driving, but that's fine,' said Rosie when the three were armed with flutes filled with sparkling fizz. She held her glass aloft. 'To Livvie and Zander, have an amazing wedding day.'

'Here, here. Have a totally amazing day. You make a perfect couple,' said Noushka, a wide smile spreading across her pretty face.

'Thank you both so much. I've had the best morning and I really appreciate you coming up here, you've certainly cranked up my excitement levels which I think will be pretty much stratospheric by the time I've finished this glass of Prosecco.'

'Which is just how it should be on your wedding day,' said Rosie as they chinked glasses, beaming at one another.

56

Not long after Rosie and Noushka had left the snow started. Just light at first, but it wasn't long before it was falling in huge, feathery snowflakes, swirling down and obscuring the view of the sky. Livvie looked out of the window in disbelief. 'Couldn't you have waited?' She puffed out her cheeks and sighed. 'What's going on with this silly old weather, Alf?' She bent and ruffled the Labrador's ears. 'Oh, well, how about we get you fitted with your wedding bow-tie?'

Alf sat to attention, pressing his paw against her leg, the eager expression on his face making her smile. 'Now, sit nice and still while we get this done, okay? None of that wriggling about you do when you're feeling mischievous.' She was pleased to see he did as he was bid and tickled his chin once she was done. 'There you are, you look very dapper. All the lady doggies will be wondering who the tall, dark and handsome boy is.' He trotted about the room, pleased with himself.

Worrying about the snow was setting Livvie on edge; she'd seen the forecast on the TV last night and hadn't wanted to dwell on it but the speed at which the flakes were falling meant she couldn't help it. Zander would be worried too. She'd spent the last twenty minutes gazing out of the window, watching it fall thicker and faster. A spike of anxiety shot through her as she wondered how the wedding car was going to get to the cottage, never mind to the castle – the road leading up to it was notoriously bad and liable to deep snow drifts. *What exactly made me think having a winter wedding was a good idea?* She glanced over in the direction of Withrin Hill Farm which was barely visible so dense was the blizzard, wondering if Camm had been out ploughing the roads, doubting it a second later; he'd be getting ready for the wedding himself. Thoughts segued to her bridesmaids; were they at Rosie's beauty room? Had Annabel managed to join them? Had they finished getting ready? What was the snow like in the village? Jeez, all this worrying was setting her nerves on edge and putting her mind in a turmoil. Did all brides have this much stress on their wedding day?

She checked her phone to see if she'd heard anything from anyone but there'd been no more since the slew of upbeat texts wishing her well first thing. Her eyes caught the time. Eleven fifteen; her stomach flipped, it was time to get dressed. With a deep breath, Livvie made her way up to the bedroom; she'd worry about the weather afterwards.

Slipping the cover off her gown she hung it on the back of the door, the sight of it sending a thrill rippling through her.

Carefully, she lifted her delicate wedding-day underwear out of the tissue it had been wrapped in. The matching bra and knickers were exquisite, made from silk and vintage-style lace in a rich shade of clotted-cream, trimmed with tiny bows and pearls. They complemented the lacy-topped stockings she'd bought for the occasion. She felt special as soon as she put them on.

Next, she eased her dress off its padded hanger and carefully stepped into it, the sumptuous fabric rustling against her skin. Pulling up the hidden zip in the back proved tricky without an extra pair of hands, but she finally managed and made her way over to the full-length mirror.

She gasped at the reflection looking back at her. Rosie had made her look like a glossy, shiny version of herself. Her auburn hair had been tamed into rich, sleek waves, pulled back at the sides, while her skin was glowing and dewy. Noushka had been right about her make-up, it really did emphasise the colour of her eyes.

She was overjoyed with her dress, which had been cut to flatter the curves that Zander loved so much – she was proud of them and there was no way she was going to disguise them for her wedding. It was made of cream raw-silk with a loose-weave lace over the top, lending it a boho vibe. The V-neck was perfect for Livvie's ample bosom without revealing too much cleavage, while the floor-length skirt gently flared from the waist. The bishop-style sleeves were made of lace, and the deep silk cuffs were trimmed with matching covered buttons. Thousands of tiny pearls and crystals had been painstakingly sewn onto the fabric; it had been time-consuming but worth it. They glittered prettily in the light of the bedroom.

Once she'd put in the tiny snowflake diamanté earrings Annie had given her as her "something old" and put on her diamond drop necklace, she slipped her feet into her shoes. They were made of butter-soft cream leather that fastened around the ankle, edged with tiny silvery-gold beads. Their two inch heel meant they'd be comfortable to wear for the long day ahead.

Livvie was just fastening them when the landline rang, pulling her out of her musings. She jumped up and hurried downstairs, her heart thumping. 'Hello.'

'Livvie, it's Camm. I assume you've seen the weather?' His voice had an urgency to it that set her stomach jittering.

'I have, it's not good. What are we going to do?'

'Look, I'll be honest with you, the roads to the village are dicey; there's no way the wedding cars will be able to get from Middleton-le-Moors to Lytell Stangdale, never mind tackle the roads up to your cottage. And I don't have time to plough all the way to the main road to the moors and get back to you.'

'Of course, I appreciate you ploughing any at all. But what can we do?' It wasn't really a surprise to hear about the wedding cars but Livvie couldn't help but feel disappointed. If they couldn't get here, then more than likely, the guests that lived further afield would struggle. Bryony's face flashed through her mind; she still hadn't heard from her friend. *Why did it have to snow like this today of all days?*

'I'm afraid there's nothing for it but for me to come for you in the tractor with the snow plough attached to it. We'll get to the castle in that, no problem. I've already ploughed the road leading to it and Ollie's set off with Kitty, Lucas and the bridesmaids from the village, so they should be there now. Jimby's taking Zander as you know, as well as Rhoda and anyone else who wants to squeeze into his Landie.'

'Okay, that sounds good.'

'Yep, and Ben's just set off with Molly, Emmie and Moll's parents in our Landie. And, unless you've got any objections, I'm going to set off for you now.'

Livvie felt a cocktail of nerves and excitement swirling round inside her. 'That's great. I'll make sure I'm ready.'

'You might need to put a coat and your wellies on, just in case.'

'Right, yes.' *Wellies? Just in case? Oh flippin' heck!* 'Thanks, Camm, see you soon.' She groaned inside. Nowhere in her wildest dreams did she imagine she'd arrive at her wedding wearing a pair of wellies.

She turned to Alf who'd been watching, wondering what was happening. 'Oh, well, Alf, if that's what it has to be…' With that, she dashed upstairs to finish getting ready.

Ten minutes later Livvie was downstairs looking out for Camm. She'd managed to fix her veil with the tiara to her head as best she could; she'd get Rosie to adjust it when she got to the castle, if she could find her. It felt odd to be wearing her wedding dress underneath her heavy wool coat, her clumpy green wellies on her feet. She glanced down at her hands for the umpteenth time to make sure she was still holding onto the bag containing her shoes. It would be a disaster to forget those. She was clenching her bouquet tightly in her other hand. She'd tried texting people but the signal was down. Rather than worry about the situation, Livvie had decided to go with the flow, stressing and fretting wasn't going to help anything and she wanted to enjoy today.

Her heart leapt as she spotted the tractor as it approached the cottage. She called for Alf. 'Come on, lad, time to go.'

57

Outside, winter was well and truly baring its teeth; the wind was howling, driving snow at them unrelentingly. Livvie was thankful she'd tucked her veil down the back of her coat; she had visions of it flying off down the dale, lost forever.

'Mind how you go, that wind's strong enough to blow you off your feet,' said Camm linking his arm through hers and guiding her down the path.

'Oh my God, I can't believe how cold it is,' said Livvie as she climbed into the cabin of the tractor, glad to be out of the wind; her cheeks were stinging with the cold.

Soon they were heading down the lane and onto the road leading to the castle. It was a tight fit with Alf in there too, but Livvie didn't care, she was just glad to be on her way.

Camm drove calmly and carefully, pushing through the snow-drifts effortlessly as she took in the wintry scene around them. He was concentrating hard and she didn't like to distract him so she sat quietly, looking out at the moors that had vanished beneath a thick eiderdown of snow.

Soon they were heading through the castle gates and she could feel her heart rate up its speed. Camm climbed down from the cab and ran round to help her out. She was pleased to see the courtyard had been gritted and was snow free albeit for a few slushy piles around the edges. She was making her way towards the entrance, holding her dress up and feeling ungainly in her wellies, when Caro opened the door and Mr Tubbs shot out. He and Alf were friends of old and after an initial sniff of one another, they started leaping about, snapping giddily at the snow. Out of nowhere Livvie felt herself being propelled sideways as the Labradors collided with her. 'Arghh!'

'Alf! Stop!' She heard Camm call out her name and saw Caro's look of horror as Livvie landed in a pile of slush.

'My dress,' she said, gasping in disbelief as she felt herself being pulled back to her feet. From the corner of her eye she saw someone retrieve her bouquet and give it a shake.

'Thank goodness the flowers are okay.' If Livvie wasn't mistaken, the owner of the voice was Lady Davinia.

'Oh, my goodness! Are you okay, darling?' Caro appeared beside her looking concerned. 'Are you hurt anywhere?'

Livvie shook her head; if she was hurt, she was sure shock would have numbed it. She could barely speak, all she could think about were the huge dirty stains that covered the skirt of her beautiful gown. 'My dress … it's ruined.' Tears swam in her eyes. How could she get married in it now?

'Come with me, we'll get you cleaned up, it'll be as right as rain. My mother's a whizz at getting stains out. And you're early so time's on our side,' said Caro kindly, taking her by the hand.

Livvie felt herself being swept into the castle, a sea of chattering voices in her ears.

Once inside, she was whisked off to a large, private kitchen where Caro and her mother assessed the damage. Livvie looked on, fighting back tears for fear of ruining her make-up too.

Lady Davinia pressed her hand to her chin. 'Hmm, I'll try with soap and water first, see how we get on with that.'

'Do you think it'll come out?' Livvie asked.

'I'll give it a jolly good try.' Lady Davinia smiled kindly at her, showing a very different side to her personality.

Fifteen minutes and several methods later, the vast stains were showing no signs of disappearing. Livvie felt her panic levels rising, making her feel nauseous. 'What am I going to do? I can't wear this, I look a mess.' Her voice cracked and a plump tear ran down her cheek.

'Oh, my darling girl, don't cry.' Lady Davinia looked distraught for her.

'Is there nothing we can do, Mother?' asked Caro.

'Actually, I think there is. Follow me.'

58

LADY DAVINIA TOOK Livvie's hand and strode out of the room. 'Caro, you go and find Livvie's friends; we need them to fix-up her make-up. Meet us in the Blue Room, quick as you can.'

'The Blue Room?' Caro frowned. 'But there's only … oh!' Her eyebrows arched as she shot off down the hall.

Livvie's mind was too much of a blur to comprehend what was going on; it was only when they arrived at the Blue Room and Lady Davinia pressed the security code into key-pad of the glass case of the display that it slowly began to dawn on her. Her hand flew to her mouth. 'Surely, you don't mean…?'

'I surely do, my dear.' Davinia removed the arms from the mannequin and started to manoeuvre the dress carefully over its head. 'Well, that was easier than I expected.'

'But, I can't … what if it doesn't fit?'

'Oh, I think it'll fit perfectly. Actually…' Lady Davinia looked from the mannequin to Livvie, '…your tiara looks remarkably similar to the one here.'

'It's the original,' Livvie said hesitantly, touching it with her hand. 'Freda, or rather, Lady Phaedra lent it to me.' She hoped her revelation wasn't going to cause trouble for her friend.

Lady Davinia digested the information, her eyes fixed to Freda's tiara. 'Well, that settles it as far as I'm concerned. You absolutely must wear this gown, the two are meant to be worn together.'

'Found them.' Caro burst into the room followed by Livvie's

friends all dressed up in their wedding finery, their faces etched with concern. They bustled over to her, asking if she was okay and what they could do to help.

'I'm fine but my dress is ruined, look.'

Four sets of eyes took in the damage. 'Oh, flower,' said Kitty.

Once they'd recovered from the initial shock, Rosie was the first to speak. 'Right, come and sit over here while I fix your make-up.'

Livvie sat down and her friends chatted away, doing their best to lighten her mood.

'There, good as new. I'll fit the tiara and veil as soon as you've got changed.' Rosie gave one last sweep of the highlighter brush and stood back to admire her handiwork.

'Thank you, Rosie, you're a life saver.' Livvie smiled though anxiety still fizzed inside her.

'Now, my dear, it's time to get this dress on.' Lady Davinia guided her to a side-room, carrying the gown across her arms.

'Oh, gosh, I feel nervous.' Livvie pressed her hand to her chest.

'Don't be, I promise you you're going to look every inch the goddess Zander says you are when you walk towards him,' Vi said sincerely.

'You might want to lose the wellies though, chick. They're not screaming "goddess" to me, more like "farm-yakker",' said Molly making them all fall about in a fit of the giggles, even Lady Davinia.

'Oops, I'd forgotten about those.' Livvie heeled them off, then took the dress from Lady Davinia. 'Are you absolutely sure about this?'

'I couldn't be more sure of anything.'

There was a collective gasp when Livvie returned to the room. The feather-light fabric felt exquisite against her skin. Her cheeks flamed and she cast her eyes down self-consciously.

'Oh, you look absolutely stunning, darling.' Caro smiled, wiping a tear from the corner of her eye. 'Mother, you're an absolute genius.'

'Can I have that it writing, Caro?' Lady Davinia's mouth quirked into a smile.

'You look absolutely gorgeous, petal. That dress could've been made for you,' said Kitty, her face glowing with happiness.

'It could; I think Great Aunt Veronica was a little taller than you but you're pretty much built the same.'

'It feels a little snug around the bottom, but not uncomfortably so.' Livvie caught sight of herself in the mirror. She loved her wedding dress, but Lady Veronica's gown was out of this world, the plunging neckline, mirrored at the back, was cut to be perfectly tasteful and not at all revealing.

Caro peered around Livvie. 'Oh, darling, it actually makes your backside look fabulous.'

'No one's ever said that to me before.' Livvie chuckled.

After a quick check over of the fit by Kitty and Vi, Rosie fixed the tiara and veil. Livvie slipped her shoes on, thankful she hadn't forgotten them.

'You're an absolute vision, chick, but we'd better get to our seats or we'll be in trouble for holding things up,' said Vi.'

'Happy wedding day, beautiful.' Kitty gave her shoulder a squeeze.

'Yep, see you on the other side.' Molly leaned in and whispered, 'Lady D's redeemed herself big time.' She gave Livvie a grin before heading into the hall in search of her family.

59

LIVVIE STOOD beside Camm at the entrance of the Great Hall, her heart fluttering wildly in her chest. With Lady Davinia and her friends coming to her rescue she was at last free to take in the splendour of her surroundings. The floral displays were striking in their rich, festive colours. Annie had done a wonderful job. A thick conifer garland with echoes of Livvie's bouquet, decorated with deep-red roses had been wrapped around the bannister of the large staircase. Rich red voile ribbon had been woven through it and it had been trimmed with matching baubles, sprigs of eucalyptus, trailing ivy and fir cones. Warm white fairy lights twinkled amongst the foliage. It was quite the statement piece. Above the doorway to the hall was a matching swag while large floral displays in ancient pewter pots filled the mullioned windows. All the while, the scent of Christmas filled the air.

Noushka and the gaggle of bridesmaids stood patiently behind them looking wonderful in their claret-coloured silk bridesmaid's dresses, each one a little different, festive-themed flowers in their hair and hands. It was warm inside the castle and they'd dispensed with their white faux-fur shrugs with diamanté clasps for the moment.

'Ready?' Camm offered Livvie his arm, his smile crinkling the corners of his eyes.

She took a deep breath and adjusted her hold on the bouquet, its winter-green and dark-red roses matching the rest of the floral decorations. 'Ready,' she said, returning his smile as butterflies took flight in her stomach.

The music struck up and Livvie made her way towards Zander at the other end of the hall where a fire crackled in the enormous inglenook and fairy lights glowed on the mantelpiece. With Jimby standing to his right, he had his hands clasped in front of him, his shoulders shaking with laughter at something Jimby was saying in his ear. Like Camm, the pair looked smart in their petrol-blue suits with floral ties and pocket handkerchiefs. Alf sat beside him, panting, waiting patiently. After a moment, Zander turned around. His wide smile morphed to a look of awe as he watched her walk towards him, her dress shimmering with her every step. "Wow!" he said, mouthing the word. Her happiness soared right up to the ancient rafters; Livvie couldn't have smiled any wider if she'd tried.

AFTER THE CEREMONY, the guests were milling around sipping Prosecco and chatting away, laughter and Christmas music filling the air. Livvie was talking to Zander's cousin, Beth, when she sensed someone standing beside her. She turned, her eyes widening in surprise. 'Freda! You came.' She bent and hugged her friend.

'I couldn't miss your special day.'

'Well, it's extra special now you're here.'

Freda smiled shyly. 'And you look lovely in that dress, it's only right you wear it with the tiara; they're meant to be together.' She looked at Livvie for a moment. 'Funny how things turn out, isn't it?'

'You heard what happened?'

'Aye, lass, we all did, but I'd recognise that gown anywhere. And you look absolutely beautiful in it. I'm thrilled to think it's come to your rescue.'

'That makes me so happy, thank you, Freda. And I feel very honoured to wear it.'

'Do you ever think that things happen for a reason? That fate has a hand in the things we do?' Freda asked, tipping her head to one side.

'Always,' Livvie said with conviction.

'Livvie, can I have a word? Hi, Aunt Phaedra, you look lovely.' Caro appeared beside them.

'Of course,' said Livvie. 'S'cuse me a minute, Freda.'

'It's a couple of things, both weather-related, which probably doesn't come as a surprise.'

'Er, not really, no.' Livvie felt her spirits sink a little.

'It's nothing serious, or at least nothing that can't be fixed. Firstly, I think having photos taken outside is going to be impossible. The snow hasn't stopped, it's bitterly cold and—'

'And I wouldn't dare go outside in this dress after what happened earlier.'

'Yes, quite, but that's not what I was going to say.'

'Oh?'

'I'm afraid the photographer couldn't get here.'

'Ah.'

'And neither could the band or the DJ.'

None of this news came as a surprise to Livvie, but it was still disappointing.

'But all's not lost. I'm a keen amateur photographer and, if you'll let me, I'm more than happy to take some informal photos – I always think they work rather well. Of course, I can take some posed ones too.'

'I'm happy to go with that.' In Livvie's mind, it was better than having no photographs to remind her and Zander of their wedding day.

'And as far as music for the disco's concerned, we can just swap the current Christmassy playlist for dance music and, here's the best bit, how do you fancy having Gabe Dublin stand in for the band?'

'What? Are you serious? Gabe Dublin singing here? Tonight?' She looked at Caro, her eyes wide with disbelief.

Caro nodded, giggling at Livvie's reaction. 'Yes, yes and yes.'

'How? Why? What?' she asked, suddenly feeling giddy again.

Gabe Dublin was a world-famous musician who was a friend of Caro's sound engineer husband, Sim. 'It's a long story but, basically, he's split up with his girlfriend which has caused quite a stir amongst the paparazzi, so he's hiding out here until things calm down a bit.'

Livvie was aware of the split, it had been splashed all over social media. Surely he'd be too upset to perform for their wedding? 'Oh, right, but are you sure he wouldn't mind playing for us?'

'He said he'd love to; it'll help take his mind of it and it's better than being stuck in a room listening to everyone having a good time.'

Livvie couldn't argue with that. 'Wait till I tell Zander.'

THE RECEPTION HALL WAS STUNNING. A huge Christmas tree stood at one end, festooned with hundreds of fairy-lights and shiny plum-coloured baubles and topped off with a dramatic angel. The tables were covered with crisp white cloths, with deep-red runners down the centre, set with antique-gold candelabras and mercuried tea-lights. Gold, sparkly wedding confetti was sprinkled liberally over the cloth. The floral theme continued in the room, with a vast centre-piece on the main table, and smaller versions on the other tables. Place names were in a gift-tag style and decorated with pine cones and sprigs of fir tree, the names written on by Molly in a cursive hand. The wedding favours were Christmas crackers containing handmade chocolates made by Becca from the Chocolate Cherub. 'Let's hope they don't look anything like our efforts at your hen party,' Molly had said with a dirty laugh.

The wedding cake – or rather, cakes – was set on a huge cake stand. On top was a traditional top-tier-sized cake with ivory-coloured icing and a matching trim of lace at the base. Atop, three roses made from royal icing in subtle shades of peach were clustered together; they looked convincingly real. Beneath that were tiers of plates, increasing in size and filled with cupcakes. Some of the cupcakes were decorated with smaller versions of the peach roses, some with small ivory-coloured flowers with tiny petals, others with large peach roses that covered the whole cup-cake. The whole effect was jaw-dropping.

It had been agreed to get speeches over and done with as quickly as possible so everyone could get on with the task of enjoying themselves.

Camm, standing in for Livvie's father, gave a brief but warm speech describing how he and Molly had first got to know her. 'I'd like to thank you from the bottom of my heart for asking me to give you away, Livvie. It's been an honour.' His words brought a tear to Livvie's eye and once he'd sat down, she kissed him on the cheek.

'Thank you, Camm, there's no one else I'd rather have do it.'

Next up was Zander, fiddling with the pages of his speech. 'I'll never forget the first time I set eyes on Livvie...' Livvie clapped her hand over her eyes and winced; she knew what was coming. '...I thought she was the most beautiful woman I'd ever seen.'

A collective 'ahh', went round the room and Livvie felt herself blush furiously.

'I know it sounds soppy, but it's true. And the fact that Alf here wouldn't leave her side told me she was a keeper, isn't that right, fella?' Alf looked up from his place by the Christmas tree where he'd been investigating the fake presents. His tail thudded against the carpet. 'But seriously, folks, joking aside – and I'll apologise in advance for getting mushy on you – don't let anyone tell you there's no such thing as love at first sight, because they're wrong. Completely and utterly. I fell in love with Livvie the minute I clapped eyes on her – I should probably point out it had absolutely nothing to do with the fact that she was naked – that was a bonus. I just knew, in that moment she was "the one". And the more I got to know her, I just fell deeper and deeper. And, just when I think it would be impossible to love her any more than I already do, she goes and does something that makes me fall a little bit deeper again.'

Oh, Zander!

By the time Zander had finished his speech there wasn't a dry eye in the house and Livvie was frantically dabbing her eyes with a crumpled tissue. 'Thank you,' she said with a sniff when he sat back down.

'I meant every word but I didn't mean to make you cry.' He turned her face towards him and kissed her gently on the lips, resulting in another collective "ahh".

'I reckon it must be my turn now,' said Jimby, wearing his habitual wide smile, rubbing his hands together. 'From hearing what Zander had to say in his speech about Livvie, it looks like there's a bit of a naked theme going on here. I mean, when I first met Zan, I ended up seeing a *lot* more of him than I expected. I think one of the first things I said to him was, "Hiya, mate, I didn't recognise you with your clothes on".' The room erupted with laughter while Zander shook his head, laughing in disbelief. 'I should probably point out the reason he was knack-naked was for our charity calendar shoot, just in case you were wondering where this was going.'

By the time Jimby had finished his speech the guests had tears of laughter pouring down their cheeks as they applauded him effusively.

'Encore!' Cheryl's husband, Gavin, had been indulging in the free-flowing Prosecco and was slightly merry. 'Ouch!' His comment earned him a dig in the ribs and a frosty look from his wife.

LIVVIE WAS DANCING and laughing with her friends when she felt a tap on her shoulder. She turned and it took a moment before she realised who was standing before her. 'Bryony! Oh, my God! You're here! What happened?' She threw her arms around her friend. 'It's so good to see you.'

'It's good to see you too, you look gorgeous. I love your dress, did you make it?'

Livvie shook her head. 'It's a long story. Come on, let's go somewhere quiet so we can have a catch-up.'

It transpired that Bryony had had quite the adventure in getting to the castle. She'd got as far as the outskirts of Middleton-le-Moors when the roads had become too bad for her hire car to manage. A passing farmer in a Landie had stopped; he was heading to Arkleby, the next village on from Danskelfe, and offered her a lift. 'I could've cried with happiness,' Bryony said to Livvie.

'Another thing we can put down to fate,' said Livvie.

'He was really good-looking too. Gave me his number.'

'Oh? What's his name?'

'Connor. Connor Mortimer. Think I might actually give him a call.'

'Are you and Josh—'

'We're through. I'll tell you about it later; tonight's not the night for that. Anyway, there's a party going on through there, and I've got some boogying to catch up on, come on, we're wasting time sitting her here gabbing, let's go and dance.' Bryony grabbed Livvie by the hand and ran back in the direction of the music.

They hadn't been dancing long when the music stopped and a voice in a lilting southern Irish accent said, 'Good evening, everyone. I hope you don't mind me interrupting but I thought I'd sing a few songs, if you don't mind, that is?' He brushed his floppy dark fringe out of his eyes and gave a lopsided smile.

There was a collective gasp in the room as people looked at the stage in disbelief.

'Oh, my days. He looks exactly like Gabe Dublin; sounds like him too. Have you got a tribute act?' Bryony asked Livvie.

Livvie grinned and shook her head. 'Nope, he's the real thing.'

Bryony looked at her askance.

'It's another long story I'll tell you about later, and something else fate has had a hand in.'

'Wow! Fate's a babe.'

'She sure is.'

Before they could say anything more, Gabe launched into a rousing rendition of his new Christmas single. The dance floor was packed with people singing along at the top of their lungs. Even Livvie's mum and sister were on their feet enjoying themselves.

AFTER PLAYING FOR A SOLID HOUR, Gabe declared it was time for a break. Sweat was pouring from his brow and his black t-shirt was drenched. 'I need to wet my whistle, folks, but I'll be back soon.'

Livvie and Zander were heading to the bar when Gabe caught up with them. 'Zander and Livvie, right?' He gave them a warm smile. 'Congratulations, and thank you for letting me join your wedding party.'

'Honestly, you're so welcome, it should be us thanking you. You were awesome,' said Livvie, feeling a little star-struck to be talking to one of her favourite singers.

'Yes, huge thanks for coming to our rescue and making our night so special,' said Zander.

'Hey, guys, it's a real pleasure.'

Noushka bounded over as they were talking, her pretty face lit up with a smile, her golden hair shining like a halo in the soft light. 'That was totally awesome, I can't believe you're here at Livvie and Zander's wedding.' She beamed at Gabe who was staring at her with his mouth open.

Livvie felt Zander nudge her; she nudged him back. Clearly she wasn't the only one who could sense the chemistry.

'Oh, erm, hi, thank you. Livvie and Zander were kind enough to let me join the celebrations, it was the least I could do.'

'Cool. It was amazing and I love your new song. Anyway, I'd best dash, Annabel's waiting for me. See you later.' Noushka disappeared in a whoosh of blonde waves and floral perfume.

'Who is that angel?' Gabe looked like he'd been struck by a thunderbolt, as he followed her with his eyes.

'That's Anoushka, or Noushka as everyone calls her,' said Livvie, an amused smile on her lips.

'Anoushka,' Gabe said slowly as if trying her name out for size. 'She's beautiful.'

Livvie and Zander exchanged knowing smiles.

~

'RIGHT, since it's got to the magical hour of midnight, I think it's time to slow things down a bit, folks. So grab the person you love and hold them close,' Gabe said, strumming on his guitar.

Zander took Livvie by the hand and led her to the dancefloor. 'Come with me, Mrs Gillespie. Time for our first smooch as a married couple.' He pulled her into his arms and looked down into her eyes.

Mrs Gillespie. It felt good to hear him call her that. 'Takes me back to last year and the party in the village hall,' said Livvie, looking up at him. She wrapped her arms around his neck as they swayed to the music.

Zander gave an easy smile. 'Yeah, that was a great night. I knew then, I couldn't let you go.'

'I felt the same about you.'

'That's because you'd had too much Prosecco.'

'I had not,' she said with a giggle. 'I can remember thinking you were lovely.'

'Hmm. You said as much.'

Livvie felt a warm glow envelop her as she cast her mind back to that night exactly a year ago.

Zander dipped his head and kissed her, slow and deep. 'Mrs Gillespie, you rock my world.'

'I can live with that,' she said, her eyes dancing with happiness.

The End.

AFTERWORD

Thank you for reading A Christmas Wedding at the Castle, I hope you enjoyed it. If you did, I'd be really grateful if you could pop over to Amazon and a leave a review – if you click on the link below it will take you right there:

Eliza J Scott - Amazon UK

Eliza J Scott - Amazon US

It doesn't have to be long – just a few words would do – but for us authors it makes a huge difference. Thank you so much.

If you'd like to find out more about what I get up to in my little corner of the North Yorkshire Moors, or if you'd like to get in touch – I'd love to hear from you! – you can find me in the following places:

Amazon author page: Eliza J Scott - UK or Eliza J Scott - US

Website: Eliza J Scott

Twitter: @ElizaJScott1

Facebook: @elizajscottauthor

Goodreads: Goodreads.com

Instagram: @elizajscott

Bookbub: @elizajscott

THANK YOU!

I do hope you enjoyed your visit to my fictional corner of the North Yorkshire Moors, and the chance to catch up with Livvie and Zander – not forgetting the rest of the gang. I'm so pleased the pair got their happy ending.

I always love popping back to Lytell Stangdale and finding out what the folks there have been up to; it feels rather like home to me. I regularly get asked by my lovely readers if I'll be writing any more books in the Life on the Moors series, and the answer is, yes, there'll be plenty more. In fact, a couple are simmering away quite nicely as I write this. Noushka's itching for me to tell her story! And I'll be introducing a couple of new characters who I'm keen for you to get to know. Watch this space!

So, now's when I get the chance to thank the people who've helped get this book ready for publication. First of all, I'd like to say a wholehearted thank you to my wonderful editor Alison Williams. I love working with Alison and always enjoy getting stuck into her edits – it's become one of my favourite parts of the writing process, I guess it's because it's a step closer to my manuscript being transformed into a book.

A great big thank you goes to the fabulous Berni Stevens for yet another gorgeous cover. Berni always manages to create the most beautiful covers for my books. I feel like a child in a sweetshop when she sends out the visuals for me to choose from.

As ever, I must say a special thank you to Rachel Gilbey of

Rachel's Random Resources whose blog tours are just incredible. Rachel has the impressive skill of keeping everything calm when the rest of us are melting into pools of panic. She's also kind-hearted and incredibly organised (just as well with the chaos I have a habit of inflicting on her!).

Thanks also to all of the amazing book bloggers who have taken part in the blog tour for this book, for taking the time to read and review it and feature it on your awesome blogs. I'm so incredibly grateful for your kindness and generosity.

I can't close without saying thank you to the wonderful book community which is full of the very best folk. I'm so happy I've got to know you.

Wishing you all a very merry Christmas and a happy New Year!

THANK YOU!

ALSO BY ELIZA J SCOTT

The Letter – Kitty's Story (Book 1 in the Life on the Moors Series)

You can get it here:

UK: www.amazon.co.uk

US: www.amazon.com

The Talisman – Molly's Story (Book 2 in the Life on the Moors Series)

You can get it here:

UK: www.amazon.co.uk

US: www.amazon.com

The Secret – Violet's Story (Book 3 in the Life on the Moors Series)

www.amazon.co.uk

www.amazon.com

A Christmas Kiss (Book 4 in the Life on the Moors Series)

You can get it right here:

UK: www.amazon.co.uk

US: www.amazon.com

ABOUT THE AUTHOR

Eliza has wanted to be a writer as far back as she can remember. She lives in the North Yorkshire Moors with her husband, two daughters and two black Labradors. When she's not writing, she can usually be found with her nose in a book/glued to her Kindle, or working in her garden, battling against the weeds that seem to grow in abundance there. Eliza enjoys bracing walks in the countryside, rounded off by a visit to a teashop where she can indulge in another two of her favourite things: tea and cake.

Printed in Great Britain
by Amazon

25220049R00172